A CHALLENGE FOR NO OTHER WOMAN

Judith P. Joiner

12-7-07

Safe travels
Judy Joiner

PublishAmerica
Baltimore

First printing

At the specific preference of the author, PublishAmerica allowed this work to remain exactly as the author intended, verbatim, without editorial input.

ISBN: 1-4241-8434-7
PUBLISHED BY PUBLISHAMERICA, LLLP
www.publishamerica.com
Baltimore

Printed in the United States of America

IN DEDICATION TO

Ralph, my wingman.
Perry, who so longed to be riding with us.
Milissa, my little sprite and free spirit.
Amanda, whose voice I constantly heard on the Haul Road saying,
"Don't come home, Mama, until you have reached the Arctic
Ocean."
My other two boys, William and Taylor.

And to my Mama, who gave my soul, the road, to travel down.

The Last Shakedown Cruise
Early May 2005

Over the past several months, Ralph and I had made many weekend trips trying out new equipment and various packing techniques in preparation for our grand adventure. Some had worked well. Some we would not have wanted to repeat. Nevertheless, all were learning experiences. My advice to anyone about to make an extended journey into the unknown is to test and retest new equipment. Also, try various packing techniques to find out just which one will work the best. This weekend was to be the last shakedown cruise before our May twenty-first departure. We packed the motorcycles as we thought we would for our upcoming journey of one hundred days. This last shakedown cruise was going to give us an idea of how the extra weight on the bikes would feel on the road and whether or not things were packed in the right places on the bikes.

My bike, though fully loaded, handled quite well. I was expecting the bike to feel top heavy and unmanageable. However, the extra weight only felt like I had a passenger on board. At least this passenger didn't wiggle like most human passengers I have had the pleasure of carrying.

The fuel cell that was added to my motorcycle functioned properly and more than doubled the range I could travel without refueling. I now had a range of approximately two hundred and seventy miles depending on my speed. I could now make fewer gas stops and would not be worrying at the one hundred mile mark where there might be a gas station in the next twenty miles.

I only had to make a few minor packing adjustments, shifting things from one place to another, and I thought I was set. The fuel cell needed a small adjustment as it had a teeny, tiny leak. There was nothing pouring out but it was leaking just enough to soak into one of the canvas backpacks I had attached over my hard saddlebags. Everything inside the backpack reeked of gasoline. I decided to leave the adjustment to Ralph, Mike Sachs and his team of expert mechanics. As it turned out a little Honda Bond smeared around the washer and fuel line exiting the fuel cell did the trick.

Mike, the director and instructor of the Motorcycle Maintenance Program at Dekalb Technical Institute in Atlanta, designed and engineered the platform for the fuel cell. Ralph, my husband of twenty-six years, worked on the mechanics and assembly. My Honda Shadow had a totally new look. The rear seat was removed and the platform was attached in its place. Without the fuel cell, the platform on my bike looked like the launch/landing pad on an aircraft carrier. That baby was not going anywhere. The platform had to be extremely secure to endure the abuse it was going to experience in the next three months. We had read many accounts of the rough roads in Canada and Alaska.

Ralph and I departed Atlanta on our last shakedown cruise on Friday afternoon around two-thirty en route to a campground called 29 Dreams southeast of Birmingham, Alabama. 29 Dreams is a motorcycle camp and lodge for motorcyclist. Unfortunately, our reserved campsite was only a newly deposited area of gravel in the back of the campground. The front part of the campground was really nice and if we manage to go back to 29 Dreams, we will be sure to secure a spot in the front of the campground close to the bathrooms, showers, and lodge.

Other campers on bikes surrounded our site. The distance between tents was approximately ten feet. Hey, but that was ok, after all 29 Dreams was a motorcycle campground and we were staying only one night anyway. We were just going to make the best of things. We were fifteen yards from a covered area with picnic tables and a port-a-potty and a very short fifty yards from a train track.

There were no fire pits or grills in the back of the campground where we were so my plans to cook a dinner of pork chops and fresh corn on the cob and asparagus hastily disappeared. We dined in the restaurant on chicken salad sandwiches, which were good. We enjoyed sitting on the deck in the rocking chairs and talking to other bikers whose numbers were mounting as evening approached.

Our friend Mike Sachs and a friend of his were spending the night at 29 Dreams also and met us at the restaurant for drinks and dinner. Around ten P.M. we decided to mosey on back to our tent and call it a night. There had been some talk at the bar about some bad weather that was expected to move through the area during the middle of the night. Someone suggested that we move our bikes under the covered picnic area. The bikes might tip over if the ground got too soft from the expected rain.

Everyone else had the same idea. There were about thirty bikes parked under the covered area. As it turned out, social hour had moved from the bar to the covered area fifteen yards from our tent and talk of the bad weather moving in was the main topic. My ears perked up somewhat. I had been in a tent during a severe storm with my twin daughters, Milissa and Amanda. They had thought they were going to die. Though I had been scared at that time, I did not feel threatened. That was about to change, however.

Ralph seemed to have little difficulty falling asleep but I was wide-awake listening to all the bikers exchange tales and hearing the door bam shut on the port-a-potty a million times. I guess the beer that had been consumed earlier was now making its exit. Finally, around two-thirty in the morning, the last biker called it quits for the night and crawled into his tent. Then the stereo snoring between our tent and the camper ten feet from my head started revving up. Ugg!

By now the train had come through a few times and each time my eyes popped open thinking I was about to be run over by a train. The ground rumbled and even the air vibrated with the train's whistle. Somewhere between two-thirty and four-thirty, I must have fallen asleep. At four-thirty, the first drops of water began to fall on the tin roof on the covered area protecting the multitude of bikes. It sounded to me like acorns hitting a metal drum. Hints of a breeze ruffled the sides of the tent. I drifted in and out of sleep until five o'clock when all of hell's horsemen broke loose through the dark black sky. The thunder started beating its large bass drum, followed quickly by lightning. The sky dumped buckets of water directly on our tent.

I was totally and fully awake now, sitting up in my sleeping bag, watching the sky light up through the thin nylon walls of our tent.

The lightning was getting closer and closer. Ralph sat up too and we watched as the area around us light up just like a strobe light going off in a dance club. The sides of the tent were being sucked in and out. I thought the tent, with us inside, would take flight at any moment. I was really getting scared. Wind, rain, thunder, and lightning were coming down all around us and on top of us. I briefly thought of all the other campers in their little tents and wondered if they were as tense as I was.

I now admit that for the very first time in my life I did something that has never, never happened. I think lightning struck and knocked right at our front door because there was a flash and the crack of lightning at the same time. A noise so loud I thought my eardrums were ruptured. I screamed and hit the dirt —literally. Then I cried. I think it must have been the adrenaline dump into my nervous system. I have never screamed out of fear in my life much less cried. That gives you some idea of how terrifying this storm was. It is one thing to be in the house when a bad storm is raging outside. It is another thing entirely to live through it in a nylon tent!

After a few moments of whimpering, I sucked it up and sat up again. Ralph pulled out the laptop computer and went to the weather site. I fussed at him for pulling it out, accusing him of attracting electricity. Who needed the weather channel at this moment anyway? I knew exactly what was happening!

Just about that moment, another lightning strike sent me prone again. I never knew just how close one could get to the ground when necessary. I became one with the earth at that moment. During the height of the lightning storm, a train chose that moment to come barreling down the tracks blowing its whistle full bore. Now what was it they said about tornados sounding like freight trains? Was it a tornado or a train? Hummmm. After a very long hour, the storm let up and moved on east.

Campers started unzipping tents and surveying the area. All the tents were still standing, as were the bikes that had been moved under the shelter. Only my nerves were rattled. At least some of the other campers said that they had gotten a little nervous. I only felt a smidgen better and really did not want to admit to anyone that I had been that scared.

Our new tent got a good test to say the least. The inside was surprisingly dry. There was only a small puddle near the front door. Of course, the helmets we had left by the front door had soaked up most of the water. I made a mental note not to leave my helmet by the door again. Putting on a helmet whose foam had soaked up a gallon of ice-cold rainwater was rather uncomfortable.

We managed to get things packed without too much difficulty as the rain continued to come down. The eight-pound tent now weighed twenty pounds. Other than the helmets and the tent, the rest of our gear was dry.

Mike, his friend, Ralph, and I left the campground at around seven-thirty A.M. and headed toward southwest Alabama for the "Ride to Eat" event held at a local catfish restaurant. When we pulled out onto the main road, we discovered just how bad the storm had been. Debris was everywhere. Tree limbs, pinecones, leaves, pine straw, and chunks of unidentifiable things littered the road. We were running an obstacle course on the road. The debris field went on for miles and miles.

We came to one town only to be stopped by a roadblock. Power lines were down in the town and traffic was being rerouted. The police officer gave Ralph the directions for the detour and we followed Ralph back out of town. On the detour, fire trucks and bulldozers were moving a very large tree out of the road. I was just counting my blessings that one of the many trees we had been camped under had not taken the opportunity to come crashing down with me under it. Without a doubt, we would not have survived.

Four hours later, we made it to the catfish place on the river and met about forty other riders for lunch. We saw a few familiar faces from some of the other rides Ralph and I had been on. Touching base again was nice. Since I don't eat bottom feeders I ordered the chicken fingers and fed half of them to the adolescent kitten that begged for food. Her stomach bulged with her free lunch and she kept asking for more. I obliged.

Ralph and I spoke with two members of the Iron Butt Association who had ridden the Ultimate Coast to Coast ride from Key West, Florida to Prudhoe Bay, Alaska. We were asking questions to prepare ourselves for our arduous trek to the Arctic Ocean. I started getting a queasy feeling in the pit of my stomach listening to these pros talk about their experience. At the time of my questioning these fellow riders, only twenty-six men and absolutely no women had ever accomplished this extreme ride. A little voice in my head kept asking me if I really wanted to take such a challenge but then that other voice yelled back saying, "You can do this and be the first woman." Yep, it was full steam ahead for me. But what was I possibly getting into? Only time and actually attempting the challenge would tell.

After being told good luck by many well-wishers, some of whom were genuine and some with that sarcastic tone that spoke of "you'll never make it," we headed out to look for a campground for the night. Mike's friend was leaving for Tennessee and Mike was riding to Birmingham to stay with some friends so they would not be joining us for another night of camping. A few of the other bikers were staying near a small town called Moundsville in Alabama.

The state park at Moundsville was beautiful. A nice flat area beneath the pines and hardwoods had been designated as a campground. The campground was adjacent to acres and acres of Indian mounds.

After the tent was set up, I had to soak up a great amount of water on the floor of the tent. The flood from the storm, combined with the tent being stuffed into the carrying case, had caused the entire tent to be saturated. At least the floor of the tent got a nice mopping. The sides were drying out quite nicely in the evening breeze as I cooked port chops and corn on the cob over a charcoal fire. The asparagus had soured and smelled gross. I tossed it into the fire and watched as the asparagus was quickly consumed.

Our tent site was directly by the path to the bathroom. Other campers, who happened to be some of the bikers from the lunch, stopped by, chatted, and shared our fire. We spoke of our upcoming adventure and all wished us good luck. As usual, when bikers get together, they love to share stories of where they have traveled and their experiences. They also invited Ralph and me to come join them at their fire and to have dinner with them as well.

Unlike the previous night, this campground was mostly silent with just the pleasant sound of the wind in the pines, a lullaby of sorts. Unlike the previous night, the train was about a quarter mile away and had a soothing, lonely, far away sound.

I slept like a log, and was only briefly awakened by the sweet sound of the lonely train and the whispering wind through the pine needles and the new spring leaves. Sleep returned quickly and pleasantly.

Morning brought the sunshine and the chirping birds. They were happy and were announcing their happiness to the world. After a wonderful shower with hot water and plenty of soap, I felt pretty good considering the rough start Saturday morning. We were looking forward to a beautiful day to ride, a rider's dream, sixty-five degrees, clear blue sky, and dry roads. We took the scenic route home and enjoyed riding on some back roads though rural Alabama. After a huge, tasty feast of barbeque in Jasper, Alabama we high-tailed it home arriving around six o'clock in the evening.

I can't begin to tell you how good my bed felt that night. As I drifted off into sweet slumber I wondered how I was going to handle one hundred days on the road. I was excited, nervous, and giddy all at the same time. The great unknown and the unexpected awaited me. The start of my adventure was not too far off. As my eyelids grew heavy and sleep overtook me, I dreamed of Alaska.

May 20, 2005
Mile 0

Dear Folks,

After many, many years of dreaming about taking such a trip and many, many hours, days and months planning our journey it looks as if Ralph and I are about to realize our dream. Years ago, while still very young and childless, both of us wanted to journey to that far away place known as Alaska. To make the trip even more challenging we added journeying there on motorcycles to the mix. Over the past several years, Ralph and I have become completely enamored with the wind in our faces and the three hundred and sixty degree experience.

Our first date was on a motorcycle and after that, we enjoyed many fun times in the sunshine. After the birth of our first child however, the motorcycle was sold and we traveled by car. About seven years ago, when the not to be denied wanderlust hit again, Ralph purchased a used bike. He, along with three other friends, decided to celebrate turning fifty years of age, and made a cross-country trip. Motorcycling was reborn in our family.

I reminded Ralph of the dreams we had had when we were young and carefree about traveling cross-country on bikes. I took the motorcycle safety course, bought a big bike, and was hooked immediately and seriously. Not a bad addiction if I say so myself.

Over the past seven years, we have had many wonderful trips and fun times traveling around the country. However, we were usually under time constraints and had to be back home within two to three weeks. This time things have changed. Technology has become advanced enough that we can now carry a virtual office and communications. Another main event in our lives that will enable us to travel to the extent that we have planned is that our youngest will graduate from high school. Our wee small babes are all grown up. A lifetime has passed since our young dreams were born along the dusty back roads of Georgia.

Our first born, Perry, will graduate from college at the end of May. Our last two biddies, twins Milissa and Amanda, will graduate from high school today. Ralph and I plan to leave at six A.M. tomorrow. I don't know who is more excited: us for starting our grand adventure or the girls for being set free. Personally, it is hard for me to think about being gone from my children for so long. There are too many emotions running through my heart. I feel anxiety about being separated from my children and at the same time, I am filled with unbridled excitement of traveling into the unknown.

Now, with all that being said, the story of our journey will be recorded with pictures and journal entries. We hope it will be something for Ralph and I to enjoy in future years and something for our family and friends to enjoy while we are journeying north to Alaska.

We look forward to hearing from anyone and everyone while we are journeying. We can be contacted via our e-mail addresses. Please stay in touch.

Until next time, love to all always,
Judy and Ralph

May 22, 2005
Key West, FL
Mile 834

Dear Folks,

The last two days prior to departure were spent getting all the last details wrapped up, but most importantly, celebrating the graduation from high school of our youngest two children, Milissa and Amanda. I have had mixed emotions for quite a while, all of it bittersweet. Our two youngest are now out of the nest. Maybe I should say Mama and Daddy are the ones that are out of the nest since we are the ones that left home.

Two days ago, I watched proudly as our girls walked across the stage and received their diplomas. I cheered and Milissa's boyfriend, Bryan, stood up and yelled at the top of his lungs, "I love you, babe", professing his love to her in front of five thousand people. Wow!

After the graduation ceremony, we had a party for the girls and their friends and families. It was well attended with around fifty guests. I don't know what I was thinking when I planned a party on the eve of our departure. After cleaning up and returning home, we managed to get to bed around one in the morning.

Sometime in the middle of the night, I felt Ralph pushing on my back really hard. I thought he was trying to push me out of the bed. I thought he was telling me it was time to get up! I yelled at him, "What are you doing?" He was having a dream and he thought he was opening a door with a vacuum on it. So much for my five hours of sleep. Getting back to sleep took a while, only to really be reawakened by the stinking alarm clock.

My eyes burned, my stomach was really nauseated, and I was starting to get overwhelmed about our impending departure. I was starting to panic about leaving my children. I threw all the last minute things just anywhere I could find a cubby hole on the bike, all the while hearing our friend Mike's voice in my head saying, "You're just going to wind up leaving it somewhere on the side of the road." He's probably right.

When the bags and bikes were finally packed departure was imminent. Our daughter Milissa, her boyfriend, Bryan, and our neighbors Dave and Mary came outside to see us off. I had said my goodbyes to Amanda and Perry the night before. One final hug to Milissa and then the floodgates opened. All the tears I had been holding in for the last several days came bursting forth. Three months will pass before I see my children again. I have never been away from them that long. Would I be able to cope? At that moment, I did not think so.

With our horns blaring, we scooted out of the neighborhood and were on our way on our grand adventure. I sobbed all the way down I-575, and all the way down I-75. Once we crossed the north end of I-285 I was almost down to a whimper and a trickle, but the lump in my throat was still causing me great difficulty swallowing. The longing for my babies was still squeezing tightly at my heart, but the excitement of the unknown and the quest of that far away dirt road in Alaska pulled me quickly down the interstate.

The first day was going to be long as the plan was to get to Lake Okeechobee some six hundred miles away. Being extremely tired, stressed out and emotional made the trip harder and was not the most ideal way to start a trip of such magnitude. When planning a long trip of many miles, many long distance riders cover more distance in the first day and then taper off. Around the third day, distances decrease. As the days pass, daily mileages decrease. By the third day, riders are riding at about sixty-five percent of the first day's ride. Our plan after the first two days was to be averaging around three hundred and fifty miles a day. We have spent many days riding that distance and are comfortable at that range.

Riding the interstate is my very, very least favorite way to travel on a motorcycle, but was necessary the first day. We stopped for breakfast in Perry, Georgia, for a caffeine stop an hour later, and for burgers somewhere on the Florida Turnpike around four-thirty in the afternoon. We arrived in Okeechobee, Florida and headed for a campground I had found on the internet. We pulled into the parking lot at exactly six thirty-three P.M. I unglued my butt from the seat and walked over to a staff member sitting up nice and pretty in his golf cart next to the office.

Ralph told the guy we would like a tent spot for the night. He told us that if we did not have reservations and it was after six P.M. then we could not have a place to stay for the night. I turned around and looked at a virtually empty campground! What was he thinking? It was six thirty-three; thirty-three minutes too late and we could not stay in their empty campground. Am I missing something here?

Back in the saddle again and back over the same five miles of road back to the KOA Kampground where they welcomed us and our money with open arms, air conditioning, and a bar to boot. Since the KOA costs more than the place we originally wanted to stay, we were now close to being over our daily budget on the very first day of our trip. We had come up with a budget of one hundred and twenty dollars a day for gas, food and a place to sleep for both of us. The budget was tight and manageable but left no room for extras. If we stayed under budget then the extra money could be saved for tee shirts or other souvenirs.

I do not do heat very well and by now I was a sweaty puddle of addled brain mass. Ralph set up the tent and I numbly went about throwing my stuff into the tent while mumbling about it being too damned hot. We spent the last ten dollars we had on us for the day not on food my friends, but on a beer for Ralph and frozen daiquiri for me. Alcohol instead of food was worth the price on this first leg of the journey.

We listened to an old crusty country music singer bleating out the words on a karaoke machine while we drank our dinner in the bar in the campground. After sharing a basket of free popcorn and a few cups of free water, we headed back to our tent. Our neighbors in the next site stopped to say hi and ask us about all the bags and equipment we had on our bikes. We told them about our plan to travel from Key West, Florida to Prudhoe Bay, Alaska while they listened with open-mouthed astonishment. Most people just can't believe we were tackling a trip of this scope on motorcycles.

As I was sitting talking to them and petting their beautiful dog, Nikita, I noticed something out of the corner of my eye. I thought I was seeing a juvenile squirrel hopping across the campsite. I thought our daughter Amanda would have been having a hissy fit right about now as she has had unpleasant relationships with squirrels. On closer examination, I discovered that the squirrel was not a squirrel at all, but a very, very large frog. I don't think I've seen one quite the size of a saucer before.

Well, he hopped on his merry way, and I hopped on my merry way down to the shower swatting mosquitoes all the way. I stood under a cold shower for twenty minutes trying to cool off my poor old brain. It worked only briefly. As soon as I got back to the campsite, I was all sweaty again and mad about it too.

However, the campground was very quiet and I slept out of sheer exhaustion. I actually got a full eight hours of sleep. Prior to nodding, off Ralph asked me if I thought we should set the alarm. "*No!*" I said. I was convinced that Mother Nature would probably handle it for us.

At six in the morning, we were awakened by two crows yapping at each other right over our tent. That was followed shortly by the chorus of doves sounding like desperate housewives searching for their mates.

We were up at six-thirty, packed by seven-fifteen and on the road shortly thereafter. Today's ride was much better and of the type we generally enjoy. Our ride started out in just the right temperature, but the day heated up quite nicely and we were roasting in the Florida sun after a few hours.

Our route down the Florida back roads proved to be pretty in some parts, rather boring in others. We saw many new foals on the ground sleeping in the hot sun. I chuckled at a dozen or so cows in a field next to the road. All of the cows had their heads deep in the feed trough and their big black and white butts and huge pink udders full of milk faced the road. We had been moo-ned! I am sorry, I could not resist.

We finally reached the Florida Keys and its staggering, unpleasant traffic. The water surrounding the Keys was spectacular. The ocean was a swirling mixture of beautiful green, turquoise, and blue. I loved going over the bridges connecting the Keys but hated the roads in between. There are too many cars and it is entirely too hot.

Arriving in Key West around two-thirty P.M., we found the hostel where we had reservations. The hostel was the cheapest place in town at seventy dollars a night. The room was nice enough, the beds great, the sheets clean, the shower grand and we had one of my all time favorites: air conditioning.

While I showered in a completely cold shower to cool my skin and brain, Ralph was out in the common area of the hostel making new friends. I had to completely repack my clothes and other items. What started out as a good packing idea quickly became a problem. Everything seemed to be in the wrong place. Even though our shakedown cruises were in preparation for this exact problem I just had not been totally satisfied with how my clothes were packed. Happy now with my new arrangement, I went to find my husband. Ralph had made friends with three young Germans, one man and two women. They were traveling around Florida for ten days before going home. Since we had been in the Florida so many times, we suggested some top spots to visit.

The young man had a very interesting job. I have never before met someone who sold tanks to foreign countries for a living. He showed us his business web site and told us about his job of selling tanks. The young German spoke to us of the countries who were his company's prospective customers and the recruitment practices of the soldiers who would be driving the tanks. It was my turn to listen with a slack jaw. I had some of those chills that creep up one's neck when hearing something scary. I was ready to move on to another subject other than war, tanks, and mayhem.

Around seven P.M., Ralph and I rode over to Mallory Square to join the rest of the tourist to watch the sunset and the entertainers hawking their talents for money. As we sat and watched the sun set, Ralph and I shared a Key West pretzel. The pretzel was dipped in butter then thrown on the grill for a few minutes. I had a hard time deciding which was better, the pretzel, or the sunset.

Ralph and I shared old times of a prior trip to Key West five years ago with our son, Perry and laughed recalling seeing Key West through the eyes of a youth. After the sunset, we wandered over to the Hog's Breath Saloon for dinner. We sat outside in the bar area and listened to a young, hottie from Nashville sing and entertain the crowd. After our celebratory drink to commemorate the start of the Ultimate Coast to Coast ride sponsored by the Iron Butt Association, I chose to eat dinner. Ralph chose to drink his.

After my dinner and Ralph's drinks, we strolled up Duval Street. I was searching for a cheap ring to replace my wedding ring that I had put in the safe deposit box back home. I felt naked without it. I found the perfect ring in a junk store and we both picked one. As we were trying them on Ralph said he would marry me all over again. So, we were married again, so to speak, in a junk store, in Key West with our two, three-dollar rings. I wondered what color our fingers were going to turn.

We certainly enjoyed the local scenery and could have people watched for the remainder of the night but knowing that the morning would bring more excitement and a very long ride we headed back to the room. We slept so good in our little air-conditioned room.

So until later, much love to all always,
Judy/Mom/Mommy

May 23, 2005
Kissimmee, FL
Monday
Mile 1202

Dear Folks,

After a great night's sleep, we got started around eight o'clock. We headed for the ocean that was two blocks away to collect our little jar of seawater from Key West. The tradition on challenging rides to collect water from each ocean visited. I think my little jar of salt water is going to look quite nice along side the one I plan to collect from the Arctic. I plan to display each of them on my mantle back home.

After collecting our water, we rode a few blocks to the buoy marking the point furthest south a person can get in the United States on a road. We had to get our pictures with the bikes as part of the requirements for the ride. While Ralph and I were pulling out the instructions, and I the camera, a taxi pulled up to the buoy. A young girl and young guy jumped out and raced over to the buoy. The girl tells us that we had to be in their picture. Ok, what ever, but I noticed that the young man started taking off his clothes. Ooops, maybe this was just something I did not want to see but my curiosity could not stand not knowing why he was taking his clothes off in a very public place.

Under his shorts and tee shirt, he had on his girlfriend's bikini! I have to admit she looked much better in hers than he did in hers. The young kids quickly explained they were in a contest sponsored by a local radio station. They were trying to win five thousand dollars by racing to various locations around Key West in bikinis' and having their pictures made in front of those locations along with a witness. Ralph and I were their witnesses for this location. They got their picture with us and I tried to get their picture but my battery went dead on the camera. Ooooh! What timing. They had no time for me to reload my camera and off they raced down the narrow street, the cab taillights blinking goodbye.

After we captured our photos with our bikes and buoy in the background, we struck out to find a police station or fire station to have someone there sign our witness form verifying that we indeed were in Key West when we said we were. We found the fire station at just the same time as the young couple in the taxi did. This time my camera was loaded with new batteries. The young man had given up putting on the tee shirt and shorts. He was now strutting around in his girlfriend's bikini. He should have won the money just on sheer guts alone.

Ralph and I got our documents signed by a firefighter. The fire chief was thrilled to be a part of our challenge. The chief gave me one of their patches, which I immediately confiscated, and a writing pen, which Ralph quickly stashed away in his tank bag. As we were getting our documents signed, the firemen were preparing a meal. I wish I could have stayed for the meal because it sure smelled good and my stomach was empty.

The next stop was the gas station to fill the tanks and get a time stamp for the official start of our Ultimate Coast to Coast journey. I was sweating so much it looked like I had jumped in the ocean. I hate being sweaty like that and it makes me very cross and really foul to be around.

The situation only got worse as we proceeded out of Key West back north. Hot, hot, hot, hot, is the only way I can describe my feelings on the matter as we headed north over the back roads of Florida. At a later gas stop, I poured water all over my head and clothes trying to stay cool.

We thought it would be in our best interest to take a cooling rest stop in a little crossroad town in Florida called Yahoo Junction. The only facility at the junction was the Desert Inn. I had some serious doubts whether the place was open or if we should even go in, but we were so hot we needed a break even if it was to stand in the shade of the building.

Ralph and I elected to try the door. We were greeted immediately by cool air and I knew at once that I was staying. We sat at the bar, drank cokes, and cooled off. The locals started filtering in, as it was late in the afternoon and getting close to quitting time somewhere.

The middle-aged waitress behind the bar started hitting on one of the young, attractive male customers sitting two seats down from me on my left. One of the locals at the bar, sitting two seats down on Ralph's right, started talking some serious trash about the waitress to the rest of us at the bar. Ralph and I were caught in the middle. I was convinced it was time to leave. What were about to get ourselves into? I envisioned flying fists and broken beer bottles.

Since the Desert Inn advertised rooms for rent, we gave a thought to actually staying, as it was six-twenty P.M. We were tired, sweaty, and ready to stop for the day. The room cost thirty-two dollars and that would keep us well within our daily budget.

I should have known things were not going to be desirable when the waitress said we could inspect the room before we paid our money. Once the money was paid, there would be no refunds. Ralph took the key, went and took a look, and was back in record time. He shook his head quickly at me as he returned to the bar where I was still sitting between the young, attractive male and the foul-mouthed local. I did not ask any questions but asked Ralph to get out the laptop. A quick search on hotels.com located several cheap hotels in Kissimmee.

As we left the bar and were putting on our helmets, Ralph told me he pulled back the sheets in the room to inspect them and found all sorts of creepy things between the sheets. I did not want to know any more. I had to pee badly but I figured if the sheets were gross, the bathroom would be even worse. Yep, Ralph said it was even worse than I could imagine. I held it all the way to Kissimmee.

We easily found the hotel and are happily settled in for the night in a forty-dollar room with clean sheets and clean bathroom and again my all time favorite, air conditioning. Yeah!

We're off early tomorrow, hopefully, to reach southern Alabama.

So until later, much love to all always,
Judy/Mom/Mommy

May 24, 2005
Gordon, AL
Mile 1593

Dear Folks,

Ralph and I left Kissimmee, Florida at eight-thirty this morning. We drove through hellacious traffic that consisted mostly of heavy industrial trucks screaming by us throwing sand and dirt all over us. Combine the industrial trucks with the rest of the tractor-trailers, school busses, cars, and extreme heat and that made for a very lovely traveling day. There is not much to report about today's ride because we were trying desperately to get out of Florida. Today was a butt and brain burner. We were so very hot and made several stops to drink water and pour ice water on our heads and torso. The coolness only lasted briefly. We were dry completely in about ten minutes of driving on the road.

Finally, we made it to some pretty back roads after traveling the majority of the day in unpleasant conditions. We rode through areas of freshly plowed farmland and newly sprouted crops. I kept wishing it had not been so darned hot. I do not do the South in the summer very well. Today it felt like late August and it is only May. Our thermometers registered a cool ninety-eight degrees. Oh, my poor brain. Combine the heat of the air, the heat coming off the bike engine and the heat radiating off the black asphalt and a person can get in trouble very fast if not careful. We stop frequently for a cold-water hose down.

We made our way into the most southeastern point of Alabama. Tucked away in the corner of Alabama, with the Florida State line forty feet away and the Georgia State line across the lake behind the trees, is the Chattahoochee State Park. The park is absolutely lovely.

We pulled off the hot Alabama road into an immediate covering of hardwoods and pines. The road that wound back far into the woods was sand and gravel. I thought I might be getting a tiny taste of something remotely like an Alaska road we plan to travel down. I think this road probably pales in comparison though, from everything I have read.

The campsites surrounded a lake about ten acres in size. I had second thoughts when we pulled up in front of the lake and I saw a sign that said, "No swimming, alligators." Humm. Was I going to be awakened in the middle of the night by a seven-foot gator crawling through the campsite?

The place was pretty and we decided to stay. After picking a campsite near the lake but still under the trees, the tent was quickly erected. We had no food with us and since there were no restaurants in the vicinity, we had to go in search of grub. We drove another eight miles on a tiny, narrow, back road until we found a Chevron station complete with a small food store. We bought dinner there which consisted of two cans of tuna, eight slices of American cheese, saltine crackers, a can of pears, a can of peaches, potato chips, four bottles of water, one Pepsi, a bear claw, and a brownie. That purchase combined with the two bagels, cream cheese, and two honey granola bars I swiped at the hotel this morning, we prepared our feast at the picnic table in front of our tent.

Ralph and I ate our dinner as we watched the fish jump out of the water over the lake. The fish were eating the hordes of mosquitoes that were humming and buzzing. The jumping fish, I took as a sign that maybe it would be a good time to cover myself in Deet.

Just as we were finishing our feast, the park official came by to get our names and tag numbers and to collect the money for the campsite. We found out from the park official that the gator living in the lake really is about seven feet long. He said that someone was coming to catch the gator soon. Soon, was not good enough for me. Right now would be fine and dandy. Since our tent backed right up to the deep, dark woods, I asked if there were any deer in the woods that might be wandering around. I just wanted to be prepared mind you. "Oh, yeah", he said, "there are deer, gators, panthers, boars, and all sorts of animals." Great, just what I wanted to hear.

We are the only campers in this park tonight. We are all alone with the bugs and animals. Deep darkness has descended upon the campground. The frogs have started croaking and the crickets are fiddling. The light from the computer screen is attracting too many bugs, many of them very large. So that is it for me tonight! I hate bugs flying up my nose and down my shirt. The bats have started swooping in search of their dinner. Good, maybe they will eat some of these monster bugs that are irritating me.

Until next time, much love to all always,
Judy/Mom/Mommy

May 25, 2005
Tombigbee, MS
Wednesday
Mile 1966

Dear Folks,

I am bone weary tonight. My back hurts very badly and my knees are not functioning too well either. We are staying in a very rustic cabin in Tombigbee State Park in Mississippi. How nice it will be to sleep in a bed after last nights fight with the bugs.

As I left you last night, the bugs were honing in on the computer screen and the mosquitoes were having a feast. The evening under the stars was rather relaxing even though there was an element of fear in it for me. Pitch-black darkness surrounded us, and then suddenly the summer lighting bugs came out in full force lighting up the sky and woods like little firecrackers.

Since we were the only ones in the campground, we pulled our chairs out onto the dirt road and watched the stars. Several satellites made arches across the blackness of space. The frogs kept up their chorus talking back and forth to each other across the lake. When the frogs got silent, I got worried. In my mind, if the frogs were quiet, there must be a predator in the area. I had a chill to my skin thinking about all the critters that would surely come visiting as soon as I got in my sleeping bag, not to mention the big, gigantic seven-foot alligator that was lurking somewhere in the dark water of the lake.

The bugs and mosquitoes left us alone as soon as we turned out all the lights. The darkness to me was spooky. Just as I expected, when I got ready to settle down on the air mattress, I heard the first animal. The owl was the loudest I have ever heard and I swear it was right over where we had just been sitting. The owl was extremely close and his hooting getting louder by the second.

He must have spotted his dinner because he kept hooting very loud and then we heard some rustling right behind our tent. I

26

whispered to Ralph, "I don't like this at all." The nearest Holiday Inn was nowhere in sight. I am not generally scared of creatures, animals, and insects. It is the darkness that gets under my skin. In the darkness of the campground, with all the unsettling noises, I was fast-forwarding several weeks down the road. How on earth was I going to deal with the unknown critters and bugs that would surely be coming my way somewhere in the wilderness of Alaska? I was very familiar with the animals and bugs in my own back yard in the south and some of those held absolutely no appeal what so ever. What was I in for? I was not sure I had bargained for one hundred days of having the willies and goose bumps and things wandering around in my campsite at night. But, then again, I think being just a little scared adds an element of thrill to the experience. I was probably going to be totally thrilled for the next three months.

Mr. Owl must have taken his dinner off to some other part of the forest, because his hooting became fainter and fainter. In a spine tingling way, though, it was rather exciting to hear the rustling of bushes and the crunching of leaves around our tent in the darkness of night. Off and on through the night there were unidentified creatures rustling through the bushes. They were not too loud, but every footstep awakened me. Every footstep, added to my snoring tent mate, made for a very restless night for me.

At one point during the night, I could have sworn Ralph had gotten up and was peeing outside. There was definitely some water being poured on the ground near the picnic table. However, it was not Ralph, I realized as I peaked out from under my sleeping bag. What could the splashing noise have been? There was no way in hell, I was going to stick my head out of the tent and find out. At least for the night a mystery it would have to remain. Maybe I could figure it out in the morning's light.

Dawn came at five-thirty with the lightning of the sky and the chirping birds. Mr. Owl was still hooting a tune far off in the woods. The call of the hawk and the pile driver hammering on the tree behind the tent added to the chorus. Sunrise was beautiful over the lake. The morning sun cast a pale pinkish, yellow color to the lake. The fish were still jumping at the bugs but I had yet to see the gator. I had no regrets about not seeing the seven-foot monster. The peeing I heard in the bushes last night, which I had blamed Ralph for, turned out to be the melted ice I had left in a bag on the picnic table. I watched it spill out of the bag, onto the leaves next to the picnic table, duplicating the exact noise I had heard in the darkness. I have an active imagination, my friends.

Ralph and I were all packed and ready to move out by six-thirty over the sandy road. We had to cross over an earthen dam at the end of the lake. The dam was covered in cobblestones and they were not round like I would expect, but were square and rough.

I now know I can go as slow on my bike as the fastest duck can waddle. Just as we started to cross the cobblestone path over the dam, a mated pair of Canada geese and six babies decided to go first. I had no idea geese could waddle as fast as those did. Eight duck butts waddling and sixteen feet just a flapping over the cobblestones was more than I could stand. I was laughing so hard the tears rolled down my face. As we approached the dam, I assumed the geese would head into the bushes along the dam. They figured they had the right away and made a beeline as fast as they could for the other side of the dam with us directly behind them on their tails. After crossing the dam, they scurried out of our way, stood under some pines twitching their ruffled tail feathers, and watched us with uncertainty as we continued on our way.

Our ride today was pleasant as I think a cool front moved in last night. We enjoyed the ride but I am now ready for a good night's sleep and a good rest for my tired bones, painful back and sore knees. The clean sheets and comfy bed are calling me.

So until next time, love to all always,
Judy/Mom/Mommy

May 26, 2005
Thursday
Ozaraks, MO
Mile 2309

Dear Folks,

Ralph and I left Tombigbee State Park at seven-fifteen this morning to a beautiful, cool morning, with clear skies. We stopped by Elvis' birthplace, which was just a block off the main road and got our tourist picture. Since we were close, I thought I should at least see it, even though I have never been a big Elvis fan. His boyhood house was smaller than I imagined even though I have seen pictures.

Since it was still very early in the morning, we got busy and put some serious miles behind us quickly before the traffic got heavy. Ralph and I were still looking forward to some back roads that were not crowded. Later in the afternoon, we were greatly rewarded.

After riding through billions of trucks, speeding cars, crap roads, and crossing over the mighty Mississippi in Memphis, we were treated to State Road 19 in Missouri. Just as soon as we turned onto Route 19 off Route 63, the road immediately turned beautiful. The road was just the kind that we have been longing for. The road started through small, rolling pastures dotted with hardwoods. Lucky, lazy cattle grazed in the lush green pastures. Shiny horses, some with new foals, stood peacefully swatting bugs.

Soon the road became more hilly and there were fewer pastures and more woods, mostly hardwoods. As we traveled down the road, yellow finches and bluebirds darted across the road in front of me on their way back to nest, maybe full of babies. A hawk came in low, just above head level, and soared into the dark woods to my right.

Wild flowers consisting of white daisies and yellow, black-eyed Susan's, along with fuchsia pink flowers as big as my hand, were bunched together in masses of color along the roadside. The smell of freshly cut hay and honeysuckle was pure delight to me.

The road started to get more and more hilly and before I knew it I felt as if I was on a stretched out roller coaster. Up and down the hilly landscape we rode. My stomach began to take a small flight when I crested a hill. As we rolled over and over, up and down the hills I could not help myself but to yell with glee. Weeeeeee. Weeeeee. Ohhhhhh. Over and over again I laughed with childish pleasure.

Unfortunately, as I loved the up and down motion, the hills evened out and turned into curvy mountain roads, just like the ones in north Georgia. I have never been in the Ozarks before, but they reminded me of home and a small twinge of homesickness awakened in my heart.

The day was starting to wind down and we needed to find a camp spot for the night. The road passed by a canoe campground that also had camp store and firewood. We turned around and headed straight for the office. After setting up our tent under a magnificent oak tree, Ralph went back to the office for goodies and I headed into the woods for extra wood for a fire.

Ralph is on his way back now, I see him coming with his box of firewood and Margarita wine coolers. Oooh, it is going be a good night!

Until next time, love to all always,
Judy/Mom/Mommie

May 29, 2005
Sunday
St. Paul, MN
Mile 3,038

Dear Folks,

I think last time I wrote, I left you with the picture of Ralph coming across the campground with drinks and firewood in hand. We built a grand fire and I actually cooked dinner. Yep, I pulled out my expanding fork, stuck hotdogs on the end of it, and cooked those suckers. Boy, they were good. Roasted hotdogs, chips and bean dip, chocolate chip cookies and Pepsis was what I fixed for a feast of a dinner. I am forever amazed at just how good an old hotdog cooked over an open fire can taste. I guess that will keep up my cooking skills for a few days at any rate.

Watching the fire was better than taking a Valium, it was so relaxing and calming. Soon, we both were noodles and ready to snuggle into the sleeping bags. The night would be cool as we were in the mountains. The beauty of the stars at night was breath taking. There were so many in the dark sky. They looked like pin pricks of light punched out of a black cloth.

I actually slept deeply, but was awakened only once by a varmint rooting around in the bean dip can we left on the table. I think he liked Pepsi, too. The cans and bottles were strung around the campsite when we climbed out of the tent the next morning.

We were awakened very early, around five-thirty, to the sound of sweet birds announcing the arrival of a new day. We both felt rested and after taking a shower that we had to pay for with quarters, we were ready to tackle a new day.

About the time we were finishing packing our gear on the bikes, out of the misty shrouded woods came bounding, two dogs. Great, I'm thinking, now we're going to be eaten by wild dogs protecting who knows what. As they got closer, however, I noticed tongues hanging sideways out of their mouths and wagging tails. I talked sweet, silly baby talk to them hoping that would indicate to them that I was friend, not foe, and not something to eat.

Both hounds were tickled pink to see me and both jumped up on my clean tee shirt covering the side with dark brown mud. So much for taking a shower and having clean clothes. Anyway, the dogs were sweet and I fed them chocolate chip cookies, a bagel with cream cheese and a squished bear claw. After gobbling their breakfast, the dogs proceeded to fall asleep behind my bike, making it hard to finish packing. I had to gingerly step around the dog that looked like a husky. My impression was that he was so hoping I would throw him some more breakfast.

With the bikes finally packed up tight in spite of our furry friends, we were at last on our way back on Route 19 in Missouri. The roads were empty due to the early hour and absolutely beautiful. I hope I can come back to this stretch of road some time in the future. Route 19 in Missouri from the bottom of the state to the top will definitely be put on my list of favorites. The road is another motorcycle riders dream.

We came out of Missouri and into Iowa on Route 61. The road was still enjoyable, but as we traveled further north, the winds picked up great speed coming barreling out of the west. Ralph and I were being blown everywhere. My shoulders and upper arms were burning from holding the bike in the lane. We had to stop several times just to give the muscles a break, not to mention my sanity. I am not fond of wind either. I knew in a few days we were heading to the area of the country that is known for wind. I was getting a good taste right now, though. It is beginning to sound like I am not fond of much anything but I think the list only includes heat, darkness, wind, the interstate and tractor-trailer trucks. I wondered just how many more things would be added to that list as our trip progresses.

The landscape turned to farmland with rolling hills of freshly planted corn. Sprouts were coming up everywhere looking like a fuzzy green beard across the land. Clouds of giant white cotton balls filled the bright blue sky. I was enjoying the landscape, except for the wind.

However, because of the vast open spaces, there is nothing to stop the wind when it gets rolling. You can see trouble coming in the form of rain, tornadoes, dust, and other forces of nature. Off in the distance, just in the direction we were heading, I noticed two pockets of rain. One on the right side of the road and one on the left. I was thinking, with any luck, we could ride right down the middle of them and be on our merry way. How wrong I was.

Out of the west came trouble in the form of high winds and heavy rains. Ralph happened to be in the lead for a while and I watched as he was blown all over the road. Combine the rain, high winds, and the tractor-trailers coming straight for us and that makes for a pants wetting experience.

If we stayed staggered in our lane as we were supposed to, one of us would get blown off the road. That would probably be me since I like to ride on the right side of the lane. We both stuck to the center of the lane so when a truck came by going fifty-thousand miles per hour we might only be blown over to the right side of the lane and not off the road.

I mean to tell you, it was one hairy experience. I did not like it one bit. But, I figured that if Ralph was not being blown over, I probably was not going to be either. Small comfort that was though. Riding through that cell took about twenty minutes but they were very long minutes.

When we finally rode through it, I started laughing. I could not figure out if it was from the adrenaline dump in my body or if I was just happy to be alive. I know one thing though; I needed a dry pair of under drawers and a Long Island Ice Tea, neither of which were available. I had also white knuckled the grips on the handlebars so hard I had to pry my right fingers off the throttle.

After all that excitement, we finally reached Davenport, Iowa and drove right up to our friend's house. We were going to stay with our friends, Janet and Terry, for a couple of nights. Low and behold, there was an unexpected party waiting for our arrival. Family and friends were there to greet us and all of them had brought food!

What a tremendous surprise and treat that was for me. We were warmly welcomed into Janet and Terry's home and all the family and friends made us feel like they were anxiously awaiting the road warriors. I was totally thrilled.

The food was grand, the company was even better. Everyone was interested in our journey and our stories. One of the friends of the family, Burley, gave us tee shirts that had been brought to him from Egypt. How cool was that? Thanks Burley, I look forward to showing off my Egyptian shirt.

Utter chaos reigned king at Janet's house. Little, squealing kids were laughing and running around the house like it was Christmas Eve. The dog was bouncing up and down trying to get into anyone's lap, the two birds were squawking and screeching and all the adults talking. I thought it was wonderful. I also thought it wonderful that Janet had all that family around her now.

I last saw Janet three years ago. She had moved back home to Iowa from Atlanta. I was happy for her. She seemed content and settled. People she loved and who loved her surrounded her. In turn, that made me content for her.

We had a non-travel day on Saturday. Ralph had to do some work so he spent the day at the house working while Janet showed me around Davenport. I loved seeing the town with its different architecture and style. She showed me where she grew up and the two houses that she and her husband, Terry, had refurbished last summer and were now renting. Lots of hard work had gone into them but the houses were very cute.

We then went to the Rock Island Armory and the cemetery there to put flowers on her father's grave. Every grave in the cemetery had a flag. Being Memorial Day weekend, they were ready for the memorial ceremonies. I think that was the first time I have been in a military cemetery on Memorial Day.

All the tombstones were lined up just like the soldiers buried beneath. All were in straight lines whichever direction you looked and all with United States flags fluttering gracefully in the warm afternoon breeze that blew off the nearby Mississippi River.

We drove past the Confederate part of the cemetery. Apparently, Rock Island had been a prison for Civil War prisoners of war. They had their own special memorial. I walked down between the rows and noticed the dates on the head stones. Eighteen hundred and sixty-three, eighteen hundred and sixty-four, eighteen hundred and sixty-five marked the marble stones along with the names of the fallen soldiers. Confederate flags, some faded, some wrinkled, some new, hung from their sticks stuck in the Iowa soil. Most of the soldiers, who were just boys, were from Tennessee, Alabama, and

Mississippi. There were a few Georgia boys scattered among the buried southern soldiers.

After a late dinner, Ralph and I packed our freshly laundered clothes and climbed into bed. We planned to get an early start in the morning. We had not planned on quite the early start we did get. At five-thirty the sun and birds woke us up. I am starting to notice a pattern of five o'clock wakeup calls. I have never been an early riser but is sure is hard to stay asleep with earth's racket going on around me.

Ralph and I tried to be quiet but we figured we would wake the household getting our stuff out of the house and onto the bikes. I guess everyone must have been exhausted, as we did not manage to wake any one. We left without getting to say goodbye to our friends. In a way, it was better that way as goodbyes make me sad. I would have only started crying and then that would have fogged up my face shield on my helmet. Better to just leave silently.

We scooted out of town at close to seven A.M. and were delighted by the completely empty roads. The sky was full of dark, grey clouds and it did not look like we would escape the rain. After riding for forty-five minutes hoping to avoid the rain we had to pull over and cover Ralph's tank bag with the waterproof cover to protect the laptop computer. I was freezing so I took that opportunity to put the liner in my jacket, and close up all the vents. I pulled out a heaver pair of gloves and put the grip heaters on the handles.

That solved my cold body but it did not stop the rain. However, the rain did make the air smell good and we cruised on down the road smelling freshly plowed Iowa fields mingled with fresh cut hay. The sweet smells of wild flowers blooming mixed with the wet pavement, creating one of those smells I wished I could bottle.

Mother Nature served up a pure banquet today on a large platter. The landscape kept changing ever so slowly. From flat Iowa corn fields to Wisconsin's hillier farms, we rode through the day. The small towns had funny names and lots of charm. My favorite, though, was Coon Valley, Wisconsin.

We stopped for a short period of time to get gas, and then rode on for about four more miles to a place that advertised breakfast. About two miles down the road from the gas stop a deer popped her head up out of the grass along the side of the road.

Now just why didn't she run into the woods on her side of the road? I don't know what possessed her but she ran right out onto the road to cross over to the other side. Both of us did some serious breaking but Ralph was leading and he was closest to the deer. He missed her by mere inches. We got an up close and personal look at her hindquarters as she tucked up her hind legs under her just as Ralph passed her. All three of us survived though Ralph and I had to swallow hard to get our hearts back where they belonged in our chest and not in our throats. We lived to enjoy our breakfast of eggs and pancakes and the deer returned to her grazing.

Making our way north on Route 61, we followed the Mississippi River. Having never seen the Mississippi up this far north, I noticed it was much prettier up here than down in Memphis. We stopped in a small town called Lake City. We sat on a restaurant's deck and had lunch while we watched the sailboats cruise the river. Wow, what a day. Mother Nature gets an A+ today.

All is well with us today and we are tucked in for the night in a motel somewhere north of St. Paul, Minnesota. Our plan is to head for northern Minnesota tomorrow and hopefully make it to Canada if time allows.

Until next time, love to all always,
Judy/Mom/Mommy

May 30, 2005
Karlstad, MN
Monday
Mile 3367

Dear Folks,

We stayed in a motel last night so Ralph could have internet connection to work. We used the last of our budget money on the hotel leaving us just a few dollars for doing the laundry and for dinner. We were not really hungry, thank goodness, so we shared a bag of microwave popcorn, a coke, and a bag of M&M Peanuts. With my belly satisfied and a good long shower, I went immediately to sleep and left Ralph working into the wee hours of the morning. He got to sleep around two-thirty in the morning.

Our start today from St. Paul was very late, as Ralph had to finish the special study he was doing for a client. We did not actually start rolling until around two in the afternoon. As for me, it was such a late start, I was thinking to myself why even bother. That bed in the motel was looking mighty enticing.

We left St. Paul this afternoon with the idea we would ride about two hundred miles then see how we felt and whether we felt like stopping. As the miles rolled by the countryside got more and more beautiful. Farms stretched out as far as the eye could see on the horizon. Dark, rich earth freshly plowed and sprouting green plants, gave off it's aroma of warm dirt.

Farmhouses were tucked up in the fir trees that had been planted years ago to protect the houses from wind, snow, and summer's heat. Neat two story houses rested close to bright red barns and silver silos.

Lilac bushes, with a riot of purple blossoms and the heady perfume smell, were divine to the senses. The aroma reminded me of the gardenia bushes that must be blooming now at home. Lilac bushes grow in colder climates than in the south or else I would plant one first thing when I get home.

All along the road as we traveled, red winged blackbirds perched on dried up stalks of cattails or weeds. They looked to me like black and red suckers stuck on sticks in the grass.

The further north we went the more wet areas I noticed. The ducks were paired off and were interested in only one thing if you catch my drift. Copious amounts of lakes and small ponds were in every indention of the land. The landscape was getting wider and wider and more stretched out. The sky was larger and full of more clouds, all with flat bottoms and puffy tops.

We rode longer that we expected and I was starting to get a little worried about finding a place to stay. The sun was going down; shadows were stretching out in long fingers across the road and the air was cooling quickly. As we passed through each tiny town on the northbound road, no campgrounds or hotels were to be found.

I was also worried about the deer that might pop out of the grasses beside the road. I was concerned about moose also, as I had seen a sign a few miles back stating "moose crossing." Hitting a moose on a motorcycle would be disastrous.

We pulled into a small town about fifty miles from the Canadian border and found a small park. There were only about five or six buildings in the town but the town had a very nice park complete with campground. There were no showers though, so we are going to be quite stinky by this time tomorrow. Ralph got our tent set up just in time to see the sun go down. Ralph asked the only other camper where we were suppose to pay the five-dollar fee and they said we could pay anyone in town, it didn't matter, anyone could take our money. We both chuckled to each other as we walked about one hundred yards back to the main road to find a local resident. We found a young waitress at a little restaurant on the road and paid her our five dollars for the night. What a deal. When was the last time anyone paid five dollars for a place to sleep in the United States? We were well under budget for the day.

The campground is about seventy-five yards from the train track that runs through the center of town. Now how come I did not see that when we came through the town? A very long train complete with a very loud whistle just rolled through town. I shudder to think how many times that will happen tonight.

It is late and I know the sun and birds will be awake early, probably at the predictable five o'clock hour so I'm going to snuggle down quickly in my bag and sleep while I can.

So, until next time, much love to all always,
Judy/Mom/Mommy

May 31, 2005
Tuesday
Yorkton, Canada
Mile 3766

Dear Folks,

Just as I expected, we were up early with the chirping birds, quacking ducks, and croaking frogs. However, it was a very pleasant way to be awakened. The air was very cool and if my hand or leg escaped from the warmth of my sleeping bag, it was quickly drawn back inside.

We were blessed with another clear blue sky today for our travels. We have been fortunate so far with the weather but I have probably jinxed it now. We got on the road to the gas station by seven-thirty in the little town called Karlstad, Minnesota where we stayed last night and filled the tanks with gas and put oil in both engines. I noticed on the ground at the gas station, copious amounts of dead beetles about the size of nickels. They were the perfect size that would have me kicking and screaming a plue perfect hissy fit if one were to land on me. I am not a friend of flying beetles and roaches. The thought of one landing on me and its flapping wings on or under my clothes makes me want to gag.

Fortunately, they were all dead or crunched up. I know now what was hitting the side of the tent last night. I knew it was something large popping and tapping on the tent just waiting for an opportunity to gain entrance. I get the willies just thinking about one flapping around the inside of our tent. I sound like a real sissy, don't I? I have always been of the nature that if those undesirable creatures leave me alone, I will leave them alone. I never go out of my way to kill other living creatures but just let one of those nasty things land on me and it is all over, at least for the bug that is.

Back out on the road we realized we were just thirty-four miles from the Canadian boarder. As we got closer to the boarder, another deer ran across the road. Fortunately, this time though, there was a car in front of us and the deer was faster than the car. After the doe made it to the other side, she turned around with her ears perked up and eyes big as black saucers and looked at us like we were freaks.

The border crossing was easy. The crossing guard looked at our passports and asked us to take off our helmets so he could match the pictures. I told him I would take my helmet off if he promised not to faint. I had a bad case of helmet hair combined with bed head and no shower. I felt really nasty. He just laughed and asked me to take it off any way. Thank goodness, he did not faint.

Ralph and I were only asked a few simple questions and we were on our way in a matter of minutes. When the time comes, it will be interesting to see how quickly we can get back into the United States.

The road at once became rough, torn up and bumpy. I knew it was going to be a long day on that surface. The first small Canadian town we came to visually announced their Ukrainian ancestry. The names of the stores reflected as much as did the cemetery with its unusual crosses for head stones. I thought for a brief moment we might have been somewhere in the Ukraine.

One thing I did not expect was to be traveling through the great plains of Canada. Our surroundings were flat, flat, flat with farm fields as far as the eye could see. The vastness of the fields was so large that my brain had a hard time conceiving how many square miles the area covered. Some fields were already knee deep in crops and in other fields, their black dirt waited for the sun to do its ageless warming.

Some of the smells were overpowering. Nasty smells, like rotten feces assaulted my nose. I tried holding my breath but could not for very long. Of course, when I could no longer hold my breath, I would have to take a big gulp of air and suck all that nastiness down into the depths of my clean lungs. About the time I was about to gag, the air would clear and the smell of lilacs blooming would be a welcome relief. Such opposite ends of the spectrum, these smells were to me, in this area.

On several occasions, I thought a crop of bright yellow flowers had been planted. The yellow was so intense and bright it hurt my eyes. I kept seeing more and more of the yellow flowers along the road. I finally realized it was just dandelions, millions of them! They were so incredibly thick and beautiful though and so many in one place. I could envision the upcoming cloud of fluffy, tiny white parachutes that would soon be floating on the air.

The roads were very rough for the most part but every now and then, a newly repaved stretch of highway would calm my rattling teeth. From everything I read before we left Atlanta, I know there is more of this rough terrain to come further north on our route. Is my body going to be able to handle it or will I just become accustomed to the roughness of the environment?

Unfortunately, the trucks were back in full force today. I just love being blown around by shit filled cattle trucks, gravel trucks, and tractor-trailers carrying extra large farm equipment. My muscles tense each time we encounter one. My sunglasses, face shield, and windshield get sand blasted with each passing truck. You cannot imagine how large the farm equipment is up here. Ours down south looks like miniature ponies compared to the big boys up here. All sorts of equipment in all sorts of various shapes and sizes travel the roads and fields. Most of the equipment I cannot even begin to tell for what purpose they are used. But, of course, logic tells me they are all for planting and harvesting the crops grown here. One of the crops is wheat but I do not recognize the other crops. If it is not grown in the South, I can only use my imagination.

After five days of rain before we got here, the ground is a black quagmire. I kept noticing black globs on the roads. I was sure it was pieces of tires or something that had been torn up or maybe black rocks had been scattered all along the road. I was having a hard time avoiding the black stuff and continued weaving around it until I realized it was just black mud that the farm equipment had on its tires when it came out of the fields. Deciding to run over the mud after that, each mound squished silently under my wheels. Then it became a game to see just how many mushy mounds I could run over.

As we proceeded further northwest, the number of small ponds and large puddles were increasing. In each and every pond or puddle, no matter how small or large, there were ducks. I saw mallards, Canada geese, loons and many others I could not identify. Most ducks were nesting. I saw one pair of geese with so many babies in tow I could not count them. It must have been a good year in the aviaries.

Ralph and I reached our limit for one day after riding about three hundred and ninety miles. Stinky and tired to the bone, we decided to find a hotel, eat dinner, and go to bed. I am going to have to hose off my riding pants somewhere as the legs are crusted with yellow bug guts. I am not kidding; there are bug guts on top of bug guts and it looks as if my legs have been spray painted with school bus yellow paint. Later, in our room, as I took off my riding pants and boots, dead bug carcasses fell out onto the nice clean bathroom floor.

I am clean now, smell much better and it feels great. Ralph just read the weather report and we are expecting to be traveling into rain for the next two days. I guess the riding gear will get another test but I am not looking forward to it at all. Riding in the rain has its own set of tricks.

Amanda, the bear is holding up just fine strapped onto the back of my bike. Daddy did not have room for him on his bike so I am carrying him. He is not too dirty yet but I think that is about to change. I guess you meant for this bear to come with us since he was on Daddy's motorcycle seat the morning we left Atlanta. If not, let me know and I will ship him home. I think he needs to have his feet dipped into the Arctic don't you? I have had to give him a new name. Grizzle Bear fits him, don't you think?

Perry, I will download all my pictures onto a disk and ship it home to you. I know you are waiting for pictures and they are coming soon. You just will not believe the beautiful scenery. You must come someday.

Milissa, I think I saw a coyote today. Looking rather sneaky, it was all alone in a field. Though I think it was a coyote it could have been an ugly dog. After all, the other day, I did actually see a dog that at first, I thought was a pig. That was the most butt ugly dog I have ever seen in my life, poor thing.

My new favorite name for a road that I happened to see yesterday is Oink Joint Road. That combined with Otter Tail Town ranks right up there with my list of favorite names.

The clean sheets and soft bed are calling me and enough is enough for one day.

Until next time, love to all always,
Judy/Mom/Mommy

June 1, 2005
Wednesday 6:45pm
Lloydminster, Canada
Mile 4138

Dear Folks,

I forgot a few things about yesterday that I will now tell you about. I do not know how I forgot them, as at the time they were very impressive.

Yesterday, we stopped in a very small town, which had maybe, three or four buildings. There was a small restaurant offering breakfast for three dollars and ninety-nine cents Canadian. Since we were starving and the towns we had already been through were so small with no facilities we decided to take our chances in this town since there was a small restaurant. There were several cars parked outside which is always a good sign. There were no motorcycles though. Seeing a motorcycle outside any restaurant always draws more motorcyclists. One favorite pastime of bikers is riding to eat. Therefore, following an unwritten code, if a biker is parked in front of a diner or restaurant then the food must be good. I have routinely found this to be true.

As we walked into the restaurant, there was a table of six old codgers sitting around a small table drinking a final cup of coffee for the morning. They were pleasant enough and asked us where we were traveling. They did not seem the least bit impressed nor did they really care.

The owner came over and asked us what we wanted for breakfast. There was no menu mind you, just tell her what you wanted and she would fix your meal. I ordered scrambled eggs with cheese, hash browns, bacon, and white toast. Ralph ordered scrambled eggs without the cheese and sausage instead of bacon, hash browns, and his usual wheat toast.

The lady went back into the kitchen and we could see her starting our breakfast. I knew it was going to be fresh. There is nothing like the smell of bacon frying to get those old taste buds working overtime. While our breakfast was cooking, the lady came out and asked me to sign her guest book. I gave a quick glance to see who had signed recently. The most recent date was two years ago and was signed from someone about fifty miles down the road. So she really wanted our entry from Georgia in the United States. At least she was impressed.

When she came back out of the kitchen with our breakfast, the plates were loaded. Good, I was hungry. When she put the plate down in front of me, my heart sank. I could not tell which were the hash browns and which were the eggs. Both were brown and crispy and there was absolutely no hint of cheese anywhere on the plate. I think it was brown, too. The eggs were in small bb size pellets. My visions of soft, fluffy, scrambles eggs oozing with cheddar cheese quickly evaporated. Now just where did she learn to cook?

I forgot I was in Canada and the bacon I ordered was Canadian bacon not hog fat bacon from the tables of homes in the South. I was so hungry I ate the pellets anyway along with the hash browns, Canadian bacon, and toast. I wish I had taken a picture of the eggs but Ralph told me I would be rude and insulting. I tried to remind him that my pellet eggs were insulting but he silenced me with a dirty look. No one I know would have believed the eggs I had been served. The lady was nice and she took our U.S. dollars so I guess it was best that I had not insulted her cooking. We departed with our bellies full of pellets, brown stringy hash browns, meat, and toast.

Our environment had been relatively calm for hours but as we traveled on down the road the wind picked up somewhat. As we rounded a curve, I noticed off in the distance, huge, monstrous windmills. Seeing windmills high up on a hill is not a good sign when riding a motorcycle. Those windmills are there for a purpose and that usually means that there is the force of Mother Nature to turn them. High enough up on a hill to catch the wind, they were all white, on columns at least twenty stories high. The blades reminded me of a big turbine on a spacecraft in some movies I have seen. Monster size windmills were spinning in the wind like no body's business. We scooted by them without incident and moved on down the road leaving them twirling in the wind and me breathing a big sigh of relief.

Now, back to today's events. As feared, we woke up to very gray clouds, rain, and cool temperatures. After leaving the warm, dry hotel room, we only got a sprinkling and misting of rain. Ralph was insistent that we were going to be camping tonight after spending the last two nights in a hotel. Off in the distance, however, lurked trouble and trouble had our names written in the darkness of the clouds.

I figured that today being overcast and rainy there would not be much to write about and that we would just put in the miles to get closer to our destination in Alaska. But, even on what you might think would be just another day, there are events, sounds, smells, and visuals that can provide plenty of material for storytelling.

Today, I noticed that the smells are different when riding while it is raining. Some smells are good like the damp earth and the heavy scent of wild things blooming. Those smells make you want to take deep breaths. Some smells are really nasty. I keep talking about the nasty smell. I cannot figure out where it is coming from. The smell is like a rotten stockyard on a hot day after a few days rain. The odor hangs heavy in the air covering the land with a pungent blanket of stench. I will be extremely happy to vacate this nasty smelling area.

I have also become somewhat an expert on winds. While riding my motorcycle I have discovered that there are basically four types of wind. First, there is the rather rare time when there is no wind. I believe this one speaks for itself and I naturally like this one the best. Second, is the tail wind. This type ranks high up there with no wind. A tail wind will push you along from behind and feels like it did when you were a child and your daddy or big brother pushed you on your bicycle. It feels effortless as you scoot down the road. Getting great gas mileage is an extra-added bonus. The wind rushing through the helmet ceases and it is almost silent as we rush down the road.

Then, we travel around a very long curve in the road and what was a tail wind now becomes the third type of wind: a cross wind. Look out for those, they will catch you by surprise and send you flying all over the road. Remember that trouble I was talking about earlier? More about that in a moment. The fourth type of wind to me is the head wind. Not as bad as a cross wind but it is a struggle to get through. Getting nowhere, it is like being on a treadmill going seventy miles per hour.

I think I am deaf from the wind in my helmet. I am thinking about buying some earplugs but then I could not hear Ralph yell at me when we pull into the small towns at the lights or stop signs. Humm, maybe earplugs would be a good idea after all.

As we traveled along today in the mist and rain, I started to see more and more different types of birds. I chuckled within my helmet at one bird. He looked like a smaller version of a crow. His whole head right down to his shoulders looked liked he lost his way at the picnic and dipped his whole head in mustard.

There were more ducks I could not recognize but they all were so beautiful. One, I noticed, had a red head the color of rust but as I flew by at seventy-five miles per hour, it was difficult to distinguish which color. Today was a good day for ducks as the rain and mist continued.

One thing I am constantly amazed at is the size of the balls that some of the smaller birds have when it comes to protecting their nests. On many occasions along our trek, I have noticed several small birds attacking hawks that have ventured too close to a nest. The hawk is high tailing it as fast as its feathered wings will carry it the other way.

I have seen many hawks soaring. One today actually stooped from a lofty perch right into the ground next to the road. As I whizzed by I did not see what he captured but I hope the hawk was successful.

Today, I saw the perfect commercial today for Chevy trucks. Traveling down the highway, coming our way, hogging their lane and part of ours were two tractor-trailers pulling flatbeds. On the flatbeds were huge pieces of farm equipment, so large that they hung over each side of the flatbed and into part of our lane. Right behind the two tractor-trailers was a white Chevy truck pulling its own flatbed trailer with a piece of farm equipment just as large as the ones the tractor-trailers were pulling. Too bad a camera crew was not available. I was impressed. I guess the next truck I have will be a Chevy.

I have not figured out what other crops are grown here but it must be something industrial, feed the world, size. The farm equipment used to plant and harvest the crops is massive. Other than wheat, maybe it is canola or something of that nature.

Ok, now for the crosswind from hell. All day we had been skirting around some very large storm cells. Since we could see so far to the horizon in all directions, we could see the clouds building and determine where the rain is coming down. So far today, we had been lucky but that changed after lunch. Trouble came a knocking.

The road wound up between two of those cells. I had to stop and take a picture it was so menacing and impressive. The picture cannot capture the three hundred sixty degree experience like the eye can. No sooner had we gotten back on the road and were one hundred yards up the road from where the picture was taken, than a cross wind from hell came thundering out of the north. Instantly, we were blown all over the road. Since I was following Ralph, I watched him lean into the wind at an angle that he would if leaning into a mountain curve in north Georgia. I knew that just a mere fraction of a second would pass before I would be hit by the same fist slamming into me. My heart rate flew up instantly and my intestines did some interesting things as well.

We were battered and torn, twisted and bent by the wind. Then the rain came down in buckets. Those dark, troubled clouds let loose their icy mother load straight from the heavens and right down onto us. The lightening that accompanied the dark rain clouds was an extra-added bonus. I just love lightning, particularly when I am in the middle of nowhere and it is fifteen miles to the nearest town, with the wind howling, rain blowing sideways and the trucks flying by sending up their spray of crud. I had a momentary flashback to a sunny road in South Georgia but it immediately vaporized with the next lightning bolt.

In the middle of the downpour, with the wind blowing us sideways and the lightning flashing long, white bolts to the ground, Ralph's bike quit. Right in the middle of the road it just died! We rolled to a stop on the paved shoulder of the road, which, fortunately, was relatively wide.

There we sat, on the side of the road in total disbelief. At that exact moment, the icy water from outer space found the opening between my helmet and the collar of my jacket. I got goose bumps right down to the sock lint between my toes. I hunched over my tank bag and Ralph just stood there in the soaking rain, looking at his bike, all-forlorn, as if his best friend had left him. I was thankful that I had chosen the riding gear that I had.

With torrential rains, hellacious wind and a fantastic lightning and thunder show all around us, Ralph started mentioning something about me towing him to the next town that was fifteen miles away with the rope he had stashed in his saddlebag. I looked at him, then at the clouds and yelled above the roar of rain, "Can't we just wait a few minutes and see if some of this blows over? Oh yeah, and by the way, I'm not camping out tonight."

I noticed a small dirt road about thirty yards up ahead and a small covered picnic area. I suggested we try to push the bike over there and get out of the rain. There was no response from Ralph so we continued to sit there. Ralph made several attempts to restart the bike with no luck and a plethora of colorful language issued from his mouth. After standing in the vicious weather another few minutes, Ralph went over and tried to start the bike again. Miracles of miracles, it started. Ralph took off at once leaving me behind on the roadside watching the rooster tail from his wet rear wheel grow smaller and smaller. I knew he was headed to the next town as quickly as possible and I would find him there if I could not catch up with him in the pouring rain.

My bike started right away and I caught up with Ralph a few miles down the road. We managed to make it to the next town safely and pulled into a hotel that had a covered awning. We checked in immediately. Ralph can set the tent up outside the hotel room if he really wants to camp so badly tonight. Me, I am going to sleep in a nice dry bed with a hard roof over my head and the only shower I am going to get is the one with running hot water and a nice dry towel.

Once in the room, Ralph got on the phone immediately to our trusty motorcycle mechanic instructor, friend, Mike. Ralph got a few insights from Mike but not a good solution to what might have caused the bike to suddenly stop. Ralph refused to let the situation go as a freak occurrence. He took his bike apart in the parking lot in front of our hotel room. By now, the storm had moved on further east and we were treated to just a little drizzle.

Ralph made trips back and forth between the bike and the room, which had now become a motorcycle spare parts lot. There were pieces of the bike everywhere and I had instructions not to touch anything. Yeah, like that was my top priority. He had placed the parts in a certain order so they could go back on the bike in the same order in which they were removed. No way I was getting anywhere near anything that remotely looked like a motorcycle part. I am not that stupid.

Besides, I was too busy drying off my wet gloves and one wet Grizzle Bear. I had covered his head with a plastic bag this morning to keep him dry but the bag had torn in a place and poor Grizzle Bear's head and clothes were soaked. His rain gear did not work as well as mine did.

While I was busy drying very important things like the bear and the cuffs to my jeans, Ralph was filling the trashcans in the room with water and dumping the whole contents on the running bike outside. He was trying to duplicate the problem he had had earlier. Gallons and gallons of water, like Noah's flood went out of the room and onto his bike. The bike ran like a champ, not one little cough, not one little sputter. The bike was drowned with the likes of being dumped in a swimming pool! The bike continued to run on and on.

Ralph put all the parts back on his bike, came back in the room, and announced he had fixed the bike. Here I thought I would have nothing to write about today since it was going to be a soggy one.

We are off to Edmonton tomorrow. We are stopping at the BMW motorcycle dealer to have a worn out front tire replaced on Ralph's bike. He has plans to ask about the nature of the stalling problem as well.

So until later, take care and lots of love,
Judy/Mom/Mommy

PS. Our riding gear got a super endorsement today, truly passing the test. My feet were dry as a bone, my pants, and tee shirt were dry as well. Only a spot around the cuffs of my jeans got wet. I believe that was caused by some wicking from an exposed part of my jeans. All in all, I am really impressed with the way our riding gear performs.

June 3, 2005
Fort St. Johns, British Columbia
Friday 8:00 pm
Mile 4,750

Dear Folks,

As I left you last, we were recuperating from a heavy downpour. Ralph's bike worked perfectly fine the next day. We made it to Edmonton without incident, got his tire changed, and were on our way in record time. The BMW dealership failed to diagnose the stalling problem. That left Ralph puzzled and a little nervous.

Once again, the landscape was slowly starting to change. The farmland was changing from flat fields to hills. Animal crops were becoming visible and they were replacing some of the plant crops. My mouth watered at the cattle in the pastures. Recognizing my place in the food chain, I was hankering for a good piece of Canadian beef.

As the miles rolled on and on, I have ample time to absorb my surroundings and take notice of those surroundings. Sites along the way will stay with me forever. There is an abundance of hawks here, much bigger than our beautiful red tail hawks in the south. The hawks here sit upon the tall telephone poles waiting for a tasty morsel to venture by beneath them. Sometimes, I see them majestically soaring in the wind currents looking for a meal. While at other times I see them being chased off repeatedly by small birds protecting nest.

Traveling along over this grassland prairie, I have become aware of the many graveyards. Most are just off the road and are very well tended. But, to me, the graveyards are so very forlorn and silent as we pass. To think of them covered in a blanket of winter's snow, that surely must cover this northern part of Canada when the cold winter descends, makes me shudder with chills of coldness and loneliness.

I have enjoyed seeing the trains crossing this vast and endless country of fields. The countryside is so open and flat that I can see the entire train. The track runs close to the road and as I get closer to the train coming my direction, I wave with great determination to see if the conductor will blow the whistle. Even expecting the whistle, it is so loud it startles me, when the conductor sees me waving and waves back with both his whistle and his arm. I have fun sharing a hello with a complete stranger. We are ships that pass in the night, as my Mama would say.

I noticed, also, passing by several large pastures, that there appeared to be orange and blue tents set up in the grasslands. At first, I wondered what was going on and how unusual it was to have tents set up in the middle of huge pastures. Then I figured though, that the tents must be shelters for the cows to huddle in when the weather turned foul or are in need of a bit of shade.

Yesterday was just a day for pumping out the miles. We were trying to get some distance behind us and put us closer to Alaska. I was so bone weary by the end of the day I could hardly see straight. Every muscle in my body hurt. We found a nice provincial campground about three miles off the main highway. Once we got further into the woods, the road down into the campground turned out to be gravel. I was thrilled to say the least.

The campground was actually very beautiful but very primitive. I had to find the potty immediately and noticed that I had to walk down a trail back into the woods to find the outhouse. Ugg. There were no other facilities were around, so I went in the women's side only to find it humming with mosquitoes. Now what a lovely combination that was: mosquitoes and a bare butt. Just think about all the possibilities! One learns to take care of certain necessities rather quickly when faced with having one's ass chewed.

The campsite was infested with the bloodsuckers. I now have a new perfume fragrance. Deet works as promised but leaves quite an aroma. The mosquitoes will not bite but the repellant will not keep them from swarming. Unfortunately, I have discovered that Deet tastes much worse that it smells. After coating all of my exposed skin, I accidentally wiped my hand over my mouth. That mistake is one I will only do once. It also has a numbing effect on the lips and tongue.

We built a small fire last night and between the smoke from that and the Deet, the monster size mosquitoes did not bite, but they did buzz. We have been fortunate to keep the pest out of the tent so far on our trip. Ralph and I have developed a method that has worked consistently. I stand by the door to the tent and make great fanning motions with my jacket. This disturbs the air so much that anything with wings leaves the area immediately. While I am fanning, Ralph quickly unzips a small opening in the door to the tent and throws our gear inside. This is repeated until all our belongings are inside. Then we quickly jump inside and zip the tent enclosing us in a mosquito free environment. There is nothing worse than having that high-pitched humming in your ear while you try to sleep.

We picked this campground because it had showers but it turned out they were not any where near the campsite we had picked. After Ralph did an inspection of the showers on the other side of the campground, he said he would pass. They must have been really bad. I knew I was going to stay dirty another day also.

The sounds of wild birds woke me this morning at five-thirty. They had such a sweet song I imagined them being fairy-tale birds of all sorts of pastel colors. The little birds were a much nicer wake up call than the loud raucous caw of the stinking crows. The crows are always in pairs, yakking at each other. I'd like to stick a sock down their gullets. We were on the road early this morning and had plans to ride only a short distance so we could rest in the afternoon.

As we venture further north, the landscape is changing dramatically. Instead of rolling hills of crops, evergreen forest and aspen tree forest have appeared and surround the green pastures and planted crops. There are many horses with foals on the ground. I really enjoy watching the horses as we pass their pastures. The horses remind me of our own we had long ago.

Today, as we were coming around a long hilly curve in the road, suddenly there was a deep valley off to our right. Down in the valley, there was so much smoke, it looked as if the entire valley was on fire. I was getting worried thinking we would be stopped at any moment on the road by a forest fire until I realized it was river fog coming from the river down in the valley. As we rode up and over the hill, I saw the sign that said Smokey River. Well duh, and how stupid did I feel?

On we rode through the fresh scent of the fir trees and wildflowers. The road signs posted were calling for caution for moose crossings. Just as I had gotten use to looking out for deer, I now have to look out for moose. Today, I saw many deer off in the woods near the road but only one moose. Unfortunately, for the moose, he was dead as a doornail and stinking to high heaven. As we whizzed by I got a quick look at his rotten, swollen butt carcass and caught a whiff of a smell that would stop a bear in its tracks. Along with the many deer and the dead moose today, I spotted a fat and healthy coyote hunting and pouncing for food off in a pasture.

Around lunch, after traveling almost five thousand miles over the past thirteen days, we finally made it to Dawson's Creek and the zero milepost for the start of the Alaskan Highway. We took the tourist picture in front of the milepost and started on our way down the fifteen hundred mile infamous road to the far reaches of Alaska.

As we got closer to our final destination for the night, we came around a curve and noticed a sign that warned trucks to check their brakes. That is never a good sign. There were steep grades ahead. I downshifted into third gear and started down the incredibly steep slope. We descended a mountain I had no idea we were even on and saw a bridge off in the distance. I knew Ralph was not going to like the bridge. The bridge went across a deep canyon with a rushing river at the bottom. I was getting a little nervous too. Down and down we went, out onto the canyon ledge, then onto the bridge.

Oh, I got the willies. This was a rather long bridge made entirely of the type of bridge one sees on drawbridges. A sign before we crossed said, "Caution bridge may be covered in ice during frost." Great. Well I knew it was sixty degrees so there was no threat of frost but it is not much fun to ride on that type of surface. On the grated surface the front tire and handlebars wiggle and play loosey goosey too much for my taste.

As we crossed the bridge I kept telling myself not to look down, don't look down, hey stupid, don't look down! Well that is just what I did and all I could see was the rushing river down in a deep canyon. My heart jumped immediately into my throat and my sphincter muscles geared up. We were riding over a bridge that was a metal grate. I might as well be riding on glass.

At the next stop, I sarcastically asked Ralph if he liked the bridge and did he happen to look down as he crossed over. He had not even thought of looking down. He wanted to go back and do it again. I would gladly wait right were I was for him if he would like to go back and experience the bridge again. He thought better of the idea so we kept on going and found a real nice provincial campground similar to the one last night. This one had paved roads through the campground but no showers. This is day two without a shower and I feel gross. Dirty fingernails, dirty hair, I smell like Deet, firewood smoke, road dirt and just plain dirt.

The birds up here are absolutely incredible. So very many songbirds fill the woods around me with melody. I am really enjoying the birds on this journey. Bright yellow finches are singing as we speak right in the tree above the picnic table. A beautiful woodpecker is having a blast, eating bugs out of one of the birch trees behind our tent. I can only imagine the size of the pile driver that is hammering in the woods across from our campsite. That bird sounds like a member of a marching band is taking his drumsticks and beating a cadence on another piece of wood. I have truly never heard anything like it. The natives are restless.

Wow, we have had another good day. Ralph and I have ridden in and out of rain for the past three days and I am ready for some solid sunny days. Sunshine or rain, we take what we get, and keep on following that mysterious road to our dreams in Alaska.

Grizzle Bear is getting his share of rain and dirt on him too. His little leather jacket has gotten some tiny scratches from flying debris, just like ours. I have also had to dry his clothes out just like I did mine. He is quite a trooper, never complains, and is always ready for the next day's journey strapped upon the back of my bike.

Ralph is keeping the fire warm for me. It is late but the sun is still shining and it does not get dark now until around eleven at night. I am off to sit by the fire and to listen to the sounds of the wild mountain birds lull us into tranquility.

Until next time love to you always,
Judy/Mom/Mommy

June 4, 2005
Ft. Nelson, British Columbia
Saturday 9:00pm
Mile 4978

Dear Folks,

As expected this morning we were awakened to the chirping of the bright yellow finches and the pile driver working away deep in the woods. Last night one bird sang until the last drop of sunlight, which was around eleven P.M. and was up bright and early going at it again. When does he rest? I know all during the day he or she is singing for a mate, building a nest, or trying to find food. The activity of this little bird wears me out just thinking about it.

It rained during the night, not a downpour, but a nice light rain pattering down on our little green tent in the deep woods of Canada. Though not enough rain to even worry us, it was just enough to lull us back to sleep.

Ralph got up to go to visit the bushes sometime after daybreak and I groaned thinking it was time to rise and shine. Trying to ignore him, I quickly turned over in the bag and went back to sleep. I woke up solidly at five-thirty with the birds. Ralph was snoring away. He later told me it was around four-thirty when he got up. At that time, it was already light! These short hours of darkness mixed with the time differences is really messing with my poor old brain.

Our early start this morning took us directly into the wilderness. Before us was pristine forest of evergreen mixed with the white bark of birch and aspen. My brain was continually clicking off pictures of the beauty before me. We saw several large deer today and all looked so startled that we were even riding down the road in their territory. Everything up here in British Columbia is much bigger. The further north we go into the wilderness the vastness increases, from the mosquitoes, to the crows, to the hawks, to the deer, and most impressively, the landscape increases.

Describing the way the landscape has changed is difficult for me. I can ride up a very long hill and around a curve in the road and all of a sudden the land before me explodes in a depth I find hard to believe. For miles and miles as far as I can see, the land is stretched out with wild forest of dark green evergreens and is completely void of any development. As I crest every hill, I see the road many, many miles ahead of me wandering through more dark forest. I am humbled at the vastness and grandeur and so delighted to see the wilderness before me.

Oh, and the smell. We try so hard at Christmas time to bring the smell of fir trees into our homes with just one little tree. Up here, this is a whole world of Christmas trees and the smell is intoxicating and divine. I breathe deeply so often that it becomes dizzying.

Speaking of Christmas trees, as we were traveling down the long road today, through virgin forest with absolutely no other soul around, a bright shiny object caught my eye off to the right. As I got closer, I started laughing. Someone had decorated a fir tree with Christmas balls and shiny garland of red and gold. All alone, in a giant forest of Christmas trees, stood this one lone tree, beaming colors of red, silver, and gold.

Today we encountered the first of the motor homes that we had been warned about in the books we read while doing research for our trip. These motor homes are houses on wheels pulling their full size cars and boats. I did not see one other motorcycle other than Ralph's! Today it was just the motor homes, the trucks and us. This country of Canada and ours moves very much so on the backs of the trucks. They are mega trucks, all pulling an extra trailer behind them. Having to pass one makes it more hair raising when the trucks are doubles.

The winds have died down for the time being and I am glad, as it is not much fun riding in the winds. My shoulders, arms, and wrists are sore from holding the bike steady and the muscles have burned for days. I am wondering if I should have been lifting weights to strengthen my arms and shoulders before we left Atlanta.

In addition to the sore muscles, my fingernails are all ragged and I have many hangnails even though I try to get them straightened every night. Even though I smear enough Vaseline to lubricate a freight train on my lips many, many times during the day, my lips stay chapped. My face had finally scabbed over and healed from the hefty burn I got in Florida. I have an awful tan in the form of two triangles, one for each cheek. I call the tan my bat wing tan for not much is exposed to the sun but the cheeks when wearing a full faced helmet and sun glasses. I have bruises in places I did not even know I owned and for the life of me cannot figure out when I even got the bruises.

I do not think my poor ole body can figure just what it is I am doing to it. But, despite all the abuse my body is taking, I am thoroughly thrilled with the challenge. My brain is alive with the thirst for what is around the next bend in the road, over the next mountain and down the rivers we follow along the road.

We stopped this morning in a little place called Pink Mountain at a road house and had a wonderful breakfast of yummy warm pancakes dripping in maple syrup. The cook knew perfectly well how to cook scrambled eggs with cheese. The bacon was good old hog fat, too. After breakfast, we got our first glimpse of the Canadian Rocky Mountains, complete with snow from the winter past, way off on the distant horizon.

We are seeing more and more warning signs for wildlife on the road. The signs are also an indication of our changing environment the farther north we travel. We have graduated from deer signs to moose and now caribou. With each new sign comes the warning of larger and larger animals. I have also seen many buffalo herds grazing. These are not wild herds though, but someone's business now that buffalo meat has become so popular. I will pass on the buffalo thank you and stick to cow.

The further north we travel, we see more evidence of the natural gas industry. The smell of wonderful evergreen was interrupted quickly in one location by the smell of natural gas. I looked over to the left side of the road and there was a pipe about twenty feet in the air burning a bright red flame. It reminded me that this area of the world is rich in these types of resources.

I am getting closer the goal we have set out to achieve. There are only seventeen hundred miles left to the Arctic Ocean. We have covered almost five thousand miles so far. As we traveled down these beautiful roads over this vast country, I see my goal coming within reach. Each day and mile brings me closer to fulfilling a dream a long time in the realization. I cannot quit now nor would I want to. My spirit is alive with the life and world around me and it is hungry for adventure.

Milissa and Amanda, you just thought you liked the trucks in Atlanta. They totally pale in comparison to the ones up here. Y'all would be in truck heaven. Everyone drives a truck with a capital T, not those little sissy things at home. I am talking huge four by four's all pumped up or lifted as y'all say, and covered in mud. It is not the red Georgia clay but a grayish brown. Here, I think it is a status symbol to see who has the most mud on their trucks. The trucks all look like they are on steroids as they flash by us as if we are standing still. You girls would love them. I saw a beautiful red Dodge Ram today with silver maple leaves fanning out from the front bumper and swirling over the front fender and door. I know y'all would have loved it.

We are in a hotel tonight as Ralph had some work to do and it required internet connection. We are about to enter a section of country where there will not be any connection and maybe not a good phone signal. Do not worry if you don't hear from us for a few days. Maybe we will get lucky and a little signal will creep in just when we least expect it.

Grizzle Bear stayed dry today but got a little cold. The temperature dropped and I was glad I had the liners in my pants and jacket. I will have to add a layer tomorrow as I was still a little chilled. Ralph is definitely adding layers as he has been riding without his liners. Burrrrrr!

Take care and I will have lots to add in the upcoming days I'm sure. I miss you kids, Perry, Amanda, and Milissa. Big hugs and squeezes to all of you. Milissa tell Bryan hi for me and if maybe if you feel like it give him a hug from me.

And as always I love you bunches and bunches.

Until next time, love always,
Judy/Mom/Mommy

June 5, 2005
Watson Lake, Yukon
Sunday 9:21 pm pacific time
Mile 5301

Dear Folks,

When we got up this morning and looked outside, I just knew it was going to be a miserable day. The skies were very overcast, gloomy, starting to mist heavily and very cold. I was not looking forward to today's ride. Knowing that I would not be seeing anything at all due to the weather, I resigned myself to just putting in miles. How wrong I was.

How could I have known that this would be one of the most gorgeous and challenging days I would have since we left home fifteen days ago? As left the town of Ft. Nelson we headed up into the mountains, which were totally socked in by rain, heavy fog, and mist. The fog was so heavy I could not see thirty yards in front of me. I knew I was missing some beautiful scenery and that made me mad, as I did not want to miss a single thing on our trip. There was nothing to do but gut it out and keep going.

We had completely ridden out of the flat roads; they had become mountainous and rocky. After about an hour, the mist lightened, the clouds loosened up and the breath taking scenery opened up before us. Suddenly, we were in the Rocky Mountains of British Columbia and they were stunning.

As we rounded a downhill turn, before us was a very deep glaciated valley with a riverbed that must have been two miles wide, running through the middle. Although now there was a small stream running through the valley, during the snowmelt the river must be vicious with fast moving run off from the towering mountains above.

I stood at the edge of the road over looking the valley below and was breathless with awe at the magnitude of the size of the mountains and valleys. There was snow still on the mountaintops in spots but the rivers ran wild with the remnants of the melt. The sides of the road bloomed profusely with wild roses of pinks and reds and with bright yellow dandelions and some pretty purple flowers on stalks. I have not identified them yet but will have to ask someone what the purple ones are.

Continuing our journey, the surroundings, of such immense rocks, valleys and mountains, closed in around us. I felt the size of an ant next to these mountainous giants. The mountains were practically void of all trees. Sheer rock faces of mountains greeted us around each turn in the road. Twisted layers of mountains showed the force of the shifting plates of earth beneath me. Millions of years of effort had been required to push the mountains into shapes and designs of serpentines and checkerboards.

I could see where the raging waters of snowmelt had flowed, racing down the slopes into the waiting riverbeds below. The area was all a jumble of rocks and boulders that looked like the debris field of an explosion. Mile after mile after mile of beautiful twisted rocks and mountains were welcoming our journey through them.

Our journey today made me think that the earth must have looked much like this when it was formed millions of years ago. Raw and powerful, this landscape must look the same way it did thousands and thousands of years ago. I cannot imagine it has changed very much at all. Layers of sediment once flat are now twisted at odd angles, some pointing vertical, others at sharp angles to the earth.

The sharp faces of the mountains leveled out somewhat and we traveled through more pristine forest along side wild raging rivers still full of snow melt. The road was a narrow ten feet from the riverbank. I kept thinking it would be a very unpleasant experience to hit a bump in the road and go flying into the icy water.

Coming out of one mountain pass, we approached Muncho Lake, a place I had spotted on my map and hoped to see today. The lake extended between mountains that had been carved by glaciers eons ago. Muncho Lake was a brilliant turquoise about the same color as the waters of the Caribbean.

We stopped and had lunch in a lodge that overlooked the lake. I had a great burger that was very costly. The price of food had increased dramatically since we are getting further north. I am starting to live off a diet of cheeseburgers and French fries. They are just about the cheapest things on the menus. I guess it is a good thing I love them.

We knew that the Alaskan Highway would have parts of the road that would be under construction and today I got a good taste of the repairs underway. We were brought to a stop at a bridge to await a pilot car to take us over the part under construction. We must have waited roughly thirty minutes for the pilot car to come lead us over the bridge. The bridge was over the Laird River and the hot springs we wanted to visit was on the other side. I had visions of soaking my weary muscles in an outdoor natural hot tub. After crossing over the bridge we turned into the hot springs and found out there was a charge per person to go in so we turned around and left. Our budget today did not include any extras. My muscles groaned and whimpered with disappointment.

Unfortunately, we had to wait at the entrance to the hot springs for another pilot car to take us over the rest of the construction. While we were waiting in the gravel parking lot of a roadhouse, several other motorcyclists, who had just come from the other direction over the stretch of highway under construction, had stopped for a breather. One man said the stretch of construction was horrible and covered in about ten inches of deep loose gravel. His wife, who was riding her own bike, had dropped her bike twice along the three-mile stretch of road. Great, just what I wanted to hear. I had already ridden over more gravel in the past two weeks than I have in the entire seven years I have been riding. Now I was really worried. But, I figured if I dropped my bike I would be in good company and the nasty road conditions would be my good excuse. I already had plans to just pick the bike back up and keep going.

The pilot car came eventually and we pulled out behind five motor homes and a tractor-trailer. I made an assessment that the weight of all those vehicles in front of me would help pack down the gravel and mud we were about to go through. This is the first time I have been glad to follow motor homes and tractor-trailers. The road was much worse than I imagined. I followed directly in the path the tractor-trailer had made thinking that would be safe but I hit one ten yard stretch of loose, muddy gravel that just about sent me sprawling in the mud. My bike started fishtailing making a new s shaped track of my own. Somehow, I managed to keep the bike upright. The front tire caught some solid hard packed dirt and I got the bike back under control. I was glad no one could hear what I was saying to myself as I slipped and slid my way through the Canadian mud and gravel. I even embarrassed myself.

I made the three-mile stretch of dirt, mud, loose and flying gravel without any loss of face and got a real good taste of traveling over that kind of terrain. About the time we got going good again, the road got bumpy. There were many places on the road ahead where repairs had already been completed and small signs were on the side of the road strongly suggesting a slow speed. A bucket was next to the sign indicating the tar and small gravel that had repaired the hole.

Never knowing just how much loose gravel was on the road, I would always slow down upon seeing the warning signs. A particular warning sign ahead of me said nothing about the dip in the road. I hit it going about sixty miles per hour and though the bike stayed on the ground, I went air born! I came completely out of my seat and my feet came off the pegs. It scared me so completely that I lost all good sense and control of my mouth. Once again, I tested the limits of my vocabulary. I came down with a good thud and continued down the road acting as if nothing had even happened. However, my spine had compressed nicely and sent nice shock waves down my left leg reminding me of the ruptured disc I had had repaired several years ago.

Today was great for seeing wild life. I had a deer run in front of me today. Fortunately, I saw her coming right out of the woods on my right and cross in front of me. I braked hard and had plenty of stopping room. Ralph did not see her until she had crossed in front of me. He had to do another rapid stop to miss the deer. It is a little unnerving to hear Ralph braking hard behind me. I was waiting for the bikes to make contact.

Later, a yellow-bellied marmot crossed the road in front of me, scurrying off into the grass by the road. He was big enough that if I had hit him, he might have caused an accident. Earlier at the hot springs were we were waiting for the pilot car, there was a buffalo standing right in the middle of the parking lot. He was looking all around, waiting for a handout I think. Not receiving one he then moseyed off into the woods. We passed another lone buffalo on further up the road doing the same thing.

noticed it was a very large German Shepard doing its business. I felt very foolish at not
being able to tell the difference between a bear and a dog. In my
defense though, the dog was the right size and color.

However, later this afternoon, as we were getting close to our
stopping place for the night I really did see a big black bear munching
something in the grass. He looked up as we passed, chewing with his
mouth open and went back to his business. About a mile further up
the road there was another black bear doing the same thing. It was
feeding time in the woods of Canada.

I noticed what I thought were horse droppings along the side of the
road for quite a distance. I did not think it could possibly be horse
droppings. Maybe it was elk or the caribou that the signs kept
warning us about. I knew that elk, moose, and caribou droppings
were a different shape from horses. What animal could these
dropping belong to? The area we were in was complete wilderness
and not, in my mind, conducive to horses. We came up over a hill and
around a corner and there in the middle of the road was a herd of
horses just standing there. People had stopped in the middle of the
road and had gotten out of their cars to pet the horses and take
pictures. I think everyone was in such a frenzy to see wildlife that even
if it was a loose herd of domesticated horses in the wilderness, they
qualified.

We drove right on by and about twenty yards down the road was
a huge sign to watch out for buffalo. I think the road crew put up the
wrong sign. The horses were pretty though and one of my personal
favorite animals wild or otherwise.

After all the excitement of the day, we made it to Watson Lake,
Yukon and found a campsite. This is probably one of the worst
campgrounds I have stayed in. There is nothing appealing about this
place. After all the wonderful sites we have seen today, the
campground is a disappointment. We are staying only one night and
we will be moving on in the morning bright and early so I guess we
can stomach it. There are not even any birds chirping, no crows either
but the monster, steroid mosquitoes are plentiful.

We cannot even have a campfire tonight, as the place does not sell firewood. Now just what kind of campground is that? Even though there are showers here, I do not think I am going to partake. The last time was the place was cleaned must have been weeks ago. I am pretty dirty but I just do not think I can stand the facilities. I may be dirty again tomorrow. I smell of Deet anyway and that covers up just about any odor.

The sun is now setting and it is ten-thirty at night. The sun will be giving us a wake up call around four-thirty A.M. so I am off to try to get some sleep.

Today proved that though you think your day just might be a crappy one, it can turn out to be spectacular if you only stop, take the time to enjoy and embrace the journey.

Love to all always,
Judy/Mom/Mommy

June 6, 2005
Monday 8:30pm Pacific time
Kluane Lake, Yukon
Mile 5720

Dear Folks,

One small mocking bird with a very loud mouth awakened me at four-thirty this morning. The sky was already light and I had only slept five hours. Trying desperately to go back to sleep, I was startled fully away, thirty minutes later, at five, when a motor home, diesel mind you, left the campground making a pass within ten feet of our little tent. Both Ralph and I bolted straight up in our bags thinking the motor home was coming right through the tent. Returning to sleep was hopeless so we crawled out of our warm sleeping bags. I decided to brave the nasty shower to get the bug spray off as well as road dirt. My disgust with my present aroma and hygiene was much worse than the dirty shower facilities.

Unfortunately, our early start down the road led us into rain clouds that promised a downpour. Another dreary morning, I was afraid, with not much to look forward to until the next stop awaited us. Experience is teaching me quickly that adventure, excitement and beauty can be found at anytime and any moment. Being unprepared for that experience makes it all the more intense and enjoyable.

On our way north out of town, we passed Watson Lake's famous signpost forest. It was started by Carl Lindley, a U.S. Army soldier in Company D, 341st Engineers, working on the construction of the Alaska Highway in nineteen forty-two. Longing for home, the soldiers in Company D nailed signs to trees pointing in the direction of their homes. The tradition has continued to this day and there are over fifty-four thousand signs nailed to trees and posts in the signpost forest. Visitors are still encouraged to add their signs to the growing forest.

As we left Watson Lake and drove for miles outside the little town, I noticed a new kind of graffiti. At first I thought it was funny and cute but as the miles passed, I thought it a scar upon the beautiful outdoors.

Instead of people taking spray paint and marking walls with their form of artistry, people had taken the round rocks that were part of the glacier and riverbeds and had written their names or professions of love to a girlfriend or boyfriend in the side of the banks that lined the road. To see the beautiful wilderness scarred by human hands was to me, discouraging.

I saw my first eagle today. A golden eagle was eating her breakfast of rodent or such close to the road but near the tree line. Other than the eagle, no other wild life was seen today.

We crossed over many, many bridges that hovered close to the swollen rivers fresh with melted snow. If I looked left or right as I crossed over these bridges, it was like looking back into an unspoiled and unexplored geologic time. The Laird River, which we crossed many times, is very wide and I think it is wider than the Mississippi in sections.

At our first stop of the day, in Teslin, for breakfast, gas and potty, five bikers that we had met last night at dinner, came rolling in for the same. They were a little friendlier this time. I guess they were very tired last night from riding for such a long day. Our paths crossed several times over the day finally ending in Whitehorse where they were going to stay the night. We were going to continue on to Haines Junction.

Though there were many beautiful mountains to look at today the first part of the day was just barely tolerable as it started to rain and turned cold. We could not see much except the road in front of us and the trees we passed through. Hours of riding in that environment can at times become tedious. But, ever hopeful, around every turn in the long road ahead of us, I kept hoping for a break in the weather and more wondrous scenery. About the time we got to Whitehorse, Yukon the clouds looked as if they would finally break up.

North, from Whitehorse, we ran into several patches of bad road. But wait, there was no road! The road was completely gone, and under reconstruction. At one such area, Ralph and I came to a complete stop and just looked at each other and cussed. Before us was a steep grade with no road. The area was just dirt and mud and appeared to me to look like a small mountain completely scraped clean of all trees and vegetation. I was sincerely hoping that there was some semblance of a road on the other side of the hill. Ralph and I looked at each other, nodded acceptance and took off carefully up the muddy side of the hill. Surprisingly, we scooted right up the hill without incident and found pavement on the other side. We continued riding as if we had been riding on such surfaces all our lives. I was getting tremendous practice riding on all types of road surface and my confidence was building. I have no idea, however, what to expect as we venture further into the wilderness to the Arctic Ocean.

As I resigned myself to this being an average day, the scenery changed dramatically again. Mountains with snow graced us and surrounded us in majestic splendor. Great expanses of large mountains with snow were resting on top of smaller mountains of dark green forest. I would stop and take a picture then round another bend and have to stop and take another.

Along the road were new flowers I had not seen yet. Hot pink and purple flowers mixed with yellow ones, bloomed in the foreground of the forest and snow capped mountains. The area is so large and the wilderness and mountains defy words but my spirit is so alive. I am so blessed to see this incredible earth.

In Haines Junction, where we had planned to spend the night, the only two places to stay were for RV's. They were so unappealing that we decided to ride another fifty miles to a campground that appeared, from my map, to be in the wilderness and nestled along a lake.

The ride was well worth the extra effort. The mountains got closer together and bigger and higher and covered in more snow. Every turn we went around brought more snow covered mountains, more breath taking vistas and more wilderness with wild rivers and streams running right through it.

Up and over a long tremendous stretch of wilderness, around a long curve in the road and I was completely consumed by the remarkable vista. Before us was a tremendous ice blue and turquoise lake stretching the length of a glaciated valley and surrounded on all sides by snow-covered mountains. The road wound around the lake right at the water's edge. I had trouble not wanting to stop every ten feet and take pictures but the road was very narrow and full of potholes. There was not enough of a shoulder to pull off onto without the possibility of falling into the glacier, cold water.

Just as we saw a sign for the campground, road construction stopped us again. Each time we have come to construction the situation has become progressively worse. Each time I am convinced that this time was probably the worst piece of messed up dirt we have been over and each time I am yet again surprised at how much worse it really has become. Here again there was no road at all but something that resembled a mud pit full of large pot holes filled with brown water. We had no idea as to the depth of the potholes. The cars in front of us were struggling and sliding through the mess. Every pothole they hit sent a shower of liquid mud several feet into the air.

There was only one way through the mess and that was straight ahead. We sloshed through the mud and holes somehow but not before getting our bikes and ourselves wet with mud and ground water that had settled in the potholes. I was certain this time I would drop the bike; the chances were looking mighty good. But, luck was on our side and we made it to the campground covered in black mud. The shiny chrome on my bike has lost its luster, now being a lovely shade of brown mud. No more silver shows and the bike has taken on one color only. But, the wonderful thing about the way the bike looks is it tells the story of our journey.

When we pulled into the campground, we both thought heaven had made an appearance and had been set aside just for us. We picked our campsite directly on the ice blue water and faced our little tent toward the water and snow covered mountains. This place is an imagined dream. Snow that looks like powdered sugar drapes over the mountains like a white blanket. Long expanses of green forest march skyward to meet the mountains. The lake water, a deep blue from the ice melt, laps gently at the rock beach before us. The water is so clear we can see the rounded rocks of all sizes on the bottom.

There is a squadron of swallows flying and darting quickly overhead eating the mosquitoes. They fly in pairs like fighter planes, one in the lead, one a wingman, both flying in unison turning at the same moment. They fly so close over my head, twisting and turning at the last moment, missing me. I am getting dizzy watching their aerial acrobatics but so fascinated at their precision that I cannot stop watching.

The sun behind us is trying desperately to sink behind the mountain and is sending long shadows across the blue water. The wind had shifted and has turned cool giving me goose bumps. Ralph has built me a fire tonight. The smell of burning wood and the yummy heat from its flames is just the icing on the cake. My soul is content tonight.

After starting a day that held little promise, here we are at day's end in a place that looks like heaven. What a magnificent end to another memorable day. I have learned on this journey that each day is a wonderful new chapter in my life. Some open wounds I still carry with me are starting to heal. This raw nature and world around me have become, to me, a life giving force. I embrace it with open arms and ask, with each passing day, to heal me more.

Grizzle Bear had a rough ride today. He was rained on and had his fur blown dry in the wind. He got dusty from the road construction and a little mud slung on him in the process but the little guy took it like a champ and is now in the tent sleeping it off.

According to the GPS that Ralph has on his bike the sun will not set tonight until eleven-thirty and will be up at four-thirty in the morning. Ralph wanted to stay up until darkness set in to see the first star appear but I just do not think I will make it. I had a very long ride today and I am going to have to crawl into the tent with Grizzle Bear.

So until tomorrow, much love to all always,
Love,
Judy/Mom/Mommy

June 7, 2005
Tuesday 8:00 Alaska Time
Chicken, Alaska
Mile 6019

Dear Folks,

This morning, instead of being awakened by birds, we were awakened by the sound of waves hitting the rocky beach below our tent. The breeze had picked up bright and early and the tent billowed in and out. I thought at one moment the tent would take flight. The morning was brisk and sunny for once.

I took a nice hot shower in the very clean bathroom that was complete with bathmats. Unfortunately, when I opened my toilet article bag, my big bottle of shampoo had opened up in the bag and more than half the shampoo was oozing around everything. Everything was slick with soap and no amount of wiping and washing could get it all off.

Before we left our beautiful campsite, I looked across the side of the lake we were on and noticed back in the construction area we had come over yesterday, a blast going off followed quickly by a series of six blasts. Not only was the blast very loud, the rock explosion went very high. We were probably about a mile from it but I was definitely impressed. The area we had come over yesterday was bad enough. I wondered what it looked like now after the dynamite blast.

As I was getting on my bike, I looked down and noticed a sizeable oil leak on the chrome around a seal. After feeling the oily spot, we decided to get to the next station, check the oil level, and see if we could find out the problem. When we got into the small town of Destruction Bay at the one gas station there, the oily area on the bike had totally dried. A sudden realization dawned on me about the oily spot. I figured out that what I thought was an oil spill was actually an animal's territorial marking. Oh, yuck, and I had my fingers in it! I immediately found the bathroom and scrubbed my hands.

As we left the camp earlier and started down the muddy road, it dawned on us that we should have had a pilot car take us over the road to the north. Apparently, the sign at the entrance to the campground had been knocked over and we did not see it when we left. One hundred yards down the road the monster trucks and cranes were working. I have seen these dump trucks on The Learning Channel about monster machines. I wish I could have had a picture of me facing off a three-story dump truck. The cab of the truck was literally three stories tall and the wheels were way over my head. I stopped in the mud and waited for him to come by because he was much bigger than I was and he would win in any showdown. However, he was kind enough to let us pass and we went on our merry way. I guess he figured it would be better to have us out of their way.

Off we went into the early morning sunshine with the plans to stay in Chicken, Alaska tonight. I only thought I had had challenging riding days so far on this journey. This day made it to the top of the list. My body took a beating and my brain is still addled. Though the scenery was spectacular, I think, as I caught a glimpse here and there, I was not able to take my eyes off the road the entire day.

Of the three hundred and thirty miles we traveled today, virtually the entire length of it was either gravel, mud, torn up pavement and frost heave. Having ridden for miles and miles on gravel and other interesting road surfaces, I have decided that I would much prefer to ride on gravel than frost heave. Frost heave will destroy your back, shoulders, knees, and butt. I could see it coming, ripples in the pavement that look like sounds waves. Upon hitting the dip in the road, everything bottomed out on the bike and my spine compressed sending pain down my legs and up to my brain. My brain, thinking I am about to meet an untimely end, sent out warning signals coursing through every nerve and muscle and each contracted, tensing with fear.

I found the only way to get through miles and miles of frost heave was to act as if I was jumping a horse. Upon coming up to a deep dip, I would grip the tank with both knees as I would if I were in a saddle and lean forward over the tank as if taking a jump. This technique helped some but after hours of jumping, combined with slick mud, loose gravel and just plain no road, I was beaten up badly and every muscle in my arms and back was screaming in pain.

We passed the Canadian border and drove thirty more miles through no man's land to the U.S. border. Just before we reached the actual U.S. customs, up on a hill on the left was a huge sign that said "Welcome to Alaska." I was not expecting the sign and it hit me head on that we had actually made it to the far reaches of the United States! I was so overcome with emotion that by the time we reached the actual customs station another half mile up the road I had tears rolling down my face. Ralph, too, had a lump in this throat. As we waited our turn at customs, we looked at each other and again nodded confirmation. Ralph said to me quietly, "You made it, no one can ever take this from you." I cried again.

So much research and planning went into this trip. I looked at so many maps and learned the names of roads and towns. They came alive as we actually passed through them. My dream of seeing Alaska had come true and discovery of new scenery and new experiences lay just up ahead around the bend in the road.

My first view of Alaska was one of snow-covered mountains, fast running rivers, and glacial lakes. The road was horrible. More frost heave and potholes awaited us around every curve. We had plans to go to Chicken, Alaska which was sixty-five miles off the Alaskan Highway. I had discovered Chicken on the internet when planning our trip. The pictures I saw were of a little town with only three connecting buildings. One was a gift shop, one was a bar, and one was a café. All three were connected. The picture I saw on the internet showed the narrow bar's ceiling covered in hats that people had left when passing through.

About ten years ago, Perry had given me a hat for my birthday. The hat was very colorful and was my favorite. I wore it everywhere. Every motorcycle trip, every trip to the beach, every sporting event or any place there was sunshine, my hat went with me. Over the last ten years it has become extremely worn. All the colors had faded and the bill around the edges had become frayed. The material was thin with age and some small holes had starting to appear. The time had come to get a new hat and retire the old one. I thought that the little bar in Chicken would be the appropriate place to leave the old beloved hat.

After bumping, sloshing, bouncing over three hundred and thirty miles today, and riding through miles and miles of burned out forest (six million acres I found out later), we ground our way the last three miles on a dirt road, finally reaching Chicken in the late afternoon. Chicken was everything we both hoped it would be. Sure enough, in the bar, the ceiling was covered with hats, torn up shredded underwear and dollar bills. The bar was approximately fifteen feet wide and maybe twenty feet deep. Bar stools surrounded an old wooden bar and logs placed around the base of the bar was just the right height for resting weary feet. We loved it.

With a Mike's Hard Lemonade in one hand and a black marker in the other, I wrote a message to Perry on the bill of the hat and the bartender stapled it to the ceiling. The message said: To Perry, Thanks for the hat and the many trips and memories with this hat. Love Mom.

Perry, someday, you must come see the place of honor your hat has and maybe someday you can come retrieve it. Our experience so far has been quite a ride and worth every speck of mud, dust, grime and pot hole.

Shortly after hanging the hat, two huge tour busses pulled into the dusty, gravel parking lot. Dozens of tourist got off the bus and came in the bar and gift shop. I walked outside to get Grizzle Bear to take his picture in the bar and got attacked by the people on the tour bus. Our filthy, dirty, nasty, mud coated bikes were parked out in front of the bar and I became the subject of interest to the many foreigners on board the bus. I had to answer boo koos of questions about where we started, where we were going and why were we doing such a trip. I had inadvertently become one of the tourist attractions in Chicken, Alaska.

I sampled every flavor of Mike's Hard Lemonade the bartender had. I believe there are five flavors. Exhaustion and an empty stomach are the perfect way to enjoy happy hour. In my state of delighted happiness, my brain registered hunger pains from my stomach so Ralph and I asked the cook to fix us some hamburgers. Oh boy, they were good. That combined with the homemade cherry pie with vanilla ice cream was just about more than my senses could handle.

While we inhaled our dinner, we continued talking with the bartender and some of the locals started to stop by. All were very friendly characters and ready for a new ear to bend. We happily obliged. Along with the locals, came the mushroomers.

The mushroomers are people from all walks of life that have flocked to the area due to the tremendous forest fire in the area last year. Apparently, after such a fire, a particular species of mushroom sprouts and are very prolific in the ash of the fire. These gourmet mushroom, called Morels, are sold for large amounts of cash. The mushrooms look to me like the seedpod of the magnolia tree only much smaller. I have not tried one yet but I have not been offered any yet either. The mushroomers don't want to give away any of their profits.

Due to the amount of alcohol we had consumed and the lateness of the hour, we are bedding down in Chicken for the night. The woman that owns the place said we could set up our tent in the willows behind the bar or we could stay in her trailer behind her house. Now that is what I call hospitality. I think we are going to opt for the tent in the willows. While we appreciate the offer, we really do not want to impose on her hospitality particularly after she said she could not guarantee the condition of the trailer. The proprietor warned us about not setting up our tent near the path into the willows. She said that a moose had been seen several mornings lately wandering out of the woods and down the path into the area in front of the bar.

Apparently, moose have poor eyesight and cannot distinguish the difference between a green tent and green bushes. They will stumble right over a tent and trample a camper. I cannot say as I am up for the experience of being trampled by a pissed off moose. At it turned out the ground in the willow trees was saturated and floating in water. The only place we could set up our tent was in the gravel area behind the bar. Though not at all scenic, it was free. Our daily budget was safely within its limits.

Grizzle Bear had quite a day too. I thought I heard some whimpering and grumbling coming from behind me. I guess he was worn out too from all the bumping and jumping down the road. Chicken and the tourists were just too much for him. I let him belly up to the bar for a nice tall mug of root beer and he has forgiven me for the rough day. We are off tomorrow to Fairbanks. We hope to find a hostel to stay in and maybe an actual bed.

Until tomorrow, much love to everyone,
Judy/Mom/Mommy

June 8, 2005
Wednesday 10:59
Fairbanks, Alaska
Mile 6361

Dear Folks,

Our camping spot last night, in the gravel parking lot of the bar in Chicken, Alaska was behind the buildings right next to the tents that were set up for the employees of the Chicken establishments.

As usual the sun was up at four-thirty A.M. and we were not far behind. I groaned as I had to get up and I felt just like I had been run over by the loose moose. After packing everything, we went back down to the café and had a wonderful breakfast before we took off for Fairbanks. While we were eating breakfast, three tour busses showed up and all occupants of the busses attacked the three buildings.

I went outside, sat with Chicken Pete, and talked about the area and his life. He was quite an interesting, colorful character. He spent winters in Arizona and summers in Chicken. He left for his house down the road a little before we did. Chicken Pete called his little dog and up she hopped onto the back of his four-wheeler and off they went in the dust.

As did we. The road back to the main highway did not seem as bad this morning as it did yesterday when we were so terribly tired. This day's ride was committed solely getting to Fairbanks. As we got closer to Fairbanks, the Alaskan Range came into view. The mountains are very impressive and still covered in really deep snow. I could feel the cold air issuing off the mountains and reaching to embrace me.

We arrived in Fairbanks in the late afternoon and found a hostel. This is a new experience to me. We are staying in a dormitory room with a young man from Finland. There is a community kitchen, living room, and bathroom. Ralph and I love meeting new people and I hope this will be a positive experience.

This is going to be a short letter tonight as we are going to have to really get up early in the morning and get our butts moving. I am within two days of reaching my goal! I cannot believe it! I am thoroughly convinced that it is really happening. We are so close, just a mere five hundred miles left to go to reach the Arctic Ocean. The roughest part of our journey awaits us down a desolate stretch of gravel road heading for the sea. I am so very determined to achieve that goal that nothing short of a blizzard will stop me.

Ralph checked the weather report on the computer and it seems that sometime in the next few days it is going to start raining up near Prudhoe Bay and then turn to snow. So we are going to have to scoot up the Dalton Highway and try to do it in one day. All five hundred miles of it. I think I am tired now, I do not have the slightest idea how I will feel by sunset tomorrow, which happens to be around eleven-thirty at night. The sun does not actually set; it just circles the sky and dips below the horizon slightly at "sunset." There is constantly light now.

Unless we can get an internet connection in Prudhoe Bay it will be a few days until we can send any journal entries or pictures. So be patient and do not worry. If you have not heard from us by Monday then get worried and send out the search parties.

Bright and early tomorrow, it is on to the Arctic Ocean and on to becoming the first woman to reach this finish line on this ride. Wish me luck, cross your fingers and say a prayer that all goes well.

Nighty-night from here in Fairbanks. Grizzle Bear is excited and having trouble going to sleep. He cannot wait to go swimming in the Arctic Ocean. He is wiggly with excitement.

Love to all always,
Judy/Mom/Mommy

June 10, 2005
Friday
Prudhoe Bay, Alaska
Mile 6804

Dear Folks,

**MISSION
ACCOMPLISHED**

Love,
Judy/Mom/Mommy
PS: Details and photos to follow

June 10
Late Friday night
Prudhoe Bay Alaska
Mile 6804

Dear Folks,

Where do I even begin to tell the story of the last two days? Mine is the story of unbelievable challenges, scenery and pure sheer gut and determination. Ralph and I left our hostel in Fairbanks around nine on Thursday morning after unloading about fifty percent of our gear to lighten the load. We stored our unloaded items in the garage of the hostel. We carried two empty extra gas cans in case of emergency. We knew where the gas was located along the Haul Road and we would fill the cans when we left Coldfoot. There would be no gas between the two hundred and forty-four miles separating Coldfoot and Prudhoe Bay also called Deadhorse.

We carried only survival gear. The tent and sleeping bags were the number one priority. We also added fire starter, a hunting knife, a one-burner stove, and a change of clothes to the survival gear. We knew we were heading into the wilderness and had no idea of what to expect even though we had read so much information. We did know that the area we were heading into was void of civilization and the weather could be brutal. Off we headed for the wild woods of Alaska. The nice paved road that headed due north turned into dirt and gravel approximately seventy miles north of Fairbanks.

I chose to follow Ralph into the wild woods of Alaska; he would guide the way. After a few miles of following Ralph, the dust was horrible. It got into everything. Most of all the eyes were a problem. The more I blinked away the dust, the more my eyes watered and ran. My eyes ran tears that turned the dust to mud. I was convinced, at that time, I would not be able to handle five hundred miles of burning, stinging eyes. But of course, I had no idea of what lay ahead of me along the desolate road to the Arctic Ocean. The dust was to be the least of my worries.

As we drove along between the woods on both sides of us, an eagle came out of the woods on my right and flew just above my head and in between Ralph and me. I could have reached right up and touched him as he flew by. The sight of the magnificent bird gave me goose bumps. He was huge! I thought this might be a sign of some of the wild animals we might see on our journey or at the very least, a good omen.

As we bumped and giggled over the dirt road another biker passed us and we were surprised to find out it was the same young man we had meet two days before on the road north of Lake Kluane. We had passed each other several times and on one particular time we stopped to see if he needed any help, as he was stopped on the side of the road in a gravel area. We struck up a conversation with him and found out he was headed the same direction as we were. We wished him luck and a safe ride. Needless to say, we were surprised when he passed us on the Haul Road but glad to have another biker on the baron road with us.

After what seemed like forever, we had only gone about thirty miles. I was saying to myself that it was going to be a longer stretch of road than either of us speculated. Finally, we made it to the Yukon River and across the long bridge. The long bridge over the very wide Yukon was made of wooden planking and was torn up in places making the passage over it scary. We gassed up, had a quick sandwich, and headed back out on the bumpy road to the next event stop.

Only a small post and a little history marked the Arctic Circle. Getting off our bikes to get the tourist picture, we were attacked immediately by the hordes of mosquitoes just waiting for a tasty morsel. We got going again quickly, spitting mosquito carcasses as we continued on our journey.

The road became very bumpy and very tiring. My arms were getting sore and the muscles were burning profusely. I slipped several times in the loose gravel and worried how I was going to handle the road conditions for so many miles.

After many hours, we arrived, covered in dust, in Coldfoot, Alaska. Coldfoot was the last fuel stop and the last services, period, for the next two hundred and forty-four miles. I had missed the not so well marked road down into Coldfoot and had to turn around in the dirt and back tack. Only the change in the speed limit alerted me to the fact that I had missed the smaller dirt road down into Coldfoot.

Coldfoot, Alaska consisted of several buildings: a restaurant, shower facilities for the staff and truckers, a hotel that was really a few trailers turned into rooms with beds, and a gas pump.

The day had been brutal beyond anything I had ever known and I would have happily put my sleeping bag down in the dirt and gone to sleep. We were so exhausted at this point that we decided to take a chance on the weather and wait until morning to finish the remainder of the Haul Road. Our decision was a very wise one.

Our fellow rider had arrived in Coldfoot about an hour before us and was already chilling out in the bar. We were going to get a hotel room but the room cost one hundred and fifty dollars and we could camp for fifteen dollars, so guess what we did? There was a soft grassy area behind the hotel, in front of a small lake surrounded by fir trees and mountains in the background.

After setting up our tent, our fellow traveling companion, Erick, and we went back to the restaurant for a glass of wine and dinner. Two glasses of wine and my brain went south back to Georgia. I was so tired, my stomach was very empty, and I was probably a little dehydrated. The wine went well with that combination and in no time, my aches and pains were forgotten in the fogginess of my brain. Our dinner was so delicious and it was hard to imagine in this wilderness town. We were really not expecting much being in such a remote location. But they must have had a gourmet cook in town for the night. The food was unusually good, either that, or I was just so exhausted and tipsy I could not tell otherwise. I think a peanut butter sandwich would have been grand at that point, however.

Exhausted, I finally gave up and went to bed even though it was broad daylight and would be all night. The constant lightness has really taken a toll on my body rhythms. I would wake up every two hours or so look at my watch and realize it was the middle of the night! I woke up once at three A.M. and it was so light I thought it was morning.

Wind and rain blew in through the night and tossed our little tent around, sucking the sides in and out. It blew over, the sun came out, and it was still quite warm when we got up and packed our belongings back on the bike.

Our new friend, Erick, was heading out the same time and we agreed to watch out for each other along the way if necessary. Slightly renewed from a few hours sleep, we once again headed out on the bumpy, dusty road. The bumps smoothed out somewhat and the ride was actually quite pleasant. I was convinced the worst was over and at the rate we were going it would be a breeze the rest of the way. How terribly mistaken I was. I had been teased and fooled.

The mountains started closing in on us as the road went further and further into the wilderness. Wild rivers and creeks rushed by us and under the wooden bridges we crossed.

The Alaskan Pipeline followed the road but it was actually the other way around. The pipeline was an impressive vision to see for miles, and miles and miles. The road was rather smooth for a gravel road and we cruised right along enjoying the morning and the mountains and the rivers and streams. Then the terrain changed and we started to climb in elevation.

We were heading into the Brooks Range and the Atigun Pass. I had seen pictures of this pass and I have to admit I was nervous about climbing the pass on gravel. Our motto over the last several days had become a chanting of "there was nothing else to do but up and onward." That is exactly what we did. We climbed and climbed and I looked over my right shoulder and gasped at the valley below and the road we had already maneuvered over. The road below was tiny like a baby snake. Ascending the pass, I had stopped to take a quick picture of the mountains and road behind us but Ralph went right on by me and shouted my name. I thought he was upset with me for stopping so I continued forward without getting my picture. At the top of the pass he and I both pulled over and he told me that he was not about to stop on the way up or down but I was welcome to. I will try to get the picture on the way back if the weather holds.

As we were starting down the pass, a large cloud was racing out of the canyon right on the road we would have to travel down. Down we went, Ralph going first because he felt safer that way. The cloud came rushing up and we descended into solid whiteness with just the gravel below us.

The feeling of seeing nothing but wet gravel ten feet in front of me was eerie to say the least. I loved it. As we descended into the valley floor, the rugged mountains all around us soared jagged toward the sky. Rocks, due to the freezing every year, had broken away from the mountains and created a rocky surface all black and wet with mist and fog. The whole landscape appeared to me to be prehistoric. I would not have been surprised if dinosaurs popped out from behind the rocks. I felt like I had stepped back in time and was witnessing the raw earth being formed.

This road for me was like a time machine. I could visualize the earth being created. The earth is raw and wild and renews itself every year with a changing landscape caused by harsh winds, ice, snow, and temperatures. I cannot believe that conditions have changed much in the last million years.

On and on we went, traveling now through a heavy fog, seeing not much further in front of us than about thirty yards. I was worried that the tractor-trailer trucks would come screaming out of the fog and run us off the road. The tractor-trailers have the right of way on the Haul Road and it was evident repeatedly today.

To be safe, we had read, it is advised to pull over when you see a truck coming. They own the road and they sling dust and rocks when passing. I did a lot of duck and covering today. Most trucks were considerate and shared the road, slowing down when they passed but others, laughing, roared by, enveloping us in a cloud of brown dust and flying rocks.

After we had been about one hundred miles, I was absolutely out of energy and ready to be at our destination of the Arctic Ocean. I could not imagine having to go another mile mush less the last one hundred and forty-four left on our journey. But the worst was yet to come. The road at this point got viscous. We had already been over so much rough road, but it only got worse. The next eighty miles was the most bone shattering, teeth jarring, muscle stretching, and mind exhausting thing I have ever done. If I looked away from the road one second, I would put myself in jeopardy by loosing control of the bike. The rocks changed from regular gravel to those now the size of tennis balls. Maneuvering over and around the cobblestones was at best, difficult. Some were round, most were sharp sided, just right for slicing tires. While trying to avoid the ball size rocks the only way around them was directly into deep potholes. I think we averaged around twenty miles per hour during these stretches of horrible road.

Every now and then when the rocks got smaller and the bumps less, I would look around me at the awesome expanse of territory surrounding me. The mountains were now rounding into the North Slope and we were venturing out onto the tundra. Wild, prehistoric, vast, earth forming, uninhabited, undeveloped, raw earth stretched for hundreds of miles. I know I keep using the same words to describe this environment but no others come to mind.

Every time we would round a curve, below us or around us was another scene of hundreds of miles of wild tundra. Ice and snow were still in pockets and had a beautiful blue green tint. Before coming here, I could not imagine the vastness of this space. Every turn brought more and more land stretching far beyond what my eye could see.

The temperature had dropped dramatically after crossing the Brooks Range and though I was mostly prepared, I was very, very cold. Exhaustion was taking a huge toll on me. This was such a harsh land and getting harsher with every mile north we continued. I really had to dig deep into my soul to grasp what little energy I had left. I was running on sheer determination alone.

With about fifty miles left to go, we finally saw some wildlife. Caribou crossed the road in front of us, swans floated in the melting ponds and geese were prevalent. A pair of snow geese followed us at very close range right over the road above us for about two miles. They would fly in close as a pair then veer off for a moment then come close again. They were not afraid of us.

Ralph had seen an Arctic fox earlier and the fox had blended in with the brown color of the tundra. Ground squirrels raced across the road in front of us with their tails stuck high into the air like pencils.

I was freezing in this harsh environment and I was shivering. I was ready to be inside when I finally, after eighteen days, saw the tiny dots of buildings on the frozen Arctic horizon. We had spotted the oil field and we were just about to reach our goal. Ralph and I were riding side by side and we looked at each other, nodded again, and smiled broadly. Ralph raised his fist up high into the air, a sign of victory. I kept telling myself, "you're almost there, don't quit now, don't give up, just a little further." I dug deeper in my spirit and recalled the words of my daughter, Amanda, that had been my constant companion. Her words kept me strong: "Mama, don't come home until you have made it to the Arctic Ocean."

Across the tundra and into the icy environment we rode, into the town of Prudhoe Bay we came, together, after six thousand and eight hundred miles. Wingman and point, coming, riding in side by side. Destination complete, mission accomplished.

When we pulled into the parking lot in front of the hotel, which was once crew quarters for the oil well workers, I had to be helped from my bike. Numb with cold and exhaustion, I was stuck like glue and extremely stiff after eight hours of very intense riding.

We had to find witnesses to verify that Ralph and I were actually in Prudhoe Bay and get them to sign our forms. Then we had to get our picture made in front of the building with the name Prudhoe Bay on it and we were official. Since there was absolutely no camping, thank God, available, we got a room at the Prudhoe Bay Hotel to the tune of ninety dollars per person. Fortunately, the room included three meals each.

We collapsed shortly after getting dinner since we had not eaten anything all day. There are no picnic grounds or stores along the way, just pure wilderness. Since we were not sure how the journey would go and concerned about the weather, we decided to just keep moving forward today. We were really starved and exhausted. Add a nice hot shower to my full belly and I had instant sleep. Which is exactly what happened to two weary, rode hard, put up wet, road warriors.

And for me, how can I even begin to describe what this first leg of the journey means? I set an unbelievable challenge for myself. I wanted to be the first woman to accomplish this ride from Key West, Florida to Prudhoe Bay, Alaska. From the searing heat of the southern most tip of the United States in Florida to the most northern icy tip on a road in Prudhoe Bay, Alaska, I did it!

I finished the ride with pride in my heart and tears in my eyes. This achievement was a personal success and something, that for as long as I live, will be a milestone. I have been to the far reaches of this continent and have had the privilege and honor of seeing lands and sites that most people will never see. I am thankful I had the opportunity. Though the journey arduous, trying and exhausting both mentally and physically, I would not trade it for anything. I have grown personally in sprit and my heart bursts with joy at my accomplishment. I thought only briefly of those back home that doubted my ability. That did not matter anymore. I knew in the very core of my soul what I had accomplished and that for me, alone, was enough.

Now, we have to make it back over the five hundred miles we have just covered. That journey also will be hard but I know I can make it. I must admit to dreading the road back. My shoulders ache in places I did not know existed and it feels as if someone is sticking a knitting needle under my right shoulder blade. Every bump toward the end today made my spine compress with pain and my head was beginning to hurt with every jar it took.

In the morning, we are going to take the trip onto the oil fields and step into the Arctic Ocean and collect our other container of ocean water. Grizzle Bear has been promised he can dip his feet in the water too. He has had a very rough two days stuck on top of the pack and arrived in Prudhoe Bay dirty beyond belief, covered in arctic dirt, freezing even though he has fur and a leather jacket. He was none to happy with his transportation but he is warm and snug in the bed with me and has forgiven me for his bumpy ride. I just might let him ride inside the saddlebag on the way back and give him a rest.

So until later, with much love as always,
Love,
Judy/Mom/Mommy

June 12, 2005

Sunday
Fairbanks
Mile 7246

Dear Folks,

We got up early the next morning in Prudhoe Bay because we had an eight-thirty A.M. bus ride out to the oil fields and the Arctic Ocean. It was springtime in the Arctic, thirty-three degrees with the wind blowing making it somewhere in the twenties. Oooh, just how cold was that going to be on the bikes riding back to Fairbanks?

We boarded the bus and bumped over the washboard gravel roads out onto the oil fields. I found it very interesting that that is where a fair amount of the oil and gas comes from for the United States. All the science and technology necessary to discover the oil and gas was of interest also.

Prudhoe Bay is strictly a work environment. The people work on two-week shifts. Two on, two off. They have to fly in on the company plane; can have no personal cars, no spouses or other halves, and no alcohol. The environment is strictly one of, come to work, do your shift, eat, go to sleep and then go back out to the oil fields. The buildings are worn and weathered due to the severe conditions. A lot of the actual work, finding new drilling sites and such, is done during the time when the ice is frozen everywhere so the scientist, drillers and machinery can have ice roads.

The site is not at all pretty to look at, just purely functional and strictly business. I got all warm and sleepy on the bus and I was suddenly awakened when it dawned on me that the long road back to Fairbanks was still ahead of us. I knew by the time the tour was over and we found the gas pump it would be around eleven A.M. when we would actually be on the road. Then it would be eight to nine hours on the bike back over rough roads to Coldfoot. The aches and pains in my body were saying a definite no to the challenge, but what choice did I have?

The last stop on the tour was the Arctic Ocean, which was still frozen. As I looked out over the bay, I could see tinges of blue green in the frozen water. Just at the edge of the water there was some thawing taking place. So, as promised to Amanda, I stood on the ice of the Arctic. I could come home now with my head held high. I dipped Grizzle Bear in the cold, cold water of the Arctic Ocean. Both Ralph and I stood on top of the frozen water and reveled in the fact that we had actually made it to the frozen tundra and Arctic Ocean. Another item on my list of life's things to do I could now cross off.

Back at the hotel, we bought a few tee shirts that could be proudly displayed back home. Back on the bikes, we headed out to find the only gas pump available to us. We had to search up and down a few roads before we found a tiny little hut with two oil drums outside that had hoses and pumps attached to the top of the drums.

Totally fueled, we headed back out onto the ice and tundra in a most southerly direction. The day was cloudy, bleak, and cold and I took many long looks at my surroundings, as I knew I probably would never be this way again in my life.

As expected, the road grew worse and worse. At least this time we knew what was coming and I do not think it made it quite as hard mentally. Physically, it was the same but worse in some spots due to the severe pain in my right shoulder.

We slowed as many caribou crossed in front of us. Along with geese and duck, swans swam in some of the melted lakes. Ralph, at one point honked, I thought at me, but turned out he was just irritating the caribou crossing in front of us. He wanted to see them run, which they happily obliged. I personally thought it rude to upset the wildlife with a loud man-made noise and scolded him.

We made a pit stop, which by the way, is on any long stretch of road where we could see in both directions for miles. When no one is coming, I had time to go to the side of the road and do what was needed. There are no toilets on the Haul Road but my bladder has taken such a beating that there was no choice but to use the side of the road as a pit stop. There are not even any trees to go behind either on the tundra. I became very quick in my potty maneuver however, because just as soon as bare skin was exposed the mosquitoes attacked.

It was at one of these pit stops that we noticed that Ralph's back tire was having some serious issues. The wire was showing on one spot and we still had over three hundred miles back to civilization! We kept our fingers crossed with every rock we rolled over. I was nervous that his tire would give out at any moment and we would be pulling out the tent and sleeping bag and spending a scary night on the tundra. Since Ralph was following me, he had to stay a good distance behind me due to the severity of the dust. I would loose sight of his headlight if I went over a hill. I found myself anxiously waiting to see that spot of yellow coming through the dust.

We made it back to Coldfoot without any problems and I was in quite a bit of pain. My right shoulder now felt like it had a railroad spike driven through the joint. Under my right shoulder blade was the knitting needle and my back had started to act up not to mention the gravel pounding headache I had. I was a mess on the verge of tears just from the pain alone not to mention the exhaustion. I was not about to allow myself to cry at this point but it was difficult to hold it back. Pain has to be considerable for me before I cry and my eyes were welling up quickly.

But my spirit was not to be toyed with, however. We were three-fourths of the way back and we felt the last fourth was going to be easy after all we had already been through. The lady at the café at Coldfoot, who was interested in my quest to be the first woman to make this trek, came out on the front porch at the exact moment we, all covered in dirt and mud, pulled in. She was genuinely happy to see me and very happy that I had accomplished my goal.

I pulled off my jacket, which was coated in dirt and mud and she gave me a big hug and bought me a glass of wine. I was so delighted at her interest in our journey and it felt like I had a welcoming committee waiting for me when we rolled into Coldfoot. Her attention to me brought a lump to my throat and some tears too. She also gave us the tent site for the night for free. These seem like such small gestures but were grand in my heart and mind's eye.

A dinner of burgers and fries, which tasted like filet mignon, and three glasses of wine made the tent and sleeping bag feel like the Ritz. Our friend, Erick, who had been traveling with us along the way, was there to greet us also. In the morning he would be heading back to California and back to his job in the Navy.

We headed out early Sunday morning for the last leg of our dirt, gravel, and mud journey. We passed on breakfast in Coldfoot, as it was eleven dollar each for breakfast. I decided I was not that hungry after all. We had plans to eat lunch at the roadhouse on the Yukon River anyway.

At the Yukon River roadhouse, I found a conversation of real interest when we were sitting eating lunch of over stuffed bacon, lettuce, and tomato sandwiches. I overheard conversations of other people traveling by car, talking of making the journey to Prudhoe Bay. They were full of excitement and wonder, just as I had been three days earlier. Just as I, they did not have a clue what they were getting into. I was not about to spoil their fun either. Let them find out all on their own. I went into the wilderness full of spit and vinegar and came out wizened, worn, and aged like a good stiff shot of scotch.

One thing about the Haul Road that has impressed me is, when going over the mountains there are no twistys like back home. In our mountains, the road snakes back and forth until it gets up and over the mountain. Here in Alaska, and particularly the Haul Road, the road just goes straight up and over the mountain. The grades are very steep. One particular stretch actually had a sign on it calling the ascent or decent, depending on which direction you were riding, the Beaver Slide. I am not kidding, the road looks straight up as if it is right in front of my face. It is all gravel and full of potholes both the north and south sides. It was very scary to drive both directions. Going down it felt like we would slip right off the mountain and going up I kept thinking that the bike would give out at any moment and I would just roll back down in a big heap of bike and body. On many of these steep grades, I had to use first gear to get over them. First gear was used going down as well but some additional braking with the rear brake was needed. Never use the front brakes on gravel unless you want to loose control and eat a dirt sandwich.

But my trusty Black Shadow kept chugging and pulling those mountains. The old bike never let me down, not once! My trusty companion is no longer a cruiser. The Black Shadow has morphed into a dirt bike in the biggest order. I think Honda would be proud.

We were counting the miles in reverse now, getting closer and closer to pavement but not before the Haul Road threw one more nasty trick at us. We were following a rain front and that mixed with the tanker trucks full of water they were dumping on the road for grading purposes, created a muddy mess. Muddier and slipperier than any thing we had seen previously. I was convinced that after all the rough terrain we had been over in the last seven thousand miles this was going to be the stretch where we both would drop the bikes. We were covered in mud as well as the poor bikes as we snaked our way through the black gook. To my dismay, we fishtailed our way without incident back onto dry, solid pavement.

When we finally reached solid blacktop after four unbelievable days and I had to stop in the middle of the road and savor the moment. We had done it. We had safely conquered the Haul Road and I had safely conquered my quest. Ralph and I looked at each other, smiling with satisfaction. I slowly let the clutch out and drove the last seventy miles of black top to Fairbanks as if we were riding on glass, unbelievably smooth glass. I immediately got sleepy.

We got back to Fairbanks in the late afternoon and pulled into the hostel where we had stored our belongings and found that we had no place to sleep even though we had reservations. There was a convention of biologist studying evolution at the University of Alaska and the hostel was full of participants. I was so tired I could not even tell you my name if I had too but I was conscious enough to be displeased, to say the least, that our room had been given to a biologist.

I have slept in some interesting places in my life but I think this one takes the cake. The owner of the place had a greenhouse out back behind the house. I was not happy about the situation at all and I was just about to show my rear end. I was tired, I wanted a bed, I wanted some darkness, I wanted food and I wanted some privacy.

I slept in the glass house on a cot. Ralph slept on the floor. It rained last night and the roof leaked, but I did sleep like the dead and woke up in a decent mood. We are going to spend the next two days or so in Fairbanks doing laundry, shipping stuff home, cleaning the poor bikes, changing oil, and getting Ralph a new back tire.

Our odyssey of the Haul Road is physically over but very much alive in my heart and spirit. Mission complete. So what's next?

Update on Grizzle Bear. He was not happy with his feet being dipped into the Arctic Ocean. He thought that should have been left to his cousin Mr. Polar Bear. Then he did not get to ride in the safety of the saddlebag like planned. He rode in the freezing cold with wet feet and mud being slung on him and dust and rain and bumps and jolts. He did not speak to me the entire trip back. He finally warmed up, dried off, and slept on the rocking horse last night in the green house. He is still not speaking though.

Until next time, love to all always,
Judy/Mom/Mommy

June 14, 2005
Tuesday
Denali National Park
Mile 7476

Dear Folks,

We had a maintenance day in Fairbanks yesterday. Ralph washed the bikes and you should have seen the clumps of mud that came off the bikes. Grapefruit size, mud balls hung from the bottom of the frame and there must have been half of the Dalton Highway under the fenders. Even after washing and washing, when the bike would start to dry there were still many missed spots that popped up like brown beacons. Ralph finally gave up because he knew that more dirt would gather there soon.

Ralph had to locate a back tire for his bike. What a stroke of luck that we just happened to be staying in the hostel that was down the same little street that the BMW dealer was located. To make matters even sweeter the tire was in stock.

Ralph walked up to the dealership, came back shortly, and told me to get my camera and follow him. Ok, I'm gamed. Ralph rode his bike down the two blocks to the dealership and I followed on foot. The dealership was one place, that in your wildest imagination, description would be impossible at best. I could not believe the place passed for a business.

When I got to the end of the street, which happened to be a dead end, the entrance to the dealership was to the left, down a heavily wooded, gravel path. At the head of the path was a small three foot by three-foot plastic sign with the BMW logo on it. I looked down the path thinking that surely I must be in the wrong place. The entrance was not really a road but a gravel path into over grown bushes, trees, and grasses. I wondered where Ralph had disappeared to but I had seen him turn down this direction.

I followed warily, looking around me in total disbelief. Ancient rusting trucks and cars lined the path as well as thousands of discarded motorcycle tires in various stages of decay. There, in the midst of all the old worn out tires thrown everywhere, the old broken down cars left to rot and rust, a multitude of motorcycles in various states of repair and a copious amount of motorcycle pieces, was a little wooden shack. This shack was the BMW dealership of Fairbanks, Alaska. The proprietor is a man I will long remember.

A man of advanced year, he was an unbelievable character and quite a legend. He had the look of the village smithy of long ago. His face was weathered and wrinkled but kindness shown from his eyes. Over his clothes was a leather apron, scuffed and worn. He emerged from the wooden shack and placing each hand on each side of the door opening, he smiled at me. He already had Ralph's bike up on the center stand working on it when I finally made my way back in the woods on foot to the shop. I do not even know how Ralph rode the bike back through all the junk lying around.

To make things even odder, another man who was riding a fully loaded BMW GS with all the bells and whistles, CB radio attached to his tank bag, satellite phone and tracking devices, was waiting also to get a tire because he was making the journey to Prudhoe Bay that very day. Another young man, all six feet, eight inches tall and three hundred fifty pounds of him, showed up on his tiny KLR 650 needing a tire as well. For such a remote place that this was, it was suddenly very popular.

I stood around for about ten minutes and realized that I was not very interested in the business of changing tires. The atmosphere was totally male and testosterone dripped from the trees as each attempted to out do each other with tales and experiences. The idea of being eaten by mosquitoes, that had suddenly sprouted and swarmed from the standing water resting in the millions of discarded tires, was unpleasant. I left the boasting boys with their puffed up chests and hoofed it back to the hostel to wait for Ralph.

Ralph disappeared for five hours. I thought the goblins of the woods had gotten him but it turned out that he and the old man had had some serious bonding time. Ralph decided to get the oil changed in his bike also. While the oil drained, Ralph and the owner of the BMW dealership went to get coffee. Five hours later Ralph came back with a new tire, an oil change, and a new friend. The proprietor is all motorcycle. I think our friend, Mike, and this gentleman should meet. They could spend hours and hours discussing the finer details of motorcycles and riding.

When Ralph finally showed up at six in the evening, we went in search of a place to wash all our nasty clothes. We ate dinner and then went in search for a cot for me. Sleeping on the hard ground even on a Therm-a-rest has had my back and left leg in knots and fits. I wake up in the night with wild pain and cramping in my left leg and back. Some nights, I have cried with the pain. I should have known my old back would fight back someway and pay me back for the abuse it has endured. We had looked into taking a cot with us from the start of our trip but then decided to take a regular air mattress. That was a big mistake.

When we had to sleep in the greenhouse there were two cots inside. I put my Therm-a-rest on top of the cot and thought I had gone to heaven. For two nights I slept this way and without any back or leg pain. So, we went on a hunt for a cot that would fit on the bike and found a sporting goods store with just the ticket.

We had, earlier that morning, shipped things back home. I could hear our friend, Mike, speaking in my ear as I packed those things he said I would leave on the side of the road. Some of the items I packed were things we did not need anymore but others were goodies for the kiddies. I shipped home more in weight than the new cot weighed so I am still ahead.

Later in the day, we started to put our documentation together for the Iron Butt Association and found it was going to take much, much longer than we expected. We were itching to leave Fairbanks and be on our way south to Denali. We packed up all our receipts, maps, and witness forms and decided to do a few days documentation at a time instead of trying to do it all at once. Hopefully, by the time we get home it will all be done and we can send it off to become official.

The next morning we headed down the road to Denali National Park but not without first having to deal with more road construction, more gravel, and more mud. So much for the semi-clean bikes. I am not the least bit intimidated by the gravel now. I wonder why?

The drive was pretty, like some scenes I have seen in the Rockies in Colorado. We stopped for lunch in a little charming town called Nenana. Beautiful hanging baskets of brilliant purple, pink, and red petunias mixed with yellow daisies hung in front of every storefront and home. Nenana was a one street town on the Tanana River and I would have loved to have taken the time to visit every nook and cranny in the town.

We found a restaurant on the river and while we ate lunch, the Irish proprietor entertained us. He had come to Alaska for a visit thirty years ago and never left. He let me borrow the binoculars to look across the river at the native cemetery. He also convinced us to buy a ticket each for the Nenana Ice Classic. Stupid me thought it was a local ice skating show.

No, that is not the case. Sometime during the months of October and November the river freezes. The ice gets thicker throughout winter and by April first, the ice is about forty-two inches thick. Then, the ice begins to melt on the top due to the warming temperatures and melts on the bottom because of the water flow. Every year when spring comes, bets are made as to when the river will break up and start to flow. That always occurs between April twentieth and May twentieth. A large black and white tripod is planted two feet into the frozen ice of the Tanana River and three hundred feet from shore. The tripod moves and the clock connected to it at the bank stops as the ice begins to flow. The exact day and time of the breaking ice is bet on and if you are the lucky one to guess right, you win three hundred thousand dollars. Not to miss a chance at three hundred thousand dollars, we each placed our bets and dropped them in the large metal drum near the door.

After a lovely lunch in the sunshine on the back deck over looking the Tanana River, we headed south trying to get to a campsite near Denali. The sky suddenly turned black, the wind began to blow, and the lightening started to flash. We stopped on the side of the road to button down the snaps and Velcro on our jackets and continued down the road. I became a tad nervous as the rain poured and the lighting cracked and lit up the dark black sky. Then, in the middle of the storm, we approached a railroad crossing. Suddenly, the arm came down and the alarm sounded. We had to stop rather suddenly on the slick road because the train was right there upon us.

I personally do not think the crossing arm and alarm came soon enough for the closeness of the train. Well, there we were, stopped in the rain, with the lightening all around, waiting for the passenger train to cross. Since we were the first in line, we were able to wave to the people on the train. Most waved back. I imagined that those on the train were thinking that they were glad they were inside the dry train and not on the back of a motorcycle in the middle of a soaking rain and lightning storm. I would have loved to experience the train trip.

Soon enough the train passed, the arm came up and we scooted over the tracks only to face a very large metal grated bridge crossing the wild turbulent river. Oh great, I thought, now I am really going to be struck by lightening and I am going to die somewhere in the back woods of Alaska on a bridge in a lightening storm. If the lightening didn't kill me first then I would probably drown when thrown off my bike into the cold rushing river below me.

Fortunately, luck was on our side, I didn't get struck by lightening and die, and we made it out of the storm and into Denali. We past Denali National Park as our campground was six miles further south down the road. We found our very pretty campground in the woods right next to rushing river. I think it was the same one we crossed earlier in the electrical storm.

We went to the little camp store and bought dinner, which really amounted to junk food since there was not anything else. With the tent set up, my belly full of junk food, my new cot is waiting for me. I am going to bed now. Ralph gave up about thirty minutes ago and is snoring so loud I can hear him out here by the river. And I get to sleep next to that!

Grizzle Bear was happy to find a new friend tonight. A little mountain squirrel chattered in the tree next to our picnic table and I threw him some of my pecan granola bar. The squirrel and Grizzle Bear chatted for a while then Grizzle went off to the mosquito free tent. And that is just where I am headed folks.

Love to all always,
Judy/Mom/Mommy

June 15, 2005
Wednesday
Denali National Park
Mile 7496

Dear Folks,

Ralph woke up bright and early this morning thinking it was time to get up. He made all sorts of noise only to discover it was four A.M. He went ahead and got up and took a shower and I turned back over on my new heavenly cot and went back to sleep. Ralph, upon returning from his shower, climbed back into his warm sleeping bag, fully dressed and went back to sleep too.

Around eight I got up, took a shower and we took our sweet time getting ready this morning. There was no rush as we planned to stay in Denali for a few days. We moseyed on into the national park to see if there was a chance we could get on one of the shuttle busses that would take us into the park. That is the only way the average tourist can see Denali.

As luck would have it, there was space on a one P.M. bus. We purchased our tickets and went into town to get some lunch and to purchase food to take with us on the trip. There would be no food or water to purchase on the eight-hour trip.

We found a Subway in the town of Denali. Plenty of tourist stores, a jumping off place for white water rafters, bus tours, and junk stores line the main highway leading to the park. While we waited in line for our turn to order sandwiches, we had the unfortunate experience of being behind the customer from hell. We have a saying in our house that sometimes someone just needs to be slapped. This woman certainly did! She had several orders and each one had to be prepared just exactly to specifications. When the girl behind the counter put the cheese on one side of the bread and the meat on the other, she was soundly corrected by the customer and told to put the cheese on top of the meat before melting it. Then when the other employee was adding other ingredients to the customer's other sandwich, the employee could not place the banana pepper correctly on the customer's sandwich.

The customer eventually snatched the sandwich from the poor guy and did it herself. She wanted only one large banana pepper on her sandwich broken in one long piece and put exactly down the middle of the bread. By now, a sizable line had formed behind us and all of us were exchanging exasperated looks. I wanted to scream. Like I said, some people just need to be slapped.

We ate our lunch, gathered our belongings, and headed back to the park to catch the shuttle bus to take us on our tour of Denali National Park. Months ago, when we were planning this trip, we were sure we would not want to ride a tourist bus into the park. We changed our minds when we got here and decided to do the tourist thing. We were lucky to get a seat, I thought, especially since every book I had read said we needed reservations six months ahead of time.

As we started on our journey, the road turned to gravel, as usual. It was a nice wide flat, well-maintained road back into the interior of Denali National Park. I really wanted to see Denali Mountain and thought this would be the only way we might get close to it. The flight seeing tours were a bit pricy and Ralph was not under any circumstances getting on one of those small planes to fly around the mountain.

So, off we headed on what seemed to be a very tame ride into the back woods of Denali National Park. The beautiful clear morning had now turned cloudy and storm clouds were moving in from the west. They were similar to the late afternoon thunder boomers we see in Atlanta on a hot summer day.

We were on a very large school bus shuttle painted green. The bus cruised at a reasonable speed viewing the beautiful mountains and rivers and valleys that stretched forever it seemed. I was comparing this landscape to the one we had just seen on the Dalton Highway. At first, it didn't even compare though all around me was wild, untamed beauty.

But then things changed. If I had had any inkling of what was up ahead and about to happen I would have gotten off the bus right then and there and hiked back to the parking lot. The road suddenly narrowed, to at best, a one lane, gravel road and we started to climb in elevation. Several pit stops were made in the drizzle but even the drizzle started to change the higher we got in elevation.

Just as we started to climb the tallest, narrowest pass in the park, which is called Polychrome Pass, the entire sky opened up and "there come a flood." There were no guardrails at all and the drop off was at least one thousand feet to the valley floor. I noticed a sign as we started up the pass that said Slide Area. Great! Ralph and I were on the inside next to the mountain and the other side of the bus was hanging right on the edge of the road.

I was so nervous I thought I would throw up. Then, with the sky dumping the mother load of all storm water, the side of the mountain was sliding down in several places in front of the bus as we watched! Huge rocks the size of basketballs rolled into our path. There were several areas where the mountainside had actually washed into the narrow, gravel road, but the bus kept climbing higher and higher and higher, the engine straining with every foot it climbed. I was saying just about every cuss word I knew and even made up a few new ones.

I wanted to get out and walk even with all the rain, rockslides, and oh yeah, lightening. I felt I stood a better chance of surviving on foot than on that bus. I was so very scared. Put me on a motorcycle, let me drive all over the country, let me take a treacherous ride to the Arctic Ocean and I will do just fine. But put me on a big, green bus with thirty other people and have hell fire and brimstones thrown at me on the side of a steep mountain with the lighting flashing, torrential rains and the mountain giving away as we watched, and I was in a major state of panic. I was glad I had my living will in order. I just hoped the kids remembered where I put it.

I thought I was the only one upset. Everyone in the back of the bus was laughing and having a gay old time. Ralph was rather silent but appeared right calm. The man in the seat across from us was so stoic and silent and looked to be enjoying himself. I was a wreck and starting to become very vocal about it. Hyperventilation only adds more chaos to an already stressed brain and nervous system.

I do not know if the bus driver was worried or not but he appeared nonplused by the falling debris, torrential rain and washed out road and continued up the mountain. Just as I was literally about to get off the bus, we crested the top of the pass with all its switchbacks and started down the other side. The situation was still nerve wracking and the mountain was still sliding into the road but there is something about the feeling of going back down that made me feel that the trouble is almost over.

That was all the excitement I thought I could handle for one day but then I realized that, just with the Dalton Highway, we had to come back over this same pass to get back out and this time I would be sitting on the drop off side. My lunch crept up my throat.

We got to the end of the first leg of our bus journey safely. The mountains and valleys, braided streams, wild rushing waters of rivers, and snow on the mountaintops were breathtaking. The raw wildness of earth surrounded me. I can understand why this is the only way one can see the park but I really missed the photo opportunities that I would normally have taken. We just have to remember them in our brains forever and play them like a video over and over again.

The few chances to take photos I did get were at the pit stops and these were not exactly in some of the most scenic spots.

We struck up conversations with some of the other passengers and we all shared stories of travels. Along the way back to the visitor center we watched for wild animals and saw quite a few. We saw a mama moose and twin calves, several caribou munching grass in the valley, many Dall sheep, all white, standing out against the black rocks, and a grizzly bear playing in a stream. But to me the most rewarding was the wolf.

We came around a corner and there he was trotting down the middle of the road. He was all wet and muddy and looked rather scraggly but that was just because he was wet. The driver told us that the wolves liked to travel the gravel roads because there was usually an easy meal to be had. The squirrels and other rodents dart across the road and make easy pickings for the wolves. They also get to feed on the unfortunate rodent that gets squished by the bus. A real easy dinner, it is fresh kill and the wolf does not even have to hunt too hard.

At least this time when we had to cross the pass it was not raining but the road grader was out plowing the rocks off the road. We had to pass him in very tight quarters and as I said before this time, we were on the outside. I had to physically turn in my seat so my back was to the drop off. I was practically sitting in the aisle. It was at this moment that the Dutchman, who had traveled the world and had seen many extremes, said to me in a very quite voice, "that was the first time in my life that I thought I was going to die." He was talking about his stoic ride up the mountain pass. I burst out laughing. I was so relieved that I was not the only one scared to death. Neither one of us looked until we got to the bottom of Polychrome Pass and felt reasonably safe again.

After all the incredible scenery, the frightening experience and the wild animals we did not get to see the mountain, Denali. The mountain was completely covered in clouds. I was really disappointed but maybe we will see it somewhere else down the road.

The bus made it safely back to the visitor center and I climbed off a little weak kneed and headed straight to the toilet. Afterward, we headed into town for some dinner and found a nice pizza place. After dinner, we rode back to our campground and as we pulled into our secluded campsite, we found we were surrounded by a group of bikers and tents. I thought how convenient that we should all be in one place and was tickled at the prospects of a party.

We went and introduced ourselves and spent the remainder of the evening laughing and telling stories around their campfire. They were a lively bunch and made us feel so very welcome. They lived in Alaska and were on their way to the motorcycle rally in Fairbanks.

We told them our story of traveling to Prudhoe Bay and that I was the first woman in the Iron Butt Association to finish the ride. They were all so congratulatory and genuinely happy for me. Toasts were made all around. The women in the group were exceptionally proud that a woman had done something that is usually saved for a man. I felt so proud and these new friends made me feel so very good about myself.

This group of bikers lived in Kodiak, Alaska and they will be heading back on the ferry from Homer, on June twenty-first, the summer solstice. Since Ralph and I wanted to go to Kodiak anyway, they invited us to join them on their journey back home. We are going to try to get reservations on the overnight ferry to Kodiak Island. I can't wait! I feel like we have made some new friends that we will stay in contact with for quite a while.

Today was another day that we thought would be rather tame and who knew what the day would bring. It brought a treasure chest full of beauty, terror, excitement, and new friends.

What a winner of a day.

Until later. Much love to all always,
Judy/MOM/Mommy

June 18, 2005

Saturday
Indian, Alaska
Mile 7746

Dear Folks,

Thursday we spent the day around the campsite, enjoying having a day to do nothing. I wrote a bunch of postcards to friends and family while Ralph surfed the net. As I sat in my chair with my feet propped up on the bench of the picnic table, I watched the little squirrels chatter and fuss at each other. They made many trips back and forth between our tent site and the others around us, picking up dropped food and scattered seeds from the evergreens above us.

One little rascal popped right up on the table, with me sitting there, looking for food scraps. He must have smelled something particularly yummy as he sunk his teeth into the side pocket of the little collapsible cooler I carry with us. I shooed him off, looked into the pocket, and found several individual packets of peanut butter and several of jelly.

I had taken a few of these from a Super 8 motel from the free continental breakfast bar we had eaten at many days back. I figured if we were stranded somewhere the peanut butter and jelly would come in handy to spread on a few crackers.

Mr. Squirrel must have had a radar nose because he was about to tear a hole in my cooler to get the forgotten treasures. He scurried off when I got up to see what he was after. I put all the peanut butter and jelly packets on the table and went back to other things.

Ralph and I took a ride back into the town to get some lunch and to explore the visitor's center in the park. When we returned to camp a couple hours later the peanut butter packets were missing. Not the jelly mind you, just the peanut butter.

While in town, I found a gift shop and bought a few goodies to ship home. Then we bought some sandwich meat, bread, chips, fruit and of course chocolate candy and returned to camp for more rest and relaxation. I threw some bread out into the woods for the birds but Mr. Squirrel found it first and made about twenty trips back and forth to his nest with the feast.

We read for a while, listened to the threatening thunder, and wondered if we were going to have to scurry into the tent any moment. After a day of doing not much of anything and enjoying some much-needed rest, we climbed into the tent and went to sleep.

Friday morning we got up early with the sun shining right in our eyes. After packing all our stuff, we hurried back to the visitor's center in the park to catch the bus to go see the dog sled exhibition. During the winters in Denali, the rangers use dog sleds to patrol the park, as no roads are passable due to snow.

The rangers gave a little demonstration and talked about the use of sled dogs in the park during winter. They hooked up the dogs up to a sled and showed how the dogs pull a sled around an area set aside for the demonstration. Before the demonstration, they let the spectators walk through the kennels, see, and pet the dogs.

Some of the dogs were put in fenced off kennels for various reasons such as illness or females getting ready to be bred. The rest are in roped off areas with nice doghouses. The dogs are tied to a spike in the top of the doghouse with a long chain. They can move freely around the area roped off for them. I could go up to the roped off area and call them over to be petted if they so choose.

Three other dogs were not in roped off areas but were tethered. We could go right up to these dogs and pet them. All the dogs were very friendly and absolutely loved the attention they were receiving. I got to pet one dog named Muddy. He found something very, very interesting about the smell of my pants legs. I guess it was all the mashed up bug guts on my riding pants. I do not know what it was that attracted him but he could hardly be torn away.

We left Denali National Park around eleven-thirty and we did not get too far before we stopped for lunch at a ranch down the road called the Lazy Jane. I had my usual huge hamburger and fries and immediately got sleepy. I guess all the rest we had yesterday did not help any.

The light, or lack of darkness, has tortured my internal clock. After almost three weeks of no darkness, it has taken a toll. Both of us are exhausted at odd hours and sleep patterns have been altered. Add into the mix of being four hours earlier than home, our bodies just do not know what to do.

After lunch and followed shortly thereafter by a caffeine fix, we continued down the road toward Anchorage. Today was supposed to be a short travel day. We were planning to stop in Anchorage for the night but had no reservations anywhere nor any idea where to stop in the big city of Anchorage. We knew the hotels in Anchorage were extremely pricey. Ralph and I thought we might find a campground somewhere in the area though.

As we left Denali behind, the road continued through a glacier valley between high mountains on both sides. The river raced right beside the road and was muddy grey with silt runoff. The sky was clearing into a beautiful blue freckled with puffy white clouds.

We rounded a corner and off to our right was the mountain we missed in the park: Denali or Mt. McKinley as some still refer to it as. Denali was so impressive standing there tall, high above the rest of the snow covered mountains. The longer we continued down the road the closer we came and the larger the mountain became.

I was glad to at least say that I had seen Denali even if it was rather far off in the distance. As I rounded a long curve heading away from the mountain, I took a last look in my rear view mirror and there in all its splendor was the huge mountain framed on both sided by the fir trees and the road behind me heading toward it. Darn, that was the best shot ever and I missed it. I was going too fast to stop and there was not a good place to turn around but I will forever remember that big white mountain in my rear view mirror.

One nice thing that has impressed me about most of the roads here in Alaska is the lack of advertisement along the way. For the most part, until you get very close to a town, there are no signs other than highway signs marking the route. There are no billboard or advertising to spoil the beautiful scenery. As soon as you get close to a larger town though, that changes.

As we got close to Anchorage, it looked like it could be Anywhere, USA. Too much clutter, too many advertisements for this or that eating establishment or gas station, or Wal-Mart littered the roads. All the commercialization was smack dab in the middle of the most breath taking mountains and snow.

As we got close to Anchorage, we finally saw salt water. The road followed the water right into downtown Anchorage. We had not made any reservations and the campground we located in the city was only a gravel parking lot made for RV's, not tents. I was getting very frustrated as it was late Friday afternoon and we had no idea of where we would stay.

Ralph stopped into an Econo Lodge where we were told they had one room left. When Ralph went in to register, he found out that it was a mistake. There were no rooms in Anchorage. Apparently, there was a mayor's marathon going on in the city and rooms were scarce.

Out we headed, going further south out of Anchorage. The road we were on was the only one that goes south out of Anchorage and down to the Kenai Peninsula. The road is right on the water and follows it for miles. The mountains drop right off into the water and the view is very dramatic. The traffic was fast moving and it was hard to sight see as everyone was in such a big hurry. Welcome back to the big city.

Ralph told me when we left Anchorage that he would stop in the first place that came along on the road. Things were starting to look a little bleak when the Brown Bear Saloon and Motel popped into view just south of Indian, Alaska.

We pulled into the gravel parking lot and realized immediately that we had found, quite by accident, a biker bar, complete with motel. A wooden, weather eroded, sign outside claimed rooms available for half the price in town. Oh, great, what could that mean?

I did not get off my bike this time and let Ralph go in to find out the details. Meanwhile, five bikers immediately came over to inspect the bikes tags to see where we rode in from. I immediately thought of dogs sniffing the new dog on the block. One look at our Georgia tags and jaws started dropping. They were duly impressed and became friendly immediately.

Ralph came back outside with a smile on his face and said we had a room above the bar for the night but the bartender said it might get a bit loud later in the night. Oh, me. So happy to have a place to stay, I unloaded all my stuff and Ralph carried it up the steps to the room, which was directly over the bar. Our gear filled the room and the bed was small but it appeared clean and it had a toilet and shower. I would not have to fight mosquitoes tonight and I would have a convenient potty in the middle of the night.

Well, we have slept in the parking lot behind the bar in Chicken, Alaska. We are now going to sleep over the bar in Indian, Alaska. I wonder where in Alaska we will spend the night inside the bar. I just hope that if we do wind up inside a bar sleeping, I am so inebriated that I will not notice where my head rests.

With all our gear stacked against every wall in the tiny room, we went back down stairs to have a drink and see if we could rustle up some dinner. The bartender offered to fix us "bar food" which consisted of frozen pizza. We gladly accepted and our cheese pizza was rather good, especially after being so tired.

We played songs on the jukebox, tacked a dollar bill to the wall to keep the many others company, talked to some of the locals and played pool with the bartender, Chris. A few hours later, we moseyed up to our room, fell into bed, and went to sleep to the sounds of the jukebox, people laughing in the bar and loud motorcycle pipes singing a song of farewell as they roared down the highway.

Sometime during the night, the rain came in. Clouds socked in all the mountains and the inlet across the street and poured for hours. I was glad to be out of the rain as it would have been a miserable riding day. We had set aside today to catch up on some administrative things and Ralph had some work to do for a client. Today was a non-ride day and nothing noteworthy to report for today. Oh, but the three hour nap we got to the sound of the rain was heavenly.

Tomorrow we are heading toward Homer, Alaska at the bottom of the Kenai Peninsula and will stay there a couple of days. From my Milepost bible, there is a campground there but it is out on the spit, right next to the water and very windy. We have opted to try another hostel located in town. So far, our experience with hostels, while not terrible, has not been wonderful either. We both prefer the privacy of our tent to sharing space with too many strangers. While we both love meeting new people, the occupants of hostels are generally of a much younger generation and mostly stick to their own age group making it difficult for us to strike up conversations.

Grizzle Bear has been snug as a bug for the last two days. I have heard him snoring a time or two over in the corner. I don't think he much cares that he has to sleep on the floor, he is just happy he did not have to spend the day riding in the rain on the back of my bike.

So until later, much love to all, always,
Judy/Mom/Mommy

June 19, 2005
Sunday
Homer, Alaska
Mile 8020

Dear Folks,

As soon as we left the Brown Bear Saloon this morning the scenery became our main focus. After the downpour we had all day yesterday, the clouds were beginning to lift over the mountains and the rain was gone. Though it started out cold and cloudy we were warm and toasty in our riding gear.

The mountains stepped right out of the water and soared right into the grey sky. The tide was way out leaving mud flats for miles and miles. Signs were posted frequently warning people not to walk out onto the mud flats as it would quickly turn to quicksand and be extremely dangerous. Not interested, no thanks.

The area that we rode through today was devastated back in March, nineteen sixty-four with the largest earthquake ever recorded in North America. Nine point two registered on the scale that day. The land dropped six to twelve feet in some areas. The trees killed in this area due to the salt water, still stand as reminder of the devastation. I kept getting a creepy feeling as I looked upon the scared landscape still visible today. I have to admit to being a little nervous as well.

The road followed Turnagain Inlet for miles and the scenery got more and more rugged and more beautiful. We were now entering glacier country and several could be seen on the mountains across the inlet.

Portage Glacier was just a few miles off the road we were traveling and we decided to take a little side trip to see the glacier. We knew there was a boat trip on the lake in front of the glacier but this glacier did not actually come right down into the water. I am saving my money for the boat trip in Seward, Alaska to the Fiords National Park, which does take you up to the glaciers.

As we got closer to the Portage Glacier, the air definitely turned cooler and the ice on the mountains became more prevalent. There were several glaciers in the same area and all very close to the road. Parts of the ice were the most radiant blue green color.

We pulled up into the visitor's center and the boat dock and were able to get a good look at the glacier without going on the boat. I wore out my index finger I took so many pictures of the glacier and the turquoise icebergs still floating in the lake. With my curiosity satisfied, we headed back down the road south toward the Kenai Peninsula and Homer, our destination for the day.

The road itself, wandered through mountains and valleys surrounded on both sided by lush green mountains and some even with snow still in the crevices. We reached the peninsula and were struck by the color of the Kenai River.

If it had not been so darn cold I would have love to jump into the water. The Kenai River was the color of the Caribbean and flowing at a rapid rate between the mountains. Several boatloads of rafters were rushing down the river. I wanted to be on the boat with them. I like rafting very much and this place was so alluring I wanted to be on the water right in the middle of it.

But then again I was in the middle of it, just on a road not in the water. A little bit further down the road and we came upon dozens and dozens of cars parked on the side of the road. Curiosity got the best of Ralph and he wanted to find out what all the commotion was about. We found a spot between two trucks and backed out bikes onto the dirt shoulder.

The commotion was that the salmon were running and every fisherman or fisherwoman in the vicinity had a pole out and waders on, standing in the cold Kenai River, pulling in the salmon as soon at they bit the hook. And boy howdy, they were biting. We could see across the river when a salmon bit because there would be a big splash and then the fishing pole would appear to bend in half.

Too bad for Ralph, as he left his fishing pole at home. It is just as well though, I do not cook fish. Don't know how, don't want to learn. He has to enjoy his fish from the restaurant, not my kitchen.

I would love to see the natural fishers though but don't think that is going to happen this trip. I would love to see the bears standing in the water waiting for a juicy fish to jump upstream and be caught "bear handed."

Our curiosity satisfied, we headed back out on the road toward Homer. The wind had picked up and it was becoming increasingly hard to ride. We had head winds combined with swirling cross winds. Two of my personal favorites.

Just when I thought I had seen the prettiest, grandest site I could possible see, I would come around a curve in the road and was struck by another breath taking view. I came up over a hill earlier today and off in the distance was a huge snow and ice covered mountain that was just as impressive as Denali any day.

The closer and closer we got to it, more and more mountains, just like the first one started to appear. The wind was strong and it was hard to take my eyes off the road but I did get a look off to my right. Off to my right was Cook Inlet and on the other side of the inlet was a completely new mountain range I had not seen before. They were stunning. There are no other words to describe it.

I was hoping, at some point on this trip, to see some eagles. I had seen one on the Dalton Highway, a golden eagle. I had heard that in Homer during the winter the eagles were very numerous. I was hoping that maybe a stray eagle or two would be around for me to feast my eyes on. I dearly love birds of prey.

At the next opportunity to pull off the road, I did so to take a good long look at the incredible vista before me. Suddenly, I was treated to many bald eagles soaring in the currents above the inlet. As I sat on my parked bike, the strong wind was all I could hear and my eyes beheld the splendor of these magnificent birds soaring and turning in the wind. They looked as if they were playing in the wind, wings tilted perpendicular to the ground one moment and then next parallel with the ocean and ground.

The eagles made circles and came back over and over again to the same spot to soar. Imagine, deep, blue ocean, navy blue, almost black mountains with icy tops, as a backdrop, ice blue sky dotted with white powder puff clouds, green sea grass on the cliff's edge wind blown almost over and the eagles playing in the wind. I stood alone in the wind blown grass and watched the eagles play. The moment was almost too much for me. I wanted to stay and watch but the wind was very cold and getting colder by the minute. I had gotten my wish of soaring eagles on currents of Alaskan air.

Off we went, fighting the wind, to finish our journey into Homer. Our journey through the wind was not as graceful as the floating eagles. They were in their element; we were but passengers through their world. When we were just about to Homer, I saw a sign for a scenic view. Since we were climbing a steady hill, I hoped the view just might be good. I was stunned when we came over the hill and off to our right were glacier-covered mountains and ice covered volcanoes sky rocketing right out of the water reaching for the sky. The water was various shades of blue, turquoise, navy blue, almost black in spots. The scene completely surrounded the end of the peninsula. For miles and miles there was nothing to see but mountains, ice, glaciers, snow, cold blue water and soaring eagles.

If I had not already had goose bumps from the cold air, I would have gotten them just from the view below. This view was more than anything I hoped it would be when I was reading about the area months ago.

Back on the bikes, we went on in to Homer, found our hostel we were going to stay in, and unloaded our things. This hostel is much better than the one in Fairbanks. It is cleaner and we have a room to ourselves.

I had done some research before we left home about the camping on the spit in Homer and I had seen some pictures of tents turned over because of the wind. I had these pictures in the back of my mind when we decided to try a hostel again. I am sure glad that we are staying here for the next two nights and not out on the spit of land that juts out into the windy ocean.

After dinner, Ralph and I rode out onto the spit and were immediately sand blasted by the sand and dirt being fiercely blown from a sinister crosswind from hell. The crosswinds were so intense and it felt as if we were going to be blown off the road and over into the rocks and sand. Once committed to riding out to the spit there was no turning around until we reached the end four miles later.

Out on the spit were many restaurants, gift shops, and fishing boats for hire. And just like the pictures I had seen before we left home, the tents that had been set up on the beach were blown over, some turned inside out. Some were standing, how I don't know, but most were not faring well at all. Gee, let's see what the choices are here: a nice room in a dry, windless hostel or tent, contents blown inside out, sand blasted and freezing on a rock pile of a beach. Hummm? This bed sure feels good right about now! Guess you know where I am spending the night.

I hope that the wind will die down some tomorrow. We are going to take some back roads around Homer that will get us closer to the glaciers. I have to get some minor work done on my bike tomorrow. The oil is in desperate need of changing, as it has not been done since we left home. The dipstick broke somehow, maybe on the Dalton Highway, I don't really know.

My bike has run like a champ. I thought I got a serious rattle on the Dalton Highway. The bike was making a real loud rattle when I hit a bump and then again when we were in Fairbanks when I hit a pothole or bump in the road. I thought for sure the bike was destroyed. I was greatly relieved and slightly embarrassed when it turned out only to be a can of peaches bumping around in one of the saddlebags.

The only new noise or rattle I have gotten so far is not even on the bike. The noise is on my helmet and is just about to drive me crazy. The sound is like Styrofoam squeaking together right in my ears. I have to find some lubricant of some sort to grease the hinges of the face shield before I throw my helmet in the trash. Ralph later found the proper solution to my squeak. All it took was a little spit on each hinge and I had immediate silence. I wish he had thought of it sooner.

Grizzle Bear had his breath taken away today with all the new vistas. He is silent again, asleep in the corner, too tired to even take off his little leather jacket and black jeans. I threw him a blanket out of the kindness of my heart and I hear him snoring right in tune with Ralph as we speak. I cannot go to sleep with all the log sawing.

Happy Fathers Day to Ralph. I know he missed his children today. Milissa got the first call in this morning at six A.M. followed by William, Amanda, and Perry. Maybe I can cook him a belated dinner sometime soon in a campground over the open fire.

So, until later, with much love always,
Judy/Mom/Mommy

June 20, 2005
Monday
Homer, AK
Mile 8075

Dear Folks,

The sun shining in my eyes this morning woke me as usual at a very early hour. However, I turned back over, put my back to the window, and went back to sleep. The wind blew itself out last night and we awoke to the clear blue sky and temperatures like very early spring in Atlanta.

We walked outside and were greeted by the sight of snow-covered mountains and the ocean. Wow, what a sight to wake up to each morning. I sure have not missed the fire engines roaring down the street behind our house at home a zillion times a day in Atlanta. Actually, I have only heard one siren in the month we have been gone and that was in Fairbanks.

We had some unpleasant chores to do today so we got about it. I got the oil changed on my bike finally but if Ralph had not carried the oil filter and the wrench with us, it would have been a problem. With that over with for a few thousand miles, we went about finding a place to stuff our faces. We had the unpleasant task of laundry, too.

Since our harrowing experience driving out onto the spit last night in the hellish winds we were a little reluctant to do it again. The winds had died down so we gave it another shot. This time it was manageable and we made the four-mile journey to land's end on the spit.

There were all sorts of places to eat, shop and take boat charters for fishing and nature watching. We decided to do a little nature watching ourselves and sit out on the porch of a restaurant that sold fish and chips. As most of you know I do not do fish at all so I had my usual cheeseburger and fries to go along with my coke. I have sampled my way across the United States and Canada eating cheeseburgers and fries. You would think I would get tired of them but not so far.

I have been eating cheeseburgers for breakfast, lunch, or dinner since I was a little girl. I don't think I will be able to stop now. But, Ralph ordered the local catch of the day, halibut. While we waited for our order to arrive, I sat outside in the warm sunshine. Ralph wandered around inside the place looking at the pictures and items of interest.

I was watching the sea gulls coast and bank in the air current over the rocky beach and listened to them screech at each other. As I looked further down the beach, I saw a dark bird come gliding in at about rooftop level. At first I thought it was one of the many ravens that are common here. But at a closer glance, I realized I was looking at a bald eagle coming my way. Oooh, I was so excited. This one was coming in close. He soared in right over the roof of the fish and chips place. I was speechless. Where was Ralph?

I looked back down the beach and saw another one heading my way. I quickly grabbed my camera, extended the telephoto, and hoped for the best. I told myself that I would get a picture, whether I could see him or not, out of focus or not, I wanted a picture of an eagle.

As the eagle approached, he slowed his flight, spread his wings out far, extended the feathers on the wingtips, and lowered his legs, ready for landing in the tree post right beside the restaurant. Snap went the shutter on the camera. My heart gave a little squeal of delight.

He hovered over the tree in the air current momentarily then decided on another fallen tree on the rocky beach. Fortunately, I got Ralph's attention in time for him to see the eagle bank, make a circle and land.

The eagle stayed on the driftwood for quite a while and I was able to get close enough to him as I walked over to the rocks where he was perched. I was close enough to see a water drop hanging by a thread to the end of his beak. I suspected I could have gotten closer but he was looking rather nervous at my presence and I reminded myself that he was a wild animal and he had a very large beak and very sharp talons.

I stood for a few moments savoring my close encounter with the eagle. I had been truly rewarded. I do not think I will ever forget the way he looked coming up the beach heading right toward me, wings stretched out fully, legs tucked up, streamlined, white head and yellow beak turning in the wind, looking, I suspect, for prey. Oh, what goose bumps I had. Oh, what a gift I had received.

On the advice of the owner of the hostel, we rode up a road today that is not traveled by too many visitors. It is off the beaten path and not many tourists know about it. The road goes for twenty miles along the edge of the peninsula and climbs way above sea level. Many local people have houses out this road. Some have small farms and a few horses dot the landscape.

But the higher we climbed the clearer the ocean, inlets, glaciers and volcanoes became. The pavement was a very narrow, winding road and there was not any place to pull off to take any pictures. But, I did manage to get some photos at the top of a hill when I pulled into someone's driveway.

The road dead-ended in a turn around at the end of the mountain. Apparently, there is a Russian community at the end of the road. The road turns from pavement to gravel and descends sharply into this community. We turned around at the end of the pavement and headed back to Homer, getting another perspective and another view from a different angle. I cannot even begin to imagine what it would be like to wake up every morning to the views of the glaciers, mountains, and ocean. I think it must change on a daily basis depending on the weather, clouds, and air currents.

As we descended the twisty road back into town, straight out ahead of us several hundred miles across the inlet stood a huge volcano covered in ice and snow. It must be magnificent up close.

The road going back into Homer was under construction so we did a little experimenting and followed some of the local traffic that looked like they knew a way around the torn up road. The detour led us right back to the spit. As we headed back, into town we crossed a lake and I was struck with something rather funny. There were houses on the lake like you would see at most any lake but instead of boats on the boat docks there were airplanes on skids tied up at the docks. The lake is used as a runway.

Back at the hostel, we unloaded our clean clothes we had washed earlier and walked down to a restaurant called Fat Olive's for dinner. We had a nice dinner but unfortunately, we reek of garlic. I don't know which one of us is worse. We had to apologize when we walked in the hostel to the people around us.

We are off to bed early tonight, if you can call it night. The hour is late but the sun is still very much awake. Tomorrow is the summer solstice and up here it is called the land of the midnight sun. The sun will just stay in the sky tomorrow and make a small circle. But then again we have been seeing this amount of daylight for a long time now. We go to sleep with the sun shining in on one side of the tent only to awaken with the sun shinning in on the other side.

I have to admit that I am ready for a little darkness. Grizzle Bear has been looking at me with one eye open, one closed wishing for some place dark to sleep too. Hey, if I can't sleep neither can he. Right?

I must read Ralph his bedtime story. These journal entries are written at the end of the day and after writing them, Ralph likes me to read to him. I call them his bedtime stories. Grizzle Bear likes to be read to also. The story of the day and the sound of my voice puts everyone is a contented sleepy frame of mind and helps us go to sleep in this bright sunlight.

Tomorrow we are heading for Seward for a couple days.

Until next time, love to all always,
Judy/Mom/Mommy

June 21, 2005

Tuesday
Seward, AK
Mile 8355

Dear Folks,

Today is the summer solstice. That means that at any point above the Arctic Circle the sun does not set. At midnight, the sun is still high in the sky. But of course we have had a good dose of that anyway the last few weeks and it wasn't even the official summer solstice. Since we have moved further south now we actually have about three hours of semi-darkness. In other words, the nighttime looks just like our cloudy day in the south.

We left Homer this morning and headed back over the same road we came in on two days ago. This time the wind had died down and the skies were blue. Going in the opposite direction and having clear skies we saw all we missed when coming into Homer.

I sound like a broken record I know but just when I think I can't be impressed anymore, bam, there is another scene or another spectacular lake or river or gigantic mountain for me to feast my eyes on.

Today, as we left Homer, the volcanoes were very visible out over the inlet. Even being hundreds of miles away over the water they were impressive. Leaving town and coming up over a hill there was another volcano we had missed due to the earlier cloud cover. Gigantic, it was, jagged and ice covered stretching skyward.

These mountains seemed larger than Denali but that is because they are at sea level as are we. They jut right out of the ocean reaching heights where the snow and ice stays on them year round.

As we made the turn toward Seward, the mountains closed right in on us and it seemed we were just a zipper closing up a seam in between the mountains. The remaining snow on the mountains was stripped in places reminding me of a zebra with his strips. White, against the black mountains looked like the zebra cakes of chocolate cookies and whipped cream I made as a child.

All along the route, we saw many bald eagles above us. It was as if the eagles sought me, knowing I would watch them float above in the currents of cool mountain air. We also had a very close encounter with a female moose. We came around a bend in the road and there the big mama was, just on the side of the road, munching her heart out in the sweet tender grass. She didn't look the least big skittish and didn't look like she was interested in running out in the road. She was totally focused on her spring grass to fool with the likes of two bikers rolling down the road.

As we came to the Kenai River again, there were many more anglers than the other day. According to a man I spoke with in Homer yesterday, this was the hot spot in Alaska to be right now for the salmon run. I would have loved to watch but felt rather sorry for the fish having to run the obstacle course of hooks and nets.

As we got closer to Seward, the wind picked up again and came swirling down the canyon to meet us head on. The wind tossed us around a little but we rolled into Seward only to be greeted by Resurrection Bay. Wow, mountains and heavy, dark fir trees surrounded light sea green water in the bay.

We had located a campground via the internet a few days ago and had reservations. Once again, after coming through a town, the paved road ended and we traveled the remaining four miles on a wide dirt road that ran right along the bay.

The campground is right on the bay and we are tucked in beneath the old fir trees, nestled in the pine straw. Fishing boats come right up to the dock at the camp store and unload their passengers and catch of the day.

Since we were about six miles from the store in Seward, we decided to scrounge around in the camp store for dinner. The pickings were slim as the store is only stocked once a week but we found some canned tomato soup and a pound of bacon.

Back at our campsite, Ralph siphoned gas out of my tank into the duel fuel stove. I fried the entire pound of bacon and heated the soup. That combined with some left over cheese and we had a feast of sorts. Other than a good campfire burning sweet smelling wood, the smell of frying bacon in the woods is a delight to the senses.

The smell of frying bacon brought the camp dogs around sniffing and waiting for a handout. No such luck for them. We weren't sharing. The dogs finally gave up and went on to some other sucker.

After all the greasy dishes were cleaned, Ralph built a fire with wood purchased at the camp store. We popped our last bag of popcorn in the store microwave and ate it around the fire with the M & M's purchased at the camp store. Junk food never tasted so good.

The old camp dog thought she would come around for another try and put her head in Ralph's lap begging for an M&M. Ralph was mean and would not share them either. The old dog gave up and left.

For some reason tonight, our bikes have attracted a lot of attention. I believe it must be the Georgia tags on the back of the motorcycles. People have come into the site to ask us about our trip and about the bikes. We are always happy to tell our story. People are shocked that we have ridden as far as we have. I'm a little shocked myself.

Tomorrow, we are going to take a boat trip to the Kenai Fiord National Park and hopefully see some wildlife and glaciers. There are no roads to this park so the only way to visit the park is by either plane or boat. I'm excited as I love riding on boats and we are going to venture into new territory. As I look down the bay from the dock at the camp, it looks like we will be venturing into the islands of Jurassic Park. The water looks rather choppy tonight. I wonder what tomorrow will bring.

But that will be another story won't it?

Our fire is going good now, it is popping and crackling just right, and the smoke is blowing in the other direction. How perfect. The campers around us are settling down for the night. The Grandpa in the next site is singing some sort of Russian song to his grandson. The camp dogs have gone home, thank God.

Grizzle Bear is in the tent pouting and silent. There were no marshmallows to cook over the fire and I wouldn't share my popcorn with him. I guess he'll get over it won't he? After all, he did get a spectacular ride today and he is warm and dry snuggled down deep in my sleeping bag. What else could a little ole Grizzle Bear ask for? Marshmallows I guess.

So until tomorrow, love to all always,
Judy/Mom/Mommy

June 22, 2005
Wednesday
Seward, AK
Mile 8365

Dear Folks,

Ahoy maties, thar she blows! These two landlubbers are quite exhausted after our trip on the bounding main today. The day dawned today grey, bleak, misty, and cold. But not to be put off, we boarded the boat that would take us for an eight-hour trip into the Kenai Fiords National Park.

The park ranger told us that the weather today was typical of the environment. Yesterday had been so pretty with blue sky, lots of sunshine and clam seas. The boat had cabins that were heated fortunately, but the brave could venture outside if they liked. The upper deck, the bow, and stern were available for open-air viewing of the environment.

Everyone was assigned a table and had to share table space. It is always a lottery as to whom you will wind up sitting next to on excursions such as these. Since we had booked our trip late, it looked as if we might have our table to ourselves but at the last moment a young girl, traveling alone from Wyoming, slipped on board and sat with us.

Marie was working on her doctorate at Michigan State University in Decision Sciences. She was a very bright, intelligent girl and very interesting to talk to. She seemed to enjoy talking to us as well given the fact that we were old enough to be her parents. She had finished high school at seventeen, college at twenty, her masters at twenty-two and was working on her last year of her doctorate. She was twenty-three, very bright, single, and cute. Now that must to some seem like a dating ad but that is not the intention. We just thoroughly enjoyed the time we spent getting to know her.

Lunch of prime rib and salmon were served along with rice, salad, and bread. Of course, I bypassed the local salmon and chowed down on the prime rib. After lunch, which was served while underway, I donned my silk hoodie, stocking cap, added my gloves, and headed out to the front of the boat.

We had already planned ahead and were wearing our motorcycle gear so we were a lot warmer than the others on board. As we traveled out of Resurrection Bay the mountains around us became wilder and wilder. Low hanging rain clouds threatened but held their moisture.

The water was a unique color of dark teal unlike any color I have seen in an ocean environment. The park ranger pointed out evidence of World War II cannon tunnels that had been used for protection. I had not even thought of the necessity of such in this far away place.

More history of the earthquake of nineteen-sixty-four was told and it was making me nervous. This is such a very young geological area with moving tectonic plates. I believe this area is still called the ring of fire. Hey, if it happened once…

We chose this boat trip because of the possibility of seeing wildlife such as eagles, puffins, sea lions, whales and, of great interest to me, the glaciers. We were not disappointed.

As we ventured out of the calm bay, we turned out into the Gulf of Alaska. The ocean out there became rolling and swollen with large swells. The boat rolled up and over sending crashing waves the size of a dump truck and the color of lime sherbet, beside us.

I sat in the front on the starboard side and rode the waves just as the boat was doing. Then it started to rain and the cold became bone chilling. My rain proof riding gear lived up to its promise and I stayed snug and dry except for my face, hands, and hat.

Puffins with their pretty red beaks and sleek black bodies floated on the water. When the boat came close by all the little puffins would dive deep into the water to escape. I watched for them to come up but we always passed before they did. Along with the puffins, there were some birds, which I can't remember their names that looked just like small penguins. They were so cute. I love penguins too.

Large sea lions wallowed on the slabs of rock jutting out of the frigid Alaskan waters. A few even bothered to lift their flabby heads and give us a queer, unconcerned look. There were several large bulls but most were females. One even had a pup that poked its little head over mama's large brown body resting on the rocks and eyed us with mild curiosity.

As we moved on, suddenly a school Dall Porpoise appeared off the bow of the boat. They were so awesome. They looked like miniature orcas, jet-black with white stomachs, and they raced and flew through the water like black bullets. They would come swinging in very close to the boat then swerve out and jump out of the water and dive back down for another turn. They were playing in the cold, food rich waters, taking a moment from the abundant undersea buffet available during the summer months. What sheer freedom they represented to me, what speed, and agility.

As quickly as they appeared, they vanished. Like magic. Little black and white streaks of flying underwater animals, showing off to us, then, poof, gone, as if we had only been seeing things, like they hadn't even been there. What a precious gift I had been given.

On we rolled and crashed through the deep green waters; the rain clouds were hanging heavy now and dropping their payload. Suddenly, off to the right, came the spray from a large humpback whale. Then it disappeared. The pilot of the boat cut the engines and waited for the whale to resurface. We waited about ten minutes with no luck and just as he restarted the engines, the whale resurfaced about fifty feet from the boat.

Everyone oooohed and ahhhhed. Slick black and mammoth in size, it surfaced repeatedly, each time blowing water out its spout in a tall plume of water vapor and taking another deep breath before diving again. Water spout, hump, dorsal fin, repeating itself over and over until the last time when the whale had a stronger arch to its back. We knew it was going for a deeper dive this time and with a final arch, showed us his fluke as it slid silently into the deep ocean water.

It was very hard to get pictures as the boat was rolling something fierce and I was having a hard time with my sea legs. Every time I even tried to get a shot, the boat would lurch and I would manage to take a great picture of out of focus water or boat deck. I gave up on the wild life and just stored away the images in my brain along with the experience.

Between small rocky islands and much larger ones covered in moss, green bushes, and trees, the boat rocked and rolled. Monolith mountains emerging from the ocean were all around us sending their melting snow down in towering white waterfalls and falling in feathered spray into the sea.

We sailed into a fiord and immediately started seeing small chunks of ice. That was when I realized we were getting close to the glacier. The closer and closer we got to it the calmer the water became and the more ice we saw floating in a stream heading out to sea. As we rounded a turn, I saw what I wanted to see most on this voyage. The glacier.

The closer we got to it the bigger it became and the bluer it appeared. My camera at this moment chose to die. At first I thought the camera had gotten too cold in the freezing ocean air. My hands were like ice so I naturally thought the camera was suffering too. But it turned out the batteries went dead and Ralph went scurrying back downstairs to get some more. With new batteries restored, we captured some pictures but unless you are right in front of this glacier, there is no prospective. But I will tell you that the face of the glacier where we were was as tall as a sixty-five story building!

The boat engines were cut and the ranger told everyone to be silent and we would hear the glacier speak. For moments, there was the silence of the earth and then the voice of the glacier rumbled in vibration. The ice was moving and cracking and it echoed across the mountain walls. The glacier's voice sounded to me like a large tree cracking and breaking in half. Then we actually saw the glacier move in a process called calving. Part of the ice blue glacier broke off, tumbled down the face, and splashed into the cold water.

We slowly left the fiord and glacier and headed back out into open waters to the rookeries. This is when the ocean became nasty. I have no idea how high the swells were but it was enough to make many people sick. And yours truly, too. Up until this point I had experienced not the first moment's motion sickness. Given my propensity toward any kind of motion sickness, I had been pleasantly surprised. I had just enjoyed a nice cup of hot chocolate with whipped cream when the boat started doing some very funky things.

The woman in the seat behind us was already throwing up and her husband wasn't doing too well either. I started seeing the crew passing out barf bags and I knew I might just be in trouble. The hot chocolate was squirming around, rolling, and swirling, becoming a hot chocolate milk shake. I had to go to the potty but knew that would be a bad idea with being seasick. Close quarters like that is a death sentence.

I couldn't wait anymore and stumbled for the head. Sure enough, it was a mistake. I was thrown all over the place in the toilet, bruising my side on the latch on the bathroom door. It was a pure miracle I was able to hit the hole of the toilet. With that mission accomplished, I was just about to throw up and a quick look in the bathroom mirror confirmed my green face. I couldn't decide whether it would be better to throw up in the tiny bathroom or over the side of the boat into the water. I chose over the side of the boat because at least I wouldn't have to aim. I had hoped that the cold ocean air would help if I could just make it outside. I managed to reach the rear of the boat and leaned over waiting for my lunch and hot chocolate to emerge but the cold air immediately helped calm the nausea.

I stood there without my jacket, freezing, but looking at the horizon, trying to focus and keep from throwing up. I gagged more times than I care to recall. After about ten minutes in the cold, freezing air I thought I would try the indoors again. As I sat down at the table again, someone spotted another whale. This one had a calf with her. The captain stopped the boat again and the boat rolled with a vengeance. The poor woman behind me puked with each dip and roll of the boat. I felt sorry for her. I felt sorry for me.

The ranger now wanted to show us some more puffins. For those on board that were not sick, they were delighted. I don't think anyone of us that were nauseated much cared for any more puffins, any more sea lions, or any more glaciers. I just wanted back on some calm water and quickly.

After seeing an incredible place on this earth, wild ocean, wild animals, sea life, and a lone otter floating on his back watching us roll by, we made it back to the calm water of Resurrection Bay. My seasickness immediately disappeared.

The boat trip was everything I had expected and hoped for, well except for the seasickness. Wildness, primitive, earth unspoiled by man, and I was there. The thirst in my spirit and soul was quenched today with the elegance of the wild earth.

Back on shore, we rode down to the grocery store in town and bought the fixings for homemade chili for dinner. With the dishes all cleaned up and bellies full of warm, flavorable chili we sit by the campfire now warming our toes and reflect on the astonishing day we had at sea.

Grizzle Bear is in the tent still recovering from his day at sea. It seems he didn't get his sea legs today either and turned down the combustible chili and opted for a warm place in my sleeping bag. He's not talking to me again. Maybe a marshmallow or two tomorrow might help.

Well, the fire is just about out, the red coals winking at me, it is midnight here, and the day has caught up with me.

Until next time,
Love to all always,
Judy/Mom/Mommy

June 23, 2005

Thursday
Seward
Mile 8372

Dear Folks,

After all the clouds, misty rain, light rain, rolling seas of yesterday, guess what? We woke up to perfectly clear blue skies and smooth as glass seas. I would like to know why the only two times we chose to do the organized tourist thing, it rained, and the very next day was absolutely beautiful? I know why but I think I would have enjoyed the sun.

We got the full extent of the experience with the rain thrown into the mix and extra added excitement that otherwise wouldn't have happened if it remained sunny. So I guess I should be thankful, huh?

We had planned to mosey around town today but Ralph had some unexpected work to do and while we had good internet signal we stayed in camp today and tele-commuted. I think we have the best office in the world. Imagine your office in a nice wooded campground, surrounded by tall sweet smelling evergreens. Your desk sits next to a nice warm campfire and the view is wild Alaskan wilderness. I can't imagine a nicer office, can you?

I pondered what I would write about today as we were not moving or seeing anything new. I was observing things around me nonetheless.

Today, I have decided to write about campground observations and experiences. Those who love to camp have in their minds the perfect campsite. Mine is a flat but padded pine straw site tucked up in the trees, next to a stream that rushes over rocks creating a melodious tune. The site would have a fire pit and plenty of dry firewood available either in the woods or for purchase. It would also have a clean potty with hot and cold running water and a nice clean shower that I don't have to put quarters in the box for a quick two-minute shower. Add to that an incredible view and perfection is at hand.

Oh yeah, internet access for Ralph, and a grocery store within striking distance to purchase steaks and corn to cook over that fire pit is a must. Oh, and one more thing, a laundry to wash those nasty, smelly, dirty clothes that reek of campfire smoke from the fire pit.

Well, we've come close on some of our campsites, but some were really pitiful. The one we are in now in Seward has most of the criteria but is lacking is some. We do have the pine straw bed under the fir trees, a fire pit, a beautiful view of the ocean, a laundry, a grocery store six miles from here, but the bathroom has gotta go, my friends. It is ancient and smelly. I think there must have been an outhouse here before there was running water. The area still has that outhouse smell to it. There is no hot water in the bathroom and the cold water is enough to cause hyperthermia in a heartbeat and frostbite to the fingers instantly.

There is a sink attached to the shower house to wash your dishes that I think was built for leprechauns. I swear it comes only up to my knees. And there is no hot water there either, just a spray hose like in the kitchen sink that is like using a fire hose, the pressure is so great. One good spray on a plate and you have an instant ice cold shower down your dry warm clothes. No amount of soap will get congealed grease off dishes in ice-cold water.

Now, I have seen some showers in my lifetime that go from one end of the scale to the other but this one takes the cake. There are three stalls in the women's side and no privacy. I'm sorry y'all but I like my privacy when showering and dressing. The guys can strut around all they want. I like to dress all by myself, thank you. Out of necessity, I did have to shower and was perplexed when I climbed into the metal walls and found no water knobs. I saw the water pipes coming out of the ceiling and down the shower wall and saw the kitchen sprayer, but no knobs!

Just out of curiosity, I picked up the kitchen sprayer, pushed the button and wonders never cease, warm water came out! Now just imagine how tricky taking a shower in that was. It was hard to soap up and wash my hair with a kitchen sprayer that would only stay on when I pushed the button. I managed, but I came out slick with soap and cream rinse residue still in my hair. At least I smelled good.

This is a popular campground and reminds me of a twenty-four hour truck stop. Since its daylight almost twenty-four hours, campers come in at all hours. They are not the least bit respectful of the others who have just managed to fall asleep in spite of the sunlight.

Two nights ago, in the site right behind us, the party girls came in drunk as skunks and were happy as all get out. I had just dosed off and I think it was somewhere around two in the morning. I quickly started thinking of ways to pay them back in the morning when they were hung over and trying to sleep.

There are many human noises here in camp. Men burp and fart in the dirt road in front of our campsite thinking that no one hears them. Well, hello! Here I am sitting at the picnic table. Can't you see me? Pots and pans bang in other campsites, campers hoping to prepare a fine dinner to be eaten outside. Twelve boy scouts across the road tried cleaning up dinner pots by hitting them together hoping the food clinging to the inside of the pots would fall out. While some scouts clean pots others banged rocks together to see if they could make sparks. One Boy Scout had a large pot down by the water faucet trying to clean it out and wound up pouring the entire contents down the front of him. I guess that was his shower for the week.

Lots of vans, cars, and trucks moving around on the gravel create a particularly nice sound, especially combined with the diesel engines. That has such a lovely ring to it doesn't it?

Today, there was the lovely man made sound of dump trucks unloading gravel and spreading it around on the road we will be leaving on in the morning. There went my nap I had been thinking about. Now I'm worried how deep the gravel is going to be and whether or not I will be dropping my bike.

Last night when we got back to camp from the boat trip and the grocery store, a young family with a toddler had set up camp in the site behind us next to the party girls. Dad was sitting by the fire he had started and poor mom was in the tent trying to get the baby to go to sleep. Baby wasn't interested and he cried for four hours solid. I'm not kidding. The poor baby was totally exhausted but was just not in his own bed and couldn't settle down. I knew exactly what that was like but I was not about to go over and offer any friendly advice. If mama had cuddled the baby next to her while she and dad both enjoyed the fire there would have been instant silence in the campground.

Today though, as we were wrapping up the days work, a mega motor home the size of one of the humpback whales we saw yesterday rolled into the site right next us and suddenly all the nice warm sunshine that was warming my back and head disappeared. Gone in an instant and the temperature dropped ten degrees immediately. The guy stuck his head out of the window and said, "Is this ok to park here?" Well, no, I thought since he was now taking up both entrances to his and our campsites and was blocking the path to the potty.

Seven people piled out of the motor home, four adults, two of which were as large as the motor home, and three children. Oh me. Grandpa was friendly enough and the little boy with his brand new popgun pretended to shoot the little squirrels that had been coming to the tree stump right in front of our tent. Earlier, I had placed some stale bread on the tree stump for the critters to enjoy but I wound up only baiting the poor things for this little boy's personal shooting gallery. It was his little sister I could have gladly turned the pop gun on and with pleasure stuffed a sock in her mouth.

She whined and cried and moaned and groaned and yelled and cried some more because things weren't going her way. She reminded me of a girl Milissa and Amanda grew up with. Oooh, what are parents thinking when they let a kid go on that way? Well, I'm not going to go into child raising techniques here but I will say that paybacks are hell and they are going to get theirs ten fold. Do you think I'm going to be quiet when we pack up in the morning? After all, they are literally ten feet from our picnic table. You snooze you loose.

Now, besides the human noises there are the animal noises. This camp has five camp dogs. All are running free, collared, and tagged, thank goodness, but a nuisance never the less. One looks like she is part Border collie as she acts just like our neighbor's dog Chelsea. She was trying to get me to throw a lid to a container like it was a Frisbee. She had the same body language. I was suckered in and I threw it once then ignored her after that.

One of the other dogs is at the bottom of the food chain. She is so shy but sneaky. She is the one that put her head in Ralph's lap begging for popcorn. Since Ralph was so mean and didn't give her any, I saved our pork chop bones from dinner to give her should she show up.

Sure enough, she did and as we sat by the fire, she weaseled in between us, inched her way up to the paper towel, and got the bones. One bone she had to retrieve from the dirt as a crow flew in low, landed near the paper towel, and tried to haul it off before I shooed him away.

Then there are the other three dogs that I really do not like. They look like hyenas and are so double butt ugly it just plain hurts my eyes to look at them. They wander around the campground chasing cars, barking at the hundreds of squirrels in camp and just generally making a nuisance of themselves. I wish they would go away.

Now I have a problem with the crows here. Every morning one comes to a branch right over our tent and starts to caw, caw. Such a lovely alarm clock don't you think? This morning the crow and the chattering squirrel were in competition with each other.

Some other lovely elements about camping are the things that can accumulate inside the tent. Forget the usual sleeping bag, clothes, etc. I am talking dirt. You should see the inside of our tent right how. Last night as I was getting ready to slip into the sleeping bag, I was sitting on the side of the cot rubbing my feet together. Ralph looked at me as if I was crazy and asked me what I was doing. I told him I was getting the dirt off my feet, as I didn't want the fir needles, dirt balls, pebble size gravel, and sand in my sleeping bag. "Oh," was all he said.

Along with the dirt which is to be expected somewhat comes some extra critters that are very much unwelcome. For instance, the tick that Ralph found on the side of the tent right over his pillow. I wanted the gross, nasty thing, killed immediately. Ralph got out his trusty, handy dandy all-purpose tool and squished that sucker flat. Of course, we itched all night anyway in spite of witnessing the demise of the tick.

Before settling in on our first night here, Ralph noticed a nice size spider in the top of the tent. He started to kill it but just as he was going for it, the spider captured another bug in the tent and wrapped him up in silk. Now just what do you think happened to the spider? He has a nice web spun over my side of the tent. Unfortunately, I think he will be squished anyway tomorrow morning when we take the tent down. But for now, he's welcome to catch all the bugs he wants. I'll try to gently remove him in the morning before we drop the tent and leave.

About mid-day today, we drove into town to get some lunch. Going down a side street we passed a house with at least thirty sea gulls all facing the same way, all enjoying the nice warm sunshine. They weren't on any other roof in town, just this one. I was puzzled by their choice.

We ate lunch, went back to the grocery store for dinner fixings and headed back to camp. Along the way back, in the bay close to shore, were the otters. The warm sunshine had brought out the playful otters to float upon their own little brown floats in the incoming tide. They are so cute. I would love to pick one up and give it a squeeze but I'm sure that even if I could get close to one, it would take my hand off.

There are many bird noises in camp. The raucous crows are my least favorite; the gulls here have a moaning cry, not like the loudmouths on the beaches back home. Today we heard a new bird sound, like a hollow knocking on a piece of wood. The bird came closer but we were never able to see it.

But my favorite bird song is from the veery. So many times, on trips to the Smokies I would hear the veeries singing in the early evening. I thought these were southern mountain birds. But I heard one today. It will always remind me of my southern mountains back home. I've never seen one but I recognize the song right away. Her song is sweet and melodious and it sounds like she is singing down a tube. So very pretty. Such a sweet reminder of home.

And that is how I will leave this camp story, with the sound of the campfire crackling and the tinkling song of the veery.

Until later, much love to all always,
Judy/Mom/Mommy

June 24, 2005
Friday
Glennallen, AK
Mile 8592

Dear Folks,

The crows this morning chose someone else's campsite to bother instead of ours, but the squirrels stayed true blue and chattered and fussed with each other over the breadcrumbs and the tips off the ears of corn I left on the tree stump. The party girls, in the site behind us were up early, laughing and banging pots and pans and announcing pancakes in five minutes. I was ready for some pancakes but figured they would know that I wasn't part of their group if I snuck in with my empty plate. Instead, I had a box of cold cereal that had no sugar on it.

Another beautiful day awaited us. Today there was a vast amount of blue sky complete with small white puffy clouds. The temperature was in the upper sixties making for perfect riding conditions. With every thing packed up, we rolled down the newly graded gravel road without any problem and into town glancing around one last time as we passed right on through.

Just out of town was a road we missed when entering Seward three days ago. The road was to Exit Glacier. The sign was so small I can see why we missed it, as we missed it again and had to turn around in the middle of the road. It was an eight mile, beautiful road back to the only glacier in Kenai Fiord National Park that can be reached by road. The rest are only accessible by boat or air.

A river ran right by the road and the mountains were tall and gorgeous around us as we made our way to the glacier. Just before the end of the road at the visitors center, was a turn out and the glacier could be seen very clearly. The side trip was worth the ride to see the glacier sparkle ice blue in the sun.

Back on the main road, we headed back north toward Anchorage. Our destination today was to be Glennallen. Since there are few roads in Alaska the ones you do travel going to a location generally have to be traveled back over in the other direction. There are no short cuts.

On our way to Homer and Seward, the skies had been overcast and rainy in some spots. We got to see the mountains and waters under those conditions and they were beautiful even though it was rainy. Today, we got a different view on the return trip, and beautiful weather to add to the vast scenery before us.

Mountains that could not be seen several days ago now shown brightly with a covering of snow in the brilliant summer sky. Shasta daisies had popped out everywhere and swayed and bobbed in the wind as we passed. Numerous glaciers that had been hidden by the clouds now appeared at just about every turn in the road.

Swans swam in the marshes made by the rivers and other wild flowers had bloomed along the edge of the water in the warm sunshine. Purples, pinks, yellows, and cream-colored flowers lined the side of the road.

The traffic increased also as we got closer to Anchorage. There was only one road on and off the peninsula and it was busy with fast moving traffic. I had to bypass several good pictures of the Alaska Range over the water on the inlet, as there just wasn't a safe place to stop on this busy highway.

Once clear of Anchorage, I was hit in the eyebrow by a monster, juicy bug and his guts ran into my eye and stuck in my eyelashes. I was unsuccessful in wiping the innards out of my eye and I was looking through a greasy film. Just then, we were blasted with grit thrown up by a passing dump truck pulling another dump truck trailer. I spit into my gloved fingers and wiped my right eye clearing it to most of the gunk. My vision was however, a bit blurred still. That is one of the unpleasant experiences of motorcycle riding.

As we turned onto the Glennallen Highway and went through the town of Palmer, the landscape once again changed. Briefly, there was some farmland and freshly cut hay. That ended suddenly, as we came over a hill and there in all of Mother Nature's splendid glory was one of the biggest glacial valleys I have ever seen. Off to the right side were endless mountains, some with snow, and some without. I gasped with surprise at this new visual treat.

This was a different type of forest we traveled through. There were hardwoods mixed with the evergreens. These marched up a good part of the mountains covering them in swirling green velvet. In the valley was a braided stream traveling through the massive gravel riverbed.

Higher and higher we climbed and as we did, the vistas became like a painted canvas that surrounded us. The artistry was priceless. The road narrowed and became more rough due to the traumatic weather changes. We traveled through many avalanche areas over the narrow, winding road as we continued to climb. The guardrail had been severely battered and bent from all the rocks that had tumbled down on other occasions.

I looked in my rear view mirror and noticed that Ralph was riding the centerline, not getting any where near the edge. I figured that was where he would be when I saw the sheer drop offs on our right. I knew then that any chance of me stopping to get a picture just went over the cliff.

The road reminded me a good deal of the Going to the Sun Highway in Glacier National Park in Montana. It seems that every time we think things can't get any prettier it does. This highway was different from the rest we have traveled. The vistas are vast in distances and the glacier valley was tremendous. On our decent, I noticed a small area of what appeared to be snow at a low elevation. I thought that odd but as we got closer the white area turned out to be another glacier. It snaked out of the mountains and twisted onto the valley floor. I imagine that ten thousand years ago this glacier was responsible for the gigantic valley floor below us.

Due to some road construction, I was once again foiled in any attempts to get any good photos of the glacier. Upon descending the mountains, we came out into a forest of fir trees. Most looked like bottle brushes stuck up straight in the land. For miles and miles, fuzzy sticks covered the land. The mountains that lined the left side of the road were bare for the most part but the rocks and soil were bright shades of orange, rust, brown, and grey. They were quite a contrast to the snow and ice mountains on the other side of the valley.

As we were getting closer to our destination for the night, way off in the distance blue, black sky could be seen for miles and miles. We were heading right for that area. The temperature dropped dramatically and it looked as if we were in for one hell of a storm. I was dreading setting up a tent in the rain and was making plans to ride the storm out in some gas station parking lot until it passed.

Then, off to our right, between the green fir trees and the black clouds, a gigantic area of sky appeared in rainbow colors. The closer we got to it, the colors changed into the normal arched shape of a true rainbow. All the colors of the rainbow, against a black sky, in a huge arch across the landscape, appeared before us. Now what more perfect way to end a day's ride could there be?

Another mile down the road and we were at the campground we had selected for the night. It seemed that we were riding the tail of the storm and we missed most of it only catching the scattering of rain in its aftermath. When we stopped at the campground, the storm kept going and we were left with clearing skies and a muddy road.

Back into the woods we drove and came to a rustic, wooded campground right on a little stream. Other than the foul mosquitoes that are driving me crazy tonight the place is perfect. We have our little tent set up next to the babbling stream, that is after I removed a huge pile of moose dung from the middle of the tent site. We have hot showers, a laundry, firewood, fire pit, a little store and internet connection.

The sun is supposed to set at eleven-thirty tonight and rise at three-forty A.M. That will give us about two hours of dusk darkness tonight. It will be nice not to have the sun shining in my eyes as I try to go to sleep.

Grizzle Bear had a great day today. He enjoyed his ride through the countryside and I can hear him in the tent now humming and purring. He is busy licking his whiskers and his paws clean. You see tonight he got his marshmallows.

Until next time, love to all always,
Judy/Mom/Mommy

June 25, 2005
Saturday
Valdez, AK
Mile 8735

Dear Folks,

The campfire we had last night was too smoky to really enjoy but it did run off some of the vampire mosquitoes. We roasted a few marshmallows and they were deliciously sweet. The campground was so silent compared to the one at Miller's Landing in Seward. The only sound was the running of the creek next to our site and the humming and buzzing of the mosquitoes.

The sun shown strong through the tent this morning and warmed the tent up very fast making our sleeping bags feel like Reynolds's cooking bags. We packed our things inside the tent first due to the varmints winging outside the screen waiting for their breakfast of warm blood. As soon as we stuck the tiniest bit of skin out of the tent door, we were attacked.

I have, most of my life, been pretty much immune to the mosquitoes. They leave me alone generally. But I'm here to tell you, the blood suckers attacked in full force. They were flying up my nose, in my mouth and ears and biting my neck and hands. I was to the point of screaming. I've never packed my bike so fast. I should have known that the camp that had the name Wil-der-ness in its name would have been trouble.

We left that place on the muddy gravel road as fast as our wheels could carry us and scooted into the town of Glennallen where we had a wonderful breakfast in a lodge. We had hoped to visit with our friend, Jack, who lives in Glennallen. After calling him a few days ago, we found out that while we are here in his hometown in Alaska, Jack is in South Carolina. I cannot believe our timing. I was really looking forward to seeing Jack again.

While we were eating breakfast, four other bikers pulled up each on a BMW and heavily packed. There were three BMW GS's and one BMW RT just like Ralph's. The four men sat right behind us and at first they were not the least bit friendly. They tried to ignore us, which I thought was so silly and childish.

Ralph kept talking to them anyway trying to draw them into a conversation, and not give them the satisfaction of ignoring us. The guys were from New Mexico and had also been traveling in Alaska. They had just completed their trip to the Arctic Ocean at Prudhoe Bay and were moaning and groaning about how horrible the road was. Since we had been there before them, we knew exactly what they were talking about.

As it turned out, one of the men, the one who rode the same bike as Ralph, actually gave up on the trip and turned around at the Arctic Circle. Well, the road wasn't even that bad at that point! He just had no idea what was up ahead. The other three continued on, one having a flat tire that required plugging, and all were met with strong head winds.

I kept my mouth smartly shut to the fact that here they were on bikes designed to make a trip on roads such as the Haul Road, and here I was on my big stock Honda Shadow, designed for touring on pavement. One had quit and turned around and the other three were totally amazed and dazed at the dangerous road that Ralph and I had been on two weeks ago. All their comments did was to verify to me the fact that the Haul Road was a brutal stretch of gravel into the wilderness. I just smiled to myself and kept my mouth shut.

Out front in large flowerbeds were flowers the likes of which I have dreamed of on my front porch but have never been able to accomplish. Vibrant colors of yellow, orange, red, pink, and purple were so bright I was glad for my sunglasses.

After our bellies were sufficiently stuffed, we took the road to Valdez. Like most of the roads in Alaska, this one we will be returning on tomorrow.

We were lucky today as the weather cooperated and was another glorious day of sunshine and white puffy clouds. For the first seventy miles, we just cruised along enjoying the mountains and valleys along our route. More Shasta daisies bloomed along the road and competed for space with the fireweed of reddish purple. Clumps of some sort of grass with their seed stalks looked as if they were paint brushes dipped into an iridescent pink paint. They swayed in the breeze as if painting a magic canvas.

In the lower forty-eight, the geography has some predictability to it. On the east coast, there are the coastal plains with the oceans and small hills, then the Appalachian Mountains with their soft rounded mountains of blue. Then the flatness of the Great Plains meets again mountains of rugged rock jutting quickly out of the ground. And once again the ocean.

Here in Alaska it looks as if Mother Nature took a big stick and stirred up all the dirt, mountains, trees, oceans, and grass and poured it out of her big cooking pot. When it cooled, the shape of what is now Alaska became a jumbled mixture of mountains, valleys, and vast areas of wilderness and streams.

Today, after traveling the first seventy miles, we were struck again by the rawness and newness of Alaska. The mountains became jagged looking like a saw blade, black against the sky. As we continued to climb over Thompson Pass, we came around a curve in the road and were surprised by a huge glacier creeping down the black rock mountains.

At the top of the pass, we could look down in the valley below to see a river in it's over sized bed, running between white mountains. The scene reminded me of a reverse chocolate sundae or maybe chocolate ice cream with marshmallow topping drizzled over the top.

We made the long decent into the valley we had just been looking at from above and ventured into a canyon, named Keystone Canyon. The wind howled through the canyon. Sheer rock face guided us down between its walls and the Lowe River crashed and rushed with a torrent of liquid cement colored water.

The walls of the canyon were black with wetness from the ground water that was seeping out between the cracks in the walls. This made everything shiny and the green vegetation was prolific from the moisture.

As we rounded a curve in the canyon, a three hundred foot waterfall fell from the top of the canyon to join with the Lowe River. The sun caught the mist of the waterfall and the water seemed to fall in slow motion. The falls did look like their name: Bridal Veil Falls. They were very stunning.

On up the road a few hundred yards was another waterfall, this one looking like its name also: Horse Tail Falls.

The canyon emptied out into the valley and the town of Valdez was before us right on the water. We found a tent site right in the middle of town in a RV park that had room for tents. There was a good breeze blowing and I hoped it would keep the mosquitoes away tonight.

After setting up the tent and unloading the bikes of their heavy loads, we went to investigate the town of Valdez. This is the end of the Alaskan Pipeline, as most of you know. Ralph and I have followed the pipeline from the Arctic Ocean in Prudhoe Bay all the way to its end, in Valdez. Here the oil is loaded onto tankers and out to sea. Of course, everyone remembers the Exxon Valdez of the late nineteen-eighties. Well this is where it happened.

We went exploring the small town, riding up and down the streets in search of something interesting and we found the fishing spot. On the wharf, right next to the ferry dock, were about twenty people fishing. The tide was coming in and the salmon were running. Poles, lines, and hooks were flying in the bright afternoon sun.

We found a spot on the dock, sat, and watched the people fish. The fish were jumping everywhere as the tide rolled in. Two boys around twelve years old rode in on their bicycles. One carried two poles twice the size he was on his bike and the other carried a net so large he could have climbed into it himself.

One boy, whose name I learned was Sammy, had a bright iridescent red pole and a red lure to match. As he cast his hook out I realized that he was quite adept at fishing. He had a flick to his wrist and elbow that indicated he knew what he was doing.

Sammy's skin was browned by the sun, his curly mop of brown hair looked as if it hadn't been cut or much less brushed in at least a month. He was very patient with his fishing and within about ten minutes, he caught his first pink salmon. That was followed quickly thereafter by two more.

He and his friend helped the other people fishing, net their fish, and lift them onto the wharf. There were pink salmon flopping all over the weathered wooden wharf. As each fisherman caught his limit of three, he would pack his tackle box and take his treasure and go off home or back to a campground in the area.

I asked Sammy if I could take a picture of him and his fish and he ignored me while he was getting the hook untangled from the net. He had already thrown his fish up on the wharf. Whatever you do, you should not disturb a fisherman at his work. I slunk off back to my place on the dock to mind my own business when I noticed that Sammy had picked up his fish and was looking for me. Of course, I obliged and took his picture. I don't think he even said two words to me but I could tell he was mighty proud of his catch of the day and loved the attention I had given him.

As I was pulling out of the wharf, I noticed a gigantic otter floating on his back riding the tide into the harbor. The otter looked like he was body surfing upside down.

Our stomachs were now empty and we went looking for our own supper and found it on one of the little side streets. We dined in a little Greek restaurant. At first, I was skeptical, as most restaurants in any seaport serve fish. Alaska boasts of the catch of the day being halibut or salmon. I wish my stomach had been bigger as the food in this Greek restaurant was wonderful. After dinner, we rode back to our campsite and we are ready to call it a night in a little while.

Grizzle Bear much prefers marshmallows to the fish he would usually eat like his cousins but he had a bellyache today from all the marshmallows he ate last night. He has decided to just eat ice cream tonight for supper. The little brown bear had a good day today.

So until later, much love to all always,
Judy/Mom/Mommy

June 27, 2005
Monday
Haines, AK
Mile 9426

Dear Folks,

First of all, just in case anyone has been reading the news, we are not the older married couple attacked and killed by the grizzly bear in Alaska. We were however, at about the same time, through that same area of wilderness on the Haul Road in the Gates of the Arctic National Park and Reserve, but we were not camping in the backcountry wilderness. We are safe and sound as we speak in a campground in Haines, AK.

Yesterday morning we packed up our belongings as quickly as possible due to the biting bugs. They weren't mosquitoes but as bad or worse because they were biting *me*! They found my last nerve and I was about to have a full blown hissy fit right there in the campground with the whole world watching. You know it's bad when you have to spit bugs out of your mouth and blow your nose to get them out of that orifice. Oooh! Though the mosquitoes have been as bad as all accounts we read before coming to Alaska, they have, for the most part, not bothered me too much. After the attack in the Glennallen campground and the attack this morning, I fully understand how a person could go completely nuts. I reached my limit this morning and I was about to get very ugly.

I got packed first and I circled the campground on my bike, waiting for Ralph to finish his packing. After outrunning the persistent bugs, we finally left the biting insects and Valdez. As expected, the return route was very gorgeous and we got a different view of the same incredible country we crossed yesterday. The further north we went the more the weather changed. More and more dark clouds built up as we moved up the road and the temperature dropped a good twenty-five degrees making me wish I had put on more layers under my riding gear. I had goose bumps all day.

We traveled over some very rough road. We came to a section of about ten miles of torn up road that was void of any pavement. The section was a muddy, gravely soup full of water filled potholes and deep washboard. It was bone jarring. This was a section of road that was under repair due to a serious earthquake a couple years ago. Miles of road was being reconstructed due to the drop in elevation of the surrounding area.

Ralph started to run low on fuel and it appeared he was going to run out in the middle of nowhere when, like a vision, there appeared out of the clouds, a roadhouse complete with gas and café.

While we were eating lunch, three other riders rolled in and seeing our huge juicy hamburgers, decided to eat lunch as well. We got into a lengthy discussion with one of the men and it turned out he claimed to be one of the founders of the Iron Butt Association in Canada. I am thoroughly convinced that he and his buddies did not believe us when we told them we had gone to Prudhoe Bay and particularly on the bikes parked outside and me being a woman.

After he asked us more questions he became convinced that the tale we told was entirely true. One of his traveling buddies even went so far as to go outside and check out my bike. I think he was convinced also when he saw the fuel cell mounted among my gear. All three men warmed up to us after that.

We finished our lunch before they did and headed off on down the road. During our conversations with the three riders we found out they were heading in the same direction to Haines. I knew we would be playing leapfrog all day, which usually happened when riding in the same direction as other bikers.

We covered ground that we had been over three weeks ago, but it still looked different as much of the snow had melted. Also, when we came through the area before, the sky was clear and lots of beautiful sunshine beamed down on us. This time it was overcast and threatening some serious rain.

I knew we just might get a tad wet when the area we headed toward was completely black. It's not a good sign when the sky and the black mountains match in the color black and you can't tell which is which. I was not looking forward to what the immediate future was about to hold for me.

Closer and closer we drove until finally we were right in the middle of the blackness. Swirling winds picked up and then the rain came down in earnest. In order to get to our destination for the night we had to ride right through it. There were no other roads to take to get around the storm, no place to stop and wait for it to blow over. Fortunately, there was no lightning this time, just heavy rain.

Everything under the riding gear stayed nice and dry, but my gloves were soaked and my hands were freezing. I went through two pairs of gloves and ten frozen fingers.

We had decided to push on a little further than planned and make our favorite campground, Cottonwood, on Lake Kluane south of Destruction Bay. That was the campground we fell in love with on our trek north; our little place in heaven. It would mean riding for five hundred miles and I had only planned on three hundred and fifty for the day.

We rode on through the rain several times during the day and at the end of each storm we were rewarded with a beautiful rainbow. Yesterday was a day for rainbows. I saw three.

As I said earlier, we were riding over roads we had traveled over three weeks ago. One thing I found astonishing was the road we traveled on was torn up in places that were paved three weeks ago! There were places now where the road didn't even exist. Gone! In its place was gravel, dirt and mud and still plenty of frost heave.

The section of frost heave that just about wrecked my back three weeks ago just about did it again yesterday. Toward the end of the day each hole in the road or dip would compress my spine and each time it would mash on that bad disc in my back sending shock waves down my leg and cramp up behind my knee. It was agonizing.

The day was getting very late, most everyone was already tucked into a motor home, hotel or camper, but on we went. When we came around another bend in the road and saw another area of black sky that I knew we had to go through, I thought I would cry. I was so very tired and we still had to go through some serious construction areas.

After being rained on one more time, we finally saw the lake and we knew we were getting close. Cottonwood Campground was up the road just a couple more miles. Those miles were over slick, brown, gooey mud and gravel. As we neared the campground, I was praying that they would have an empty site.

As we came over the final hill before the campground, off to the left, over the water was a beautiful rainbow. The end of the rainbow went into the water and the water around it seemed to sparkle like green sequins. We had found the end of the rainbow and it was in Kluane Lake. What a gorgeous way to end a very, long tiring day in the saddle.

We did get lucky and not only did they have a campsite, but we got the exact spot we had three weeks ago. We got a fantastic fire going and cooked hotdogs over the open fire. It was now eleven P.M. and there was still plenty of daylight.

The remaining marshmallows I had been carrying for several days had managed to become one big blob of sticky mess so I threw them into the fire. The fire pit was a metal ring with air vents in the bottom to feed the fire oxygen. Suddenly, out from the bottom of one of the vents came an oozing, white mass of liquid, melted marshmallow. We both thought of Mr. Staypuff marshmallow man in the Ghostbusters movie.

We tried to contain the marshmallow flow but as soon as Ralph scooped up some and threw it back in the fire, more took its place. What a mess. The goo finally stopped flowing or else it burned as originally planned.

Exhausted beyond belief, we gave up and went to bed around midnight. I think I was unconscious the entire night. Wild and crazy dreams and the bright sun shining in my face brought me out of my stupor in the morning.

After moaning and groaning a while, I finally climbed out of my warm sleeping bag and headed for a nice shower. After cleaning up, I was sitting at the picnic table putting on my boots. I noticed the cutest little chipmunk heading directly for the fire pit. I now have an idea for a better mousetrap. Poor little thing, thought he was going to get some sweet, sticky, roasted marshmallow. What he got was stuck! One of his hind legs had gotten stuck in the marshmallow ooze and was wiggling and tugging but was stuck fast.

I couldn't figure out what he was doing. I thought he was having some kind of immediate sugar rush with all his fidgeting until I realized he was stuck. I felt rather sorry for him so I went to help the poor critter out. I think he was more scared of me than he was of his foot being stuck and he surely must have dislocated his hip getting himself loose from the marshmallow flow. He did manage to get loose and he scurried off to lick his wounds or his foot, I should say, in the bushes beside the tent. I threw some dirt over the remaining marshmallow so no more animals would get stuck.

All packed, we reluctantly left our campsite and continued our journey back south. This is the same road where I faced the three-story dump truck several weeks ago. He was still there and he had brought friends and brothers this time.

The two-year road project had made some progress while we had been away. New signs were up now warning of blasting whistles and their sequences. Oh, great, not only do I have to wiggle my way through three story dump trucks, I have to worry about being blown to bits in the process.

As it turns out the blasting was the least of our worries. A pilot car guided us safely through the construction over mud and gravel paths and back onto what would pass for something called pavement. The pilot car turned around to take the next waiting group through and we continued down the road.

In my opinion, we came to the most dangerous area of construction that was totally without guards or safety procedures in place. On our left was a drop off into the icy water of the lake. On our right, on the hill, was a man operating a heavy piece of machinery that looked like a cherry picker. The machinery acted like a mammoth weed whacker, except the weed whacker was cutting down small trees, sending large pieces of sharp, wooden splinters onto the road in the our path.

Wooden lances and spears with sharp spiked ends were being spit out of the cutter right at us. I quickly dodged over into the oncoming lane and got close to the lake's edge to try to avoid the flying debris. Fortunately, there was no oncoming traffic. Ralph told me later that I missed the flying missile sent out of the weed whacker that came right between us. Timing is everything isn't it?

Once safely out of the construction zone, the road improved and we made good time into Haines Junction. We had a huge breakfast and gassed up for the last leg of our journey today.

We had crossed back into Canada yesterday and were about to cross back into Alaska to reach Haines. We traveled through the Yukon and into British Columbia. Neither one of us expected to see the awesome sites we saw today. There were just too many places I wanted to stop and take pictures. My shutter finger went crazy with all the mountains. The scenery is all a little different, each beautiful in its own rite.

At one of the scenic pullouts, I, according to Ralph, had a Kodak moment. Fortunately, for me, he didn't have access to the camera. After taking a few more beautiful shots, I started my engine and slowly pulled away on the gravel and dirt. Right in front of me appeared to be dirt and I did see tire tracks and thought it firm enough for me go ride over. I was instantly wrong.

With both wheels on the dirt, I turned the wheel slightly to the left and the dirt turned out to be eight inches of deep sand and river silt the consistency of baby powder. Well, one moment I'm riding the next moment I'm standing. The bike is no longer under me but tilted to the left still running. I'm looking around totally astonished like "what happened" when I realized that the bike had gone over.

After riding my bike for thousands of miles over gravel, slick mud, boulders, potholes, frost heave and every imaginable road surface, I loose it in a parking lot in eight inches of river silt. Oh well. I did not even fall over, I was still standing, it was just the bike that left me. Ralph called it really a tilt instead of a drop but it still took three people to pick it up once I climbed off.

After the bike was picked up, Ralph hopped on, gunned the throttle, and drove it out of the sand and silt but not before sending a rooster tail plume of sand and powder shooting up from the back tire at least six feet long directly on me. I spit sand and grit immediately. Then, I experimented with some of my new language skills.

With my ego only slightly bumped, we continued on our way. I dusted myself off, spit the remainder of grit from my lips and mouth and I didn't stop for any more pictures. We made it into Haines safely and without any more incidents and found an acceptable campground for the next two nights.

Grizzle Bear had a rough two days. First, he had to ride in and out of numerous cold rainstorms and I think he got a little chilled. He had too long a ride for his liking. He had left his rain gear back in Atlanta. Then I burned up the rest of his marshmallows turning the remains over to the chipmunk. He pouted about that last night and wouldn't speak to me. Then today he got rained on again and got thrown into the sand and powder silt when the bike he was riding on got dumped. He's in the tent now, marshmallowless, picking the rest of the grit out of his teeth, lower lip stuck out in a pout and whimpering that he is tired. I guess I'll have to give the little guy a little TLC tonight and let him sleep with me.

So, until later, much love to all always,
Judy/Mom/Mommy

June 29, 2005
Wednesday
Skagway, AK
Mile 9445

Dear Folks,

Tuesday morning we woke up to the obnoxious squawking of crows and a sopping wet tent. Ralph was floating in a lake of cold, rainwater but I was high and dry on my cot. We had to pull everything out of the tent and literally tip it over and get the water out. Then we emptied the small pond that had gathered on the tarp under the tent after last night's rain. After rearranging the tarp and replacing the tent back over it, I cleaned up the mess inside with paper towels.

It rained in a steady downpour all day so we spent the day in the library in Haines. Ralph worked and I read a book. The library was an exceptional one, large and new. Around six in the evening we left the warmth and dryness of the library and went in search of dinner. Right on the small boat harbor we found a nice restaurant over looking the harbor and the fort with officers houses high up on the hill. The setting was unique and I could imagine the soldiers of old marching on the parade grounds in front of the officer's housing.

As we were finishing dinner, an eagle swooped in and perched himself on top of the tallest mast in the harbor. I watched for a while to see if he would fly off but he had the best view in the harbor for hunting and was not moving. After dinner, I walked down the boat dock to the boat mast the eagle was perched on and looked straight up at him. He eyeballed me with mild curiosity and continued his look out for his fish dinner. I eventually gave up waiting for him to fly off into the air currents and we moseyed back to the campsite and turned in early. I had planned to do a little shopping in the morning while Ralph finished some work in the library.

Those plans went terribly awry at six this morning however, with a hysterical phone call from Amanda and Milissa. Our beloved seventeen-year-old cat, Tux, was dying. The girls were en route to the

151

vets just crying their eyes out and hardly able to mutter an intelligent word. The old cat had been missing, not showing up at the front door as usual in the morning howling to be let in the house. Milissa had found Tux after calling and calling his name. He finally meowed weakly and she found him under the neighbor's porch. He was unable to move his hind legs.

I tried to comfort the girls over the phone and to prepare them for the inevitable but they were not listening. I did manage to convince them to get the vet to call us after Tux had been examined. The news from the vet was not good. It seemed that a blood clot had formed in the lower spine probably due to the clot being thrown from his enlarged, over-worked heart. Tux was not going to survive.

The decision was made to put Tux to sleep. The poor vet was left with two inconsolable girls and a tough choice for them to make. Milissa and Amanda did get through it together and our little cat was put to sleep. Milissa told me later, that after she had given the vet permission to put her kitty to sleep, she scratched under Tux's chin like he always loved and gave his pink nose a kiss good-bye. Tux was purring as the vet turned and quietly left the room leaving Milissa alone with her tears and broken heart.

It has been a hard day on both coasts. My two girls had to do some growing up today and face some heart breaking choices and I was not there to help them. I was broken hearted for two reasons. One, that I was not home for my girls to help them through this tough time and two, I felt the loss of Tux too.

He came into our lives almost sixteen years ago when, as a young kitten of about eight months, he was dumped in front of our house. He was scared and hungry and three year old Milissa was the only one who could get near the howling cat. We took him into our home, fed him, and loved him for the next sixteen years. He was Milissa's best friend and really her cat. Both girls took turns dressing him up in baby clothes and rolling him around in a stroller, which he tolerated with unending patience and total devotion.

Milissa taught him many tricks. She taught him to climb the ladder to the top bunk in her bedroom so he could snuggle up next to her while she slept. In any writing assignment in school, Milissa wrote stories about him. He was a constant companion, sleeping in her bed every night. Tux remained a fine, faithful friend to all of us into his senior years.

His sweet disposition and warm purring body snuggling up next to us for friendly comfort will be sorely missed. I will remember him as a playmate, friend, and companion. He will be missed for a very long time to come.

So, today was a hard day. I hurt for the loss of Tux and my heart aches because my girl's hearts are broken and I am not at home to comfort them. Not there to put my arms around them and tell them it will be ok with the passing of time. I wept for my children today and the loss of our little friend. The tears just don't seem to end and I have an everlasting supply. It was a tough day.

We left Haines today, later in the afternoon and caught a ferry to Skagway. Skagway was just about fifteen miles by water but over land was over three hundred miles. It was a short ride for me as I would have enjoyed a longer one. The three fellow riders from Canada had camped in Haines also the last two days and we ran into them again while waiting for the ferry. This would probably be the last time we saw them, however, as they were heading back home and we were continuing our journey south.

Skagway was a jumping off point for the gold rush. The town looked like it might have during that time. Old buildings have been refurbished and now contain many shops and restaurants but you can imagine what it might have looked like over one hundred years ago.

Skagway will be our last town in Alaska, then we will be heading back into Canada through British Columbia and down into Washington. I hate to leave Alaska, it has been much more than I ever expected. I have been living in my dream. Alaska is a wonderful place and we have had an amazing time.

The journey isn't over just because we are leaving Alaska soon. We still have a long road ahead of us and many more sites to see and places to go and people to meet.

So until later, much love to all always and especially to you girls, Milissa and Amanda. Big hugs and kisses too and know that I am there in spirit for you and that the warm arms of my heart surround your wounded souls.

Love,
Judy/Mom/Mommy

June 30, 2005
Skagway, AK
Mile 9445

Dear Folks,

Reflections of Alaska

Five weeks ago, Ralph and I were two into Alaska. Now as we leave this incredible piece of earth I feel I must reflect on what has become a permanent piece of my heart. I want to try to give you a feeling of what Alaska has become to mean to me.

Coming here in the first place had been such a long time dream, I can't even remember when that dream started, but I think it might have had its seed planted when I was eleven years old. My mother had taken us children on a three-month camping trip around the United States. I can remember her talking about wanting to come to Alaska during the trip, but the distances, time, money, and road conditions at that time prevented it.

Alaska, such a far away place, I think had called me from that far away time. So, Mama, I finally made that trip you so much wanted to make. I am here to tell you it was worth the wait.

Alaska, to me, had always meant that far away place, full of wilderness, wildness, beauty and wonder. I thought it was hardly a place that someone like me would ever have the chance to go. But I hung onto that dream of one day visiting and exploring and my dream did come true.

After many years of dreaming and ultimately many, many months of planning, Ralph and I set off on an adventure of a lifetime. Combining our love of motorcycling and traveling was the perfect way to see our dream come true.

For me, Alaska came to mean an achievement of a ridiculously hard riding challenge that no other woman in the Iron Butt Association had done. It was just begging to be ridden by a woman and I was going to be that woman. For me personally, it was an incredible challenge of physical and emotional strength.

As the challenge of the ride became a reality, other things happened to my soul along the way. Unpredictable things, heart wrenching things, wonderful things and to me, life altering.

I have seen things that will forever remain in my heart. My brain will eternally see the images. I have been to that place somewhere over the rainbow. I have seen the rainbows arching over the heavens, backlit by a black sky and ending in a turquoise glacier lake shattering into a million pieces of green glitter and sequins.

And somewhere over that rainbow, I didn't see a blue bird fly but eagles soaring. Soaring on unseen ocean currents of air in search of food or just to frolic in the warm sunshine.

I have seen the swans floating in tundra ponds, gliding across, with their necks tucked back resting on their feathered backs and others with necks straight up trumpeting to each other.

I have seen the caribou of the tundra with calves, life renewing itself once again.

I have ridden to the top of a mountain pass on an ice and mud soaked dirt road to be greeted by a white cloud bank rushing up to me, drenching me in a cloak of thick moisture. Descending into the cloud, I allowed its thickness and moisture to embrace me and blind me from my surroundings, trusting my instincts to get me safely to the bottom of the mountain pass.

I have felt the misty spray on my face from the humpback whales in the fiords of the cold Alaskan waters and watched the fat sea lions lazing in the brief sun's warmth. The little puffins, with orange beaks and feet and tiny propeller wings, diving deep into those same cold waters, amazed me with their strength and resolve to find food for survival.

I have felt the cold air issuing off the ice blue glaciers and have, at waters edge, heard the glaciers speak. Their ancient crackling voices groaned as pieces of their bodies broke off, splashing into the icy water below and drifted slowly out to a never-ending sea.

I have stood on the edge of mountains and looked out at the miles and miles of wilderness untouched by man. There before me, wild rugged mountains covered in timeless snow and ice reaching tirelessly and eternally for the blue sky of space. Forever reaching, forever failing, but forever trying.

I have watched as Mother Nature has recreated herself Mad, rushing rivers full of glacier silt and snow runoff have carved away at the rock year after year creating a new and different landscape.

I have seen the slick, silver salmon running back to their spawning grounds only to be yanked out of the emerald, green river by sharp hooks in their mouths and beaten in the head until dead by fishermen.

I have seen acres and acres of wildflowers on every road I have traveled, bursting with color. Stalks of purple balls and the fuchsia fireweed mixed with the whites of the Shasta daisies and the cow parsnip. I have witnessed fields of bright yellow dandelions turn to cream colored ones when their fluffs of seeds are ready to set sail on the winds. I have tasted and inhaled the cottonwood fluff that filled the sky and dusted the ground as if it had snowed in summer.

I have seen primitive, prehistoric landscapes that look like the beginning of time and have felt so small riding through it.

I have smelled sweet smells of wildflowers blooming, and the faint ocean's unique smell on the air. I have smelled the air fresh with ozone after a rainstorm. I have smelled just plain clean air.

I have had dirt thrown up in my face by fast moving tractor-trailer trucks. I have tasted my fair share of grit and dirt. I have had bugs splatter and pop in my face sending their guts into my mouth and eyes. I have smelled the unfortunate dead animal too close to the road and have smelled the decaying fish near the shore. I have smelled the earth.

I have ventured out onto the frozen tundra side by side with my best friend and have conquered an unbelievable road that was not meant for man, woman nor motorcycle. I have dipped my feet in the Arctic Ocean fulfilling a promise made to my children.

I have seen my soul mate and best friend experience such joy and excitement with each new day and new road to journey down. The unknown of this adventure has given his soul wings and he has found an inner contentment and a new quest to see more of this world.

In a campground, sharing a campfire with others, we have met people that will stay in our memories forever. I have had other women congratulate me on the accomplishment of being the first to make such a trip from Key West to the Arctic Ocean on a motorcycle. One bought me a glass of wine, two asked for my autograph. Can you even begin to imagine what those small gestures did to my spirit? I know what it did. Validation.

I have felt the tremendous and timeless pull of home on my heart. Like the moon pulling on the tides, my children pull me back home. Like the ebbing in and out of the tides, they pull me back. One moment of pulling me home still in need of mama and the next a moment of letting go and flying free.

For family and friends who know what trying times we went through in the last few years, know how devastated and crushed my spirit has been. For those that don't know that will just have to be a mystery to you. For me Alaska has come to mean a healing and a rebirth of my crushed spirit and soul.

Riding over the country, seeing such wondrous and awesome life around me created peace in my heart and soul. I have shared with my best friend and soul mate a time in our lives that no one can take from us. If our trip ended here, it would have been perfect and much, much more than either one of us ever imagined. Getting up everyday, we have ventured into new lands and each one more breathtaking than the next.

Each day when we get up and journey down a new road, it is an adventure and exciting and wonderful to have new experiences each day. How can that not help but change a wounded soul?

I know I have been forever changed and I am so very thankful that this dream was captured and fulfilled.

So, good-bye Alaska, and thanks so much for the memories and the healing of my spirit.

Though we say goodbye to Alaska this is only the end to one part of our journey. We still have many new roads to travel down and many more new adventures to experience.

So until then...

Much love to all always,
Judy/Mom/Mommy

July 1, 2005
Friday
Ft. Watson, Yukon
Mile 9765

Dear Folks,

Everyone who knows me knows how much I love animals of all sorts, but I tell you what, if I had a gun this morning I would have shot the raven that sat in the branch over our tent. I am thoroughly convinced that crows and ravens will inherit the earth. In every camp we have been in these loud, raucous, annoying black feathered creatures are there.

They rob camp sites of food left on the tables and when you are gone or not looking, they are prowling your campsite in search of goodies either for their stomachs or their nests. They don't wait until a natural hour to start their cawing and squawking. They seen to know just when you have turned over and settled back into slumber and are in the perfect REM sleep. Their cawing is always in a series of two's or three's and is the most unpleasant sound imaginable at four to five in the morning. And sure as shoot'n just as soon as they are sure you are awake, the damned things fly off to someone else's site and start all over again leaving you cussing and wanting revenge.

You can hear them plain as day, skirting the campground, making the rounds. Yep, one good sling shot sending their cussed black feathers up in a ball of black smoke would work for me.

In the last campground in Skagway not only did we have the crows and ravens, our campground was directly below the flight path for all the single engine planes taking off. For extra-added enjoyment, fifty yards from our little tent tucked up in the fir trees, was the train track. Much to our dismay, two mornings ago we were rattled and jumbled from our sleeping bags with what we thought was a derailment headed right for out tent. We had no idea the tracks were there when we set up our tent but we surely found out quickly enough that next morning.

I have a new creature noise to add to the multitude we have heard over the past six weeks. Last night while we were sitting around a small fire, on our last night in Alaska, I heard a full-blown turkey call. "Surely not," I said to Ralph but then he heard it and over and over again, the old turkey buzzard called and called. I was convinced in the morning he would get in on the early bird special with the crows but the turkey's alarm clock apparently didn't go off and he was late. We were already up and packed when I heard him. I bet he sure would have tasted fantastic cooked over our campfire. I guess I'll never have that chance to taste a wild Alaskan turkey.

It rained a good bit during the night and it really sounded wonderful with the rain pattering down on our little nylon tent. This time the elevated tent pad that came with the site helped the tent inside stayed dry. We left Skagway in a blanket of low hanging clouds and headed north out of town.

I found Skagway of particular interest. I liked the town, which had been kept in the original flavor of the gold rush days. The town was neat and clean and flower baskets were in colorful profusion in front of almost every shop and store. The National Parks Service had several buildings along Broadway refurbished and along with pictures and brief history, told of the mad rush to the gold fields through Skagway. The picture most everyone has seen of the miners carrying their packs and a years supply of food and goods up the side of the mountain in the snow happened right here.

I learned there was also a really bad guy living in Skagway, during that time that practically owned the town. Soapy Smith cheated and swindled most everyone out of his or her money and claims. He was eventually killed in a shoot out, by Mr. Reid, who was also mortally wounded. Soapy Smith was killed immediately but Mr. Reid died an agonizing death twelve days later.

Both are buried north of town in the Gold Rush Cemetery. On our way out of town, I wanted to see the infamous cemetery. It was on a dirt road, next to the river and up on a hill under old fir trees and hardwoods. Talk about creepy. The damp day, with rain dripping off the leaves and onto the graves, combined with the mist and fog from the river, was enough to make anyone's hair stand up on end.

There were at least seventy graves with markers in the cemetery. Some graves were the local town's people, some were children who died of a meningitis outbreak, some graves belonged to "fallen women," and one each belonged to the notorious bad guy and the local hero. What I really found bizarre was when I passed Soapy Smith's grave, someone had thrown a handful of purple flowers beneath the headstone. No other flowers graced any other grave.

As we left the cemetery and crossed the Skagway River heading north toward the Canadian Border, we started to climb in elevation. Deep gorges of rough rock had been cut by the river and the railroad could be seen climbing up in elevation also on the other side of the gorge.

The scenery disappeared suddenly in a deep dark fog bank and cloud cover. It was so thick I could only see about twenty yards in front of me. I kept seeing poles that hung over the road that looked like street lamps without the lamps. I had seen these on some other mountain passes and wondered what they were. I didn't figure it out until this morning in the heavy fog. They are markers for snowplows! Then I realized how many other mountain passes we had been over with those tall poles hanging over the road. I can't even begin to imagine that amount of snow.

Anyway, I was really sorry we couldn't see any of the mountains and gorges below. I know it must have been dramatic. Then, just as we crested the top of the pass, the cloud cover lifted and we were in a completely new terrain the likes of which we haven't seen before on this trip.

We were riding as if we were on top of a mountain valley, skimming along the top ridge of the mountains. There were numerous ponds everywhere and rough broken up boulders were covered with moss and lichen. I thought I was riding through tidal pools. The landscape looked just like the rocky coast of Maine around Bar Harbor, only there was no ocean. There was plenty of water in small ponds, acres and acres of craggy rocks covered in clinging lichens of various shades of greens and yellows and all wet from the recent rain and cloud cover. It was unique to say the least.

After clearing customs at the Canadian Border, which was really no bother at all, we started our decent into another mountain valley.

The valleys in this area are not like our short beautiful valleys of the Appalachians but ones that go on for miles and miles and miles.

The snow has melted entirely and black mountains have appeared underneath. Some are covered with fir trees but some are just craggy rock alone. We followed a lake resting in a valley carved by glaciers long ago. The lake was teal green in spots, sea green in others and the two colors swirled together in other places making the lake look like a watercolor canvas as the greens collided. And as always, the lakes, mountains, and valleys expanded into the ever-reaching horizon.

Our beautiful blue sky only lasted a short while. The clouds moved back in or else we moved into them. We rode in and out of the rain today, which really isn't too much fun, just something that we have to do to get to the next destination. Towards the end of the day, we rounded a bend in the road and saw dark, black clouds covering an area so large there was no escaping it. Black clouds matched the black mountains and the light show from the heavens to the mountaintops was dramatic.

Then come a flood! The sky opened up and sent down pelting darts of icy water. Even though I have proper riding gear, it still stung my legs and my hands. On we continued through the drenching rain and came upon the dreaded sign of road construction up ahead. I couldn't imagine anyone working in these conditions. As it turned out, the two bridges crossing the river were down to one lane and the one open lane had a stop light right at the bridge allowing a lane a turn to go over by itself. There was no construction going on at the moment as all workers had abandoned the area due to the torrential rain.

Well, there we sat, stopped at a stupid red light on a lonely stretch of Canadian highway, waiting our turn and the light to turn green. No one was coming from the other direction at all. About six cars came up behind us and we all waited for the green light. I was ready to run the red light but Ralph kept cautioning me to stay put. There was no one there to tattle except the cars behind us and I don't think that would have been a problem. The rain was beating down on us, thunder was rolling, and the Canadian sky was dumping ice-cold popsicles down the back of my neck. As an extra-added bonus, I had failed to zip my jacket up all the way and fold over the protective flap and the entire front of my tee shirt and sweater was soaked. Now that is cold! The light finally turned green and we scurried on our way. I felt really stupid sitting there in the pouring rain, in the middle of the wilderness, waiting for a red light to turn green.

We made it to Fort Watson safely, a little wet, a little grumpy and more than a little delighted to stay in a hotel tonight. After nine days in the woods and a tent, I'm in plue perfect heaven with just the thought alone of sleeping in dry warm sheets.

Tomorrow we are headed down a different road toward Prince George and on to Vancouver. We have heard many reports about this road. Some say it is horrible, some say its rough, some say it's no trouble at all. So in order not to have to backtrack over the same thousand miles of the Alaskan Highway, we are headed due south on one of the other exits out of Canada on the Cassier Highway.

As we left Alaska heading south, there were numerous bikes heading north over the paths we have covered in the last few weeks. I've been there; I know what's in store for them. They are in for a real treat. At least both of us traveling north and south are heading for new adventures. I remember the anticipation of that northerly journey and now I know what wonders await those headed in that direction. I can't wait to see what's in store for us on our southerly travels.

Grizzle Bear was plenty upset today. He was one drowned bear, shivering, soaked to the bone, little leather jacket wet, little black jeans ringing wet. I pulled his wet clothes off and put him under the heat lamp in the bathroom, his chattering teeth have quieted, and I hear some humming. His little head is getting its fair share of road dirt. I checked behind his ears and my oh my, he's going to have to do some serious scrubbing. But I will wait for a sunny and warmer day.

So, until next time, love to all, always,
Judy/Mom/Mommy

July 3, 2005
Sunday
Prince George, British Columbia
Mile 10,531

Dear Folks,

It was so dark in the hotel room at Watson Lake when we turned off the lights I thought I was hallucinating. I haven't seen darkness in about five weeks and I know in that time I haven't seen any stars either due to all the sunlight. The room was so dark and quiet that we actually over slept and woke up at nine-fifteen instead of the usual five or six. I did not hear any crows either.

We knew we had a long ride ahead of us as we were trying to reach Prince George by Sunday night in order to have internet and cell phone connection for Monday morning. There has been neither while in the Yukon.

The road we were going to take had become notorious in our minds, over the last several weeks. We have heard so many stories about how horrible the road would be. We would get variations on a theme as we talked to people about our route. It is funny to me that in this vast land there is a motorcycle telegraph that reaches thousands and thousands of miles.

No matter where we stop, we are always asked are we going north or south and how the road conditions are. Every rider has a different opinion about the severity of the road conditions. Every one rides differently and what may seem horrible to one isn't quite that bad to another. The motorcycle telegraph system works pretty darn well considering the distances up here.

Our adventure yesterday was to take us down the Cassiar Highway. Now in my mind a highway is a flat piece of pavement with fast moving vehicles that is marked with a yellow centerline and white lines down the outer edges. A highway is not what we were on

163

by any means. This was a piece of five hundred mile road that could hardly be called a road.

At best, it was a one and a half lane slice of road, scratched right through an extremely desolate piece of wilderness on this earth. The road started out just fine but that quickly changed. Many roads up here in northern Canada and Alaska are paved with something that is called chip seal. Chip seal is gravel mixed with some sort of compound then flattened by rollers. It is very rough and loud to ride on but is a dream compared to some stretches of road I've been down.

Chip seal is hard on tires, wearing them down like a fingernail on an emery board. This "highway" started out with freshly paved chip seal then graduated to torn up chip seal complete with frost heave, pot holes and asphalt repairs. The Cassiar Highway had to be ridden and watched very carefully. There was no room for error and no chance of site seeing.

As for site seeing, there wasn't much to look at other than trees that lined the road closely on both sides. This was a long road into the wilderness and after one hundred miles, it still was a long road into the wilderness.

After about a hundred miles, the tall rugged mountains had given way to softer rounded mountains. The vegetation was more lush and so thick that when looking on either side of the road into the forest I could only see about twenty yards into the darkness. On and on the road went into the acres and acres of wilderness, trees, and mountains.

I knew by looking at my map that there were going to be a few stretches of gravel on this road. I was prepared for that, but I wasn't prepared for the stretches of gravel that were not on the map.

Not only did we have gravel to contend with, it was, of course, raining. And guess what you get when you mix rain and dirt? Mud, slop, slick goo, and lots of it! The mud was actually easier to ride in than the gravel but my bike did its own kind of dancing, wandering loosely on either surface. To ride on such surfaces makes my arms ache, my shoulders hurt, and as always, my back takes a beating.

Potholes are wonderful too. When they are full of water and mud I can't tell how deep they are so it's wise to try to avoid them if possible. It wasn't possible and I hit my fair share of them. Potholes combined with washboard will make my eyeballs jiggle around in their sockets and my teeth chatter like it was freezing outside.

But my favorite of all, on a muddy, pothole filled, wet, gravely road was the tractor-trailer truck that came barreling out of the south passing a RV, going at least sixty miles per hour. He nearly ran the poor guy in the RV off the road passing him and the tractor-trailer was completely on our side of the road. I managed to skid my bike to a complete stop and off the side of the road in all that muck as the truck passed us slinging up a cloud of brown mud and rocks. I ducked and covered behind my windshield as the brown spray of mud covered my windshield, bike and body.

I got covered in a goodly amount of sprayed mud and water and rocks hit the bike but we survived, still standing and moved on down the mud pit road. There was not too much traffic on the Cassiar but just enough that there was no chance for any picture taking when there was any remote chance to take one. It was far too dangerous and there were no pullouts on this road. The road was so narrow in most spots that each lane shared the center of the road. So instead of seeing four tracks left by the cars there were only three. Now doesn't that make you a little nervous? I was glad our tires would only take up one of the three tracks.

Driving over mud and gravel isn't very much fun and I am very careful but I go as fast as I can. The bike could go down very easily if I was to get careless. I travel as quickly but as carefully as I can. It is one thing to be passed by the guys on the BMW GS's or the other dual purpose bikes as those bikes are designed to handle rough road conditions. I don't mind that but it is another thing completely to be passed by four guys going about fifty miles per hour on Harleys and one on an overgrown scooter and all of them throwing gravel and mud on us like they were bullies. Now that really pissed me off. A scooter!

But then I got to thinking, that it was ok, just let them go on and act reckless. I know my limits and it is not fifty to sixty miles per hour on a gravel and mud road. The whole idea is to arrive safe and sound. I'm not into any sort of pain associated with coming off my bike just to prove that I can go fast on a dirt road. It is too easy to loose control. Off they went passing me throwing up gravel hitting my bike and leaving me in a cloud of choking dust. I just continued to putter along to our final destination one hundred and fifty miles further down the road than where they stopped. They may have gotten to their destination faster, but I out rode them by one hundred and fifty miles for the day.

I went over so many different kinds of surfaces yesterday I lost count. First, there was the chip seal, then gravel, then mud, then mud mixed with gravel, and then broken up chip seal, then just plain dirt. Bridges had their own different surface types. Some were just regular torn up pavement, some were wooden planks, but my all time favorite was the metal grate. The bike really likes to wander on that surface. I have to keep reminding myself when I go over those types of bridges not to look down. It is just plain creepy seeing canyons with rushing water in them directly below me. It is like flying and I keep wondering when I am going to fall into the icy water below.

Mother Nature pulled out her paintbrush and covered the sides of the road with a multitude of bright colored flowers. Oranges and reds have been added to the mix of yellows, pinks, and purples. At one point when we came around a curve in the road I thought there was a snowdrift off to the left. It wasn't snow at all but a huge field thick with daisies.

On and on we went in the rain and when we came to the location we had hoped to stop for the night it was nothing more than just a junction in the road with a gas station. The gas station was just closing for the night as we pulled in. The female attendant, who appeared to me to have an immediate crush on Ralph, told us there were no places to stay in the area. Exhausted and tired from the long road we had already covered, we had to ride another ninety miles to get to a campground. At least the road had improved and was now a nicely, paved smooth "highway" complete with yellow centerline and white lines on the sides.

We rolled into the campground only to find the office closed, which I figured it would be at ten at night. There was a nice note on the window saying, "pick a site and see us in the morning." That's exactly what we did.

Now, it was ten at night and there is no way, no how, any place to get any dinner. It had been a long time since lunch. But as luck would have it, I had been storing away goodies along the way for the past week. Ralph had even scoffed at me when I picked up two apples, a bag of Fritos, and some trail mix at the little store in Skagway. Guess who was sniffing around my hoard of food?

Since Ralph only had a pack of stale peanut butter crackers in his tank bag, I caved in and shared my goodies. In our little tent in the rain, set up on some nice soft grass, we dined on cheese crackers, apples, trail mix, left over Doritos, corn nuts, fudge and bottled water. Ralph yummed and hummed his way through dinner. I was shivering too much, I think from exhaustion, and decided my nice warm sleeping bag was more important than food.

We were awakened this morning, not to the sound of damned crows, but to the sound of sweet songbirds and two hummingbirds fighting with each other. It was like comparing heavy metal music to soft classical. What a difference the little songbirds made to my ears.

As usual, as has been our fate of late, it was raining again. That was not a good start to the day. It was one thing to be caught in the rain at some part of the day but it was another thing entirely to start the day in the rain. It rained the entire day today and the road was crowded with fast moving cars and motor homes all on their way to Prince George or north into the wilderness. I'm getting real tired of the rain. The landscape had changed from rocky mountains, snow and fir trees to towns, civilization, traffic, crazy drivers and little or no scenery. I was ready to turn around and head back north.

We made it safely to Prince George and are staying in a hotel for the night. Happy Fourth of July to everyone. We'll be in Canada tomorrow and I know there won't be any fireworks. This seems a little odd not being in our own country for the fourth. So all of y'all who have some, set off some fireworks for me and have a hotdog or two. No cheeseburgers please, I have had too many.

So until next time, love to all always,
Judy/Mom/Mommy

July 4, 2005
Monday
Cache Creek, British Columbia
Mile 10,811

Dear Folks,

Guess what I woke up to today? Silence! No crows, no birds just the slight snoring of my dearly beloved. And it was dark too! Now of course if you read yesterday's journal entry you would know that we stayed in a motel last night. What sweet slumber I experienced last night. After a dinner of Chinese that was within walking distance to the motel, I took a very long shower, and climbed into nice clean sheets without dirt or bugs. The sheets smelled of clean laundry soap and felt like silk against my tattered and abused skin. I wasn't sure I would get out of the bed this morning but I did.

We got off to a very lazy start today. We pulled out of bed around nine and it was then I realized that it was a holiday and all offices were closed in the United States. We had pushed and pushed to get to Prince George so Ralph would have internet connection for Monday morning. Oh, my aching bones. We relaxed a few more minutes in the comfort of the bed and eventually packed up the bikes and headed further south.

I was skeptical about actually seeing anything note worthy today as the road we were traveling was a busy highway loaded with lumber trucks carrying tons of logs, tractor-trailer trucks, motor homes, and speeding cars some of which were pulling trailers.

Not to go without my daily fix of crows, I did see them following us down the road. At one point, I saw about eight of the little black suckers sitting on fence posts just waiting. Now of course I know that they are not following us but they are everywhere. I am starting to feel that if I go a day without seeing my feathered friends it is bad luck. I start looking for them each day and am not satisfied until I have counted at least two crows, one for each of us.

It was windy today but not raining. The clouds were threatening but we only got a small sprinkling. We needed a dry day after all the rain we've been in lately. It wears on me day after day of being damp and every thing else I own being wet. A little sunshine was very welcome today.

After leaving Prince George today the scenery was nothing to even write about. Nothing special at all, just moving down the highway trying not to get pushed out of the way by the tractor-trailer trucks and log trucks. As we moved further south, the land stretched out and farmland was on either side of the road.

The road was following the Frazer River and as we climbed slightly in elevation, the river had cut a wide canyon through the earth. On both sides of the canyon were large ranches with lush pastures. The grass looked like the color of Crayola Green; it was so bright and fresh. Hay was being harvested and it smelled heavenly.

More and more ranches took the place of big city businesses and fast food chains as we moved south along the highway. Livestock grazed in every fenced in area. Bulls sat happily chewing cud guarding their playmates that were sitting under big shade trees also chewing their cud. And the horses, wow! The people of this area love their horses. Every house, no matter how small or large had at least two horses. To me they were all beautiful. Mares stood close to their foals that were asleep in the warm sunshine, their soft warm underbellies exposed to the bright sun.

Ranch houses made of logs surrounded by fences dotted the land. I saw a perfect place that given half a chance, I would have liked to live there. Nestled up under the hardwoods was a two-story white farmhouse, like some of the ones we have in the south. In the front yard off to the side somewhat was a small garden with vegetables growing tall and lush. Next to the vegetable garden was a flower garden full of red and yellow flowers. Behind the house stood the weathered barn and paddock. Running behind the house and barn out a ways was a wide creek and to make the scene complete there were grazing horses in the thick green grass.

It was an absolutely perfect farm setting and I wanted to pull in the drive way and call it home. There were many more beautiful ranches along the highway all with cattle and horses grazing peacefully within the fences.

The geography has definitely changed the further we have moved south. Rolling hills have replaced the ice and snow covered mountains of the far north. Civilization has replaced the desolate wilderness. Both of us are having to make adjustments to returning to busy civilization. It's not easy. Alaska and far north Canada is a world in itself and I liked its environment.

We already miss the wilderness, the uncluttered highways, and the sparse traffic. I'm just hoping that after seeing such vastness and such stunning beauty that I won't be disappointed by what comes next. I do try to find some beauty in each day. If not in the scenery than in something that strikes me funny or interesting.

I did forget to mention some of the wildlife that I saw on the Cassiar Highway. There was so much wilderness that I was sure some wild creature would pop out of the woods at any moment. Well, I did see a moose with her calf off in one of the many ponds. She just popped her head up out of the water and watched us as we went by. The other wild animal I saw, at least he thought he was wild, was a beautiful paint horse running free.

We had just refueled in one of the few facilities along the way and off the side of the road about fifty yards, was the horse. He was just munching away on some green grass when we pulled back onto the road. He turned around, stared at us, and then started running. He ran directly in front of us up over the road. When he reached the road, he did a little showing off by arching his neck and slinging his head around causing his long mane to flutter in the wind. He pranced across the road, tail held high, and then kicked up his heels as he left the road on the other side. He continued to buck and prance as he ran off into the woods behind a building. I believe he thought he was king of the wind.

There are some things that I keep forgetting to mention that have given me a chuckle over the past few weeks and should give a person things to ponder. When traveling on a bike there are some things that you might want to reconsider. For instance, if you are camping, you might want to avoid following a sign that says campground and landfill on the same sign pointing in the same direction. Yes, I passed that campground up without even a second glance. You might want to reconsider whether you should continue your journey for the day when the sky you are riding into is the same color black as the mountains. If you can't tell where the mountains end and the sky begins, you might want to consider finding the next rock to hide under because I'm here to tell you the sky is going to open up and dump on you big time. Yes, I experienced this one. I never found the rock to hide under either.

Another thing you might want to pay attention to is the dreaded orange, road under construction, sign. This is necessary when traveling in the Yukon and Alaska. Don't go getting all smarty-pants and thinking that it's just nothing. These orange signs up here mean business, buddy, and not paying attention to them will find you face down in muddy gravel so fast you'll be spitting grit for a month of Sundays. No, I haven't gone face down in the muddy gravel because I've been a very good student and followed the directions, all pilot cars, and all flagmen.

But you know you are really in for a rough ride, when after already traveling twenty miles on dirt, mud and gravel, you come to one of the dreaded orange signs that states that the road up ahead is under construction. Now wait a minute, isn't the road already broken up dirt, gravel mud and full of potholes? How can it get any worse? Trust me on this one, it can, and does. The nice gravely, muddy, pothole filled semblance of a road now has chunks of chip seal added to the mix. It becomes so bumpy and jiggly that if you drank milk and added chocolate syrup you would immediately have a warm, chocolate milkshake. Yuck. You might want to check into getting a dental plan before you leave home, as your teeth will become chipped or ground to nubs from all the rough roads.

One must find humor in a situation or else one would find themselves screaming into the face shield on the helmet causing it to fog up and then probably running off the gravel road anyway. Me, I only do my screaming when my face shield is up. That way I don't fog the face shield and I don't burst my eardrums in the process. It's amazing just how loud you can get while riding and no one can hear you. Trust me on this one too.

Well, getting back on the subject of today's ride, it is over for the day. We rode into a little town called Cache Creek and we were looking for a place to do laundry and camp at the same time but had no such luck. We found the laundry but it was closed for the day. We found a hotel too. Two nights in a row in a motel. I hope these sheets feel as good as those did last night.

After getting our laundry done in the morning we will be heading for Whistler, British Columbia. It's a town north of Vancouver and we will be staying there for a couple days hopefully.

I took no pictures today. I couldn't even begin to stop for a snapshot. There were no turnouts along the road and traffic was too fast and crazy. But there's always tomorrow.

Grizzle Bear is starting to smell like a dirty little boy and I'm making him sleep on the other side of the room. I put my nose up to his little head yesterday and choked. I have smelled this exact smell on dirty little boys back home. I guess a bath is in order sometime soon. But you would think with all the showers he gets on the back of my bike he would smell like fresh air and sunshine. Wrong! Maybe a wild mountain stream would suit him better. I'll throw the soap to him after I find a good stream for him somewhere down the road.

So until later, much love to all, always,
Judy/Mom/Mommy

July 5, 2005
Tuesday
Whistler, British Columbia
Mile 10,946

Dear Folks,

After snoozing until eight this morning we packed up and headed straight to do our nasty, dirty clothes. When we got to the laundry mat the mean old fart there wouldn't give us any change for our U.S. dollars and told us in no uncertain terms that we had to go to the bank and get coins. Up until now, most places we visited either took our U.S. dollars and swapped our dollars for Canadian coins. The exchange rate kills you. The problem was the bank here in this tiny town didn't open until ten A.M. We had an hour to kill before the bank opened so we went and got some breakfast and waited until ten.

If there had been another place to wash clothes in Cache Creek we would have gone there because the owner of the only one in town was a real jerk. We sucked it up and got the nasty deed done for another week.

As we left Cache Creek, the weather was threatening to rain but we were hopeful that we might escape. We left the main highway and took a back road to Whistler that would take us over a high mountain pass. On the Cache Creek side, the terrain looked just like that of the Wyoming countryside I have seen so many times. There was tumbleweed growing everywhere and it gave off a sweet aroma as we traveled down the narrow two-lane road.

The ranches were still spotting the sides of the road and cattle and horses grazed peacefully. Soon the low craggy mountains covered with brush and tumbleweed gave way to a deep canyon cut by the wide Frazer River. The road ran along a plateau on the canyon's edge. Along the plateau's edge also were ranches and crops on any space that could be planted.

The canyon was very deep and the river rushed through the bottom madly. The road was a poorly maintained, narrow winding, two lane and the drop offs were breath taking. I kept seeing all these wonderful pictures I wanted to take and there was no place to stop. In most places, there were not even any guardrails. A quick look in my rear view mirror and I could see Ralph hugging the centerline again. I too, kept toward center. It was a long way down to the canyon floor and the rushing water.

Finally, there was one small turn out and I was able to get a few pictures of the canyon. As usual, the photos just can't capture the depth and width of the canyon. I did stand on the edge of the canyon and imagined what it would feel like to be an eagle or hawk; to spread my wings and let the cool air currents of the canyon and river lift me over the land. I got goose bumps thinking of the thrill.

As I turned around to motion Ralph over to see the splendor, he nodded his head in a negative fashion. Ralph kept to his bike on the side of the road. He was nauseated just being on the edge of the road.

As we continued our journey up the narrow road, the landscape changed once again. The mountains were back again and some still had a touch of snow left at the higher elevations. Large firs and grasses lined the road and climbed the mountains. The purple lupines blooming along the side of the road were combined with bright orange and red shooting stars. Yellow daisies were now replacing the white daisies. The sides of the road had been splatter painted with brightly colored flowers.

Stream after stream came rushing down the mountains, beautiful white waterfalls came crashing out of the sides of the mountain, and under the road we traveled. Rushing streams of silt, green, turquoise and white in color met with larger fast moving rivers all scurrying in the direction to the Pacific.

By now, we had climbed pretty high in elevation and the clouds just couldn't stand it and down came the rain. It made everything lush and green, black rocks blacker, the colors of the wild flowers more vibrant and both of us much wetter.

The road became a little more difficult but not unmanageable. It was in very bad need of completely redoing. Parts of the road next to drop offs into the canyon below or off the mountainside looked as if the very next car to go over it would completely cause it to slide off into oblivion. The road had big dips with cracked pavement around the edges the size of large dump trucks.

Many tight narrow switchbacks would either climb or descend. They were a little scary to me as the visibility around these turns was a big fat zero. Too many times a big truck or gigantic camper on narrow passes has confronted me. After climbing for a while, there was another pull out with picnic tables. The view was such an incredible surprise. A dam, that we had just come over, had backed up the water into a huge lake of midnight blue surrounded on both sides by tall black mountains. Dark grey and black rain clouds hung over the mountains and water. Wow what a site!

We continued in the soaking rain. It took a very long time to cover a short distance today. The road was not conducive to going more than thirty-five miles per hour. But the scenery was well worth the drive. The rain continued and got harder as we descended into the valley and into the town of Whistler.

I visited Whistler about twenty-four years ago when Perry was a baby. Ralph had attended a convention in Vancouver and I took a day train trip up to Whistler. I remember the ride up and back being beautiful but don't remember there being much of a town then. Now, Whistler is a big resort area. The rich and famous come here to hob knob with each other. It just so happened that a skins game was being played here today with all the golf pros in attendance. I wondered what that was going to do to our chances of finding any accommodations. Then I realized that we were camping and most everyone else would be staying in the resort hotels and lodges.

There was only one campground in Whistler and you wouldn't believe it. This had to be the most upscale campground I have ever been in. As I pulled into the parking lot, I thought I was pulling into a resort lodge. A beautiful huge log building that looked like a mighty nice ski lodge was the check in office. I thought we were in the wrong place. I thought it was a hotel. It was the office, complete with café, grocery store, entertainment room, laundry, and showers.

This place was the bomb of campgrounds. Not one speck of gravel anywhere! All pavement. That is until we found out where the tent sites were. The pavement, saved for the RV's, ended and the mud began. Slick stuff with lovely potholes greeted us at the end of the pavement. There was a general parking place for cars and wheelbarrows to roll your stuff into the walk in campsites. And of course, it was raining steadily. The campsite was really lovely, all snuggled up in the woods and all private, but after seeing the rest of the place where all the motor homes and RV's are parked I feel like we are the lower class and are relegated to staying on the other side of the dyke that holds the water from the river, back from the motor homes and RV's. What's with that?

I have to admit that I was not the least bit happy about camping in the pouring rain. I was pouting on the inside but trying with all my might not to let it show. I'm pretty much sick of the rain now.

After getting the tent set up in the rain and all the dripping wet gear thrown in the tent we pondered our fate for dinner. Neither of us was inclined to get back on the bikes and go in search of food in town so we walked from our little wet tent site in the dripping woods, down a gravel path, past all the mammoth motor homes and RV's, past the rushing river, over the dyke and into the beautiful log, lodge office and found the small camp store. There we hunted and gathered food for dinner and returned to our wet campsite the way we came, in the pouring rain.

By the time we got back to the campsite, my outer layer of gear was soaked. I was so hot from hauling our stuff back into the woods, putting up the tent and putting everything in it's place in the tent and taking an unexpected hike over and through the woods to the camp store, that my clothes on the inside of my rain gear were soaked with another kind of moisture. Clammy and wet on both the outside and inside, I was doing all I could to keep a civil tongue in my mouth. I was determined not to be a whiner and just kept silent. Usually, that is the best course for me when I am about to explode.

I made turkey sandwiches while Ralph cut cheese to add to the crackers. That combined with good old Lays Potato Chips and we had a feast in our little green tent in the pouring rain. After dinner, we sopped up all the water that had dripped off our gear and it appears that, so far, we have dryness inside our tent.

We plan to stay here tomorrow night as well; I just hope the rain lets up. It's raining pretty hard right now and even though it sounds good to sleep by, I just hope all stays dry inside. Ralph will be the one sleeping in water; I'm high and dry on the cot.

Grizzle Bear is plenty mad tonight. He is soaked to the stuffing. I have tried to dry him off but I can't get all of the rainwater off him. He looked so pitiful today that when we came to a stop at the end of the mountain pass, some native Indians standing at the corner yelled at me to cover up the poor bear. Well if we get wet, so does he. I guess I will put him inside the sleeping bag with me tonight and hope my body heat will dry him out. Poor bear.

If it's dry and sunny where you are, blow a little our way please!

So until next time, love to all always,
Judy/Mom/Mommy

July 6, 2005
Wednesday
Whistler, British Columbia
Mile 10950

Dear Folks,

Though it rained and poured and the wind blew last night, we stayed dry inside the tent. There were a few small leaks round a seam or two but nothing major. From the sound of what was going on outside the tent, I was sure we would be soaked. My sleeping bag rested against the side of the tent in the night but only got a little damp on the outside of the bag. However, we purchased these fancy sleeping bags in the event that if one did get wet, we could still stay warm. They worked well, as advertised.

By morning, most of the rain had stopped but there was a fair amount of mud splattered on the outside of the tent all around the base. Mud had splattered about two feet high in places. That gives you some idea of the amount of rain we had.

No crows squawked this morning, I could not believe it. I guess the rain ran them off. We waited around a while to see if the weather would clear but we got tired or waiting. We got on the bikes and rode into the village anyway. The village was impressive. Whistler is a big ski resort area in winter and an extreme sports facility in summer. This place reeks of money. The village looks like an Olympic village already so there won't be much to do when the Olympics are held here in 2010.

Whistler is one huge complex of resorts, lodges, restaurants, and ritzy shopping. On our budget, we decided to observe the tourist today instead of being one. We found a hamburger place and had a fancy burger then wandered over to an area with lots of stores and outside cafes and benches to sit and watch the rich and famous, the rich, and the not so rich, like us, walk the village.

We did a fair amount of people watching today and it was so fun to watch them go up and down the village area. All shapes and sizes, colors and nationalities, young and old were available for viewing.

The teenagers, who appeared to be locals, were either sporting skiing equipment or mountain biking attire. They all had their own special look. The skiers had various types and colors of beanies on their heads followed by all colors of jackets, baggy ski pants, which either were dragging the ground getting filthy dirty or were turned at the cuff to poof out at mid-calf. All carried backpacks with ski boots attached on each side and either skis or snowboards slung over their shoulders. And of course, the goggles were either being worn over their eyes for effect or raised up resting on the colored beanies. Then there was the saunter that each group had. They were all identical and all said, "look at me, I'm just too cool." Well, maybe they were cool.

They were skiing and snowboarding on one of the glaciers in the area. Wish I could have seen them snowboarding down the glacier though.

Now, the mountain bikers I thought were cool and I could identify somewhat with them. They all had protective gear on their shins, knees, elbows. They wore fancy protective helmets, gloves to protect their hands and rode incredible mountain bikes. One of the things I could identify with most was the mud they sported. Ralph and I both sported some mud of our own on our protective gear that we wore as we watched the mountain bikers.

Whistler Mountain and Blackcomb mountains are covered with ski runs and they are very, very steep. I probably couldn't even walk down one much less ski! Ski lifts climbed all over the two mountains that were adjacent to each other. On one of the mountains, the ski lifts were taking bikers up to the top along with their bikes. Then in about ten minutes, down they came flying and jumping over a course that had been designed for the bikers. There were rock cliffs that the mountain bikers jumped off of as well as vertical walls that the riders rolled over.

We sat at the bottom of the slope and watched for a couple of hours as the bikers went over and over the course. There was even a paraplegic, on a bike with four wheels, taking the course. It was fun, to me, to watch them. These were some tough, in shape, young adults. There were only a few girls participating so I naturally rooted for them. Any time women move around in a male dominated field and succeed, I get pure pleasure and satisfaction.

I can't even to begin to imagine what this place must look like with all the winter's snow everywhere, but it must be impressive. I don't know what they do to the bike course in winter. Is there that much snow that would cover the man made structures? Beats me, but I think probably so.

Ralph and I even went to see a movie today in the village. We went to see War of the Worlds and really enjoyed one of our favorite pass times. We really had an easy day today and it was nice to relax and do just nothing.

The wind blew the clouds around all day and here and there we would get a patch of blue sky and *sunshine*! We sat on a bench in the sun and dried out our riding gear since it was soaked from yesterday. The sun was heavenly and warm like fresh honey. Just as we were really enjoying the sun, the clouds would move over and give just a little sprinkle. We were teased repeatedly today, but what we had was a vast improvement over yesterday.

We are heading south in the morning, into the state of Washington and then over to Olympic National Park. Guess what the weather forecast is for tomorrow? Yep, rain. I just hope we get the bikes packed and the tent put up before it comes down again.

I took a few pictures of the boys on the bikes but other than people watching, movie watching and eating we had a nice relaxing day of being stationary.

Oh, I forgot. Do you remember how many times I said some of the landscape in Alaska, particularly on the Dalton Highway looked to be prehistoric? Well, if any of you have read any news today, dinosaur tracks were found in Denali National Park today. See, I knew it!

We have moved far enough south now that we are actually getting some darkness at night. After weeks and weeks of daylight all the time, the darkness is a little unsettling. It was pitch black in the tent last night. The sun did come up early along with the birds. The train that must have been behind the tent, blew its whistle bright and early, out doing the lovely song of the birds.

Grizzle Bear looks much happier tonight. He's all nice and dry and swinging in his hammock I made for him. I think I hear him humming a little trying to go to sleep.

So until next time, love to all always,
Judy/Mom/Mommy

July 8, 2005
Friday
Aberdeen, WA
Mile 11,478

Dear Folks,

Yesterday morning started bright and early with the sound of the train whistle in our back yard. It was overcast but not raining so we packed up in a hurry and scooted on down the road. As we left Whistler, the curvy road followed a river and the train tracks. We caught bits and pieces of the mountains through the cloud cover but for the most part clouds hung low over everything.

The trees were getting fatter and fatter the lower in elevation we went. Eventually, the road brought us to a really big bay at the ocean's edge. To look across the bay at water, mountains and sky was really pretty and eye pleasing.

We passed by a waterfall named Shannon Falls. High up on the mountain, right next to the road, the falls came crashing down onto the rocks then under a bridge and out to sea. The scenery changed from an alpine one to a coastal one. The aroma changed also from one of moist evergreen and pine to one of the sea and the creatures that live there. I enjoyed the road though it was busy with traffic.

The road eventually turned into a four lane interstate that led through Vancouver. I did not enjoy it one bit. Lots of fast drivers and too many trucks that had no concern for others at all, made my stomach turn immediately to acid. It was quite an adjustment coming from wilderness back into crowded conditions.

We eventually made it back to the United States and had to wait in line for about forty minutes until our turn with the customs agent. He looked us over, looked at our passports for all of twenty seconds, and waved us on through. So, at all of our six border crossings over the last seven weeks there were absolutely no problems and no hassles.

A CHALLENGE FOR NO OTHER WOMAN

Interstate 5 started right at the border and we road down that for about fifty miles until the cut off for the northwest peninsula in Washington. I had no idea that the road we would be taking would be so crowded. From my map, it appeared to be a back road with only small towns along the way. Well, it was a back road but it was crowded with almost bumper-to-bumper traffic. I was starting to hate civilization again with all its noise, pollution, loud cars, and crowded streets. I was ready to turn my bike around and head right back to the wilderness. What beauty and peacefulness there was to behold in the wild north.

The scenery did improve however, with farms along the way. Most were growing berries of all sorts. There were blueberries, raspberries, and cherries growing in acre after acre along the sides of the road. One farm was growing lavender. Bright purple stalks growing on two-foot tall bushes covered acres of farmland. The lavender fields looked like a purple quilt spread over the land. The valley was the bed, the mountains the head and footboard, the blue sky the ceiling in which to stare into and drift off to sleep. The sight was quite brilliant and the brief smell I got of blooming lavender was intoxicating.

At one point, a golden eagle flew right out of the woods and just above my head before veering off back into the woods. In his claws, he had dinner. I think it must have been either a small fish or small rodent. Regardless, he was heading with due hast to the nest. On down a little further we came across a few other gigantic birds. These were of the mechanical kind, bright shiny silver and roaring loudly. There was a naval air base close and the jets were A10's, whose main purpose was to destroy tanks. They were flying very close to the road at tree top level. Definitely impressive and attention getting were both of these birds, live and mechanical.

We made our way over to the dock where we would catch a ferry to the peninsula. As we rolled up, we saw the ferry just pulling away. But not to worry, there was another one coming in about an hour. I can't believe the difference in prices here in Washington as compared to Alaska. In Haines, Alaska, we caught a ferry from Haines to Skagway that took forty minutes and covered about fifteen miles. The fair was sixty dollars apiece. To catch a ferry from the Oak Harbor

183

area to Port Townsend, which took thirty minutes and was approximately the same distance cost us four dollars each!

The crossing was cold and windy but I enjoyed the salty ocean aroma and the ride was over all too quickly. The water looked like something I would not like to fall into. Kelp and broken pieces of logs floated in the current, which appeared to be rather strong.

After leaving the ferry and passing through Port Townsend, we weaved through the curves and the fir trees. As we came around one turn in the road there was an arched bridge stretching over a small canyon. A fast moving river to the left was emptying into the ocean on the right. The scenery had everybody excited because there were dozens of cars parked all over the place with people taking pictures of their first glimpse of the Pacific. The site was grand, but I was unable to stop do to all the other gawkers and their big cars taking up all the parking area.

We rode another thirty-five miles or so to the Park Headquarters of Olympic National Park. I knew, by the late hour, that it would be closed but I was hoping to find a park map. Fortunately, there was a map outside the closed building. The campground we hoped to stay in was just up the road a few miles.

We had had such an unusual day of intermittent sunshine that we just didn't know what to do with the rays from the sun. After all, we have had so much rain lately. We did enjoy not having rain but we knew the forecast was calling for more of the wet stuff. I think everything I own is damp. Not wet, as if it got soaked, but just damp from being out in the elements.

We pulled into Olympic National Park and the Heart O' the Hills campground was just inside the entrance. The area was just like what you would expect of a moist Pacific Northwest environment. Everything dripped of moisture and was lush with ferns, moss, and the biggest fir trees imaginable.

We found a campsite, Ralph set up the tent while I went to scavenge firewood, twigs, and sticks. Of course, the wood was all wet, but I lugged it back anyway. After Ralph got the tent set up he played Paul Bunyan and went back into the woods for more wood. I could hear him chopping dead logs in the woods with his tiny hatchet. But he did come back to the site dragging some sizeable pieces of wood for a fire.

We ate another dinner of turkey sandwiches and chips under the gigantic fir trees and afterward Ralph started the sticks, twigs and any paper that we had, with the fire starter sticks. We kept the fire fed with tiny sticks and twigs and eventually the small logs dried out enough to create some semblance of a fire. Now I understand the many signs along the road advertising "dry" firewood. I just naturally assumed that anyone selling firewood would be selling something dry and burnable. There is nothing burnable in this area in the forest!

Beside our campsite was a tree whose trunk was as big as a car and so tall I couldn't see the top for the rest of the trees around it. I imagine the tree was several hundred years old. Next to the tent was a very small creek that dripped down over rocks and created the most beautiful lullaby.

Safely and snuggly tucked into our sleeping bags, we were lulled to sleep by the trickling of the water, the soft fur needles falling onto the tent and the sounds of the woods. The darkness was deep and slightly spooky after so much light for so many weeks.

The night passed quickly and toward the creeping of daylight, I heard the pitter-patter of tiny raindrops on the tent. Oh, no, not again. I would drift back to sleep only be awakened again by water dropping softly around me. Suddenly, out of the deep sleep I was in, and the silence of the woods, came the lumbering, ear-shattering garbage truck. Now that is one sound I did not expect to hear in the campground.

The garbage truck went to each loop in the campground, emptied each bear proof dumpster with clanging and banging and the hissing of air breaks, and back-up warning sounds. I was popped eyed I was startled so badly. To top it off it was seven A.M. I bet that person driving that garbage truck was getting a big kick out of waking up everyone in the campground. There were one hundred and ten campsites and now everyone was awake. No way to pay him back, either.

Since we were now fully awake, we went ahead and got up, packed and headed up the road toward the summit of the mountain, whose base we had camped near. According to the map I had gotten at the park headquarters, if we went to the summit, we would be able to see vistas of mountains at the ocean's edge along with Mt. Olympus and its glaciers.

Unfortunately, the rain started again and was coming down pretty hard. Who else but the Joiners would climb up to a summit in the pouring rain to a place called Hurricane Ridge? And guess why it's called Hurricane Ridge? Gee, cause the wind *blows!* Not only was the wind blowing, but the rain was too and the clouds and fog were so low that it was like looking over into a white abyss, a witch's black cauldron of thick white brew.

Well, we reached the top, quickly determined that there would be no beautiful vistas for viewing nor any glaciers, nor Mt. Olympus so we turned around, and headed right back down. The wild flowers were available for viewing however, and I was not disappointed at all. Bright orange Indian paintbrushes were mixed in with banks of purple lupines. Sometimes these were mixed with white daisies and some other bright yellow flowers that clung tightly to the rock walls above the rest of the wild flowers.

A deer was in the same spot when we came down the mountain as she was when we went up. I think she was waiting for a handout of some sort. She was pretty but very wet. We passed on by her without giving any hand outs and she batted her pretty black eyes at us as we passed.

We reached the main highway, headed west, and found a restaurant to get a nice hot breakfast. Since we don't smoke, the only part that was for nonsmokers was in a dark room off to the side of the main restaurant. We were the only ones in there and I felt we were bad children being punished for some reason. The food and service was good and just as we were about finished another older couple came in and sat down.

We struck up a conversation with them and it turned out that the man was the retired Chief Naturalist for Olympic National Park. He was so very interesting to talk to and I could have listened to him for hours. He was a born teacher. We got the inside information on what to see in the park. Unfortunately, we had to end our interesting conversation and head on out in the pouring rain and west on the slick black top. Not only was it pouring rain but I got so very cold, at one point, I just wanted to stop right then and there, right in the middle of the road in the forest. There was no place to stop and nothing to do but continue on in the downpour. There was only one-way out of the rain and that was down the road we were headed. I had really had just about all the rain and dampness I could possible stand. For the past two weeks, we had been in and out of rain.

I really wish I could have seen the area under clear skies. I know it must be beautiful, the naturalist had said as much. He was disappointed that we were missing the gorgeous surroundings. As we got further out onto the peninsula, the road skirted around a dark teal lake. The little I could see of the water's edge, the water was clear and logs on the bottom of the lake could be seen from my vantage point on the back of my motorcycle. I wanted to take a canoe out on that lake and explore even in the rain.

I have visited Olympic National Park before, once as an eleven-year-old when Mama brought all of us children and once as a twenty-one year old when I came alone with Mama. From looking at the map, the name, La Push, of one of the areas on the Pacific Ocean, jumped out at me. It was one that Mama and I explored so many years ago. We had collected slick, wet rocks and funny shaped, drift wood and hid them in places in the van we camped in. I was anxious to see it again as the memories were so strong. I felt my mother's presence.

As Ralph and I got closer to the area, we could hear the crashing of the ocean. We pulled into the picnic area, climbed off the sodden bikes and walked down a path to the ocean. We had to cross over a field of drift wood logs and onto the rock beach. Every rock on this beach was round and smooth from the centuries of pounding of the waves and wind.

Drift wood logs, void of all bark, leaves and needles and branches, littered the beach. I stood next to the stump of one of the countless logs resting on its side. I stand five feet, nine inches tall and I was dwarfed by its size. I was in awe at the size of the mammoth trees that had been tossed around in the ocean like toothpicks and then thrown onto the rocky shore like so many pick-up-sticks. Wonders of all wonders the sun was shining on the beach. Ralph took the opportunity to stretch out on top of one of the giant, drift wood logs and sun himself like a big fat alligator.

So many, many years ago, I was on this exact beach with my mother. Now, I was sharing it with Ralph. It was a very special moment for me. My heart gave a little squeeze at the memories. Three times, in a life time, to visit such a remote place as this, was indeed special. I also snuck a few rocks into my pocket for old time's sake and as a tribute to my mother.

On further down the road we came to the turn off to the Hoh Rainforest. Well, Ralph had said we had already been in the rain forest but he didn't know what he was in for. I remembered it distinctly from the earlier trips with Mama. For eighteen miles, we rode through gigantic sentinels standing guard along the road. Their long arm drooped with rain and hung heavy with moss.

Like the perfect storm, this rain forest was sitting in a perfect set of geological circumstances. The rainforest sits in a valley with its back against the tall Cascade Mountains and fed constantly by the wet Pacific winds and rain. The rain collects there, unable to move and so the pocket of forest remains a rain forest. Rain averages approximately fourteen feet a year.

The vegetation is lush and immense. Ferns are prolific and waist high. Moss hangs from everything and the ground feels like a wet sponge. And of course, it is raining, raining, raining. We came to a big spruce tree that was over two hundred and seventy feet tall and over five hundred and fifty years old. Water dripped from every inch of vegetation creating a tattoo of water drops on the leaves and spongy moss below.

On the trip with Mama, we came here also. Where I had enjoyed the beach and its rocks and driftwood, I did not want any part of the rain forest. Mama had a particular fascination with the rain forest that, at that time I couldn't understand. But now I understand. I wish I could take back my displeasure as now, I have a new appreciation for this unique place. I said a few kind words in my heart to Mama and apologized for my youthful ignorance and displeasure.

As we left the rain forest, just for a moment, the sun broke through, filtered down through the wetness, and lit up every drop of rain like diamonds. Every tree was covered in nature's lights. The mist through the forest looked like a white, silk curtain draped through the trees over the branches. I was glad I had come back to the rain forest. Once again, my mother was in my thoughts and I carried her with me back down the road.

On the main road back down the peninsula, we ran parallel to the Pacific Ocean. The pungent ocean air smelled good to me. The sun gave up trying to shine but at least it wasn't raining out near the ocean's edge.

We were at day's end and tired and the road veered away from the ocean and headed inland. We made it to a little town called Aberdeen where we found a hotel that I'm not so sure I will be safe staying in. It looks like one of those places where prostitutes and drug dealers hang out but is right next to some other nice establishments. This is a rough, depressing looking town. I think it might just be a nervous night. Maybe I'll sleep with one eye open.

Today was a very good day in spite of the rain. My feet have just now dried out. I think my boots need a good coat of sealant, as they are no longer waterproof. Yuck.

So until next time, love to all always,
Judy/Mom/Mommy

July 10, 2005
Sunday
White Salmon, WA
Mile 11,712

Dear Folks,

We survived the night in the scary hotel and the bikes were still there in one piece this morning. As usual this morning it was drizzling rain. Packing up the bikes in the rain was no fun at all. All the dirt on the straps and the bike mixed with the water and made a nice black mess on the hands.

We got out of the depressing town quickly and headed for White Salmon, Washington. William and Jody are staying with their aunt and uncle, Elena and Kevin, for a couple of weeks finalizing their wedding plans. The wedding is to take place on August thirteenth in White Salmon on Elena and Kevin's farm. William called us about a week ago and asked if we would be coming down toward White Salmon. If so, he would like to see us since we would be in the same area. As it turned out, we were coming close to the area so we accepted the invitation.

The road we had been down around Olympic National Park and the one that took us southeast took us past millions and millions of acres of forest that had been harvested for lumber. I was totally shocked by what I saw. In south Georgia, there are pine tree farms and acres of pines are planted in row after row. There you can tell that the trees are a crop and the crop is harvested and replanted just like the corn and beans.

But up here, in the northwest, there is practically nothing but forest of giant trees. To see sections of hundreds of acres of trees cut down for harvest, was to me, quite shocking. Everything in the blade's path is cut down. The branches are gathered in large mounds the size of a house along the hillside and the remaining tree trunks stand as a witness to the devastation man has done.

190

I know I must think like most people, that wood and paper products come from somewhere but I really did not think about where that might be. Well, now I have seen where our paper and wood products come from and it is shocking. The timber company comes in and cuts down thousands of trees, scarring the face of the land. The area is replanted about a year later.

Then these timber companies put up signs along the road announcing when an area was harvested, replanted and when a new harvest will take place. I got the impression that these companies were bragging about the fact that, while at one moment in time they were scarring and destroying the forest, in another moment, they were replanting. I saw one sign that said the area had been harvested in 1920, harvested in 1984, replanted in 1985 and would be harvested again in 2045. That is a human lifetime it takes for these beautiful trees to grow. I guess I should be thankful that replanting is actually taking place but for a generation the land is scared.

Our journey finally led us to the place where the Columbia River empties out into the ocean. We headed east into the Columbia River Gorge. At first, the area was not pretty at all and as we followed the Lewis and Clark trail, I knew that if those two men could see it now, they would die from fright and disappointment. Too much commercialization, too much industry and entirely too much of the hand of man had changed the wilderness of Lewis and Clark's time.

The further east we went the more beautiful the gorge became, however. We came around a corner and there before us was the gorge and the river that could be seen for miles. Also, as we came around the curve, I noticed that the road was attached to the side of the mountain, hanging out over the gorge on stilts. There wasn't much of a guardrail at all and with the most beautiful picture before us, there was no place to stop, not that my stomach would have cooperated.

A good part of the rest of the journey to White Salmon continued next to the river but was blocked by so many trees it was hard to get a good view. When we did come out of some of the trees, the river to the right of us was very wide. The road took us through numerous tunnels and the railroad track running parallel to the road had its own set of tunnels side by side with the car tunnels.

The area was getting rocky again and was what I expect to see in a gorge of this size. We had a significant tail wind now and it was pushing us along quite nicely. I looked out over the river and could see white caps. I knew the wind must be pretty strong coming down through this gorge. Suddenly, I saw some strange things upon the river. At closer look, it appeared to be at least fifty colorful, magnificent dragonflies scooting back and forth across the river. In reality, it was people wind surfing. Back and forth, they went over the river. The sails of the surfboards shone in the intermittent sun and they really did look like butterfly wings and dragonflies dancing lightly over the white caps of the river. We stopped at one of the parks along the side of the road, sat, and watched the dance upon the water.

We found Elena and Kevin's house with no difficulty. They live on a farm about fourteen miles from town of White Salmon. Their place is absolutely, positively lovely. They have sixty acres and the farmhouse overlooks beautiful mountains and trees. The sky was overcast for the most part but occasionally the sun would stick its head out and warm up things.

William and Jody showed me where on the farm the wedding would talk place. The reception would be held in the garden behind the house. This place is so very beautiful. I already was in love with the farm when the clouds parted just long enough for me to get a good look at Mt. Adam, a snow covered volcano, off in the distance. What a scene to wake up to every day.

Across the dirt road, twenty acres was also part of Elena and Kevin's land and on it was a small house that Kevin had converted from an old barn. It was so charming. One bedroom, a kitchen and sitting area totaling about seven hundred square feet makes up this perfectly wonderful house. The deck on the back of the house overlooks a small grassy area, the fir trees and the snow covered volcano. I could spend a good deal of time here if allowed.

Elena and Kevin and their grown children, Woodley and Nate and there respective partners were here along with William and Jody. We were made to feel so welcome and we had such a good time getting to know them. A wonderful dinner of curried beef over rice was served and I ate until I thought I would pop.

After dinner some friends came over and brought their fiddle, guitar and mandolin and Diane, Roger and William played and sang songs. It was a very good day.

When Ralph and I got up to walk over to the converted barn were we would be sleeping, we were treated to unbelievable darkness. Since there was a cloud cover, it was really dark and just a little spooky. We slept like logs in the deep darkness and were greeted in the morning by the sweet singing of birds. No crows either.

As much as we would like to stay here, we will be moving on tomorrow afternoon. William and Jody will be flying back to Atlanta to finalize some wedding plans then returning here in a few weeks for their wedding. We will be on to the next stop wherever that will be.

So, until later, love to all always,
Judy/Mom/Mommy

July 11, 2005
Monday
Nile, WA
Mile 11,873

Dear Folks,

Ralph and I really enjoyed our visit with Elena, Kevin and their family and with William and Jody. Elena and Kevin's children, Woodley and Nate and their companions were such a pleasure to get to know. They are all such nice young adults.

Yesterday we had brunch, made by Nate that was to die for. Eggs Benedict and fresh fruit. Yummy, yum, yum. After the dishes were put away, everyone sort of lazed around until a round of disk golf was called for.

They played disk golf on a course the guys had made on the farm. I watched and walked with them enjoying the warm sunshine and the farm. I picked the large softball size seedpod, which looked like giant dandelions, plucked their seeds and set them sail on the wind. The sunlight caught their tiny umbrellas and the wind lifted them high above me. They looked like tiny parachutes floating on air. Nate's friend made a beautiful wreath of wild flowers as she walked along. Everyone took turns throwing a ball to the big black dog, Duke. What I couldn't figure out was why didn't Duke ever go after the Frisbee?

After playing golf, everyone settled down to do different things. Ralph and I went back over to the guest cabin. Ralph took a snooze on the sofa and I worked on my journal and pictures.

Later, Jody made a wonderful dinner and there wasn't a scrap left. The platter was licked clean. After dinner, Woodley made a pie from raspberries, strawberries and some other freshly picked wild berries. I had my eye on that pie big time and couldn't wait to have a slice with vanilla ice cream. Let me tell you it was as good as it looked but I ate way too much. It was worth it.

After dinner, we all sat in the garden in the back yard. Elena, Kevin, and I talked while Ralph and William played Pig in the Frisbee. The game is like playing horse with the basketball. As the evening wore down, we all said our goodbyes and Ralph and I wandered back over to our place. I finally saw the first stars in six weeks.

We slept until about eight in the morning when Ralph got up and did some work. I managed to pull myself out of bed around nine, took a shower, and then went on the back deck with a cup of hot tea and my book. There in the glorious sunshine, I watched the bluebirds flit around, the swallows swoop eating bugs and my first hummingbird of the year buzzed right up behind my head.

A hawk screeched high above me as she looked for food and floated on the currents of wind. I also watched the clouds cross Mt. Adam in the distance. What a view! I would read a few paragraphs then get distracted by the birds, the wind, and the beautiful mountain in front of me. Then I would daydream of actually living right in that spot in that very house. It was magical.

Unfortunately, it was time for us to move on. William and Jody were flying back to Atlanta today and we were heading north to make a loop to see Mt. Rainier National Park. As we left the beautiful farm and got back on the road that follows the Columbia River Gorge, we got to see the wind surfers again. Along with the surfers, there were those that were using a parachute in the shape of an upside down U. I know they have a name but I don't know what they are. Like beautiful U shaped kites of bright reds and yellows the parachutes pulled the surfers across the Columbia River.

I was totally dismayed and amazed at how quickly the terrain changed. One minute we were surrounded by fir trees and cool air and literally, within ten miles we were heading up a plateau to the top of the gorge. The Lincoln Plateau was completely void of trees and was almost void of any thing living. The dark rocks of past volcanic activity were all around. What little vegetation there was, was completely dry and brittle and for miles and miles was the color of camel hair.

This morning when we got up it was a very pleasant but cool fifty degrees. It was sixty degrees by the time we left White Salmon around two in the afternoon. When we reached Yakima, Washington, it was ninety degrees! It felt like we had been stuffed into hell's oven. That was a dramatic temperature change in just a couple hours. Of course, we were burning up with our riding gear on and it felt and looked like we were crossing a desert. My eyes felt like they quivered in their sockets due to the heat. Mirages were all around us.

As we rode over the top of the plateau off to our left was a beautiful flat valley with a farm. Off in the distance behind the farm was another view of Mt. Adam and off to the left was Mt. Hood. Mt. St. Helen was supposed to be there also but I don't know if any of it is still visible or not as there were clouds in the area of that mountain. Mt. Rainier was eighty-five miles away and also was not visible. It was an alluring site with all the farmland and the volcanoes in the background.

We stopped to get some water and to pour some on us to keep us cool. While we were opening the vents on our jackets, the most god-awful smell came wafting our way from across the street. I think it must have been a meat processing plant because it smelled of boiling pork. The rancid smell was heavy in the air and I really thought I was going to barf right there. The smell, combined with the heat and my already queasy stomach, just really set the tone for the ride out of town. I gagged as we hurried past the plant. I was starting to sound like the poor cat at home when he threw up a hairball. Throwing up in my helmet is not high on the list of things I want to do.

We continued in the heated desert and as we descended off the plateau, we came to a very green valley. In the valley were many orchards of cherry trees, peach trees and apple trees. Fruit stands lined the roads all advertising their crops. I'm dying for some local cherries and would have stopped but all the fruit stands were closed for the day. I hope I find one open tomorrow.

We continued out of the green valley and we rode into a small canyon that had been cut by the river we followed. The black volcanic rock was still evident everywhere and in some spots that we went through it looked like the rock would slide off and on to us at any moment. I was a little nervous about traveling under that, particularly since a sign warned of rocks slides. Trees started to appear again and the temperature dropped back to something more tolerable.

We were trying to make it to Mt. Rainier National Park tonight but the day just gave out on us. We stopped for dinner in a very nice lodge called Whistling Jacks. Ralph inquired as to the amount for a room that turned out to be way over our budget. We just settled for dinner and returned to a nice campground we had passed earlier.

The campground sits right on the river and I don't know what sounds nicer, the river flowing over the rocks right behind our tent or the wind in the tall pines on both sides of the river. Both are soothing and we are getting a double treat for our seventeen-dollar campsite. We also are enjoying a real nice campfire with free dry wood given to us by the attendants of the campground.

The moon is coming up over the mountain across the river and the stars are coming out in fistfuls. The bats are out too, swooping around above us and then darting down close to get the mosquitoes around us. They are amazing to watch and as long as they stay in flight, both the bats and I are happy.

So ends another day on the road for us. Tomorrow we hope to explore Mt. Rainier National Park and if we're lucky, the sky will be blue as it was today.

Grizzle Bear was heard complaining about his slight sunburn on his nose today. Too much sun and heat for him. Fortunately, I have plenty of burn gel with me. Also, I heard him whining again for something sweet. No marshmallows were available so I threw him a few M&M's. But for the smacking of sticky lips, all is quiet in the tent.

So, until next time, love to all always,
Judy/Mom/Mommy

July 12, 2005
Tuesday
Randle, WA
Mile 12,047

Dear Folks,

What a beautiful morning we woke to. The sky was perfectly blue and the air was just the right temperature. The campground was almost on the perfect list but it didn't have showers or internet connection. If those two items had been available we would have parked ourselves right there for several days. I probably would have even overlooked the outhouses. These days they are not called outhouses but drop toilets. They are one in the same to me. Fortunately, they now have a new ventilation system and plenty of chemicals that make these drop toilets more acceptable.

The nice breeze we experienced last night continued through the night and into morning. As a result, we had few mosquitoes last night. The river and wind in the pines sang us a lullaby all night and in the morning, we were greeted with singing birds, rushing water, a wonderful warm breeze, and best of all sunshine. Beautiful, beautiful sunshine.

After packing up and getting back on the road, we stopped after a few miles at a roadhouse for breakfast. Outside, hung along the front, were many hanging baskets of beautiful flowers.

Petunias, daisies and others I couldn't name, their colors so vibrant, were growing in splendor in the morning sun.

Once inside, we were seated next to the window that faced the backyard of the restaurant. The owner had created a haven for the birds. Several humming bird feeders along the picture windows and bird feeders full of thistle for the finches, lined the area. Along the ground, large quantities of seed were scattered.

The feast and show was in full progress. On the ground were six chipmunks gorging themselves, cheek pouches bulging and scurrying back and forth between seeds and nests. Along with the chipmunks, were many native birds and one humongous jaybird. He looked like our common jay birds at home except he was solid blue, about twice the size and legs that looked like stilts.

As we ate our breakfast, the hummers came repeatedly back and forth to the feeders and were entertaining with their hovering and zooming. Breakfast was being served at the finch feeder too. Almost on every peg was a tiny yellow finch gobbling up the tiny black seeds. A bright yellow finch popped in for breakfast along with his mate. It was a fine breakfast for all, human, feathered, and furred creatures.

Back on the road, we headed for Mt. Rainier. We climbed over Chinook Pass and when we reached the summit, we looked back over the rim from where we had come. I hadn't realized we had climbed that far up. I got some pictures of the road we had climbed and saw the place in the road that had been reduced to one lane due to half of it being washed away. I was glad I wasn't going back down that way. But then I had no idea of what we were about to experience either.

There were different kinds of wild flowers growing up at this elevation and were bright pink and clinging to the rocks. All their little heads pointed directly towards the sun.

We crossed over the pass and headed toward one of the roads leading to the north side of Mt. Rainier. The road had a fair amount of frost heave and was very bumpy in spots. Up and up we climbed and I happened to look over to my left at the mountain above us and saw what I thought was a road cut through the mountain. I was hoping that wasn't the road we would be taking.

As it turned out it certainly was. It got down right scary. To make matters worse a park service employee was cutting down bushes on the mountainside and was slinging debris out onto the road. It really did smell good, just like at Christmas time. We climbed and climbed and climbed and the drop off got higher and higher. There were no guardrails at all, Ralph was hugging the centerline, and I was pretty much in the same place.

All of a sudden, we rounded a hairpin turn and right if front of us was Mt. Rainier. I gasped it was so big. It looked to me as if someone had dropped a fourteen thousand foot mountain right in front of my face. I was stunned at the sheer size of the mountain all covered in glaciers. We only got brief glimpses of the mountain as clouds kept moving in and covering the top. We saw portions of its magnitude but the little we did see was absolutely breath taking.

By the time we got to the top of the drive, Mt. Rainier was completely covered with clouds. We walked down a trail and waited a while to see if some of the clouds would blow away but to no avail. So, back down the mountain we went to try the other pass on the other side of the park. Up over more frost heave and torn up road, up and up we went. This road seemed to be steeper and have sharper drop offs too.

As we climbed, people would just come to a complete stop in the middle of the road. Most often people stop because wild life is present or they are just too lazy to pull off to take the picture. This particular instance, a huge camper came to a complete stop in front of us. As I rolled to a stop, I saw in the lane coming our way, a ptarmigan hen standing almost off the road but in it enough to be hit. I thought the camper was stopped to look at the bird. I considered screwing things up for them by going around them and forcing the bird to scurry off into the woods, when I saw a brown, golf ball size, baby with stick legs scurry from in front of the camper. The camper still didn't move and once again I was about to go around when another golf ball baby scurried across followed by four more. They were so cute and mama waited patiently for all her biddies to get across the road. Then they all hurried off into the bushes safe and sound.

Once again, we climbed to the summit of the road to the visitor's center and could see absolutely nothing, not even a hint, of the magnificent mountain. Frustrated once more, we headed back down. It was much scarier going down than going up. This time we were on the drop off side and both Ralph and I were hugging the centerline. I did have a few moments when the sphincter muscles got a bit concerned. I did sneak a peak every now and then over the edge and decided that wasn't such a good idea. I could only imagine how Ralph must have been feeling. If I was thinking it was scary, what was he thinking?

Safely back down in the valley we headed toward Mt. St. Helen. After bouncing around all day on frost heave roads, that really should be repaved, we decided to call it quits outside the little town of Randle, Washington. We found a very nice campground that bragged about having seven hundred campsites. I think that was accurate as this place was huge. We set up camp in the very back and we felt like we had the place to ourselves. I set up my cot, placed it directly in the sun, and stretched out on it. There in the wonderful late afternoon sun with a small breeze blowing, I swore I wasn't moving one muscle for the rest of the day. But of course, that didn't happen.

While doing the rotten laundry again in the campground laundry I dreamed of having another nice fire tonight. This campground is high on the list of another almost perfect place. This one is only missing the internet connection. For some reason Ralph's hay fever acted up immediately. So we won't be staying here longer than tonight. Darn.

On tomorrow to Mt. St. Helen and then to Hood River and hopefully find a campsite around Mt. Hood. I think that any mountain viewing from now on will have to be done from valley level. Ralph informed me that he was finished with high mountain drop offs. I can't say as I blame him.

I heard Grizzle Bear gasp a few times today, then some small whimpering from the back of the bike. Once back down in the valley he did enjoy the warm summer sun. Grizzle Bear does hate doing laundry and is on the verge of griping as I wait for the jeans to dry so we can go back to camp and the fire Ralph is going to build me.

So, until next time, love to all always,
Judy/Mom/Mommy

July 13, 2005
Wednesday
Zigzag, Oregon
Mile 12,229

Dear Folks,

Damned crows! They were the very first thing I heard this morning squawking right over the tent. Two caws, then three, then his buddy across the campsite answered him. It certainly seemed to me that just as soon as the rascal knew Ralph and I were awake, he moved on to the next occupied site. And of course, when we were fully awake, the campsite was completely silent.

I looked out the tent door only to find grey overcast skies. When there is something specific that we really want to see, it has been our luck the clouds move in making it impossible. Such it appeared would happen today.

We were about thirty miles from Mt. St. Helens. After getting a rather nice breakfast at a local diner at the turn off to the mountain, we met some other bikers in the parking lot. We chatted for a few moments and found out we were all headed toward Mt. St. Helen. One of the bikers said something that made me cringe and all my warning bells and whistles went off. He was bragging when he said to us, "Yeah, I'm going to straighten out some curves and flatten out some hills." Which I interpreted to mean that he was going to go too fast on the curves and hills ahead on the road to the mountain. He and his friends took off in a cloud of dust and Ralph and I waited a few extra minutes to give them a chance to get well ahead of us. I went through a mental checklist of my medical skills and the contents of my first aid kit.

The road wound, twisted, turned, and went up and down in elevation. Right through beautiful forest dark on both sides of the road we rode. Though this is now a popular tourist destination, the roads did not reflect the traffic.

We traveled through deep forest twisting and turning until we came to the turn off to Spirit Lake. The road went back about ten miles and at first I could see no evidence of where the volcano had erupted. About four miles in, we stopped at a viewing area. It was at this location, twenty-five years ago, that some of the best eruption pictures of Mt. St. Helen were taken. On a plaque set up at the viewing area, were the actual pictures that a tourist had taken. It was astounding. I couldn't imagine standing there at the exact moment the volcano erupted, capturing those photos, and then having to run to escape the three hundred mile an hour blast.

The blast area was visible but the mountain had actually blown more to the north than where we were standing. Vegetation was coming back and the wild flowers were prolific. The bright orange of the Indian paint brush combined with low lying purple flowers grew among white daisies and purple and white foxes gloves standing on stalks of three to four feet in height.

As we traveled deeper into blast area, the curves in the road became sharper. I slowed to take a particularly sharp turn. Suddenly, two bikers came flying around the curve from the opposite direction over the centerline in my lane. We missed each other by only several feet. Guess who the fools were? "I'm going to straighten out some curves and flatten out some hills," echoed in my brain. After my heart rate calmed somewhat, my colorful language kicked into overdrive.

Riding a little further, we started to see more of the devastation the blast had caused. We pulled into another viewpoint and immediately were attacked by a herd of chipmunks. Now, I don't know how many chipmunks make a heard but there were so many I couldn't count them. One came up to me immediately, right under my motorcycle and stood up on his hind legs like he was begging. His buddies were in quick pursuit. I know I am not suppose to feed these little beggars but obviously someone has been feeding them or they wouldn't come right up to me. I have a terrible time resisting the little creatures.

Having had one very nasty experience with a park ranger in Rocky National Park when the kids were younger, I was not so sure I should participate in the activity of feeding the chipmunks again. That was the first and only time in my life I was threatened with arrest and told quite in a belligerent manner that I was a poor example for my children. I had been totally humiliated and on the verge of tears as the kids scurried to pick up the popcorn they had tossed to the rodents and birds. But, this time, desire overcame the risk and looking over my shoulder for the man in tan and green I pulled out my new package of corn nuts and opened them.

It was Katie bar the door then. The little darlings would come right into my hand and stuff as much as they could carry into their cheek pouches, then scurry off to unload and come back for more. Upon seeing more corn nuts on the rock wall, the chipmunks fought with each other for cheek stuffing rights. One stuffed so many into his cheek pouches I thought they would burst and he kept looking at me for more. Fights were breaking out all up and down the rock wall as to who would get to the corn nuts first. I've seen humans act in a similar fashion.

Other people now got into the act and one little boy fed them shredded wheat with frosting. One man pulled out a large bag of sunflower seeds. I was quickly forgotten once the sunflower seeds appeared. Just as well, I wasn't interested in Mr. Ranger catching me. It was someone else's turn.

From this viewpoint, the volcano was visible enough to get a good idea of how large it once was and what is left of it now. The devastation was catastrophic, trees leveled like toothpicks and the remaining standing ones denuded of anything living. It has been twenty-five years since the eruption and the forest floor is green again with grasses and wild flowers. The fir trees are coming back along with some hardwoods. It is a painstakingly long process. After twenty-five years, there is still no forest in the blast zone but it will eventually come back.

We didn't make it all the way to Sprit Lake. There was too much cloud cover so we gave up. But before we turned around, the clouds parted very briefly at the top and we were able to see wisps of smoke and steam coming from the new cone. I wanted to see more but it just wasn't to be today. I made a promise to myself to someday return to the area and make it all the way to Spirit Lake.

We headed back down the mountain and continued on the road back to Hood River. The road we were on had no number markings. The roads were marked in grey on the map, which indicated a very small paved road. It was an absolutely inspiring road through thick forest of fir trees and wet moss on the ground. Deer and ptarmigan were seen along the way. What a very nice treat it was to ride this road.

Hardly any cars came in the opposite direction, except for the crazy bikers and no one followed us. We had our own private road through the woods.

We made our way back to Highway 14 that runs parallel to the Columbia River Gorge and turned east. We covered the same road as we had a few days ago coming into White Salmon to see William and Jody. The wind was atrocious, much stronger than a few days ago. I wasn't liking it at all. Each time we exited the tunnels we would be blasted by winds. This did not happen last time. They were short tunnels and I could easily see through to the other side. At one particular tunnel, I could see coming my way, a tractor-trailer fully loaded with logs. I knew that we would meet right in the middle of the tunnel. I tried slowing down some but that didn't help and sure enough, we met in the tunnel. I thought I was going to die right there.

Not only was I blasted by the wind from the truck but also by the wind racing up the gorge. It was a horrible experience! As much as that scared me it paled in comparison to the experience I just knew awaited me up ahead. In order to get to Hood River we had to cross the Columbia River on a long, narrow metal bridge. My blood pressure and anxiety were reaching maximum proportions. I could hear the blood thumping in my ears even above the roar of the wind.

Now, let me tell you, remember the wind surfers, and parachute surfers I told you about on this river? They were out if full force, armies of them. And, now, there were waves on this portion of the river. If it had been on the ocean, there would have been small craft warnings. The mighty wind was racing up the gorge causing the waves to crash up against the rock sides of the gorge.

The turn to the bridge was fast approaching and I was about to throw up because I knew we were going to be hit by some monstrous crosswinds. Prior to this, I only thought I had been over some scary bridges. The bridge was unquestionably the worst one I have ever been on in my entire life. It was an extremely narrow bridge and was not a paved but one made of metal grate. One look down and the Columbia River could be seen, waves and all. This is one time I did not look down. My neck was frozen in a straight-ahead fashion, just as if I were wearing a plastic cervical collar. The minute my front wheel went onto the bridge, I was smacked with extreme crosswinds. The bike went very, very squirrelly on the metal grate, wobbling back and forth. Traffic coming from the other side did not help at all and it was very close quarters.

I was following a camper and I swear, the right side of the camper was three inches from scraping the side of the bridge. Don't laugh, but I was so scared that I was chanting "I think I can, I think I can, I think I can" over and over and over, out loud, at the top of my lungs, as I crossed over the terrifying bridge. The closer I was blown into the on coming lane the louder I got. I was just praying that the camper in front of me would not stop. He considered it as he slowed down. Between the "I think I cans" and "please don't stops" I made it over the bridge. Just as my rear wheel touched pavement the camper in front of me stopped. I was in tears I was so relieved to get off that bridge. I swore then and there that I would never, never, never cross it again on my motorcycle.

Since the wedding in August will require crossing it, I will have to be blindfolded and go by car and maybe a dose of valium would be nice. It was horrible!

Right after the bridge, we stopped and got gas and the attendant told us he rode his horse over it. I was speechless and slack jawed as he told us his story. He said that the bridge had been closed off and about twenty riders got a galloping start so the horses wouldn't baulk as they all crossed over. He said the horses were not happy about it at all and the metal horseshoes on the metal grate of the bridge was a real trip. I almost threw up again just listening and imagining.

After my nerves settled somewhat, we found the public library where Elena worked and retrieved our mail that had been sent to her house. We sat in the library and finished some administrative things. As Ralph did some work, I looked out the window below and watched the wind surfers on the river. The ones with parachutes would become completely airborne over and over. Their colored parachutes of yellows and red bounced around in the mighty wind. That is one sport I have no desire to try. Watching is perfectly fine with me.

After our work was finished, we continued down the road toward Mt. Hood. Naturally, since this is one mountain that we hadn't expected to visit nor planned to, wouldn't you know the sky was perfectly clear of clouds. The mountain was stunning. In the valley below, that we traveled through, were miles and miles of fruit orchards. The area is conducive to growing fruit due to the volcanic effects on the soil. Rich green grass and farms were interspersed with the orchards creating a peaceful pastoral scene.

The road we traveled circled the volcano and we got a real close look at Mt. Hood. It was very, very beautiful and so unexpected. We had to travel a little out of our way to find a place to stay tonight. We are in an inexpensive motel in a town called Zigzag. We will have to back track for about sixteen miles in the morning but with any luck, we'll get another glimpse at Mt. Hood. Now just because we want to see it, it will be covered in clouds, you just watch.

Tomorrow we head for Crater Lake National Park. I remembered this place from the trip when I was eleven. I was impressed then, I hope I still will be.

Grizzle Bear had his claws out today clinging helplessly to the pack he rides on. I think I heard him chanting "me too, me too" in response to my "I think I cans" as we crossed over the Columbia River Bridge. Poor thing, I felt rather sorry for him. A few M&M's helped his attitude though.

We're heading south now, out of Washington, through Oregon and then into California. We have to find a place very soon to have new tires put on my bike. They are worn out after twelve thousand miles.

So until later, much love to all always,
Judy/Mom/Mommy

July 14, 2005
Thursday
Crater Lake National Park
Mile 12,465

Dear Folks,

What a glorious and surprising day we had today. We woke up to beautiful sunshine and not a cloud in the sky. We left our cozy motel room around nine in the morning with the idea that we were not going to hurry and just take our time getting to Crater Lake.

Our first stop, about a mile from the hotel to put oil in my bike, netted some interesting information from a local man. Since we would be backtracking about fifteen miles to get to the road to Crater Lake, the man told us of several turn out spots on our return trip that would be incredible to view Mt. Hood. The best view, he told us, would be from the boat dock at Trillium Lake Campground.

The boat dock was really one only the locals would have knowledge of as there was only a small sign pointing to the campground. After driving through the campground, we really wanted to stay there but we needed to find internet access and it wasn't available in Trillium Lake Campground. We did find the boat dock and as promised the view of Mt. Hood was incredible. A nice size lake was at the base of the Mt. Hood and the entire mountain hovered right over the lake reflecting its beauty in the dark water. Several canoes floated on the lake. I wanted to jump on board and paddle out too.

We talked to a fisherman, who was packing up his gear and found out that he had lived and worked in Alaska for years. When we told him that we had been to the Arctic Ocean on the Haul Road he laughed. He had been a crane operator during the construction phase of the oil fields at Prudhoe Bay. He had made many, many trips up and down the road over that period of time. The fisherman said that when the road was first completed it was smooth as a paved road and it was constantly maintained. However, when the road was opened to the public, maintenance was all but stopped. I know from personal experience that that is an accurate statement.

Back on the road to Crater Lake, we traveled through mountain roads surrounded on both sides with wonderful smelling fir forests. It was the perfect sort of day for motorcyclists. To me that is clear skies, dry roads, temperatures in the high sixties and low seventies and absolutely eye pleasing scenery. For a while, we would descend the mountains, riding around swooping curves only to do the reverse, ascending the next set of mountains. Sunlight peaked through the openings in the forest ceiling allowing the rays of sun to fall to the forest floor in shafts of yellow white light, lighting up green mosses and soft brown pine needles.

Every now and then, I would catch a glimpse of Mt. Hood fading in the distance in my rearview mirror. Though getting smaller, it was still a very big presence on the horizon. After traveling about seventy-five miles through this beautiful, cool alpine environment, the road straightened and emptied out onto a flat plateau. The flora changed also. The thick forest gave way to scrub pines and grasses. The pines became more sparse and the grass turned to straw color. Tumbleweed became more prevalent. Off to my right as far as I could see was a line of volcanoes all covered in snow. I counted at least eight but I know there were many more.

On my left as far as I could see, were small rounded hills with scrub pines and small stunted brush. The whole area around us looked to be right out of an old western. I expected to see John Wayne come riding up on his great horse with a tribe of Indians in full pursuit. We were actually riding across an Indian reservation, also. As we crossed the plateau, more and more volcanoes appeared on the horizon. Far in the distance, some of the Cascade Mountains were visible.

We came to the edge of the plateau and we started a decent into a huge canyon. The canyon had cut through layers upon layers of volcanic rock. I was very interested in seeing where the lava had flowed and cooled and where vents full of magma had cooled into hexagonal columns. Rivers of fossilized lava and volcanic ash covered the entire area. A nice green river flowed through the canyon and the road ran next to the river as we reached the canyon floor in Warm Springs, Oregon.

After climbing back up the other side of the canyon the area slopped into a valley that spread for hundreds of square miles covered in rich farmland. Orchards and crops filled the valley along with ranches. Sleek, shiny well-fed horses grazed in the rich green grass. Mares stood over foals stretched out in the warm afternoon sun. Recently harvested wheat now awaited the bailing of the straw. Lines of white buckets stacked up along the rows of fruit trees awaited the harvest of the fruit. It was a true pastoral scene if there ever was one.

As we left the valley, the temperature started to rise and I'm not talking just a little bit either. It was suddenly hot as Hades. Up until now, the road had been ours, the weather cool, the scenery outstanding but we hit some traffic around a good size town that seemed right in the middle of no where. Things really heated up then. All my riding gear suddenly seemed like a bad idea.

We stopped at a gas station, bought water, and poured it on us and inside our helmets. That did help considerably as we rode the last forty miles to Crater Lake. As we turned off the main highway onto the road leading to the north side of Crater Lake, the road was straight as an arrow for seventeen miles. The terrain in this area was pure volcanic ash and pumice. There were plenty of pine trees in the area but the land and air was very arid and hot.

Once we entered the park, we started another ascent to the rim of the extinct volcano. We were actually higher in elevation than we have been during any point so far on this trip. It didn't seem as high though because we were not surrounded by mountains. In Alaska, it seemed as if we were in high elevations due to the tall mountains around us. Most of the time in Alaska, we were at sea level looking up at the mountains, giving us the impression we were at higher elevations.

The road to the rim of Crater Lake wound through pumice deserts and fir trees. Quite a difference in the same place. There were still large patches of snow all around. The road had only been opened since mid-June.

I saw the rim up ahead and part of it looked like a dinosaur backbone jutting upward toward the blue sky. We pulled out onto the overlook and climbed off the bikes. Below us was the beautiful blue water of Crater Lake. I had been here when I was eleven and was impressed then. I was impressed as an adult too.

About seven thousand years ago, Mt. Mazama stood at twelve thousand feet. A huge eruption of cataclysmic proportions sent magma, lava and ash one hundred and fifty times greater than Mt. St. Helen did twenty-five years ago, every where. The ash covered much of the land that is now our United States and into Canada. The ash covering the area was five feet thick. After the explosion, the inside of Mt. Mazama was so weakened and having nothing to support it, the mountain top collapsed into itself forming a caldera. A smaller cone formed and eventually sealed everything off. It took roughly five hundred years for snow and rain to fill in what is now Crater Lake. It is a sealed ecosystem, no rivers or streams flow in or out. The lake maintains itself with just the rain and snow. The annual deposits of rain and snow equal the amount of evaporation each year resulting in very little change in water level. The lake is over one thousand, nine hundred feet deep in its deepest part. The blue is the bluest I have every seen in a lake.

My brain still sees the blue from when I was eleven and it is still the same blue. I took many pictures and one I took pointed directly down through the fir trees with the lake behind. The color was distorted and it looked like I had pointed the camera skyward instead of lake ward.

Ralph and I sat a while and people watched as we drank some cold water then we headed on to the campground on the south side of the lake. We found a really nice campsite in the trees. This national park actually has a shower, and a store but the internet is a problem. Since the weekend is coming, we are planning on staying here for a few days and resting a bit.

After setting up camp, it cooled down a little and we were looking forward to a little rest and reading time. We went to the camp store and bought grub for tonight and plenty of firewood.

Grizzle Bear is humming and happy tonight. He enjoyed beautiful scenery today, a bit on the hot side, but nothing to scare him. He's swinging happily in his hammock.

So until next time, love to all always,
Judy/Mom/Mommy

July 15, 2005
Friday
Crater Lake National Park
Mile 12,465

Dear Folks,

We has stereo babies whaling last night, one each side of us. One gave up after about an hour but the other one cried, moaned, and screamed for hours. The baby was very exhausted and dad had been left in charge while mama went to the ranger program in the campground. Dad just let the kid cry, much to the disturbance of the entire campground, all two hundred and fifteen campsites. Some people just need to be slapped and I am not talking about the baby. This campsite did not follow the camp quiet hours at all. After mama got back, the baby shut up immediately. I thought I heard applause through out the campground.

I slept like a log last night and as the light was just peeping into the campground, one tiny bird started cooing. She sounded like a pigeon cooing. Such a nice gentle way to welcome the morning I was thinking, when the baby started screaming again and his big brother got into the act and egged him on. Then dad imitated both boys adding to the shock of breaking the wonderful silence of the morning and cooing birds. Like I said, some people need to be slapped and I'm not talking about the kids.

We lazed around in the tent, as we had no destination today. It was to be a day of rest and relaxation. The campground finally emptied out around ten and we were practically alone. After eating our breakfast of Fruit Loops, we sat around in the shade and read a while. Knowing that we wouldn't have to wait in line for the shower we headed off to the other side of the campground. It was locked up tight. The power company was working on the electrical box in front of the showers and everything was shut down.

I trudged back to the campsite, sat some more, read some more and swatted flies and mosquitoes. I think that our campsite is on the flight path for all flying bugs and beast. Flies of gargantuan proportions buzzed through the campsite and all of them had to take a detour to check out both of us. They were so loud it sounded like a sport bike racing down the highway. The flies were super annoying along with the buzzing mosquitoes. Poor Ralph had not slept well and he was beside himself with sleepiness. He pulled his Therm-a-rest out of the tent, as it was too hot inside and placed it up under the tree in the shade.

One fly drove him bezerk, until Ralph gave up and went back to see if the shower had been unlocked. It was and we both headed back to the shower. I think an entire hatching of mosquitoes were in my shower stall. Fortunately, they stayed in the ceiling and I hurried through my shower.

Returning to the campsite, nice and clean, I debated spraying myself with Deet. The bugs were annoying. I decided to swat for a while, as I wanted to smell of soap instead of bug spray just a little while longer.

We went back to the camp store and bought makings for lunch and dinner. Lunch was tasty and immediately after lunch, around two P.M., I got sleepy myself. With very heavy eyelids, I watched the camp animals making the rounds of everyone's campsites looking for food that had been left out. I watched one cute chipmunk hauling off something that was as big as he was. Then he came back and hauled off the same thing again. I never figured out what it was the chipmunk was hauling, but he would be if fat city for a few days.

Then the birds came through looking for a tasty morsel. They did not find anything at our campsite. We were stingy today.

One thing of note that gave me the willies. There was a notice when we checked in yesterday that said that bears were in the camp and to be sure to put up all food items, etc. This was the same warning we have been seeing for weeks and we have been very careful to follow these rules. I don't want any bears other than Grizzle Bear in my tent looking for treats. As we were riding through the campground looking for our site, I kept noticing large, brown, metal boxes on legs in each campsite. They are bear boxes! Now what does that tell you? Everything that we had that remotely resembled food, including the bubble gum and mints I have in my tank bag, was put into that bear box last night!

Poor Ralph doesn't do sitting around doing nothing very well and he had the hee-bee, gee-bees bad today. Between being bored, swatting flies, being hot and terribly sleepy he was almost beside himself. So, even though we had planned to stay here until Sunday, we are going to leave tomorrow and head for the California coast. Riding the bikes provides such entertainment that when we sit for more than twenty-four hours, we start to get bored. Our tight budget does not allow for expenditures of tourist entertainment, such as raft trips, flight seeing excursions, etc.

As late afternoon approached, I moved into the tent to read and fell into one of those sleeps that is half way between actual sleep and being awake. I could hear people returning to the campground after being out all day but I couldn't quite open my eyes. It was a lovely feeling.

New campers had moved into the site next to ours and the family provided the evening's entertainment. Mom and Dad pulled out a bright blue tarp the size of a baseball field that blinded me inside our tent. I got up then, and came outside to join Ralph and to watch our new neighbors. Next came the tent, brand new, right out of the box. While mom held and read the directions, dad and the two girls attempted to put up the tent. Mom could be heard saying, "insert peg A into yellow slot B, then red tab into black pole C." It went on like this until the nylon home was erected. I was cracking up watching them. The tent turned out to be the size of the Taj Mahal, with four rooms, one for each camper.

After the tent was erected and the hoisting crane removed, mom held up a piece of nylon tent and said to dad, "What's this for?" There was no answer. I think that piece got stuffed back into the box. Then the campers ate dinner, which mom had been cooking while the rest of the family loaded up the tent with suitcases and sleeping bags and blew up the air mattresses with an electric pump.

Now, keep in mind, that the entire time all this activity was going on, the door to the tent was wide open. And just what do you guess was making a new home within the confines of the new Taj Mahal? Yep, you guessed it, the hungry mosquitoes, and other wild, flying insects.

Dad, upon finding out new residents had moved in, went about committing multiple murder. Wop, wap, swat, pop could be heard over in our campsite and the ceiling and sides of the tent went in and out, up and down, as dad killed the mosquitoes. This activity went on for quite a while, then I heard dad say, "Dear, I think you are going to have to get the broom and sweep up all the dead bugs." I heard her reply, "The broom is right outside the tent, dear." I didn't watch to see who actually cleaned up the dead bodies, but I did hear one of the young girls say she was sleeping outside tonight. Dad politely reminded her that there were more bugs outside the tent than in.

Then it was time for our new neighbors to start a fire. I don't know what they put on the fire but within minutes the flames were five feet high. Mom says to Dad, "That's a real nice fire, Hun." I'll say! I think they threw pine needles on it to get it started. It flashed up fiercely like gasoline but died down quickly and before long they were roasting marshmallows followed shortly thereafter with a game of Uno.

I know I'm poking fun at this family but they were really entertaining. I will say in their defense that they were a very nice family, having a delightful time, sharing some wonderful memories. Everyone was getting along; there were no cross words exchanged. They were a charming family having a special time. They will always remember their camping experience at Crater Lake. More people should take a lesson from this family.

As for us, we're off to the beach tomorrow. As one Harley rider we met at the rim yesterday informed us, "It's going to be cold on the beach, probably in the sixties." Oh, my I don't think I can handle the sixties, do you?

So until then, love to all always,
Judy/Mom/Mommy

July 17, 2005
Sunday
Klamath, California
Mile 12,669

Dear Folks,

What another surprising and astonishing day we had yesterday. We left the campground at Crater Lake and stopped by the gas station in the park to fill up before our journey to the coast. As we pulled up to the pump, I noticed a popping sound. I looked around and down to see if I could locate the noise and was totally grossed out. There were hundreds of moths the size of golf balls everywhere. They covered the pump, the lampposts, and the ground and when a car would pull up to the pump and run over them, the moths would make a nasty popping noise. I was just waiting for one to fly in my face or into my jacket or up my pants leg. I couldn't get out of there fast enough.

We left the park through a forest of fir trees standing tall on each side of the road. As we came around a curve in the road I noticed what I thought was a rabbit in the road that had been run over. As I got closer and moved over in the lane to avoid it, it wasn't a rabbit at all but Bambi, dead in the middle of the road. It was a young fawn, still tiny, but whoever hit it had to have known. They could have at least gotten it out of the road. No one likes to see animals run over but it is the death of the babies that saddens more.

We traveled on through the dark, cool forest and I imagined the friends of Bambi running through the forest. Suddenly, it was just as if the forest ended and valleys and farmland immediately took its place. I was reminded of coming out of a tunnel and into the sunlight. Along with the sun light, came the heat. The sun warmed the valley where sleek horses of every color and marking possible, grazed or dozed in the sun. Where there was not a pasture, there would be farms and orchards.

While passing a farm on my left, I noticed that in one side yard of the farmhouse, about six sprinklers going full blast. In the spray of the sprinklers was a flock of Canada Geese, bathing with wings out spread and flapping.

By now, the temperature had climbed to ninety-three degrees and my head was getting hot in the helmet. I had already given up the riding pants and was considering the jacket but knew that would be a mistake. But heat, for me, is more dangerous than riding without full gear. I have a tendency toward heat related problems.

We came to a little town that boasted that they had the best burgers around. The hamburger joint looked like a hole in the wall and from experience, I know that these are usually the best places to eat. Sure enough, the burgers were great and after stuffing our faces with juicy burgers and hot French fries, we climbed back on the hot bikes and headed toward the Pacific Ocean.

As we approached a set of mountains that we had to cross before getting to the ocean, there was a noticeable drop in temperature. Thank goodness. We followed an emerald green stream for many miles. I could see the round rocks in the clear green, riverbed as we traveled along. The road became very curvy and the river deeper and the gorge it cut, steeper. I could tell we were getting closer to the ocean. Suddenly, we were in the middle of the Redwood National Park. I had forgotten how big these trees were.

I couldn't crane my neck up high enough to see the tops. Giants in height and in girth the trees were. Monster, all of them, tall and majestic and I was ant size in comparison to them. The Redwoods have been around for hundreds of years. They range in age from seedlings to two thousand years old! That is not a typo. Two thousand years old! The bark alone is over a foot thick.

The sun trickled down through the canopy, leaving a light, yellow-green path to the forest floor. I could imagine fairies with gossamer wings basking in the spots of yellow warmth on the pine needles. Maybe there were unicorns hiding there too. This was a magical forest. It breathed, it had a life force all its own. I wanted to stay, wait, and watch.

Just as quickly as we entered the forest, we came out the other side right at the ocean at Crescent City. The temperature took another nosedive and we were back to temperatures in the sixties. Just a little earlier I had wet my shirt with water from a water fountain at the visitors center and you guessed it, I was now cold.

We couldn't see the ocean due to heavy, thick fog. I couldn't believe it; we had just been in clear blue skies and were now in unbelievable fog. That is what happens here during the summer. We traveled down the coast for a few miles and the road started to climb. The feeling was a very eerie one to be looking down over the edge, when we knew the ocean was below, and seeing nothing but thick, white, fog and looking straight up over us and seeing clear blue sky. Ralph compared it to being in a plane with the clouds below us and the clear sky above.

Just briefly did I get a quick glimpse of the ocean and it was a beautiful blue but then the fog moved in again. In a heartbeat, the ocean disappeared and that was all I saw for the day. At the visitor's center earlier, we had gotten a flyer with local campgrounds in the area. All the national park campgrounds were full so we were looking for other choices. I looked down the list and found one that had internet and showers. A call ahead to the campground reserved a spot for us and we headed toward the place about forty-five minutes down the road.

We crossed a large river, turned down the road that the campground was on, and entered beautiful woods of tall aspens and fir trees. The road followed the Klamath river and about two miles back in the woods, was the campground. It was absolutely beautiful. All the campsites were in grassy areas nestled in the towering trees.

Since it was Saturday night there was a cookout to take place and live music to go with it. How in the world did we stumble onto this place? We quickly set up camp, got organized, and waited until it was time for the cookout. If we had stayed in Crater Lake as originally planned we would have missed the cookout.

Dinner of barbequed chicken or grilled salmon, rice, salad, and grilled vegetables was served and all the campers gathered around picnic tables to enjoy the feast. A couple from Oakland, CA joined us at our table and we carried on a conversation that lasted most of the evening. They were both so nice and interesting and I would have loved to spend more time with them but they were going back home in the morning.

The music consisted of two men, one who played the guitar and harmonica and the other played a slide guitar and the harmonica.

They played mostly blues but some country also. After dinner, a big roaring bon fire was built and everyone roasted marshmallows. Once the men started repeating their songs, we headed back to our tent for the night.

What a lovely day and what a fantastic evening we had. We couldn't believe our good fortune at having found this place. We had finally found the perfect campground. We had a great campsite, showers, internet connection, a laundry not far from here and a new area to investigate.

Sometime in the middle of the night, some rustling on the picnic table awakened me. I had forgotten and left the little cooler on the picnic table and Mr. Raccoon was desperately trying to get inside it. There were chips, pound cake, and hot dogs in the cooler. I was afraid he would tear it up so I woke up Ralph. He went outside in the pitch black with his head light on to get the cooler. All he could see were eyes shining in the darkness. When the glowing eyes levitated several inches in height, Ralph tried to scare him off but the eyes would not budge. Ralph peeing in the bushes did the trick, however.

The raccoon disturbed the entire campground, going from one to another. I could tell where every dog was in the campground because they went absolutely into a frenzy, growling and barking. Owners yelling at their dogs to shut up followed the growls and barks.

Things finally settled down again, the moisture from the forest dripped onto the tent, and it sounded like it was raining. There was no rain but it sure sounded like a lullaby in our little green tent tucked up in the deep, green canopy of the redwood forest.

So ended another wonderful day full of beauty and surprises, new friends and new experiences.

We like this place so much we are going to stay here a few days. We are going to ride around and explore the redwood forest and Ralph might just try his hand at fishing. They rent poles here and the campground is right on the river where it meets the ocean. Maybe if he gets lucky and catches something I might have to break down and grill him some fish. But we'll see.

So until next time, much love to all always,
Judy/Mom/Mommy

July 18, 2005
Monday
Klamath, CA
Mile 12,750

Dear Folks,

Yesterday morning we were awakened to the sound of tiny birds and dripping trees sending pattering water down on the tent. The campground had settled back down after the raccoon had disturbed the place and everyone was rather late getting up. The quiet of the campground changed quickly and human noises replaced those of the woods. Tent stakes were being tossed carelessly on the ground, car doors slamming, people clanging pots and pans readying breakfast and diesel engines were starting up and making efforts to pull away the huge trailers.

Our plan for the day included just hanging around the campground, getting some necessary administrative things done and then go exploring. The road behind the campground was part of the national park and it led to the beach.

After driving back into town for some breakfast, we filled up the tanks and went to the grocery store. Since we were going to be in one place for a while, I was planning to cook out over the open fire for a change. Back at camp, we got all the administrative things done. By then it was late afternoon but we still road the few miles on the tiny scenic road to the ocean. We parked the bikes on a little strip of gravel and started walking to the shoreline. The hike took us around a small lagoon, over rocks covered with seaweed, up over a hill of sand and driftwood and then down to the mighty Pacific Ocean.

The beach met a very deserted piece of wild ocean. Many full, tree size, driftwood littered the beach along with weathered and worn smaller pieces. The sand was a dark grey, not like our white sand beaches of Florida. The beach had once been rocks but they had worn down to sand by the crashing waves, ocean storms and the passing of time. The extra large size waves crashed with fury against the shore. This was not a place to go swimming or even stick my feet in. I would be scared of being sucked immediately way out to sea. The pungent aroma of salt sea air was strong but I liked the smell.

We sat for a while on pieces of driftwood, watched the tremendous waves crash into the shore in a pattern, rolling on down the beach at an angle, and hurtle with fury against large rocks jutting out in the water, sending a white spray many feet above the rocks. The roar of the ocean was loud. The waves did not come rolling in from long way out but curled quickly and crashed right at the shoreline. Big white, frothy, mad waves pounded the rocks and sand.

Brown pelicans glided in the currents directly above the waves making flight look effortless. I didn't see but a few seagulls. I think this stretch of beach was a bit too rough for them. There were not enough handouts from man either.

We made our way back toward the bikes and as we got closer, we took a different trail back that led us up a hill to a flat area with some wooden structures. Two small wooden structures of old weathered wood were standing next to each other. They looked to be ancestral and the workmanship of another time. The wood had been notched and supporting beams were held together with vine twisted around and around making the structures extremely sturdy. We walked a little further and came to an area of wooden benches layered in tiers and in a semicircle. In the center was a hole with a fire pit. Ralph and I wondered just exactly what this place was and I jokingly said it was a spiritual location and I expected ghosts in long white robes to pop up on the seats.

Feeling somewhat that we had stepped onto sacred ground, I wanted to leave quickly. As we left the place I saw a tiny sign put up by the park service. We were on Indian spiritual grounds and respect of the area was appreciated. Now that was just too spooky. We certainly had been respectful, only curious, but had no idea it was an actual Indian spiritual site.

We got back on the bikes and continued on the road that turned into a very narrow, winding gravel road that went to the top of a long overlook, one that looked far out to sea and a long drop off to the water. Just below us was what looked like an old weathered farmhouse. That was just a disguise however. It was really a radar lookout during World War II and the farmhouse was just to fool the enemy.

Back on pavement, we returned to camp and I cooked big fat, juicy steaks, mushrooms, and an invented rice and corn dish. Oh, boy it was so good. Ralph licked his plate and we threw the left over pieces of fat into the fire smelling up the whole campground, but good. I just love doing that except when I'm the one doing the smelling and not the eating.

After it got dark, we walked up behind the camp store to a huge field the size of a football field. We stood for a while looking for stars and found a heaven full. We watched for shooting stars but only saw a satellite. In Crater Lake, I had seen a beautiful shooting star. I was coming back from a last trip to the potty for the night when I just happened to look up to see if I could see any stars. Across the arch of space, from my right, completely over to my left, came a shooting star of bright yellow. I thought someone had set off a bottle rocket. I knew I wasn't the only one to see it as some guy on the other side of the campground exclaimed the same as I did.

Anyway, I was hoping to see another one since this was such a wide-open space and many, many stars. No such luck, but the evening was wonderful and the stars were bright. Back at camp, we readied for bed. It was so dark and since our headlamps were in the tent, we were almost feeling our way around in the dark. Suddenly, we heard a sound towards the back of the campground. Both of us at the same time said, "What was that?" The sound got louder and closer. It was not a human sound at all. At first, I thought it was some sort of bird, an osprey, or bird of prey. It was loud and getting closer to our tent by the moment.

Then the sound became a combination of a high-pitched bark and a screech. I couldn't even begin to identify it and I was getting a little concerned. Then I remembered the woman, who runs the campground, telling us about the fox family that she had been feeding. There was a mother and two kits, she said, but the mother had stopped coming by. The two kits were still showing up nightly for dinner. That is when I realized that it was one of the kits calling for the other. He called and called but there was no answer.

As he headed past our tent, we followed his calling on the gravel road in the campground and when we were just about at the office,

I saw him over in a grassy area. I couldn't make out any details, just a shape, but being able to identify the horrible noise that little thing made, gave me a sigh of relief. I thought some big bad, ugly, drool slobbering, monster of the woods was coming for me. But it was only a baby fox.

Instead of the raccoon, we had the other night at our picnic table just a few feet from out tent, I think it was the fox instead. Feeling rather sorry for the poor thing, this night, we prepared and left him four hotdogs on a plate at the table for him. Just in case.

Once again, the forest dripped through the night. It sounded so peaceful. I guess the moisture coming off the river and ocean collects in the heavy woods and then it drips and falls to the earth during the night and early morning. By about nine A.M., the dripping stopped and a clear blue sky peeks through the canopy.

The campground was very quiet this morning as it was Monday and most everyone had left on Sunday. Only the sound of the birds and dripping forest could be heard. What a lovely way to wake up. I lazed around in my sleeping bag for about an hour before I finally got up. I fixed bacon and eggs for breakfast. Nothing smells better than frying bacon around a campsite. Mmmm.

After cleaning up the breakfast dishes, which is a real trick given that I have no sink, we had to ride back into the town of Crescent City. The phone had no connection here in the campground and the e-mail server was having issues. We had to get back to an area where there was service. Ralph also had to find a place to buy tires for my bike. After all that was accomplished it was around three in the afternoon and there were parts of the park I still wanted to see.

Today I found ET's forest. A narrow road branched off the main road and we entered a place of mystery and magic. Dark and cool the forest was. Redwoods big, fat, and tall stood as guides down the road. When the sunlight was able to shine down it was the color of yellow honey and each place it hit the forest floor or a tree or ferns the sun was a spotlight on that area. In the lemon shafts of light, dust and haze lit up like powdered glitter and sparkled in the light.

I expected ET to come out of the forest at any moment. This was his place, his landing place, his place where his mother ship reclaimed him. I did not see ET or his Reese's Pieces but I did smell something that reminded me of buttery, toffee popcorn. It was not a manmade smell. It was of the forest.

We took several hikes and walked among the tall Redwoods. Pictures can't capture their size, their height, or their diameter. To walk among these giants I got the feeling of being just a fleeting moment in their time. Some of the trees we walked below were eight to nine hundred years old. Can you even begin to imagine what was going on in that forest nine hundred years ago? They were just seedlings then. What did the area look like? What animals roamed the land? Were the seedlings mere inches in size below other giants? Had other giants fallen and rotted away in the moist air.

When we stopped and listened to the forest, it was silent. So many secrets these trees could tell. But they won't. I felt so lucky to have had an opportunity to walk among greatness.

Back at camp, the breadcrumbs I had thrown out earlier were completely cleaned up. The loud raucous jays carried off the big pieces and the little, sparrow type birds got the little pieces. One little bird made a circle hopping around the tent and then back to the bushes around the campsite. He was so darling, all brown with lighter, brown speckles on a white breast and absolutely no tail. I don't know what happened to his tail but he seems to be making out ok. I've fed him enough in the last two days to keep him surviving until his tail grows back.

Its pitch black now, we have a nice fire going and I'm just waiting for the call of the baby fox to start. At least tonight I won't be half-scared out of my skin at the sound. I feel sorry for the little lone fox. We have left the remaining bacon and left over chicken at the edge of the campsite for him. I'm sure it will be gone in the morning, as were the hotdogs this morning. We never even heard him get those dogs last night he was so silent.

Grizzle Bear has had a nice rest in the hammock in the tent. He's ready to get back on the road tomorrow. He just doesn't know that we're heading straight for the heat. I'll keep that one a secret and let him find out on his own. I don't need any unnecessary complaining now do I?

We're heading for Sacramento tomorrow for new tires. We will be going down Route 1, down the Pacific Coast Highway.

Oh my God. I just had the crap scared out of me. Something in the bushes just came within two feet of me, right behind me! I had my back to the woods and was facing the fire. I don't know who scared whom worse. I wasn't expecting the fox so early! And of course Ralph is down taking a shower and I'm here alone in the dark with only the light of this computer screen and the fire. I still have goose bumps. Where is a flashlight when I need one? My heart rate has slowed some and I can see Ralph coming. Sometimes I really hate the dark.

Well, I now know what was in the bushes. It was a damned raccoon! Ralph is back from the shower and I have moved to the other side of the campfire with my back facing the tent. I can see his little white stripe across his face. He is not at all afraid of us either. As I speak he is carrying off the bacon and I can hear him smacking as he eats. Well, at least I know what scared me so bad and fortunately, I like raccoons.

All is calm now so I'll say goodnight.

So until next time, love to all always,
Judy/Mom/Mommy

July 19, 2005
Tuesday
Sacramento, CA
Mile 13,170

Dear Folks,

I had a very restless night last night. The raccoon kept coming to visit over and over. I had left the little cooler on the picnic table again last night as it only contained melted ice. I could hear the raccoon drinking out of the cooler. Then the forest would get quiet but he came back several times. On one of those times, he either brushed up against the tent or was nosing around where I had stored a bag full of chips and other goodies. The bag was right by my head and when the raccoon nudged the tent, I gasped out loud. That woke Ralph up and I think our talking ran the varmint off for good. But it was one of those nights that I just couldn't sleep very well and I knew I would be tired in the morning for our long day's ride.

Sure enough, I was tired this morning but at seven we were up and packing our gear. Stumpy, the tailless sparrow, was already hopping around looking for breakfast so I helped him out by throwing the crumbs of the Fritos and the soft tortillas out into the woods for him. I watched for a moment as he and his friends pecked away and had their breakfast.

We were on the road by eight-fifteen. I hated to leave our wonderful campsite in the woods by the ocean. Who knows, maybe someday we can return, but not likely. The sky had not cleared yet and the woods were still dripping and damp.

Today was a day of many sites and different experiences. As we left the camp and traveled south down Route 101, the fog sent long, white, solid fingers into the land. One minute we would be in sunshine and the next in pure white, thick fog. The fog was trying to race, in spots, back to the sea as the sun was trying to hurry it along. The air was cold too and I was glad I had on all my riding gear. I was wishing I had on the liner to my jacket too. We stopped for a very quick breakfast in Eureka. I grabbed my liner to my jacket. Boy did it feel good.

The road headed inland, the fog disappeared, and the sun's warmth grew stronger. When we reached Route 1 we headed directly back to the ocean. We wanted to ride down the Pacific Coast Highway and this was the route to the sea. It was actually hot now but I knew that the closer we got to the ocean, the cooler it would be. The sun was so hot, I had to stop and remove the liner again and open up all the vents in the jacket once again.

The road leading over to the ocean was full of twistys and wound its way through deep dark forests of tall ancient redwoods. There were no straight parts to this road at all. Almost thirty miles of curves up and down the mountains that were a barrier to the inland, separated us from the ocean. As predicted, the air got cooler and cooler and more fog and moisture was apparent.

We finally wound out onto the edge of the cliff and below us was the Pacific Ocean, which was cloudy and foggy, but beautiful, never the less. The road was very narrow and extremely curvy and the drop offs into the water very steep and just a few feet away from the road. At the first opportunity I pulled off into a "vista viewing" area and got a good look at the ocean and the mountains and cliffs.

Far out in the surf there were many large rocks, some the size of cars, some the size of houses and some the size of large buildings. Mother Nature had been very busy pounding down these rocks and I knew that someday the very spot I was standing would be under salt water. The smell of ocean water was very strong.

Once again, I pulled out my jacket liner and put it on under my jacket. Now that I was warm again, we set off down the coast hoping to watch the ocean as we drove south. This road was also twisty and the curves were very sharp in places and the drop offs were rather impressive also. The air was so full of moisture and fog that I got a salt water facial as we rode down the road.

There were many lovely houses along the road set up right along the cliff line. Some day those houses will be in the ocean. The little towns we went through had the look of seaport towns and had kept the look of a time, long gone. There were ranches along the way with acres of land set aside for the grazing cattle.

On a small stretch of road, a particular kind of evergreen that was short and squatty had created a dark tunnel for us to go through. Dampness, fog, and water droplets clung to most everything. All the wood fences and most of the coastal houses were dark grey with the weathering of the harsh Pacific air. Lichens and moss clung to the fences along the road. The eucalyptus trees stood tall in groves and along the road. They looked barkless, their trunks sleek and smooth. Cemeteries along the roadside looked spooky with the fog floating through the headstones and the surrounding fences.

The road did not stay on the ocean and for periods of time, we couldn't see the ocean and the cliffs at all. The road continued to twist and turn and by now was getting a little old. While I really enjoyed the smell of the ocean, the sound of the pounding surf and the black rocks and cliffs, the road was starting to take its toll on my muscles with all the twisting and turning. So we decided to cut the trip down Route 1 a bit short and cut over toward Sacramento sooner than we had planned.

Wouldn't you know it, the road we took back over the low mountains, was also twisty. This road led us through a surprise, another grove of redwoods. I have decided that I really love riding through the forest of redwoods. I love the stately manner of these trees. I respect what they surely endured to reach the age they are. I love the smell of the forest all damp and earthy. I love the way the sun lights up spots, sending their yellow swords of light to the forest floor, lighting up ferns and bits of brown earth. I love the way the sun makes the earth smell in the forest. I love the semidarkness of the woods and the way it makes my imagination work overtime thinking about all the forest animals living in their nests and homes in the tall woods. Yes, I think the redwood forests have become one of my favorite things.

Just as suddenly as we entered the redwood forest, we exited the other side into the heat and a hilly, twisty road. The land became parched, grasses along the road and surrounding hills turned tan in color. The road stayed very narrow and with so many curves, I thought I would scream. I had had quite enough of the curves. We finally stopped for lunch and once again, I had to get rid of the liner in my jacket. By now, it was at least ninety degrees of hot, blast furnace air. We had been back and forth several times already between sixty degree, wet, cool air and ninety degree blast furnace.

Our easterly route took us through another surprise, one that neither Ralph nor I expected or had experienced before. The narrow road took us past vineyards and wineries. Miles and miles and hills upon hills of bright green, grape vines basked in the hot California sunshine. The road continued to be very narrow and twisty. I thought I would scream if we didn't get out of the winding roads. But that was not to be today.

We rode through vineyards, up over large hills covered in grape vines, back down into valleys of green, twisting all the way. We rode through Sonoma Valley and Napa Valley all full of grape vines, all soaking up the heat and sun. I thought when we reached this valley the road would straighten out but no, the road would twist and turn around the grape fields making such sharp turns that we would have to slow to ten miles per hour in some areas. It was unbelievable how many curves we went around.

While riding through Napa Valley, we rode directly between the big wineries that everyone is familiar with. One thing that I found interesting was that every vineyard, big or small had a beautiful house commanding its presence among the grape vines. These houses were outstanding. Most were a Victorian style house, several stories with porches around the front. Some were of a Spanish flavor, some Italian, but all I would have moved into immediately.

It looked as if we were leaving the grape fields behind as we entered a canyon. Yellow hills interspersed with grapevines, gave way to brown hills and rock out copings. The road, as typical of the day, twisted around rocks faces and drop offs. We climbed in elevation then suddenly off to the left was a brilliant, grass green lake. The lake was in the middle of no where right in the middle of the rough landscape. The lake had been created by a damn of sizeable proportion. I didn't notice the dam as I was totally exhausted and every muscle hurt from all the twisting and turning. Ralph pointed it out to me later.

A small brush fire had started on the lake side of the road and the smoke filtered across the road. The fire crackled and spread. In the kind of heat and dryness we were experiencing it wouldn't take long for the small fire to become bigger. I noticed that someone official looking was standing next to the fire. He had a radio in his hand. As we traveled another mile or so up the road, I think the whole county had come out to the rescue. There were at least four engines all hauling our way toward the fire. I'm sure that force of firefighters and equipment could easily contain the small brush fire.

Finally, finally, we hit a straight stretch of road and made it to a small town located on the interstate. We were within fifty miles of Sacramento, our destination for the night. We drove the rest of the way on the interstate and found a hotel about one mile from where my tires will be replaced in the morning.

I was so terrified of riding the fast moving interstate that when we finally got off in front of the hotel and I removed my gloves, I had large red spots on my hands from grasping the handles so tightly. They didn't go away even after a couple hours. I really hate riding the interstates and they are avoided most of the time. But this was the only way to reach the destination of the tire place.

Of the four hundred and twenty miles we rode today only fifty were actually on a straight road. The rest was nothing but twisting and turning. Every muscle and joint screamed with protest. I told Ralph it was like riding a horse for the first time in ten years and being reminded of all those muscles that had not been used.

I was so dog gone tired that, dinner, across the street from the hotel didn't even sound appealing. Ralph gobbled down ribs and French fries and I had a bowl of soup.

Ralph and I made a deal tonight. He would take care of getting the tires done in the morning and I would take care of getting the nasty, dirty clothes washed. How lucky for me that the hotel has washing machines on the next floor.

What a wonderful day we had today in spite of its length and twisty road. Now I'm off to bed in nice clean sheets. Grizzle Bear is not speaking to me tonight. He's plum worn out and sea sick from all the winding roads. Poor bear.

So, until next time, love to all always,
Judy/Mom/Mommy

July 20, 2005
Wednesday
Sonora, CA
Mile 13,252

Dear Folks,

Though today ended on a good note, it was one of those wheels spinning, frustrating days that just sometimes happens. Ralph got up and took my bike to the shop to get the tires replaced and the oil changed. He was there by nine and I was on the floor below ours starting the laundry.

Ralph was back by about twelve-thirty and mad to boot. I was still doing laundry as there was only one washer and one dryer in the hotel and the dryer was not working very well. Doing the laundry was taking way too long. The man at the motorcycle shop tried to sell Ralph a bill of goods on other things he supposedly kept finding wrong with my bike. Fortunately, Ralph was aware of what he was trying to do but the final straw was when my speedometer/odometer cable "rusted through or broke" so the man said. Of course, they didn't have a new one in stock. The mechanic was trying to get Ralph to agree to some major repair work. The cable "breaking" was just the last straw.

After Ralph told me this story, I'm mad as a hornet. So my bike has been messed with, the laundry is still not done, and its one hundred and ten degrees outside and it's two in the afternoon.

We walked across the parking lot and got some lunch at the diner while my last load was drying. After lunch, Ralph was touching base with some clients while I went to check on the last of the laundry. Someone had moved my wet clothes out of the dryer and put theirs in the dryer. Oooh, I was angry. So now, I had to wait on their clothes to dry. So back downstairs, I went and made several more trips back and forth until finally I was able to finish drying clothes. It was four by the time everything was dry and we packed the bikes.

I was ready to leave Sacramento but really dreading the heat. Once on the bike I realized that the man at the shop had adjusted my clutch and I was really having trouble letting the clutch out. That was just the final straw. I have been driving my bike for seven years with the clutch the same way and for someone to go mess with things when I didn't even ask for it to be done just sent me over the edge. It was so very hot, dangerously so, but we wanted to put a few miles behind us and get on down the road to Yosemite.

The road out of Sacramento was through some of the hottest land I have been through. It was hilly but dry, dry, dry. All the grass was parched and yellow and if I didn't know better I would swear we were riding through a desert. My eyeballs felt like they were melting Jell-O and I was starting to sweat badly. Even on the back road out of town, I think we hit the afternoon traffic. The going was a snails pace but after about twenty minutes, the traffic cleared and we were able to pick up some speed. I had no earthly idea how fast I was going since the broken cable stopped the speedometer but I kept pace with the car in front of me and that seemed to work out for today.

We had to stop in a little town and pour water all over us. Ralph has started carrying a gallon water jug and we pulled it out and soaked heads, helmets, and ourselves. It really does help but the heat coming off the black asphalt, the engine, and the extreme heat just in the air is enough to bake our brains and have them simmering in their own juices within our skulls.

We set out goal for Sonora, a small town on the map about half way to Yosemite. We had no idea what the town held for us, it was just a spot on the map as far as we were concerned. Before arriving in Sonora, we passed through Sutter's Creek and Angel Camp. These were perfectly charming towns with the road we were on riding right through main street. These towns were gold rush towns and the street fronts were all maintained in the era they were built. I could clearly imagine gold miners walking the streets, stopping by the local saloon or maybe the local hotel.

Our route also took us through Calaveras County. The setting for Mark Twain's story of the jumping frog took place here. There was a marker for his cabin but I was unable to see it from the road.

The road continued through the hot land all yellow with parched grasses and a speckling of trees here and there. Then after about fifteen miles, we would come to another one of the towns started during the gold rush. I would have liked to investigate each and every one of them.

We finally reached Sonora after only traveling eighty-five miles but it had seemed like further after traveling in one hundred and ten degree heat. Sonora is also a neat little town with shops and restaurants lining the main street through town.

We found a bargain of a motel and immediately fell into the cool room. Once we had showered and put on very clean clothes, we lazed around the room awhile just relaxing. About eight, forty-five, we decided to walk down Main Street and get some dinner only to find out that everything closed at nine P.M. The sidewalks just rolled up with us in them. I was about to hit the gas station convenient store when someone told us that there was a Subway on the way out of town.

I went back to the room and Ralph got on his bike and went in search of sandwiches. They were mighty tasty in our air-conditioned room. Sleep followed shortly there after for Ralph, and I was very close behind.

We're off to see the granite monoliths tomorrow. We have decided to stay here in Sonoma for another night and take a day trip down to Yosemite. We have elected a change in course somewhat and not go to the Grand Canyon but head north where it might be a spot cooler.

The fur was flying on Grizzle Bear. The sun is just too much for him and I think he is starting to shed. That might be a rather ugly site don't you think I guess I will have to start pouring water into this little jacket too.

So until later, much love to all always,
Judy/Mom/Mommy

July 21, 2005
Thursday
Sonora, CA
Mile 13,402

Dear Folks,

We spent a little while this morning locating a new speedometer cable for my bike. Ralph had to find one in a town several days down the road as it has to be ordered. That place turned out to be a town between Salt Lake City and Provo Utah. It will be a few days before that problem is fixed. After taking care of ordering the part, and Ralph taking care of some business, business, we headed on down to Yosemite.

By now it was ten and scorching hot. The yellowed, dried out grass crawled all over the hills we traveled through. There were trees here and there along with some scrub bushes but mostly the landscape was just dried up grasslands and hot as fire.

Within thirty miles, I noticed that the trees were getting closer and closer together and the grass was getting greener in spots and there were more bushes and different trees. This obviously meant that there was more water on a more regular basis.

We started to climb the hills and I noticed an unusual sign saying to turn off your air conditioning for the next five miles. Well, I think I already qualified for that. The steep climb combined with the strain that air conditioners would put on engines would be too much for some cars.

The road became very twisty and winding once again. Before I had my tires changed, when we rode all day on twisting roads, I finished wearing out the tread by riding on the outside of the tires. Now I have new tires and they are getting a work out on all the twisty roads. Higher and higher we climbed in the dreadful heat. When we reached about six thousand feet, I noticed about a five-degree drop in temperature and we rode through a forest with blessed shade from the tall trees.

After the five-mile climb, we stopped at a restaurant that looked like the ones we like to eat in. The sign outside said "Play the Lottery." Well, we played the lunch lottery and lost big time. After being on the road for fifty-seven days and eating twice a day for roughly one hundred and fourteen meals this was the first time ever I have been served lunch along with a fly swatter. No sooner had the waitress placed our food down in front of us than the flies attacked. We were shooing flies from around us and the waitress brought us a fly swatter and put it on the table! I was totally grossed out and pushed the thing off onto the floor. Ralph had ordered a big fat, chilidog with cheese on top and I a BLT. Now, Ralph loves chilidogs and fries but not flies. He couldn't finish his dawg and we left as soon as possible. Dinner was a long time away.

It is amazing to me how much latitude makes a difference in climate and vegetation. Now logically, I know all this from reading and school but to actually see it happening before your very eyes it quite something else entirely. At Mt. Hood, we were at elevations of six to seven thousand feet and it was cold enough to have on all riding gear including liners. Down here in California at the same elevation, it was hot.

The forest we rode through was warmed by the sun and heat and I experienced a new wonderful smell several times while riding through the trees. It was the smell of warm baked, blackberry cobbler. I have no idea what was blooming or cooking in the forest but I sure did get a craving for blackberry cobbler with vanilla ice cream.

Imagine, if you will, riding steadily up over grass-covered hills, round and round curve after curve, continuing up through wooded areas then full forest. Then suddenly, right before you, the world in front of you separates in half and you are on one side of a gigantic canyon of massive granite domes and sheer rock faces of granite shooting straight up into the sky.

That is what it was like today riding into Yosemite. One minute we were in the woods and the next we were on the edge of the canyon with a flat valley below, separating us from the other side.

Massive granite mountains void of any trees or grasses lay before us and the flat, green valley was roughly four thousand feet below. The road took us down, down, through tunnels blasted right through the grey, granite mountains and right to the edge of sheer drop offs. I tried not to look down but had to catch a glimpse here and there.

We reached the valley floor and the road ran next to a most refreshing stream. We were both very hot and the water very enticing.

Now on the valley floor, we were surrounded on all sides by the granite monoliths of all shades of grey. Waterfalls fell from heights of twenty-five hundred feet. The water falling appeared to be in slow motion it was falling so far from above. The sun backlit the water and the mist in some places. Through the valley, ran the Merced River. In some places, the river was deep and dark green. In others, it dashed over rocks making small rapids and a wonderful noise of rushing water.

For weeks, every time I saw a stream or river I wanted to stick my feet in the cool water. Today I would not be denied. We stopped to look at Bridalveil Falls and take a few pictures. I noticed the sound of rushing water behind where we had parked the bikes. I walked over to the water and I just couldn't resist. Off came the boots and I rolled up the jeans and into the water I went. The river felt almost like ice water but my legs and numb toes adjusted quite well. I dipped my red, Georgia Bulldog hat into the cold water and dumped the icy water on my head. Oh, that felt good. It was like jumping into a refreshing swimming pool on a hot summer's day.

One thing led to another and my ooohing and ahhing about how wonderful the water felt, got Ralph to taking off his boots and joining me in the refreshing river. Then thinking about how hot it was going to be back on the bikes, Ralph went and got our helmets and jackets and I dunked them into the cold valley river. I now know that the helmets won't sink no matter how hard you push them down under water.

We carried the drenched jackets and helmets back to the bikes and when we put them on it was one of those moments when something feels so good, you just don't know what to do. I had found heaven in a cold valley stream.

Back on the bikes, we went to the Ansel Adams museum and saw some of his original photographs. He was a true master of black and white photography. We walked to the visitor's center and watched a short movie about the park. The air conditioning was on and we had on wet clothes. It was a bit cool but the movie was great.

Once again, back out in the heat, it was time to head back to our room in Sonora, about seventy miles away. Yosemite is a heavily used national park. It ranks up there with Yellowstone I think. Just about every parking lot was full to overflowing but we had found a spot that we could squeeze into. Now that we were leaving, it was about five thirty and everyone else was leaving too. I was shocked at the traffic just to get out of the park. Very slow moving and inching along made it hard on my clutch hand. By the time the traffic freed up I had a good burn going on in my hand and wrist.

Since we missed dinner last night, we were looking forward to making it on time tonight. Back over the same road, this time with the sun lower, shadows changed the way things looked. The forest was a bit cooler and the temperature, while still hot, was not quite as bad. I got to smell the blackberry cobbler cooking somewhere in the forest again.

It was another terrific day. We had Mexican for dinner tonight. Over dinner, I told Ralph, that one thing I have discovered on this trip is that the more I see, the more curious I become. I have seen things of historical or geologic interest to me and I want to know more about it. I want to explore more of the area; I want to know who walked where I am riding and what they were thinking, just as I was thinking.

I find it fascinating that, I can travel just a few miles and the whole environment changes drastically. One minute I can be in an ocean environment and within five miles, I can be in a deep, dark forest of giant trees. Then just thirty miles down the road, I can be in a desert like place with dried up grass, sparse trees, and hellish temperatures. In the environment I live in at home, I can go for miles and miles and there will be trees and trees and maybe the foothills of the Appalachians still covered with the same types of trees. Maybe if I travel a little further south I will come to flat farmland. But the area we have been traveling through lately, changes so rapidly it is amazing and I am curious.

I am glad to know that at my age my brain still is eager to learn more, see more, and understand more. It has been an awakening of sorts for me to know that, being able to explore this incredible land we live in, my brain is still very much alive. It is like a rebirth of searching for knowledge of those things around me. This is a very nice feeling. My brain and spirit are young again and that is a very nice feeling as well.

Well, it's off tomorrow in a new direction with new discoveries just around the next bend in the road to be experienced.

Grizzle Bear had the day off to enjoy the privacy of the hotel room all by himself. I think his sizzled fur has regained some luster and I thought I heard him snoring as we came in the room tonight. I don't think I'm going to tell him we're crossing the Nevada desert in a couple days. I wouldn't want to ruin his beauty sleep.

So until then, much love to all always,
Judy/Mom/Mommy

July 23, 2005
Saturday
Sparks, NV
Mile 13,587

Dear Folks,

While we are sitting in the BMW dealership in Sparks, Nevada, just east of Reno, waiting for a new tire and brakes for Ralph, I thought I would try to catch up on yesterday's travels. We left Sonora in mid-morning and it was already heating up rather nicely. We backtracked about fifteen miles to Angel's Camp to catch a scenic route over to Lake Tahoe. Ralph missed his turn off on his road and kept on following me. The road was named Jack Ass Lane. I'm sure this is one named by Mark Twain because the area we were in was one where Mark Twain had a cabin and some of his first stories were created.

Route 4 would take us over the Sierra Nevada Mountains to catch another bigger road that went into South Lake Tahoe. The road went through small town after small town with lots of traffic. The ride was pleasant enough, nothing spectacular but a very pleasant ride through the woods and small mountains. We stopped for lunch at a small café and that was the last of the traffic. It was as if the traffic vanished.

Driving on up the road, I understood why. We had been making a slow assent and the terrain had changed from foothills of dry yellow grass with sparsely placed trees and shrubs to more woods and fir trees mingled with some very young redwoods and sequoias. On the side of the road, I saw some pinecones that were the size of footballs. I have no idea which tree these came from but they were monster size.

As we traveled further up in elevation the air-cooled somewhat making the ride pleasurable. The landscape changed rather quickly and I realized why the traffic disappeared. Several signs along the road warned about the road ahead being very narrow, winding, and having steep grades. Motor homes and cars with trailers were warned it was inadvisable to continue.

Oh, me, what were we heading for? The scenery changed from nice woods to outcroppings of granite boulders and rocks. Some were the size of large houses, cars and on down is size to basketballs. This was the result of glaciers moving over the area, breaking off large chunks of the granite mountains and rolling them smooth and round.

The dirt and ground vanished and granite was everywhere. It you take the Appalachian Mountains and remove all the dirt and ground cover and expose the rock underneath, this is what the Sierra Nevada Mountains reminded me off. The area also reminded me of our Stone Mountain in Atlanta if raised from its one thousand feet up to eighty-seven hundred feet. If a whole mountain range looked like Stone Mountain, you might have an idea of what these mountains here look like.

One thing I found of particular interest was that there were trees up on these mountains too. Their root system found any little collection of dirt in the cracks and crevasses and put down their shallow root system. Some of the trees were really rather tall and old so they had been there quite a while. I was really impressed with the lack of ground cover and the amount of trees.

We came to the end of the nice two lane road and there was another sign that said road narrows and there were steep grades of twenty-four percent up ahead and no vehicles over twenty-five feet in length were allowed. I have never heard of grades that steep. Even on the Haul Road the worst we encountered were fourteen percent and that was steep, trust me.

The road became, at best, a good one-lane road. Fortunately, the traffic was slim to none. As we started to climb everything seemed ok at first, no steep inclines and no sharp drop offs. That changed quickly. The road suddenly twisted back on itself and the grade was so steep that it appeared the road was right in our face. I was so thankful that the road was not gravel, as I don't think my poor bike would have been able to pull it on loose gravel.

Down into first gear, my bike pulled and tugged, but hauled my load and me up and up and up. Even though we were pulling higher and higher up the mountain, it was as if we were riding through an area that resembled a rock meadow. Tall trees were on both sides but due to the lack of soil, we could see clearly through to the granite boulders. There were no drop offs and I was relieved, as I knew Ralph was not anxious to be on narrow mountain roads with no guardrails to block an eight thousand foot drop.

We reached the top of one pass at eight thousand feet and there in the backcountry of the Sierra Nevada's were small alpine lakes, green and refreshing. Fishermen were either wading in the water or sitting in chairs casting lures into the mountain water.

We had one more pass to go over which topped out at eight thousand, seven hundred feet and there again were more mountain lakes and ponds. One lake had several families paddling around in inner tubes and rafts. I wanted to join them. I wondered how they found this pristine place, being such a long way from any thing or any town. Of course, I wasn't thinking that if Ralph and I found this secret place, residents of the area would know about it as well.

Then came the scary down grade. As we started the descent, I kept thinking that the assent had been just fine so surely the descent would be the same. How very wrong I was. Around one sharp turn came a motor home of mammoth proportions taking up the whole lane. Some people just need to be slapped. Hadn't there been warning signs about not taking motor homes on this road? I was glad to be on a bike at that moment. I just don't know how that motor home and a car could pass at the same time. There was absolutely no place to pull off either and as the motor home zoomed by us at such a close distance, I could have reached out and gladly pounded the side of the behemoth. This episode was the reason why I did not get one single picture of these mountains.

After making it safely around the monstrosity, I noticed up ahead, a very sharp down hill turn and off in the distance clear blue sky. That wasn't a good sign to me. That meant a long drop off ahead. Sure enough, as we got closer to the curve, it was so tight that I thought I would do a somersault head over heals. Off to the right, was a sheer drop off several thousand feet to the canyon floor. I got the willies and I know Ralph behind me was spouting some of his favorite words. I could hear them clearly in my head and helmet.

The descent was just as steep as the ascent but we made it with no problems and a huge sigh of relief when we got to the valley floor. The terrain changed once again and the rock foothills changed from grey granite to ones of red and tan. The grasses were greener and large pastures with herds of grazing cattle, appeared. The air remained comfortable and I kept wondering when it was going to get blasting hot again.

The road toward Lake Tahoe took us through many canyons. Serious crosswinds came rushing down the canyon and knocked both of us around in the lane. I really hate it when the wind hits me so hard that my head jerks back and it feels like the only thing holding my helmet on is the chinstrap. When the top of my head separates from the inside of my helmet, that is a strong wind. We battled the wind for the remainder of miles into Lake Tahoe.

We stopped for a break at the local McDonalds, before deciding whether to go around the east or west side of the lake. Looking at an aerial map, Lake Tahoe looked like a great blue dinosaur egg dropped right into the middle of the mountains. I was really looking forward to seeing the lake, having heard so many wonderful things over the years, about its beauty.

Well, let me tell you. There was so much commercialization I couldn't believe it. The lake was hard to see through all the hotels and fast food places. I was thoroughly disappointed with this place. The campground we passed looked like a homeless camp and I was so glad we were not staying there. I have seen prettier lakes on our trip and our own Lake Lanier in Georgia can hold its own against Lake Tahoe anytime. No kidding. I find no beauty in commercial canyons and metal mountains.

I can honestly say I've been there, done that, and don't care to go back to Lake Tahoe. The only picture I managed to get yesterday was on the climb over the last of the mountains heading into Nevada and the desert. There was one turn out at the top and I took one picture.

As we came down over the mountain into Carson City, Nevada, then I was really taken by surprise. Below us were the flat, flat desert and the city. Squeezed right in the shadow of the mountains, was Carson City. The view was such a dramatic contrast to the one west of us back in Lake Tahoe. Since we were so high up in elevation, the view was breathtaking, very, very pretty and not at all what I expected.

When we got to the bottom of the mountain pass, I thought it would be hot since we were now in the desert but it wasn't at all. I think the mountains helped keep the area cool. The air was only eighty-nine degrees and quite comfortable. We rolled through Carson City and headed toward Reno. Just outside Carson City was a billboard sign flashing a warning to campers and cars with trailers that for the next nine miles there was a wind advisory.

I almost stopped right there in the middle of the road to find another route to take. I glanced quickly down at my map on my tank bag and determined there was no such road available. I took a deep breath, swallowed down the nausea, gritted my teeth and just said I would get through it some how. As we climbed the hill, the wind was blowing very hard and I positioned myself in the right hand lane so if I was blown out of the lane I would only wind up in the emergency lane. I knew the wind was blowing from the west and I was heading north so I didn't think I would get surprised from winds from any other direction other than from my left.

Crossing over the hill below us was a vast valley to the right and the mountains to the left. I knew that the wind was coming howling down the mountains and onto the valley. I was not excited about crossing the next nine miles in the valley. As we got down into the valley, the wind eased up some for some reason. Who knows, maybe it had blown itself out earlier before we got there. Maybe that was as bad as the wind ever blew. I don't know or care, I was happy, to say the least, that it was a piece of cake and we made it through the valley safely and on into Reno.

We found a hotel and after settling in and getting cleaned up, we walked across the road to the Hilton and the casino. After dinner, we decided how much we would loose at the casino. Setting our play money at forty dollars each, we hit the casino. I was, in no way, going to play at the poker tables since I would look like a total fool and that wasn't my style. We found video poker machines and played those. Ralph played some roulette and after all was said and done at the end of the evening we were ahead about five dollars. We spent our five-dollar winnings on the cab fare back to the hotel. We broke even for the night, stayed within our daily budget, and good nights sleep ending a wonderful day.

Well, we're ready to leave Sparks, Nevada. Ralph's bike is ready and we're going to visit Virginia City not far from here before we head out over the desert.

Grizzle Bear is sitting up on the pack on my bike, ready to go visit come cowboys and eat barbeque. He's all strapped in sitting in the shade and complaining about the wait. So, off we go.

So, until next time, love to all always,
Judy/Mom/Mommy

July 24, 2005
Saturday
Eureka, NV
Mile 13,870

Dear Folks,

After we left the dealership, with new a new front tire and new brakes for Ralph's bike, we rode down to Virginia City, Nevada. The town had been preserved just as it had been during the eighteen hundreds. Of course, now the town was for tourist, but there was still a lot of history preserved as well. Mark Twain got his start in Virginia City writing for the newspaper. The building is now a museum.

Virginia City, Nevada is where the mother load of all mother loads was found after two men sold their shares in their mine to some others. Not only was gold found but silver as well. The mother load was referred to as the Comstock Load. We took a twenty minute tour on a wagon pulled by a tractor and learned the history of the main parties of the town back during the gold and silver rush.

During the time when the city flourished as a mining town, there were over one hundred saloons and gambling houses. Today, saloons still line the street and still function as saloons, restaurants, and casinos. The sidewalks are still made of wood planks and benches that line the street, are great for people watching.

This town was steeped in history and this is another place I want to do some reading about when I get home. We left Virginia City rather late in the afternoon and we had planned on traveling just a short distance. Getting started on the days ride at three in the afternoon doesn't allow for much travel time.

The ride down the hill from Virginia City was curvy and lined with tiny houses from the era and I could just imagine who might have lived in those many years ago. Once on flat ground the air was burning up again. We caught Route 50 that would take us across the desert of Nevada. Nicknamed the Loneliest Road in the World, I had picked this route because it was suppose to be a scenic route. We were in for an unexpected surprise.

The road climbed over the foothills, which were all covered with dry dirt and some bushes. As we crested the hill, below us, spread out for hundreds of miles all around us, was pure desert. Mountains barren of all vegetation skirted the horizon on all sides and the road went right through the middle of the flat barren land.

I was surprised and in awe by the beauty before us. It was hard to imagine that, even though there were mountains all around us, we were traveling through areas so flat and dry that it could hardly sustain life. The foothills and mountains around us were just dirt and rock. No trees, no grass, just hard rock.

We came to a spot off to the left that was called Sand Mountain. And it really was. Nestled right up in a curve in the foothills of dark brown and grey, was a huge sand dune. The top of the dune looked like a tan serpent slithering down to the desert floor.

On and on we traveled through the vastness and we stopped several times to drench ourselves in water. By now, it was very late afternoon and the air was starting to cool a little. The mountains around the edges of the desert started to take on another look entirely. As we traveled east, those mountains in front of us still had full sunshine on them but the ones behind us in the west were now sending fingers of long shadows down the sides and making it look as if a cool dark hand was resting over the mountain.

We stopped in a place called Cold Springs for a Coke and found out that it was one of the stops for the Pony Express. As we looked at the map on the wall inside we noticed that the route the Pony Express took seemed to follow Route 50. I couldn't believe those horses and riders galloped across this land of heat and desert.

Our ultimate goal for the day was originally going to be Austin, Nevada but as we neared the tiny town, the air had cooled off a good bit. We thought it might be a good idea to continue over the desert in the coolness of the early evening so we decided to ride on for another seventy miles. Even though evening was approaching, there was still an abundance of light in the sky.

No sooner had we passed through Austin, a small town with just a main street with three hotels and a few cafes, I thought to myself that I should start looking out for deer, as sunset was approaching. That thought had not even left my brain as we rounded a curve and there right in front of me was a deer in the road. Fortunately, she was just on the side but I frightened her and she didn't know which way to run. I slammed on both breaks as she ran one way and then the other finally deciding to exit the road. She was big too! I decelerated so quickly that the engine cut off and I thought I wouldn't get it restarted. It turned out that, at that exact moment of rapid deceleration, the rear fuel cell emptied.

After my heart rate calmed, we slowly continued eastward. We came over a hill and before us was an extremely long stretch of highway, long and straight, and went for miles, until the next set of hills. I noticed a tractor-trailer coming my direction and as he got closer, he crossed over the centerline. I thought any second he would pull the truck back into his lane. No that didn't happen. He kept coming. It dawned on me that the driver might have fallen asleep. I just about broke my thumb from mashing the horn so hard and long. Just at the very, very last minute when I had about four feet of pavement left on my side of the road, the driver must have awakened and he jerked the truck back into his lane. But that was not until we had passed each other leaving a mere two or three feet between his truck and my body. I had one foot of pavement remaining on my right as he passed, then it would have been down in the ditch and rocks and sand. Needless to say, I had to stop the bike and regain my composure.

Here we were, on the loneliest road, in the middle of the desert, the only way out of a situation like that was to keep going even though my brain said it was time to call it a night. That's just what we did. We kept moving forward. In a space of a few short miles, I had had two near death experiences. One with a deer and one with a tractor-trailer.

When the sun goes down in most any place and the temperature cools, the animals come out of their hiding places. This is really true in the desert. During broad daylight, not an ant could be found. Now, with evening approaching, all sorts of creatures started popping out of the bushes. First was the deer, then I saw a covey of grouse, maybe five or six scurry into the bushes along the side of the road. A little bit further down the road another covey was in a big hurry hunting for bugs I assume, along the opposite side of the road. I couldn't resist and blew my horn at them and about eight birds scattered as if they had been shot.

But the absolute, most grossest thing yet, was just up the road. I stopped to take some pictures of the lengthening shadows of evening on the mountains up ahead. I noticed that something was crawling on the road. At first, I thought that maybe they were the big scorpions that reside in the desert. That would have been gross enough but instead they were the biggest, nastiest, grossest, double butt ugly grasshoppers I have truly ever seen. They were at least three inches long, and about an inch in diameter through their middles. They had legs the size of chicken legs and eyes as big as small marbles. They had some kind of spike sticking out their rear end and they were all over the road. As Ralph's bike rolled up next to mine, he rolled over several and they popped as if a paper bag had been blown up and popped. I was doing some serious checking to see if any were hopping near me or about to crawl on me. Fortunately, we got away before that happened.

The further we went down the road, the more and more of the nasty bugs we saw. In spots, they covered the road and other cars had already mashed many. I looked over to the side of the road and could see the grasshoppers coming out of the dirt and rock. Millions of them were everywhere. I was totally grossed out and was not going to stop and take any more pictures.

On we continued, heading east into the evening. The sun was starting to set, the air was very pleasant and cool. The desert put on its evening perfume and I smelled something blooming that had a hint of lemon like the Georgia magnolia trees. The light lemon fragrance mixed with the warm smell of sage and the evening desert smelled divine. The foothills and mountains before us in the east dawned a cloak of orange, pink, rust, and lavender in the setting sun. The mountains to our backs in the west had put on a cloak of dark lavender and grey. As the sun sunk lower, the mountains cast off their cloaks of color and sent them skyward, turning the sky and clouds pink, purple, orange, and red in a spectacular show.

The road before us stretched out in a long, black ribbon into the east and darkness was up ahead to greet us. Off to our right but slightly behind us the sun had sunk behind the mountains and they were now black, but the sky continued to remain red and orange like a homing beacon. Into the blackness of the eastern desert we rode, the orange beacon behind us, a friendly reminder we would not get lost in the blackness of night.

The last thirty miles of our journey was in darkness. I can't say that I particularly liked riding in the pitch black of the desert. I was praying that the bikes wouldn't break down and leave us stranded there in the darkness with those nasty bugs.

Finally, we rolled into Eureka, Nevada and of the four hotels in town, there was only one that had a room. We grabbed it, gladly paying the thirty-eight dollars for a room with two beds but no air conditioning. But it did have a fan. Thank goodness for small favors.

Eureka was another town that rolled up the sidewalks and streets after a certain hour. There was no one out or around, the streets were deserted. As we were unpacking our gear from the bikes, not twenty yards from me, came a deer, crossing the street and entering the parking lot where we were. She acted as if she were very familiar with the hotel, not afraid of us in the least. Then she wandered off behind the hotel and we didn't see her again.

We walked two blocks up to the only place open in Eureka to get some dinner. The restaurant was in the casino and that was where the locals were. Ralph and I ate in silence, partly due to exhaustion and partly because we ease dropped on a lively conversation at the next table. The cowboys were discussing the rounding up of cattle via the single engine aircraft that one of the local cowboys owned. After eating, we walked back to the room and crashed. It had been a long hot day in the sun but the desert cooled off rapidly when the sun went down and the fan in the room was sufficient enough to keep us cool.

So, we survived our first day in the desert, bugs, deer, tractor-trailers, heat, and all. The desert had been a tremendous surprise for me. It was magnificent, almost beyond words. Long vast flat areas of dry grass, sand, and rock were surrounded on all sides by barren foothills and mountains. The mountains were just bare rock, no trees, not even a stick. The mere size alone was enough to impress me. Though crossing the desert is something I wouldn't want to do on a regular basis, seeing it for the first time was wonderful and I will forever remember its splendor. The route we took was so beautiful that I really thought it should be a national park.

Grizzle Bear wasn't so sure of his trip across the hot desert. His tan fur is dirty and getting bleached by the sun. The bugs were definitely a turn off and I heard him mumbling about getting a move on when he spotted the grasshoppers. Later, in the room, I tossed him a few M&M's and that seemed to calm him down. Just teeny, tiny snores coming from his side of the room were all I heard the rest of the night.

Tomorrow we will hopefully finish this trip across the desert and get on back to the coolness of the mountains. We will be stopping near Salt Lake in order to get my new speedometer cable that was ordered and hopefully waiting for me Monday morning.

So until later, much love to all always,
Judy/Mom/Mommy

July 25, 2005

Sunday
Orem, Utah
Mile 14,218

Dear Folks,

Boy, the sun sure is up early in the desert. Our room warmed up pretty fast also with only the fan running. The morning sun was beating its way into our room with little difficulty. Ralph and I were up and rolling down the road by eight-fifteen this morning and the air was much cooler outside than in our room. We enjoyed the cool morning air and were on the lookout for more creatures that enjoy the early morning and early evening.

Fortunately, I didn't see anymore of those nasty bugs. A man at the hotel last night told us that they were called Mormon Crickets and that they were viscous and bite. Well, at least they were hopefully a thing of the past and I would not have to see them again.

We zoomed through the desert putting in the miles trying to exit the other side. As we got close to the state line of Nevada, there was actually a national park called Great Basin National Park. Since it was just a few miles off the main highway, we stopped off to get a look. When I looked at the map on the wall, I realized that the entire time crossing Nevada, we were riding over the Great Basin. The Great Basin is a vast area covering all of Nevada from the Sierra Nevada Mountains to the area around Salt Lake. There are no inlets or outlets for any water to run so anything that does fall gets absorbed right into the area.

Lines of mountains and foothills run north to south through the entire basin and from the map reminded me of a gigantic washboard road. That explained why we would see great areas of dry desert then ascend a small range and cross over into another desert area. There are even fossilized whalebones in some archeological sites along the road. We didn't see those, as it would have been about one hundred miles

251

round trip out of the way. That's a long way in the heat with no facilities to stop for water.

There were some caves at the national park and a road that led way up high into the mountains behind the visitor's center. We declined riding on the mountain road and we passed on the cave but we did go to the archeological site where there was an Indian village that had been excavated. Unfortunately, it turned out, that after the village had been excavated by students at Brigham Young, vandals started destroying things and taking artifacts. The site was recovered and now all that can be seen are markers with numbers and a book to read about the site that was there seven hundred years ago. Only an outline of several buildings was recreated above ground for visitors to see. That was a such a disappointment.

Back on the hot, hot, hot road again, we crossed into Utah. The scenery changed and the desert became a place I didn't want to be in any more. It was no longer beautiful, just a barren land with dried up lake beds that looked white like salt. All around us, the mountain's clouds thundered and threatening rain. There was rain in the mountains, we could see it coming down, we could smell it, but not a single drop fell on us.

The wind picked up also and became an unpleasant addition to the hot sun. We had to slow the pace down somewhat in order not to be blown off the road. As we got closer to Salt Lake City, the mountains closed in and the wind picked up and rained threatened. We did get a few drops on us then but nothing that even soaked the clothes.

Most of the desert was behind us now and it had been a long two days getting over the barren land. We made it to Orem, Utah, found a very nice motel for a very good price, and will be heading out in the morning to get my speedometer cable replaced. Then it's on to Dinosaur National Monument in eastern Utah overlapping into western Colorado. I hope to see some dinosaur bones. I have always wanted to see this park but it's always been out of the way or I just haven't been in the vicinity. Now we're close enough and it is right on the way to Steamboat Springs and Rocky Mountain National Park.

Well, the brain and body are totally exhausted and Ralph is already asleep. Grizzle Bear and Ralph are snoring in stereo. I don't know how I'll sleep through all that noise. I can throw a pillow over Ralph but

I haven't figured out what to do with Grizzle Bear though. Too many M&M's will keep him awake.

So, until next time, love to all always,
Judy/Mom/Mommy

July 26, 2005
Tuesday
Dinosaur National Monument Utah
Mile 14,402

Dear Folks,

Before I start to recall today's journey I must make some additions to our travel across the desert. There were so many things to remember that I was bound to forget something in my writings of the last two days.

Several miles before we got to the Pony Express station of Cold Springs, I noticed off to the left side of the road a large tree. First, it was unusual in the fact that the tree was alone in the middle of nothing but grasslands. The tree was a very large, with a full coverage of green leaves. Then I noticed that things were hanging from tree. I immediately thought it was some kind of Indian prayer tree and that the things that were hanging from the limbs were some prayer ornaments placed there by the Indians. Oh, no, I was entirely wrong on all accounts. It was not that romantic at all.

As we got closer, I noticed that what was hanging from the limbs were not prayer ornaments, but shoes, hundreds of shoes, all tied together by the laces and thrown over the branches. There were literally hundreds of them hanging from every branch and limb from the very large tree in the middle of the desert. Now explain that one. I sure can't.

One of the other things that impressed me about this desert was the long flat valleys that went on for miles and that all around these valleys were mountain ranges and foothills. As we traveled down these long stretches of desert, I looked at the map before me on my tank bag and read the names of these ranges. Their names interested me and I wanted to remember them and pass them along. Some of the names of the ranges were Big Smokey Valley, Toquma Range, Monitor Range, Pancake Range, Railroad Valley, Clan Alpine

Mountains, and Shoshone Range. Every range had a name and every valley had been named.

When I pulled from the memory of my geology classes I took in college, I remember why this land looked like it did. We were traveling along the floor of once was an ocean floor and the ranges and mountains were once underwater mountains. These long ranges extended north to south for miles and miles. They all looked different and all were beautiful.

When we stopped in Great Basin National Park there were actually mountain peaks surrounding the area that had snow on them. There was actually a glacier on one of the peaks behind the visitor's center. I was struck by such a conflict of nature. On the valley floor, it was hot, arid, and parched and all around us in the mountains thunder rumbled and rain came down in the upper elevations. There was still snow on the peaks and it was the end of July. Ice and fire in the same area at the same time.

As we left Great Basin National Park and continued eastward, we managed to make it to one of the mountain passes that had threatening rain clouds. We only felt a few sprinkled drops but the sky blackened up just a tad. Then, to me, the most unusual thing happened. Around a curve, we came, and off to our left was a rainbow! Only half showed but still there in the desert before my very eyes were colors not expected in this dry land. What a profound treat to see in the desert.

As we got closer to the edge of the desert, I knew I was starting to feel some of the effects of the heat. Even though we were sufficiently doused with water to cool us, my brain, I think must have been totally fried. Remember earlier I had stated that I am affected by heat more than most people. I was positive I was in the early phases of heat exhaustion because off in the distance in front of me, I saw something on the side of the road. I thought, at first, it must be a mirage but as I got closer, I realized it was a man walking toward me. The man was dressed in a long, flowing white robe. Across the white robe, draped from his right shoulder was a wide, deep purple sash. His long, brown hair hung to his shoulders and blended with his big beard. Upon his feet, he wore sandals and he carried a large staff in his right hand. I knew immediately who the man was; I had seen Jesus in the desert.

He waved to me as I passed and on the outside chance that I was seeing whom I thought I was, I waved back.

I just knew I had had too much sun for one day. I was hallucinating, I was sure of it. My brain must have been shutting down. When we rolled into the next town, thirty miles later, while stopped at a traffic light, I looked over to Ralph and asked him in a very whispered voice, had he seen the vision in the desert. He nodded his head yes and with a look in his eyes assured me that I was not dying of heat stroke.

No, my friends, it was not really Jesus but I have absolutely no idea of what this man was doing walking all alone in the desert. He was about thirty miles from any town. Had he walked that far? What was he doing for water and where was he going? The direction he was headed had no town for another forty miles. He was carrying nothing but his staff, no water, no nothing. I guess that is one of life's little mysteries that will never, never be answered.

Well, I think that is all I forgot to write about the other day. On Monday morning, Ralph went to the Monarch Honda dealership in Orem, Utah to pick up the speedometer cable only to find the dealership closed. Even after Ralph had been told over the phone by an employee they were open on Mondays and confirmed that the cable had arrived, the doors were locked up tight. They were open on Mondays normally but this particular Monday was Pioneer Day in Utah and the Honda dealership was closed with a sign on the door saying to come back tomorrow. I won't even begin to tell you how mad Ralph was, just don't even need to go there.

Needless to say, we spent another night in Orem, checking right back in to the same hotel. I never even left the lobby. After our tempers cooled, we spent the day resting and reading. Ralph did a little work and I dozed and read. In reality, the rest did both of us good after frying in the desert for two days.

This morning, the dealership was open, the part was retrieved, and while Ralph was at the dealership, the back break pads were replaced on my bike. We eventually got on the road around noon and headed out of town. The day was great for riding. The sky was a beautiful blue and the temperature was in the upper seventies. That was a dramatic change from the temperatures of the desert.

We traveled through the Provo Canyon, past another waterfall named Bridal Veil Falls. I think there must be one in every state with this name. The ride was pretty and we enjoyed cruising through the mountains and the cool air. That changed as we went further east toward the dinosaur area. The land became red instead of the tans and yellows we had been in for the last few days.

Layers of sedimentary rock pushed up by the tectonic plates, showed rocks millions of years old. It was fascinating to me. Rock beds and their many, many layers, that once were on the bottom of rivers were now pushed up and exposed. These layers have become eroded by time, water, and wind.

We came to a town called Vernal that was about fifteen miles from the Dinosaur National Monument and stopped in at the new Natural History Museum. There we saw many fossils of dinosaur bones, ocean creatures, river animals and leaves and trees. We also learned that the area we are in is world known for the fossil beds of dinosaurs and other living creatures and plants that lived one hundred and fifty million years ago.

Back on the bikes, we headed for Dinosaur National Monument and fortunately, made it to the quarry just before closing time. The quarry was the only place in the park that we could actually see the bones but the rest of the park contains the land they walked on millions of years ago. The land was once flat and contained rivers, trees, and such. It is a dry place now and the red sand stone and the grey shale give testament to the way it once was.

The quarry had, as one of its walls, the side of one mountain. The building was constructed around the other three sides encasing the wall of fossilized dinosaur bones. It was thought that this mound of bones was once a riverbed and the bones had been carried down stream, collected in areas and pockets, there to remain and be covered by layers and layers of sediment. Eventually the tectonic plates pushed and crinkled the earth upward and erosion did the rest to expose the bones. The area is fascinating. I can just imagine the creatures roaming these lands.

As evening was approaching, we drove back a few miles to get some food and then came quickly back to the campground in the park. We were promised shade in the cottonwoods in the camp along the Green River. Sure enough, there were plenty of cottonwoods and shade but all those campsites were closed off due to hazardous trees. Now I wondered just what could make cottonwood trees hazardous. Would they attack and eat us in the middle of the night? We did find a spot that would soon be in the shade of a hill and set up camp.

Ralph went back to pay and found out the there had been a lot of rain lately in the area. The cottonwood trees soaked up the water and the root system got very weak and caused the trees to topple over. Now that wouldn't be a pretty site having our little tent squished under a cotton wood tree.

We have a nice fire going. Yes, it is actually cool after the sun went down and the fire feels good. And boy the stars! There is no moon tonight and there is already the promise of a billion stars, the same stars that shown down on the dinosaurs that walked this land where I sit now.

We didn't get to see the entire park today, so we'll finish that tomorrow before heading out for Steamboat Springs, Colorado.

Grizzle Bear, just like a little boy, loved the dinosaurs and wants to see more. I will take him on a tour tomorrow. Unfortunately, he smelled marshmallows someone in the next campsite is cooking and is now complaining about this desire as well. Too bad for Grizzle Bear. We have no marshmallows, no M&M's, no Snickers. Maybe a few corn nuts will do.

So, until next time, much love to all always,
Judy/Mom/Mommy

July 27, 2005
Wednesday
Steamboat Springs, CO
Mile 14,584

Dear Folks,

Last night, after the wonderful fire, which lit up our entire campsite, burned itself down to vibrant red coals, Ralph and I sat in the darkness of the desert and looked at the vastness of the sky. A dark, black bowl hung over us and in that bowl were millions of stars in all degrees of brightness. Some twinkled blue, some glowed red, but most were the blue, white of stars only seen in the wide-open spaces with no city lights around.

The sky was so dark that the Milky Way shown so brightly it could have been mistaken for a huge, white cloud that stretched across the heavens. We watched for shooting stars hoping that this time we would be successful. We saw two tiny satellites and three very quick shooting stars. I was hoping for a meteor shower but no such luck. Even the moon stayed hidden.

We finally gave up after a while, and I think, we were the very last ones to call it a night in the campground. Somewhere toward dawn, roosters in the neighboring ranch started their early morning wake up call. It was still dark, what were they thinking? They shut up for a while and then when the sky really lightened, they started in again. We dozed in and out of sleep until the sun hit the tent. It was immediately necessary to clear the premises as quickly as possible because the tent reached cooking temperatures rapidly.

We quickly got everything out of the tent and packed up. Jackrabbits were all over the place this morning as well as the squirrels. Against park regulations, I threw the squirrels some trail mix and it was quickly carried off, leaving no evidence for the park ranger.

Last night when we were setting up camp, I had noticed a rather large anthill with very large red ants marching in and out. The anthill happened to be right in our path between the tent and our bikes, so, not wanting to accidentally step in the ant's home when it got dark, I stuck a sizable stick into the anthill. This thoroughly angered the ants and they went totally crazy. But, we didn't step in the anthill either.

This morning, after we were scurrying around packing up, Ralph had taken the tent poles down to pack first, leaving the tent collapsed on the tarp. When Ralph went to stuff the tent back into the bag, there were thousands of those nasty, angry, red ants crawling all over the tent! I guess they paid us back, huh? We had to shake the tent out vigorously before Ralph stuffed it in the bag. By then the tarp was crawling with them and we had to do the same thing. I was just thankful that the ants had not found a way to enter out tent during the night. What an unpleasant situation that would have been.

The morning shadows laced across the gigantic rocks in the park as we left to go do some investigation of those things we didn't see yesterday. We rode down the narrow road further into the park and into the depths of the canyons. Rocks formations of all colors soared on each side of us. Red sand stone, grey shale, tan shale, that once lay in flat layers against the earth now stood perpendicular. The erosion that had taken place had rounded many of the rocks and gave one outcropping a look of ghostly faces upon its surface. Some outcroppings had worn away the dirt leaving what looked like a dinosaur backbone along the road.

The narrow road turned to gravel and we came to a rather tall rock wall of red sand stone. There were petroglyphs carved into the rock faces and I was amazed at the artwork and at the age of these drawings.

At the end of the gravel road was a small wooden cabin that had been built by Josie Morris, a woman age forty, and her grandson back in nineteen-fourteen. She claimed a homestead back then and lived off the land, supporting herself with vegetable gardens, chickens, hogs, and cows. She lived there until the age of ninety, when her horse accidentally bumped her and she fell down breaking her hip. What a strong independent woman. She had to fight for water rights when the men who were trying to run her off said that the creek that ran through her property was theirs. She out foxed them by flooding her fields when the spring melt came.

Her grandchildren would come stay the summers with her and I can just imagine the fun they must have had on her farm. I had visions of my own children running along the creek through the grassy pastures, squealing in delight as they chased wild rabbits and butterflies.

We left Dinosaur National Monument after one more stop near the Green River where it ran right up next to the face of the canyon. Though the river ran silent, a pleasant wind echoed off the sharp face of the canyon wall. I could have pulled my cot up right there in the shade and had a real nice nap.

Back out on the hot road again, we stopped just about twenty miles on down the road for lunch in Dinosaur, Colorado. What Ralph and I didn't really realize was that we were still in a desert environment. We thought that once we got out of Nevada and western Utah that the hot stuff was over. There were mountains all around us far off on both sides of the road but the valleys we traveled through were hot and arid and the sunshine intense and bright. I was getting pretty sick of the environment. I had had enough of the desert.

Before leaving Yosemite, we had made a wise choice of cutting out the southern end of our trip. We had originally planned to go over Death Valley and into the Four Corners area. With the heat wave that was in the area at the time, we thought it would be safer to go north. I found out two days later while traveling into Utah that Death Valley recorded temperatures of one hundred and twenty-nine degrees. I'm glad we were only in the low one hundreds. We'll save that part of the country for another time. Like maybe winter.

We were both, without a doubt, ready for some cool mountain temperatures. We had visions of a campground in the trees at Steamboat Springs that didn't materialize at all. The campground, which I had found on the internet, had half of its one hundred and fifty sites right out in the broiling sun. The others had some partial shade under the cottonwoods. Before checking in though, we rode on in to Steamboat Springs and I was very shocked at how much it had grown up in the last twenty-four years.

Ralph and I came here as a young married couple before children were born. Ralph attended some sort of accounting meetings while

I went horseback riding in the backcountry. Only a little town along the main street through town existed and I remembered it very fondly. Now, there was growth everywhere and it was not attractive at all. The old section I remembered was still there and it had been preserved with nice gift shops and restaurants. We went to the visitor's center to see if there were any more campgrounds in the area but the ones available were about twenty to thirty miles further out of town. We debated what to do, as we were both very exhausted. It seemed that we both must have been suffering from a mild case of altitude sickness. Our ride today wasn't particularly long, just one hundred, eighty-eight miles, but we were both drained completely and wanted to do nothing but lie down and go to sleep.

The campground that we bypassed earlier was beginning to look a little more enticing. We turned around, headed back, and found a shady spot in the back of the campground. I was working on a king size headache and much fatigue, all attributable to the altitude I think. After resting for a bit and then getting a nice cool shower, we went back into town for some dinner. Feeling somewhat improved, we wandered around the old part of town for a bit, sat and watched people for a while.

The sun was just about to go behind the mountains so we headed back to camp, bought some firewood, and called it a night. We've had some great fires around the tent on this trip and a few that were just pitiful. This one falls into that pitiful category. I think the wood was cottonwood and all it wanted to do was smoke. The whole campground must have bought their wood from the same place as a grey, low lying cloud of smoke hung over the campground. We gave up after burning only about four logs and went to bed.

The temperature dropped dramatically and it now felt like alpine air. The stars were out in the clear darkness, well between the campfire smoke that is. They were still very bright.

Grizzle Bear wasn't feeling all to well either. The thought of marshmallows, M&M's, and such had no appeal. I put him in the hammock in the tent over my cot and he was snoring before Ralph.

Hope we all wake up feeling better tomorrow.

So until later, much love to all always,
Judy/Mom/Mommy

July 31, 2005
Sunday
Grand Lake, CO
Mile 14,740

Dear Folks,

After a few days break from writing and photography I thought it might be about time to get started again. We wound up staying in Steamboat Springs for three days. Our campsite became one we liked. Out site was backed up next to the woods and the train tracks. Beneath the trees, in the woods, were tall grasses that hid all sorts of plants and animals. The cottonwood trees sent their fluff everywhere and it looked as if it was once again snowing. I also think that Ralph is allergic to cottonwood fluff as he had a reaction to something and was sneezing his head off.

Also, in the tall grass and woods behind our campsite was a flock of, what we determined was, wild turkeys. They would gobble and cluck in one area and then move back and forth in an area that covered about one hundred yards. We never saw them but we're almost positive they were turkeys.

On our second night, before I fixed chili for dinner, we were sitting in the shade and just relaxing and talking when Ralph told me to turn around very slowly. Behind me, in the next campsite was a very large red fox. He was staring at Ralph, but as I turned around, he scurried under the fence and was gone in the tall grass. The people in the next campsite were completely oblivious to Mr. Fox and he was literally just feet from them.

Now, I did not have any idea of what was going on with the skunks, but I had had all I wanted of their pungent odor. They had been everywhere squished in the road, their odor floating heavy in the air. It was so strong to me that I almost gagged. On our last night in camp, when we returned for the night, as we were settling in, I think we must have spooked a skunk because the tent filled with the nauseating smell of skunk scent. At first, I thought we might have to abandon everything but after a while, the air carried the aroma away. Thank goodness.

Most of the time spent in Steamboat Springs was in the library. Ralph had about a day and a half of work to do and I people watched, read my book, and looked at magazines while he worked. The actual Steamboat Springs was directly behind the library and it fed into the Yampa River totally smelling up the place with its sulfa smell. The Yampa River was a brown color due to all the hot springs feeding into it and the minerals being deposited. Even inside the library, I would get a good whiff now and then. The area was a popular place for swimmers and people tubing down the river. I don't think I could even dip my feet into that stinky river.

On our last night in Steamboat, we went to the rodeo. We have attended many rodeos in Atlanta but it is always nice to experience one in the west. They served wonderful barbeque cooked out on large grills and its smell was mouth watering. The taste was awesome too. My stomach bulged from eating too much.

The rodeo was entertaining and brought back long ago memories, some incredible ones from my young, single days working on a dude ranch in Jackson, Wyoming and some, bittersweet, of a little, three year old boy. Many years ago, Ralph and I lost our second born son, Patrick, to a fatal genetic disease. Patrick was seven month old when he died in my arms. Grieving terribly, and trying to escape Atlanta for a time, Ralph and I packed our car and with our first born, little Perry, and left for Wyoming. In Casper, Wyoming, we stopped and bought Perry a full cowboy outfit. We took his picture in front of the railroad station dressed in his cowboy hat, leather vest and chaps and tiny cowboy boots. Perry was so darling as he tried to walk in his new boots. That was the first time in many, many months I had laughed.

On a cool summer evening, we took Perry to the rodeo in Jackson, Wyoming. His eyes were wide with excitement and wonder. When it came time for the calf chase, all the children scurried out of the stands and into the arena. Ralph took Perry down to the ring and a cowboy lifted him over the fence to join the other children. Perry ran as fast as his little three-year-old legs would carry him, to join the others. He was going to catch a ribbon attached to the calf's tail. Seeing how much smaller Perry was compared to the other children, the cowboy who had lifted Perry over the fence took Perry by the hand and led him into the middle of the arena where Perry would get a head start. There, my little boy stood, in the middle of the dusty arena, dressed up like the cowboy holding his hand, smiling for all the world to see. At that exact moment the announcer said, "Ok, everybody, lets give a great big hand to the littlest cowboy!" With that, the whole crowd cheered and clapped for my little cowboy. My heart and eyes filled with tears. How could those cowboys have known that such a small gesture, to such a small, little boy, at such a wounded time in his parent's hearts, could mean so much? I will forever, until the day I die, see my Perry, standing in the middle of a dusty rodeo arena, ready to catch his cow.

The rodeo in Steamboat Springs ended and I tucked my memories away in that special place in my heart as we headed back to camp. Everything was a mess inside the tent, as we had had to change campsites earlier in the morning. Someone had reserved the site we were in for that night and no amount of pleading and convincing on our part, to move the future campers to another spot, worked. It was very irritating having to move all our stuff and we just threw everything into the tent before we left for the library and then later the rodeo.

We cleared just a spot to sleep and reorganized and packed up in the morning. Then it was off to Grand Lake, Colorado at the western side of Rocky Mountain National Park. We only had about one hundred miles to cover and before we knew it, we had arrived in Grand Lake. I was shocked again to see the growth that had taken place in the area since I was here last with Perry, Milissa, and Amanda.

The town was packed with tourist and weekenders from Denver. I think we got the last hotel room in the town. The room was fine except for no air conditioning, but I was thankful for the room anyway. Fortunately, the actual town hadn't changed much at all and the one street down through town still was lined with wooden sidewalks. The old ice cream store was still there and well as some of the other places that the kids and I enjoyed twelve years ago.

We rode into the national park for a little bit but turned around when it was time to head back for our reservations for horseback riding. You would think we would have had enough of riding things but no, we had to be gluttons and take a four-hour ride back to The

Big Meadows. It was just Ralph, I, and the wrangler, Sara, on our ride. We rode about ten miles round trip and wound up being four and a half hours.

Ralph had a Belgian horse named Sunny and was marked in the typical color of Belgians, that being tan with white mane and tail. The wrangler rode a roan named Roany of all things. Now, my horse, I had been eyeing when we came to the stables and I was hoping I would get to ride her. I was delighted when the wrangler helped me onto her wide back. She was a huge, solid black Percheron and I just about died laughing when I asked her name. Oprah, yep that was her name. She and I got along just fine.

Our trip back into the back woods was grand. We traveled through forest of firs and aspens and followed a creek. The creek wound and snaked its way through the forest and grass. A nice cool breeze blew through the pines and made a soothing pleasant whispering. Along the way, we saw some elk and an elk calf. The ears on the calf were way out of proportion to the rest of the body. Even with the calf trying to hide in the tall grass, the ears were a dead give away to its location.

We also saw, in a meadow we passed on our right, a mama moose, and her calf grazing on the other side of the meadow. Then two bull moose came out of the bushes and joined in. They had a full rack each and were not the least threatened by us. Of course, they were on the other side of the meadow too.

When we got to The Big Meadow, we dismounted. I wasn't sure my legs were going to support me but they did and we had a little break, drank some water, and munched on some trail mix. I fed the horses some of the trail mix, only one of which really enjoyed the raisins and nuts.

When we got back on the horses, I realized it was going to be a long way back to the coral and I had body parts that were really making themselves known. I heard Ralph behind me saying that his knees were hurting too. Well, that wasn't the only thing that was hurting! I think the only things not hurting on me were my hands and head. Everything else was a bundle of sore muscle, tight joints, and raw skin.

On our way back, the two bull moose had turned into three and were now on our side of the meadow. All three had large racks and were so absorbed in their grazing that they hardly even gave us a second look. We stopped and I tried to get some pictures but Oprah wouldn't stand still. We were probably fifty yards from the three bull moose. They would stick their heads up out of the grass, look at us, and then return to munching.

When we finally made it back to the stable, I thought there was no way I could climb down off Oprah. Percheron horses are gigantic in height and girth. Sara, the wrangler, helped me slide down Oprah's belly and to my surprise, my knees held. My entire body from my rib cage down was screaming with protest as to what I had done to it in the last four and a half hours. I tried to apologize but my body didn't accept it. It was payback time now. I wasn't sure I could even get back on the bike and ride it the three blocks back to our hotel. Back at the room, I quickly swallowed four Nuprin and waited while Ralph took a shower.

I couldn't even muster up enough energy to shower, so we went into town and got some dinner. I was filthy but really didn't care. I knew I wouldn't see any of those people again. By now Ralph was starting to feel some complaining body parts too.

Back in the room, I managed a shower and fell into bed nice and clean. Tonight is the first time we have actually turned on a television since we left home. We both moaned and groaned about sore muscles and tender butts as we watched the end of the earth documentary on the explosion of a super volcano that is under Yellowstone National Park.

I think we are just going to hang out in the park tomorrow, due some browsing around in the shops and be lazy. Tuesday morning we'll head out again. I think we are going to go toward Idaho, as both of us have never explored that state.

Grizzle Bear had to have a scoop of rainbow sherbet to help soothe his sore butt and tired muscles. Though he's been a trooper, I don't think horse back riding is something he is going to repeat any time soon. He has to sleep on his stomach and I can hear him doing some serious grumbling and complaining over in his corner of the room. Maybe he'll feel better tomorrow.

So until later, much love to all always,
Judy/Mom/Mommy

August 2, 2005
Tuesday
Grand Junction, CO
Mile 15,000

Dear Folks,

I think our trip hit the doldrums. We were in an area of the country that we had both seen before, several times. Though it was still quite beautiful, we were looking for something new to see. Our trip is winding down with just several weeks remaining and we both were feeling a little depressed.

We originally planned to head up into Idaho today and explore that region. This morning Ralph was feeling rather antsy and got out the computer and the mapping software to see just how far Monument Valley was from our present location. Well, plans changed abruptly this morning and instead of heading for Idaho we headed southwest again and are now headed for Arches National Park, Canyonlands National Park and Natural Bridges National Monument and then on to Monument Valley. They are all in the same location of southeast Utah.

A few weeks ago, we had changed our route when a heat wave interfered with our southerly route through that area. According to the most recent weather report, the southwest area has cooled a bit. We thought we would go back to our original plan to visit that area coming in through the north.

We left Grand Lake this morning and headed west again. Our journey took us over a high pass in the Rocky Mountains just outside Denver called Berthoud Pass. Oh, my it was gorgeous. Miles and miles of tall craggy mountains followed the road. We traveled just at the timberline and then climbed up above it reaching an elevation of around eleven thousand feet. The air was so cool and smelled so clean and refreshing. I hated to leave the mountains but I was looking forward to seeing some new territory.

Unfortunately, there was a two hundred mile stretch of interstate that I had to travel over, as there was really no other way over the mountains. We went up high again, the wind picked up, and the traffic was hauling butt, too fast for me. However, the ride was incredible in spite of the road we were on.

We headed west, out I-70 over Loveland Pass and through tunnels and past Vail. I have never seen Vail, but I can tell just from what I saw from the interstate, there are many very rich people living there. Just about the time we arrived in Vail, the rain came down and the wind blew and blew. It was just the sort of riding I really can't wait to do! And, of course, please add in the tractor-trailer trucks and the speeding cars and you have a wonderful concoction just waiting to make me sick to my stomach.

We finally rode out of the rain and the mountains and we immediately were in the canyons. High walls of sandstone and sedimentary rock that had been carved down by the Colorado River, lined the interstate. The walls were monstrous and we were riding through a layer of sediment that had been put down millions of years ago. We rode through areas where cliffs and plateaus were as high as some of the Rocky Mountains we had just ridden through. It was absolutely stunning.

It was getting late in the afternoon and the cool air of the mountains was mixing with the warm air of the valleys we were riding through. Guess what that produced? Yep, wind and rain.

Over the time frame of our trip we have become quite good at predicting just when a good gust of wind would blindside us. We have learned that when traveling through canyons there will be wind howling through the walls. Bridges over wide rivers or deep canyons produce turbulence. Big valleys surrounded on one side by mountains or foothills are always good for a good blow. Entering tunnels are ok but coming out the other side usually gets you smacked here and there. Weather produces great winds particularly when it wants to rain. Always on the leading edge of a storm, there are wonderful winds. Beware, these winds come swirling at you from all directions. Then there was always the surprising, swirling, twirling crosswinds that just jump up and sideswipe you with no predictability at all. They are the most fun, let me tell you. One minute you are looking at the beautiful scenery and then wham, off to the side of the road you go. Loads of fun for all.

Oh, and I forgot the tractor-trailer trucks out here. They are no longer the single tractor-trailer of the east and they are not the double trailers either. They are now triples! When one passes me either coming at me or passing around me the wind knocks me all over the lane.

I believe we had all of these today. If it hadn't been for all the beautiful scenery, it would have been a bummer day. At one point during the ride down the interstate, it was as if the land had been divided right down the middle by the road. On my right the cliffs and bluffs were brightly lit by the intense sun and blue sky. White mounds of clouds floated here and there. At one point, I thought there was snow on the mountains due to such intense light.

On the left side of the interstate, all the bluffs and mountains were shrouded in black and grey of impending rain and storm. Rain was already falling from the clouds and fell like a black drape across the mountains. The areas are so vast out here that one can see such opposites at the same time.

The longer we continued our journey west as we followed the Colorado River, the wider it became and the canyons became deeper and more carved by the passage of time. As we entered the last canyon for the day, I thought it was interesting how the interstate had been built. It was tiered in layers. The westbound side, which we were on, was higher than the eastbound side and through most of the canyon, both directions, were built as bridges over each other. It was a most efficient way of building an interstate through a narrow canyon without destroying anything.

Just as we were about to leave the canyon, I looked high up on one wall to my left and saw something that caught my eye. I looked a little closer and saw that it was the America Flag, blowing straight out in the wind. It looked to me as if a rock climber had scaled the cliff wall and placed the flag there. Though it was rather small from where I was, I knew it was a full size flag. That image of the flag standing out straight in the wind high above the canyon floor and the Colorado River will stay with me for a long time.

As we left the canyon, our trip took us by rock walls of tan and red and I literally had my head all the way back to see the tops of the cliffs.

The area leveled out but all around us were mountains and the black storm clouds were threatening on all sides now. It was going to be a race to see whether we got to a hotel room first or were drowned in the downpour that was sure to happen.

Just as we rolled under the cover of the hotel entrance, the sky opened up. What timing. I told Ralph that I was done for the day anyway.

We have about eighty more miles on the interstate tomorrow that I'm not looking forward to at all, but then we will return to the back roads where hopefully, I can take some pictures. As beautiful as the scenery was today, I could not stop and capture any photos. It's not a good idea to stop on the side of the interstate where the speed limit is seventy and everyone is doing at least ninety. Ralph and I only managed about sixty miles per hour in the winds. That was scary enough.

Except for the ride on the interstate, the land was very stunning and it turned out to be a very good day indeed.

Grizzle Bear liked being back on his perch on my bike. He wasn't too fond of getting wet though but he dried out quickly in the hot arid air. He's already asleep and I hear some tiny snoring coming from his corner of the room. Good, now I don't have to share my candy with him tonight.

So until next time, love to all always,
Judy/Mom/Mommy

August 3, 2005
Wednesday
Moab, Utah
Mile 15,162

Dear Folks,

Wonderful new life has been breathed into our remaining time on the road. What a fantastic idea Ralph had to head southwest. Since I had never seen Arches National Park before, I mapped a route for us on a back road that was hardly on the map at all. It was barely a pin scratch on the map but took us through some incredible territory.

As soon as we got off the interstate, the narrow road took us thorough some very dry desert like land. Off in front of us I could see what looked like cliffs and canyons. As I hoped, the road took us right through the canyon area. For millions of years the Colorado River had been cutting through this canyon. Skyscrapers of bright red rock exposing their layers jutted high into the sky as we rode down the road beside the river.

This road to me seemed like one that shouldn't even be there. We were just a moment in time passing through the area. The canyon widened in parts, showing quite clearly where the river and wind had once carved its path and then narrowed just as quickly with red walls close beside us. I felt like we were traveling and exploring the banks and cliffs of the Grand Canyon. At one point, the canyon walls were so close I felt I could reach out and touch them. Black minerals seeped out of the red sandstone and colored the faces of the canyons walls with patterns and etchings that looked like a giant hand had carved petroglyphs into them. I imagined a giant cave man carving his drawings into the walls.

As we got closer to the main highway that led to Arches National Park, I noticed that there were many rafts on the Colorado River and it looked like everyone was having a great time in the muddy river waters. I was ready to jump on board. I have always wanted to raft the Colorado River in the Grand Canyon.

There were a few ranches that looked like something out of Architect's Digest. Beautiful ranch lodges, buildings with a southwest flavor, and pastures were established along the river with the red rock walls as a backdrop. I assumed that they pumped their water for the fields directly out of the river, as the pastures were a rich green among the dry red canyon walls.

When we reached the main road and took a right heading north to the park, we crossed the Colorado River and the canyon widened. The park was just a few miles up the road. We stopped, got a map of the area, and headed out into the park. I think I am at a loss for words to describe this area. I took so many pictures so I hope they will give just a tiny hint of the beauty of this land. On the map, it appears just a tiny area of this country but when actually riding through it the area is massive. The forces of nature that carved the sandstone walls and monoliths and the arches are unimaginable. Right in the middle of hard pieces of sandstone walls, pieces begin to break away due to wind and water erosion. After millions of years, a hole appears and the arch is left.

At every bend and turn in the road I had to stop and take more pictures. Every outcropping of rock had a different shape and different names. Some of them were Park Avenue, Courthouse Towers, Three Gossips, Balanced Rock, Parade of Elephants, Garden of Eden, Fiery Furnace, and the Devil's Garden.

Through out the park huge boulders of red sandstone balanced precariously atop spikes of other types of sandstone. It looked as if at any moment a puff of wind would send the house size boulders crashing down onto the road. I know some day that will happen but I'm glad to say I won't see that happen. Those boulders will fall a long way and tumble even farther until they come to rest on the canyon floor.

There was only one road into the park so we had to back track to get out but the view was different coming back and those views that were at our backs were now in front. So we got double the viewing beauty. The sun was sinking in the west and it cast its late afternoon light on the red rocks creating different shadows on the places we had already seen.

All around us for miles, we could see the afternoon thunderstorms building. Occasionally bolts of lightning would flash down. This land also had the look of a primitive time when different creatures roamed the earth. Some of the white billowing clouds were flattening out of the bottoms getting ready to be storm clouds. Their flat bottoms picked up the color of the red sandstone below and had turned the clouds a pink cast.

The trip back out was not as long as the one into the park. I didn't take any more side roads or stop for any more pictures. The clouds were looking very angry and we needed to find a hotel room in Moab.

This day was filled with unbelievable sites and it stimulated my brain and spirit. Both of us felt excited all day seeing a new area and finding surprises around every corner.

We managed to find a room before it started raining. By the way the sky looked and the lighting bolts that were coming down high up on the cliffs and mountain ridges, I expected to be blown away. Actually, it only rained just a bit and not enough to stop us from walking a few blocks to get some dinner. We ate dinner in an Italian restaurant on the main street. By far, my dinner was the best Three Cheese Ravioli I have ever put in my mouth, anywhere, anytime. Our dinners were so good that we asked the waitress to tell the cook how much we enjoyed the dinner.

Tomorrow we are going to see Canyonlands National Park, which is in the same vicinity. I've never been there either so I hope it will be a treat.

Grizzle Bear hummed along our passage through Arches National Park. I think the French fries I threw him earlier in the day kept him busy. I heard a few ooohs and ahhhs today as we viewed the rocks and canyons. The heat has worn him out and after a few of Ralph's M&M's he is already sound to sleep next to the air conditioner. I may have to throw him a towel for a blanket in a while.

So until next time, love to all always,
Judy/Mom/Mommy

August 4, 2005
Thursday
Mexican Hat, UT
Mile 15,442

Dear Folks,

There are some days in your life, that experiences, sights, and senses alter your soul and spirit forever. Today was such a day. Today we rode through the Valley of the Gods and my spirit has been forever fortified, nourished, strengthened, and changed.

I will try with my humble words to describe the experience but first I have to start at the beginning of the day in order to get to the Valley of the Gods.

After a great breakfast in a local diner in Moab, we headed north a little to get to Canyonlands National Park. The road led right past Arches National Park and past great red sandstone cliffs. The road to Canyonlands climbed steadily up from the canyon floor and up onto a plateau which turned out to be a big finger of land sticking out into the canyons. The elevation was nothing to sneeze about either, some reaching six thousand, four hundred and twenty feet.

Now imagine standing right at the cliff's edge with only a wooden fence barrier between you and the valley floor over six thousand feet below. Pretty scary huh? Today was a day for long beautiful vistas and canyons seen from way up high. My human eye had trouble deciphering the depths and perspectives so you can imagine that the camera really had trouble. There is no way the camera could do justice to the hundreds of miles of canyons below us. If I did not know better I could have been at the Grand Canyon. It was that beautiful.

Below us ran the Green and Colorado Rivers, the same ones that Powel explored. The two rivers joined right below us. Can you begin to imagine what an adventure he had on his journey? Now I'm going to have to go do some more reading about his venture into the unknown.

After seeing thousands of beautiful canyons for hundreds of miles, we headed back down south, towards Bridges National Monument. I enjoyed the ride and seeing more arches along the side of the road. I was completely surprised by the temperature. The day had started in clouds but they were trying to move out and of course, that created some pretty good winds and some brief moments of rain. Once we cleared that front, we moved into blue skies and cool temperatures for the area we were in. I think the temperatures were in the low eighties and not the usual high nineties.

The ride out to Natural Bridges National Monument ran parallel to a ridge that pointed toward the sky at an angle. From the geology classes I remember taking in college, I knew from the shape of the ridge that on the other side there would be a sharp drop off and a cliff. I was wondering just what it might look like on the other side when the road curved toward the ridge and looked like it was going to run right over the top. Instead, the road went right through the middle of the cliff. The road had been cut smack through the middle of bright red sandstone and we exited on the other side. Sure enough, there was the sharp drop off and the cliff face just as expected. The view from the other side was spectacular. The bluff and ridge ran for many, many miles as far as I could see in both directions.

For the next twenty miles or so the road ran through an area that was covered with low pines which later, I found out, were called pygmy pines. The area wasn't all that pretty and I was beginning to think that the Natural Bridges National Monument couldn't possibly be in the area. But when we reached it, I realized that we had been riding on top of the plateau and the natural bridges were in the canyons below.

The nine-mile one-way road, that led through the park, circled the canyons. In the time and water worn areas below us were the bridges that had been created by rushing water millions of years ago. These cliffs and bridges were white sandstone instead of all the red sandstone we have been surrounded by lately. I got a few pictures of the bridges but again, perspective was difficult.

Late afternoon was upon us and after completing the nine-mile circular trip around the park it was time to scoot on to Mexican Hat, Utah before the sun went down. Now, we could either back track the forty miles we had just come over, catch the main highway, and go another forty miles into Mexican Hat for a total of about eighty miles or we could take a tiny thread of a road that was only thirty-eight miles and cut off a long ride.

No sooner had we pulled onto the shortcut than a bright yellow sign just about the size of a billboard announced that the road up ahead was gravel, narrow, with steep grades and switchbacks. The sign also advised that no campers, or trailers or vehicles over a certain weight should venture down this road.

Well, the road ahead of us looked pretty tame and was paved and plenty wide. I thought that perhaps they had paved the road and had just neglected to take the sign down. We rode for twenty-eight miles on a nice paved road. I knew we were on a long flat plateau and an occasional glance to my left, way off into the distance was the flat valley. I was also sensing that at some point we would have to descend off the great plateau we were riding on. At that point, Mexican Hat was only about ten miles away and I couldn't even begin to fathom the next three miles.

Up over a hill we rode and there was an additional sign just like the one we had seen twenty-eight miles before. This time it meant business though with stronger reminders of the road up ahead. I had a flashback to the old westerns I had watched as a child, of the stagecoach with running horses totally out of control heading directly for the cliff and the drop off into oblivion. That is exactly what this road did.

It came directly to the edge of the plateau and dropped off at least twelve hundred feet into nothingness. And now the gravel started too. Ralph and I stopped right at the top and looked down at what was called a road down to the bottom of the canyon. I couldn't believe it was a road and not some goat path down the sheer face of a red canyon wall.

Out in front of us as far as we could see to the horizon was what I thought at the time, the most beautiful, breathtaking vista I have ever seen in my life. Hundreds of miles before us or actually below us were red monoliths of giant sandstone. The red giants were surrounded by green grasslands. The sun was behind us and it cast its warm blanket of light all over the earth below us. I could have stayed there and looked for a while but the decision to descend was either now or never as evening was approaching. I failed to take a picture, I was so stunned by the glory around me and the scary road below.

The road, whose name was the Moki Dugway, was one of Ralph's worst nightmares. It was very, very narrow, steep downhill, gravel and sharper than hairpin switchbacks and *no* guardrails. Ralph chose to go first and I followed him over the rim. He rode right up next to the cliff wall and he dropped his feet off his pegs as if they were landing gear. I guess he figured if the bike went over, he would stand a better chance of bailing if his legs and feet were closer to what passed as a road. He scrapped bottom a few times on the descent sending up puffs of dust from his boots scraping the gravel. He was going too fast for me but I was sure this was because he wanted to get off that cliff as quickly as possible.

For some reason, why I don't know, this road did not scare me. I was so enthralled in the scenery and concentrating on getting down safely in one piece that I didn't think about being scared. However, put me on an interstate and I immediately fall to pieces.

About half way down Ralph stopped on a narrow switchback and I right next to him. We both exclaimed at the beauty before us and Ralph said he had conquered his fear of flying at such heights. When we reached the bottom, we stopped again and I looked back and took a picture of the canyon wall we had just come over. Looking back up the cliff, we couldn't even see the road we had just come down. The road was literally built into the side of the canyon wall.

I have thought a good deal about fear over the past few weeks. I have come to the conclusion that fear is never conquered. We only experience fear because we are afraid of dying. Fear is our natural instinct to survive and without it, man would have perished long ago. I think both Ralph and I have a strong sense of survival. We both experience fear in different ways and with different experiences. That also makes us good partners as what scares one, doesn't scare the other and the one not experiencing fear gets the other one through the traumatic event.

It is very hard to run from fear and sometimes events force you to get up close and personal with it. But meeting fear face on, I think, makes you brave and bravery to me is admiral. So, Ralph I salute you. You faced one of your deepest fears head on and met it with bravery.

Now at the bottom of the cliff, the road turned back to good pavement but just a little bit further up the road was the turn off to the Valley of the Gods. It was a seventeen-mile gravel road. We looked at each other, looked back at the cliff we had just descended, looked out before us at the dirt road and both of us said, "Lets try it."

So off we went into the Valley of the Gods, with Ralph in the lead and I following. I think this must be the most beautiful seventeen miles of road on the face of the earth. The whole trip we have been on, including Alaska, we have seen such sites that the mind and heart absorb and heal the soul, but what I saw today made my soul and spirit rejoice in its beauty.

In Alaska, I saw the earth as prehistoric, raw and land just being formed. Here in the Valley of the Gods, this was a land before time, an Eden of sorts.

For the past two and a half months, I have tried with words to explain what I have seen, but today I have literally found myself speechless. I just don't think there are words in my vocabulary that can describe the splendor and the glory I witnessed today.

This tiny gravel road took us through a place that I think was set aside just for us today. Up and down, over and around great mountains of red eroded rock. How many millions of years have these stood sentinel? I felt as if I were on a different planet seeing something that no man has ever seen. Could this really be our mother earth? Yes, it is ours and what a privilege I had today.

The sun was sinking behind the cliff behind us and strong afternoon orange sun shown on the red outcroppings in front of us. It was like riding through orange marmalade colored light. While some areas were already in shade, others were lit up with the orange rays of the setting sun. Way off in the distance the rays shown like beacons, casting an eerie glow over the grasslands and the red mountains.

As we were getting close to the end of the road off to my left was a red hill and directly beside it was a rainbow. My eyes were just having trouble taking in all the beauty. My arms wanted to embrace all my surroundings and gather them next to my beating heart. We stopped our bikes, turned off the engines, and listened to the wind blowing over the canyons and rocks. This is the same wind that continues shaping the red landscape before us and has done so for millions of years. It was singing an ageless aria.

The two of us, all alone on this piece of earth, and all alone in this moment in time, with just the wind for our music and the silence for our symphony, hearts and souls joined as one, watched as the sun set and set the sky on fire with magenta, red and orange. The rainbow behind us disappeared but the clouds behind the mountain where the rainbow had been now looked like it was on fire also.

Once the sun was behind the cliff the light faded very quickly and the fiery red sky and pinks and oranges disappeared turning into dusty blues and pale lavenders. Bats, busy finding dinner, darted close to us as we moved toward our bikes. We finished the final two miles of this incredible road in the blueness of dusk and by the time we found pavement again it was dark but my soul was alive and vibrant and the colors of the day bursting in my brain.

We rode on into Mexican Hat and Ralph found us a place to stay. The adobe style lodge had a band playing under the trees and the restaurant was outside under the trees next to the live music. A large outdoor grill fed by mesquite wood cooked our steaks and as the desert breeze blew gently, we ate our dinner.

What a day, what a day. Hope everyone enjoys the pictures even though they can't even come close to what my heart, soul, and spirit experienced today. I have been forever touched.

Grizzle Bear is silent tonight. I think his little grin on his face is a reflection of the joy he also experienced today at the beautiful earth around him.

So until next time, love to all always,
Judy/Mom/Mommy

August 7, 2005
Sunday
Ogden, Utah
Mile 16,183

Dear Folk,

After our spirit moving experience in the Valley of the Gods, we left the following morning to the buzz of dozens of hummingbirds. As we packed the bikes under the trees at the hotel, dozens of hummingbirds attracted by the feeders hanging in the trees, sipped nectar. I stood and watched for some precious moments as the tiny birds hummed and buzzed back and forth between different feeders.

There were only three hotels in Mexican Hat and I think these were the only buildings in addition to the one gas station. We rounded the bend in the road and crossed the river and that was the end of the town. We were sixteen miles from Monument Valley but we could actually see the monuments far off in the distance.

Right out in the middle of small hills of grass and scrub brush were the huge monuments that made up this place called Monument Valley. They were indeed impressive but we passed through them too quickly and I wanted to see more. One thing that I did find disappointing was all the run down homes of the Navajo Indians. This was their land but their homes were tossed here and there and were not very well kept up. Junk and broken down cars littered the yards. It reminded me of the people that still live in the mountains of Appalachia.

I think it must have been round-up day, as all along the road the Navajo Indians were riding horses rounding up cattle and sheep. I had a mental flashback to another time when the Indians did the same thing except there were no fences, no commercialization and the land was truly theirs.

Today, was like to me, a day we have at home when we decide to go for a ride in the mountains. This was such a day except, that instead of mountains and streams and trees, the scenery was colorful canyons, cliffs, and dry scrub brush. It was a nice ride in the open countryside.

We made it to Lake Powel, stopped for lunch and gas and moved on up the highway. As we rode past the lake, it was amazing to see how far down the water level was. A drought for the last four to five years has dropped the water level down fifty to ninety feet in some places. It will take years of good steady precipitation upstream to refill the lake. It was still quite beautiful in spite of the water level.

We were also amazed at the air temperature. We had wisely avoided the heat wave weeks earlier and the temperature for the last few days in the southwest had been in the low eighties. What fortunate good luck.

Late in the afternoon, we stopped in the little town of Kanab, Utah about forty miles from Zion National Park. Our plans for the next day were to visit Zion National Park and Brice National Park.

The next morning in the quickly warming sunshine, we headed for Zion National Park. In the area of the southwest, we found we were either riding on top of a plateau, mesa, or cliff or we were riding in the canyons with the walls rising directly next to us several thousand feet high.

Zion National Park was such a place of towering canyon walls of bright red and creamy white. The Virgin River was responsible for the cutting of the canyon that created the park. Only one part of the park is accessible by personal vehicle and that part is a state road that crosses the lower part of the park. The only way to see the remainder of the park is to go via shuttle bus. Though this was not very appealing, we took the shuttle anyway to see the remainder of the park. Fortunately, years ago I actually drove down into the depths of the canyon with the kids. I look forward to looking at those old photos when I get home. The bus ride made us both very sleepy so we were drowsy by the time we made it back to our bikes.

One thing I had forgotten about the state road that you could drive on, was the tunnel that goes right through the middle of the mountain. The tunnel is over a mile long and dark as pitch. There are two windows cut to the outside and a quick glance out reminded me of just how high up we were.

By the time we reached Bryce National Park it was very late afternoon. We went to Sunset Point and watched the golden sun hit the red and white hoodoos. Hoodoos are what are left of the rock in Bryce when erosion does its thing. Eventually erosion wins and the hoodoos fall but for a while, they look to me like tall soldiers with red and white uniforms.

We saw just enough of Bryce National Park to get a good taste of what the canyon looked like. It isn't a very big park and only one road about fifteen miles in length. Both of us were here once before but seeing again still enriched the eyes, brain, and heart.

Dusk was upon us when we left the park and we were heading for a small town about twenty-five miles away. Just outside the park, we passed a campground that had tepees out front. On a whim we turned around and decided to camp instead of driving another twenty-five miles to the nearest town. They had one tepee left and we snapped it up. We quickly unloaded our gear inside the tepee and set up our sleeping bags. We were amazed at how much room was inside. Sleeping inside a tepee was unique and fun and on top of it, we didn't have to set up a tent. I felt sort of like a kid again and I knew without a doubt that Perry, Milissa, and Amanda would have gotten a big kick out of camping in a tepee.

We had a nice fire and as the flames died down, the stars were amazing. They were even more visible than when we were in the desert. I think the elevation and clean air had something to do with it. We were at an elevation of over eight thousand, three hundred feet and the air was thin. The Milky Way was bright and I saw several shooting stars. I wish we could be in that exact spot on August eleventh when the meteor shower comes through.

After a pretty good night's sleep in the forty-degree air, we were up early to the sound of helicopter tours over the canyon. We knew we were in for a tough day on the road and sure enough, it was very unpleasant. We were on our way back north, to Hood River, for the wedding. Today was about as miserable a day as we have had in a long time.

It was hot, hot, and hot and it was a day of riding interstates that I just love so much. I-15 in northern Utah is one strip of interstate that if I never see again, will be too soon. That piece of interstate is just one big city for over one hundred miles. When we finally stopped in

Ogden, Utah for the day, it was one hundred and seven degrees. The heat we missed a few weeks ago, we found today. The heat combined with the frightening interstate had me in a state of frenzy.

There was no other way around Salt Lake to get where we needed to be in Idaho. The west side of Salt Lake is owned and operated by the military. In the morning, we have a little more time on my favorite road and then I hope to find some cooler area in the mountains of Idaho.

Grizzle Bear loved sleeping in the tepee and I could hear him in the corner pretending he was an Indian. But the poor bear had trouble with the heat. He was whining, big time, by the time we found a cool hotel room. I think I see some thumb sucking going on over on his bed.

So until next time, love to all always,
Judy/Mom/Mommy

August 9, 2005
Tuesday
John Day, Oregon
Mile 16,804

Dear Folks,

We left Ogden, Utah around ten in the morning and it was already starting to warm up. Unfortunately, we were back on the interstate again, much to my dislike. I couldn't wait to be through with the horrible stretch of road. Just north of Brigham, Utah, the wind started to pick up and when we finally cleared the city traffic we had to deal with roaring tractor-trailers, speeding cars, and the vicious wind.

The farther north we went toward Idaho the worse the wind became. The wind roared so intensely that we could only ride about forty-five to fifty miles per hour. I knew we were in big time trouble when the signs warned that we were in a severe storm area with high winds for the next five million miles. The signs also warned not to stop on the road. Ignoring the signs, I was so frightened and so traumatized by the rushing vehicles and the vicious winds that I wanted to stop my bike right there on the side of the road, just abandon everything, and start walking. I have had my fill of interstates and will, at all cost, from this day forward, avoid them like the plague. I have had two days of terror and I'm done! I just don't think my insides can take any more.

To me, my fear of interstates, trucks, fast moving cars and the wind, it is like having a large, gaping wound on my chest and abdomen and all the nerves are raw and exposed and someone keeps irritating and scraping the raw wound and nerves. I reach the point of screaming with anxiety and fear and panic. That is terror to me. I don't really know why I get so terrified but it happens and try as I might, I just can't seem to conquer or even deal with this fear of mine.

I think it is all the noise of rushing tires, loud engines, idiots flying past me going ninety mile per hour, the weaving in and out of lanes, cutting in front of me, the crowding and bunching together of cars and trucks all speeding around me, that makes me come unglued. Also, I know if I go down on my bike, have a flat, or get blown into another lane, I am dead. At least when traveling on back roads I feel like I have a chance should something go wrong.

Well, enough of that, I get a sick feeling in my stomach just reliving the experience. When we finally got off the interstate, we headed north up into the Sawtooth Mountains. I was calm within minutes after getting off the interstate.

It was Ralph's birthday and I was sorry that the last two days had been a miserable ride. I had so hoped that we would have found a pretty road and a terrific place to celebrate his birthday. We made it to a town called Ketchum in Idaho and I thought that would be a good place. However, as it turned out it was a ski resort, Sun Valley, and the cheapest room in town was one hundred and sixty dollars. We pulled out the trusty computer, went to Google, and did a search on places in the area. I just happened to see a picture of teepees and went to that site. Just thirty-seven miles north of where we were, was a lodge, campground, and teepees. That's where we headed.

Just a little farther north of town, the air turned cool and the road took us right through the mountains. It was such a change from the awful territory we had been riding through for the past two days.

We rode through the valley and then the road started to climb over the mountains. As we were reaching the summit, I looked over to my left, back into the valley and the brief rain we experienced on the ascent, had caused a tremendous full rainbow from one end of the valley to the other. I stopped and got a picture and the colors were bright enough to show up on the camera.

On the other side of the mountains was another valley that stretched for miles and miles. Our descent took us into the valley and to the lodge where we were going to stay. It was called Smiley Creek Lodge and I tell you, it put a smile on my face.

The room we got was directly over the restaurant and was like an oven, but it did have a fan and I was sure it would cool down in the evening. We unloaded our stuff, carried it up the flight of stairs on the outside of the lodge, and dumped it in the room. The ceiling was angled on both sides, like an attic ceiling, and we had to be careful not to bump our heads.

We were looking forward to having a good dinner since the night before we ate in the truck stop next to the hotel. That meal was poor to say the least and probably one of the worst we have had on our trip.

Our meal in the Smiley Creek Lodge wasn't quite as bad as the truck stop, but not great either. The meal was so poor, that the waitress gave Ralph's dinner to him for half price since there was no gravy for his chicken fried steak. The potatoes had to be sent back to warm them up and the veggies were cold, too. The waitress threw in dessert for free and I sang a whispered "Happy Birthday" to him. I felt very sorry for Ralph on his birthday. I had really hoped we could have had a beautiful ride and a great dinner but it just didn't happen. He did get a solo birthday song from me over dessert and that made him smile.

He bought a cigar in the store and we sat outside, watched the sun go down over the Sawtooth Mountains, and waited for the first stars of the evening. We were not disappointed as the moon rose and with it, the new stars of the night. The area was very calm and peaceful. At least we weren't in some crowded, noisy city.

I slept rather comfortably, considering how hot our room was. The fan was going full blast and was pointed directly at the ceiling so it would fall back down on us. I used only a sheet for cover and managed to stay cool enough. Our room stayed warm, I think, due to being directly over the lodge and kitchen. Outside, the air was chilly. We couldn't really leave the door open to allow some of the mountain's cool air to enter because the area's mosquitoes would enjoy visiting.

This morning was like being at home and having Mama down in the kitchen fixing breakfast. I awoke to the smell of bacon frying and knew that breakfast was first thing on today's agenda. After showering and packing the bikes, we tried the restaurant again, thinking the cook really couldn't screw up eggs and bacon. Breakfast was good. I had fried eggs, bacon, hash browns, and toast. Yummy.

When we headed out for today's ride, it was rather cool and my jacket felt good. The road took us through the valley that ran through the Sawtooth Mountains. It was flat as a flitter and beautiful ranches lined the valley on each side of the road. I could have moved into any one of them, right then.

We climbed over another mountain pass and as we came down out of the mountains, we followed a stream that was as green as a lifesaver and clear enough to see the round rocks in the riverbed. By now, the temperature was rising as we were coming out of the mountains and back into the plains. I thought it would be nice to take a little dip in that nice green water.

We were just about to the next juncture in the road, when a bee came at me butt first and unloaded his entire payload into my left cheek, right under my sunglasses. Boy, oh boy, it stung and at that moment there was no place to pull off the road. About a mile further down the road, at a historical marker, I pulled the bike off into the gravel parking lot and took off my helmet just to make sure the bee was gone. He was either gone or dead, I don't know, I don't care. My cheekbone felt as if a boxer had socked me, as it ached and throbbed.

We stopped at the junction in the road a few miles further up, at a gas station. Ralph filled the tanks and I got ice for my throbbing cheek. Ralph still has me beat though; he has been stung three times.

We had a pretty ride today and experienced everything from tall, rocky mountains, green valleys, yellow, grassy foothills, and desert areas. We've had all temperatures today too, from the sixty-degree coolness of the mountains, to the hot one hundred and eight degree desert in western Idaho and eastern Oregon.

We were trying to stop at about the two hundred and fifty mile range today but every small town we went through had no accommodations, no hotels, no campgrounds, hardly even a gas station. We rode an extra sixty-eight miles in the boiling heat to make it to John Day, a town large enough to have a place to stay.

We found a reasonably priced hotel to get out of the heat for the night. Ralph's bike had been having an electrical problem and would not turn on unless the neutral light was on. The light had been taking longer and longer to come on, finally quitting all together. The bike would not start at all. At least we were in the parking lot of the hotel when the bike quit working. We rolled it into the parking space right in front of our room. I don't know what we're going to do and hope we aren't stuck here with only a few days left before the wedding.

Grizzle Bear is complaining about his empty stomach and about his little burned nose so I guess I'll have to go scrounge up some grub for the troops. I think he will quiet down if French fries and M&M's are offered up.

So until later, much love to all always,
Judy/Mom/Mommy

August 14, 2005
Sunday
Clarkston, WA
Mile 17,334

Dear Folks,

August 10

Ralph stayed up until almost two in the morning, attempting to fix his bike. He was successful in one aspect after taking the ignition switch apart and cleaning it and re-stretching the inner springs. While he was working on his bike in the parking lot in front of our room, a deer came right up to the grass not twenty feet from us. She stayed a long time, munching the bushes and wasn't the least bit frightened by us. She eventually wandered off and so did I, to bed, while Ralph kept working on the electrical problem.

Off we roared in the coolness of the morning and what a beautiful ride we had. We wound through canyons, back out onto flat plateaus, then back into canyons of small grassy hills, and finally, between dark-green, grassy farm lands.

Water is key to survival out among the desert conditions. It was really strange to ride for miles in the dirt hills and plateaus, come around the curve in the road, and be greeted by acres of rich green crops. I think the irrigation system must run continually.

One item of interest, that I have found amusing, was that some farm animals had figured out where the cool spots were in the fields. That spot was right under the industrial, farm-size sprinklers. Sleek shiny wet horses graze right next to the sprinklers. A group of very young calves had figured out that lying under the man-made rain was the perfect spot to spend the blistering hot day. There were several times during the hot ride that I thought about joining them. It certainly looked like the perfect place to me too instead of on blacktop over one hundred degrees.

Our road traveled by the John Day Fossil Beds. We stopped at one area since it was right on the road, climbed the hill to the top of the plateau and looked down at the layers of sediment and areas of serious upheaval laid down millions of years ago. The fossil beds are known to be some of the richest in the world. The fossil beds span a place in time from forty-five million years ago to five million years ago and contain such items as ancient plant life, animal life, lava flows, and riverbeds. I didn't actually see any fossils as I would have had to walk many miles down into the canyon to see them and the heat was stifling.

From our perch above the valley, we could see where the road was going to take us far on the horizon. The mountain looked to me, as if it had a large crack down the middle. That was where the road went, right through the crack in the mountain.

When we actually got close to the fissure in the mountain, we followed a stream that had cut the volcanic material just about in half. Walls of black volcanic rock stood in sheer cliffs along the road. We twisted and turned for miles through this area, riding through a time machine of sorts, as the rock around us was once molten lava thrown from the volcanoes. The lava flows of millions of years ago covered an area so large out here, that the flows covered landmasses of several states.

After we left the lava canyons, we followed the river on the flat plateau. We were getting close to the Mount Hood area again and the large volcanoes we had ridden next to several weeks ago were now shrouded in a thick haze. The entire area was covered in the haze for miles and miles. There had been some forest fires here in the last several days and the results was a cloudy haze to the atmosphere.

After lunch, we continued our trek north and climbing up the ledge of the plateau in Warm Springs, we were greeted by serious winds. We did not experience these on our trip down through the area weeks ago, but the winds were here now, and they were nasty.

We crossed back over the Warm Springs Indian Reservation and this time I thought the winds were really going to blow us off the road. They were vicious and we found we could not travel more than about forty-five to fifty miles per hour. I knew from our trip south earlier, that miles ahead were trees and if we could make the trees safely, the wind wouldn't be as bad. I felt like I was running for my life from the winds with their long arms trying to grab me from the sides. I was frightened.

As I assumed, however, when we reached the trees after traveling over a treeless, bushless area, the wind abated and we only were hit with a gust every now and then. Mt. Hood was just as impressive this time, even coming from a different direction. There was still snow on top and the air, in the higher elevation and the trees, cooled dramatically.

The closer we got to Hood River, the more orchards we passed. Fruit was ripening in the warm sun and rich soil. Harvest time was approaching. By late afternoon, we made it to Hood River safe and sound and checked into the hotel on the south side of the Columbia and the hateful bridge, for the next few days. The wedding was two days away.

Thursday August 11

Ralph spent the day working. Some much-needed time was spent resting from the past four days of hard riding. They had certainly caught up with me.

Friday, August 12

The rehearsal was held out at the farm in the morning and the dinner was held at a place called the Crag Rat Hut over looking the valleys full of orchards. Mt. Hood and smaller mountains surrounded the horizon. The setting was truly breath taking.

When we left Atlanta months ago, the wedding was, at that time a small affair with just a few friends and family. Now, several months later, it had blossomed to about seventy people. I thought it nice for William and Jody to have all their friends and family around them to celebrate their happy event.

Saturday, August 13

Some of the guest of the wedding went white water rafting in the morning. Ralph and I had to handle the usual administrative items that occur on a monthly basis and elected to stay in Hood River. We later, took a picnic down to the Columbia River to watch the wind surfers that had dotted the river for weeks, with their colorful sails. We found a nice spot in the shade and there we sat, along with all the wind surfers, waiting for the wind to blow. Now wouldn't you know it, the first opportunity to sit and relax and watch, the wind was not blowing. I couldn't believe it! After all the wind we had ridden through for days and even just the evening before when the tops of trees were being blown in half, now there wasn't even so much as a puff of breeze. The feeling, to me, was as if Mother Nature had flipped the wind switch into the off position.

The only ones on the river moving were those powered by gas and motors. But we still enjoyed the picnic and being outside in the warm air. (As if we haven't been outside enough in the last three months). I have noticed, that after being outside in the elements for so many days, that if I stay inside more than a few hours, except for sleep, I get antsy to be back outside. The indoors becomes stifling and confining.

We left the smooth as silk Columbia River, headed back to the room to dress for the wedding. I had just enough time to do one last load of laundry before we left the room to take the shuttle van over to the farm. Thankfully, I would not have to ride my bike over the bridge; I would not need blinders or valium. I scrunched down in the seat of the van and closed my eyes until we were safely on the other side of the Columbia River, in Oregon.

The wedding was sweet and beautiful. On a hill, overlooking Mt. Adam still covered in snow, and the sun setting gently over the mountains to the west, Jody walked on her father's arm to meet her new husband, William. The orange setting sun cast a sherbet color on her long silken gown and her skin glowed with afternoon sun. Her eyes shown with happiness as her father kissed her one last time, as his little girl and turned Jody over to her new love.

William and Jody spoke their own vows of love and support for each other and commitment of such for a lifetime. William's life, to me, was now complete.

With a kiss and a hug, the new Joiners were presented to family and friends and the sun bowed gracefully behind the mountains. It was a sweet and beautiful wedding.

The rest of the evening was spent in celebration with dinner and conversation. As Jody and William's first dance, they did a Tango to entertain us all. Then, daughter with her dad, and son with his mother, danced their dance. It was a sweet and beautiful wedding.

As we climbed back into the shuttle van for the trip back to the hotel, across the dark sky over the farm, I saw a bright shooting star. I saw that as good luck for the newly weds.

Sunday, August 14

Today it was time to head home and our route took us in a northeasterly direction. We headed out around ten this morning and the only choice of roads was either back over the bridge that I swore I would never do again on a bike, or down the interstate for about one hundred miles. I weighed my choices, neither of which was on my list of things I wanted to do, and chose the interstate. Since it was Sunday morning, there was very little traffic. With any luck, we would have a tail wind, so I hoped the conditions might not be so bad on the interstate where we were headed. There were no big cities to navigate, just open road. We traveled with the cliffs of the gorge on our right side and the Columbia River on the left.

I think luck was with me today. There was not a breath of wind, traffic was very light, and we encountered only three trucks on the one hundred mile stretch of interstate. Fortunately, the ride was uneventful.

The further east we went, the gorge, and river became more beautiful to me. I guess that is also because the surrounding area was less populated and the area was wilder and seemed untouched by man. I could imagine Lewis and Clark exploring the dramatic area.

When we left the interstate, our road followed the Columbia River for a little while longer then the river turned north and we turned east. The temperature escalated also. The cool air off the river and the wall of the gorge on our right had kept us cool. Now we were out in the open and it got blazing hot, fast.

Way off in the distance I could see hundreds of acres of yellow wheat. I was hoping we wouldn't be riding over that desolate area. We had made such good time today and I was ready for a break in the ride. I had planned on stopping in a good size town called Walla Walla, Washington. Just before we got into town, we hit the first detour we have had on this trip.

To our surprise, our little winding road took us right through the middle of the hills of wheat I had earlier seen. Very large hills several hundred feet high, lined the road. I was puzzled at the mountains of wheat. In the flat states of Kansas and Nebraska where wheat is grown one can see for hundreds of miles. I didn't expect to see crops grown on these small mountains that had flat tops. I couldn't figure out how the crops were planted much less harvested due to the steep angle of the land.

To ride through such eye-popping beauty of wheat fields in different stages of growth and harvest was a new experience. Once again, I thought to myself, that just when I thought I could not be surprised anymore, I was. The mountains of wheat either were ready to be harvested, or had just been cut. Those fields that had just been harvested for the wheat, were now waiting for the cutting and bailing of the remaining wheat straw. Then there were fields that had been turned over and had either been replanted or were laying dormant waiting for next years planting.

The soft-layered tones of yellow and brown reminded me of a giant, yellow cake layered with milk chocolate icing. The layers of yellow and brown went on for thousands and thousands of acres. I was glad the road had detoured, for I would probably never have had the chance to see these wheat fields.

Once back on the right road we made it into the town of Lewiston, Washington where we found a Super 8 motel that gave us a senior discount. A few days earlier, Ralph had arranged with the only motorcycle dealer in town to get a new back tire for his bike.

After that task is handled in the morning, we are headed on across the top of Idaho, into Montana and then south into Yellowstone. We hope to spend a few days in Jackson Hole, Wyoming before heading due east toward home.

Grizzle Bear enjoyed his little rest in the motel room for a few days. He slept way too much and was ready to hit the road again. He's been well behaved so far and not whining too much for French fries or M&M's. He's hoping he gets to do some more camping soon. I personally think that is because he is holding out hope for some more sticky marshmallows. We'll see. I think we can accommodate the camping but not sure about the sticky stuff.

So until next time, much love to all always,
Judy/Mom/Mommy

August 15, 2005
Monday
Hamilton, Montana
Mile 17,568

Dear Folks,

After Ralph got a new rear tire on his bike and we got the bikes refueled, oil added and lunch added to our stomachs, it was one in the afternoon by the time we left today. The temperature had already risen to more than uncomfortable proportions. We crossed the Snake River and headed out of town on a fast moving four lane.

I was just making my move to pass a tractor-trailer, when I saw the sign for Route 12 veering off sharply to the right. I wasn't expecting the turn that soon and by the looks on my map in front of me, I didn't see where the right turn was. I recovered quickly, scooted back behind the truck and we made our get away from the four lane onto a nice two lane.

Route 12, which crosses some of Washington and all of Idaho, turned out to be one astonishing ride. Although it was one of those brain melting, eyeball dissolving days, due to the heat, the beauty of the road made up for it.

Route 12 ran through a canyon and followed the Clearwater River. The river really was clear and shallow enough to see the round rocks and boulders on the bottom. Every now and then, the shallow water would tumble over rocks sticking out of the water, causing small rapids. The occasional cool breath of air coming off the river combined with the shade of the canyon wall on our right helped keep us reasonably comfortable.

As the day continued, so did the rise in temperature, until I thought I was melting. The water we followed was just too tempting to me. It was driving me crazy looking at the refreshing water babbling over rocks. I became increasingly thirsty and hotter, until I just couldn't stand it any more.

I started looking for a place to stop and finally, around a bend in the road, I spotted a sandy spot on the river with a pull off in the shade. I had made up my mind I was going in the water. And that is just what I did. I took my boots and socks off and waded into the cool mountain water. Tiny minnows swarmed around my feet as I wiggled my toes in the cold wet sand on the river bottom. I dipped my hat into the water and poured it onto my head. My, oh my, what pure pleasure I received from such a simple thing.

Ralph took off his shirt and dipped it into the water but that is as far as he went. I couldn't talk him into joining me either. Both of us dipped our helmets into the river to soak them in cold mountain water.

It was rather difficult putting on hot boots over wet feet and the sand stuck to my wet jeans that I had to sit in to put my boots back on, but it was well worth the inconvenience. I dripped water and wet sand back to the bikes and poured the water that was in my helmet, into my jacket.

I was very refreshed and feeling quite rejuvenated when we got back on the road. We entered the mountain canyons and tall evergreens had taken the place of yellow grass and scrub brush. The air was also cooler and that, combined with my soaked clothes, was delightful.

There is just something about a creek, a stream, or a river on a hot scorching day that just begs to go wading or swimming in. I can hardly resist any of them. Today was perfect for just such sport. I was not the only one to get the call of the river. Just two miles further down the road, four bikes were parked on the side of the road in a pull out. All the bikers had climbed down the riverbank, discarded their clothes, and were having a reunion with nature in the cool, clear water of the river. I laughed and waved as I went by. I truly understood.

Of the two hundred and thirty some odd miles we rode today, about one hundred and eighty ran through the canyons of scrub and yellow grass and evergreens on the road right next to the river. The road had long curves the entire way and was such a pleasure to ride. Usually, when riding I see road signs that says, "Curves Next 2 Miles." The one I saw today was a first. It said, "Curves Next 77 Miles." There were curves for the next seventy-seven miles but they were nice long curves that did not slow us down, but let us glide down the road.

The ride was good today and I came into the town of Hamilton smelling of river water and dirt but it sure was worth every moment. Tomorrow, we are going to try to make the town of West Yellowstone, Montana, which is just outside the entrance of the west side of Yellowstone National Park.

Grizzle Bear needs a bath something fierce. He just plain stinks. I gave his little head a sniff tonight and gagged. Too much time spent outside with the bugs and dirt and not enough water and soap. I have threatened a bath and he escaped under the bed and spit a raspberry at me. No M&M's for him.

So until next time, love to all always,
Judy/Mom/Mommy

August 18, 2005
Thursday
Jackson Hole, WY
Mile 18,053

Dear Folks,

We left Hamilton around ten in the morning and headed toward West Yellowstone, Montana. The ride through the valley was basically through businesses and log home manufacturers. Eventually, after about thirty miles, the road became a two lane and our junction to the east returned us into the backcountry.

The Bitterroot Mountains that we had followed in the valley were almost completely obscured by the haze caused by local forest fires. I was so amazed by just how far the smoke could float over the mountains and valleys. It covered an area of hundreds of miles.

In spite of the low hanging smoke, I knew the area must be beautiful as I could see mountains here and there, around us as we rode through the grass hills heading toward what looked like another mountain pass. Just before heading into the pass, another bee decided to pay me a visit. This time I was stung twice by the same bee before I could get my helmet off. Ralph removed the dying bee from my helmet, as I rubbed my stings in front of my right ear.

What I find hard to understand is, how, with all the wide open spaces we are riding through and the tiny exposed space on my body, a bee could be flying down the road at the exact moment I appear in its space, find that tender spot on my cheek and sting me, not once but twice? Ouch. Later on in the day, Ralph got stung for the fourth time and this time on his collarbone. Ralph is still ahead in the bee sting contest.

The climb to the top of the mountain pass was cloaked in the smoke from the fires and we couldn't see very much. At the top of the pass was a ski area, a rest stop and the turn we were looking for heading into Montana.

Just as we turned onto the road east, the speed limit changed. We were still heading into mountains mind you and the crazy DOT of Montana decided that seventy miles per hour would be a good speed to travel through the mountains. I never reached that speed having to keep it under sixty most of the time.

The ride was quite beautiful and scenic. Our road took us by the Big Hole Battlefield. We stopped and got educated and I left, feeling very depressed. This was a battlefield where the U.S. Army slaughtered at least ninety Nez Perce Indians in the late 1800's. The Indians had had ninety percent of their land taken from them due to one white man finding gold. The Indians had been forced onto the remaining ten percent of land. A band of Nez Perce, that did not sign the treaty, decided that they would flee to Canada. The Army pursued the Indians over a period of four months, finally forcing their surrender in Bear Paw, Montana. The story is much longer than this obviously but I was left feeling depressed for the Nez Perce.

Below the visitor's center was the actual battlefield. The same amount of teepee poles had been set up in the location of the battle. The wind blew their message for all to hear.

The ride was somber for me as we followed the route where the Indians fled that day, many years ago from the massacre, leaving behind dead loved ones, mostly women and children. We rode up and down the hills of the plateau and climbed another pass. As we reached the top, the view was breath taking. Behind us, way off in the distance were the faded Bitterroot Mountains. In front of us were the Madison Valley and the Madison Mountain Range. The valley was flat as a piece of paper and was dotted with ranches and homes and farm land.

No sooner had we descended the pass and got into the valley than the mighty winds began to blow. Though they were significant, they weren't as bad as some we have experienced. We had the pleasure of experiencing crosswinds from the right and just when we got use to those, they shifted to come in from the left. I tried to watch the terrain and the grasses, because I could get some idea from which direction the winds will come by watching, but I was completely stumped on all accounts through Madison Valley.

As we neared the end of the forty-mile valley, which now was following a sizable river, I noticed a ranch off to my right overlooking the canyon that the river ran through. In the front yard of the ranch was a huge windmill. The blades looked like a prop on a jet. The wind was turning those propellers so fast that they were a big white blur. I hoped he had a way to store all that energy that was being generated.

The wind continued to roar and we followed a fairly large lake that had small white caps on the surface. The rain decided to pay us a visit, since we have not seen it in many weeks. We rode in and out of splatting raindrops but the scenery continued to be pleasant. The rain made everything smell good and the fir trees gave off their Christmas smell.

We rode past a lake that had been created in nineteen-fifty-six, called Earthquake Lake. Thousands of trees stuck up out of the water like toothpicks. The river coming out of the lake had been completely displaced in its banks. I could see where the old riverbed had once been. I crossed my fingers that another earthquake wouldn't happen just at the moment we were riding through the area.

We finally rolled into West Yellowstone, Montana and started the search for housing for the night. I was floored at the prices. It just never occurred to me that this little town would be so expensive but I had forgotten that it was right at the entrance to Yellowstone Park. We found a place, after being referred, at our fourth stop. When we rolled into the parking lot, I was a little nervous. It was on the outside of town and not so nice looking. Well, we lost the housing lottery and the room was an appalling seventy-five dollars.

We have stayed in some mighty nice places for much less than seventy-five dollars. The walls were so thin that we heard everything our next-door neighbors had to say. Only trouble was the words were being spoken in French and I couldn't understand a thing. Nevertheless, we heard it all.

After things quieted down, Ralph and I managed to sleep quite well and even the slanting floor in the bathroom with moldy, wet smelly carpet wasn't too much of a bother.

After breakfast the next morning, we went to join the hundreds of others heading for the west entrance of Yellowstone. I was pleasantly surprised that the crowds at the park were not so bad. I think being late August and the kids having to head back to school had something to do with the diminishing crowds.

We hadn't been in the park for two miles when I saw two eagles, one sitting on a branch across the river and another one very close to the road sitting on a sizable, stick nest on top of a burned out tree. Within those same two miles, I also saw four brilliant, white trumpeter swans floating along in the river.

Twenty years ago, almost the entire park burned in a terrible fire. Over the years, I have had the opportunity to see the recovery of the park. It is a very slow lifetime process. The first time I saw Yellowstone after the fire, I just wanted to cry. There was nothing but charred earth, black burned trees, and the smell of fire was still in the air.

Several years later, when I saw the park, the grasses had returned and small fir trees were starting a comeback. This visit, the hills were green again, with about twenty years of growing since the big fire, the trees are now about as tall as I am. I was glad to look over the mountains and see new green trees growing again where once was a black, charcoal landscape.

I can always tell where the animals are in the park by the stupid people pulled off the road and walking in the road with cameras. We just keep rolling by and taking a quick peek as we go by. It is not so much the people stopping in their cars that is so troubling because Yellowstone is one place a person can observe natural wildlife. The problem comes when motorist actually stop in the middle of the road in both directions, blocking those that might want to continue forward. The thing that really makes me think the people are stupid, is getting out of their cars, and walking up to the wildlife. How many times, and how many signs are up telling people not to do this activity? Some people just need to be slapped, but then again, I guess the wildlife will take care of that. I'm not talking about the small rodents either, I'm guilty as charged, I'm talking about large buffalo, moose, elk, and bears. Oh, my!

At one point, I thought I saw a big, fat, ugly woman walking down the left side of the road in front of us. She had huge, bushy black hair standing out on both sides hanging down to waist level. Her gait was waddling back and forth and I thought she was entirely stupid to be walking in the road to go take pictures of some wild animal.

But I was the stupid one. The big, fat, ugly woman walking down the road turned out to be a very large, bull buffalo, just moseying down the side of the road as pretty as you please. I felt a little better later, when Ralph told me he thought the exact same thing I did, when he first saw the buffalo.

We saw a herd of about fifty buffalo very close to the road grazing and another one by himself grazing on the roadside. There were plenty of elk to observe as well as deer some with large racks of antlers. The wildlife was not the least bit frightened by the cars and people stopping and taking photos. That is just what makes them so dangerous. I was just waiting for some stupid tourist to scare one of the beasts just as we went by, unprotected on our bikes and then getting attacked. Well, that never happened, and I think all the stupid tourist stopping and getting out of their cars to take pictures managed to escape unharmed as well.

We did the tourist thing at the park. Since Ralph and I have been to Yellowstone several times before, I didn't take many pictures. We walked to some geysers and some sulfa springs, gagged at the smell, took some pictures and made it over to Old Faithful in time to watch it blow.

By now, it was six in the evening and we still had over one hundred miles to cover before we could rest for the night. While we were waiting for Old Faithful to blow, Ralph got on the internet, found the KOA campground on the south side of Jackson, and secured us a cabin for the night. I had already looked at the price of hotel rooms in Jackson Hole and that just wasn't going to happen on our budget. The prices in Jackson Hole were much higher than in West Yellowstone.

After leaving Yellowstone, we drove through Teton National Park to get to Jackson. I never get tired of seeing those mountains. They are very dramatic and they remind me now, of some of the mountains we saw in Alaska. The rugged mountains jut right out of the flat earth and soar skyward. There was still some snow left in patches but it won't be long before the Tetons are covered again. The majesty of these mountains still grabs my heart.

This area will always bring back wonderful memories of my young adult years and the fun times I had working on the dude ranch south of Jackson, near Hoback Junction. There are also bittersweet memories here too. This is where my sister Emily, died and where her ashes are scattered high upon Signal Mountain. I want to visit that place once more before we leave Jackson.

Our road followed the Tetons and they were so majestically dressed in their grays and blues as darkness approached. Some extremely, serious rain clouds were threatening the tops of the mountains and I was really hoping we would make it to our little cabin by the Snake River in time.

No such luck. By the time we passed the airport, north of town, the sky was completely black and the clouds were racing down the mountain and screaming toward us. Lightening and thunder accompanied the heavy rain and of course, the wind came along to keep us company. All the elements of a severe storm were present and I had no desire to experience any of them.

With the wind blowing us sideways, the rain pouring buckets of icy water down on us, the black sky sending Thor's lightening bolts at us left and right, we managed to ride into Jackson like drowned rats on two wheels. We still had another thirteen miles to go to our camp.

Both Ralph and I got a chuckle at the bikers in front of us in town that had on no rain gear and no helmets either. They were hunching their heads down into their jackets like they were turtles. Guess what? It wasn't doing any good. They were getting drowned. The only things wet on me were my gloves and the collar on my jacket that I failed to button up all the way many miles before the rain started.

As we rode south, out of town, I looked off to my right at the mountains and had to turn around several times before I could believe what I was seeing. The clouds had lifted just slightly over the mountains and they looked like the top was on fire with molten lava. A deep red cloud hung over the tops of the mountains as a result of the sun that had set during the severe storm. It only lasted a moment and was gone as suddenly as it appeared.

Finally, we found the campground in the pitch-black dark and got settled into our little cabin. We walked, in the heavy darkness of the night, across the road to a new restaurant, had a nice dinner and then painfully walked back to our bed. All the walking we had done during the day at Yellowstone caught up with us and we were exhausted beyond belief.

Grizzle Bear was not a happy camper at all. Matter of fact he is screaming about wanting to go home. I think the storm tonight was just the last straw for him. I dried off his little dirty head and removed his wet jacket and jeans. He's all snuggled into his bunk over mine and hopefully he will quiet down now.

Its suppose to rain tomorrow and we have to give up our nice cabin and move into a teepee. I will go shopping tomorrow and make one last shipment home. I hope that on Friday when we leave, the clouds will move off and I can get some pictures of the Tetons.

So until later, much love to all always,
Judy/Mom/Mommy

August 19, 2005

Friday
Midwest, Wyoming
Mile 18,438

Dear Folks,

Our little cabin by the Snake River was wonderful and the rain that fell during the early morning darkness sounded and smelled heavenly. I turned over in my warm sleeping bag and fell back to sleep listening to the rain fall on the cabin roof. We had left the windows open during the night and the air was delightfully cool and that made the soft warmness of my sleeping bag feel even better.

But eventually the light crept into the cabin and the campground started to stir including my bunkmate. The rain was steadily coming down but not storming. In my drowsiness, I realized that we would have to vacate our nice little cabin and move into the teepee in the front of the campground next to the road. I groaned.

After I finally got up and dressed, I took a load of stuff up to one of the teepees. We had our choice, as all three were vacant. After I inspected all three to see which one was the least wet inside, I threw my stuff into one and went back to grab more of my things.

I want you to know right now that Mama Bear was not happy at all. Our new abode smelled of mold and mildew, the wooden plank floor was dirty, the sides at the bottom of the tepee were open to the elements, the flap that was the door, was missing all but one of the small sticks that close the flap and the tepee *leaked*!

By now, the rain was coming down pretty hard and three-fourths of the teepee was wet. Water was dripping down on my sleeping bag and I had to use my dirty clothes to sop up the water that puddled on my bed. There was nowhere to stay in the teepee during the rain as the only dry spot was covered in our gear and under my cot. It was going to be a miserable night I could tell.

We had to go into Jackson because the cell phone didn't work in camp and Ralph needed to check in with the office. We moved things around in the tepee the best we could, crossed our fingers, and headed the thirteen miles into town.

I did some shopping while Ralph made his calls and waited for me in the Cowboy Bar on the square in Jackson. The rain had let up and it looked like the sun was trying to come out. Yeah, I thought. Maybe we won't be wet after all tonight.

After I finished shopping, we went to the post office to ship our clothes we wore at the wedding and some other goodies for the kiddies. Ralph and I went to the library to spend a few dry hours until we ate dinner and rode back to camp. I have found over the past few months that the library is a great place to spend a rainy day. The environment is nice and dry and there is lots of entertainment within the walls. Of course, rainy weather and reading generally puts me to sleep and it's hard to keep the old eyes open. But I was able to catch up on my journal entries and load some pictures. While at the library, the skies opened up again, water flooded everything and I knew water was also in our leaky teepee.

There happened to be a presentation at the library in the evening with slides and a talk from an author who wrote about the Arctic Wilderness Preserve in Alaska, just where we had been on the North Slope. So of course, we stayed for that. That turned out not to be what we expected. The author's photos left a lot to be desired and he was there to make a political statement about a new bill before congress about future oil drilling. I thought I would scream before I could get out of there.

After dinner, we drove in the pitch-blackness back to camp. We had just left the lights of Jackson and came around a curve in the road where a small hill obscured all vision to the left of us. As we rounded the curve and passed the hill, I thought I saw a bright white beacon, like one from a lighthouse on the ocean, shining at us from behind the hill. The beacon turned out to be the very full moon. All the rain had washed away all the dust and smog, the air was crystal clear, and the moon was brighter, I think, than I have seen in ages.

As we rode on in the darkness, the moon shown over the Snake River lighting its serpentine path through the valley. The river turned to silver in the night and looked like liquid mercury rolling through the land.

The air was quite cold too and my wet gloves felt like ice on my hands. I was glad for my riding gear and the nice warm liner that I had put back into my jacket earlier in the morning. But boy, I was dreading going into that teepee for the night. I have to say that in the three months we have been out on our trip, this was absolutely, the worst place that I have rested my head for the night.

It was pitch black where the teepees were and of course, the headlamps were in the tent, just where they belong. Ralph used the light from the cell phone for us to see to get in and assess the damage that the rain might have caused. We found the head lamps and found, fortunately, it had stopped raining early enough that part of the floor was dry enough for Ralph to place his mattress and sleeping bag.

The dirty clothes I had used to cover things up with were now not only dirty but wet as well. I threw everything over in one dry area of the teepee, wiped off the wet spots of my mattress with a dirty tee shirt and climbed into my sleeping bag. I was warm within minutes and somehow both of us managed to get some sleep. Even though my sleeping bag was slightly damp in spots, it did, as advertised, keep me warm.

The traffic on the road woke us bright and early, so early, that the sun hadn't even made it over the mountain if front of the campground. We packed up our stuff as quickly as possible and headed out of town.

The sky was blue and the day looked promising for our trip into Teton National Park but as we neared town a very heavy layer of fog filled the valley. We couldn't see anything but the road in front of us. I was hoping that once we left the valley of Jackson Hole we would be able to see the mountains.

I can't begin to tell you how disappointed I was when we climbed the hill leaving Jackson and found the entire valley completely socked in with heavy, white fog. I couldn't see the first gray rock of the Tetons.

I had looked so forward to spending the day visiting all the beautiful places in the park and going to the top of Signal Mountain where Emily's ashes were scattered. I realized that it would be futile to even spend a moment riding through the park with all the heavy cloud cover, so we just kept on going on the road east toward South Dakota. I had a large lump in my throat as I realized it might be many years before I returned to the Tetons and my sister's burial ground. I had come so close.

This road veered east away from the park and climbed the plateau. As we reached the top of the plateau and were just about to make a right turn in an easterly direction, when the clouds broke up around us, and there to my left in all their majesty were my beautiful mountains.

The clouds that had been around us in the valley were still visible at the foot of the mountains so our decision to not go through the park was a good one. Away from the valley and up on the plateau the Tetons were clear as a bell and the sky was clear blue. I was satisfied that at least I got a glimpse of the Tetons and was able to get a few photos to go with the other hundreds I have at home.

The road east was one I had never traveled on before even though I have been in this area many times. I wanted to take a different route toward South Dakota and one that would take us by the burial site of Sacagawea. Wow, what a stunning road we traveled down this morning. We rode through mountain meadows with wild flowers still blooming in the cold mountain air. Lush green grass lined the crooked creeks that snaked through the meadows. Fir trees gave off their perfume and floated on the morning air. The air was still very cool. When we left Jackson this morning, it was forty-eight degrees in the valley. We were at almost ten thousand feet in elevation in the mountains and it was very cool but refreshing.

We got to see a little bit of everything today on our tour de jour. We drove through high mountains, alpine meadows with wildflowers and crooked creeks, giant canyon walls of gray and black, forests of fir trees and then grasslands. This was all in a space of about one hundred miles.

We left the mountain area and moved out onto a plateau of red rock similar to that of Zion National Park. The red rocks then turned into grasslands with mountains off to the west and more bluffs and plateaus off to the east. We went out of our way to visit the gravesite of Sacagawea. I wanted to stand close to a woman, who had been such an influence on our young nation. But I have you know, that when we came to the area on my map where she was buried, there wasn't the first sign for her gravesite. Now you would think that someone that important to American history and someone who had a gold coin made with her face on it would at least have a sign pointing to her gravesite. Nope, not a one.

We couldn't find Sacagawea's grave and by the time we got to Landers, Wyoming I knew we had missed it. At least we were in the area where she is buried and could see her valleys and mountains. It was a very peaceful area in which to rest forever.

Disappointed, we headed on to Casper, where we had planned on stopping for the night. We had a wonderful tail wind that pushed us along nicely. Sometimes too well. We rode over grasslands, plateaus, hills, and valleys.

About thirty miles outside of Casper, I got very sleepy and had to fight to stay awake. We were in the middle of nowhere with no gas stations or rest stops so I sung to myself and chewed gum and popped bubbles to stay awake. When we reached the junction in the road at Casper we had a choice to go straight into Casper or head north on the interstate that we would have to get on in the morning.

We opted for the interstate thinking that at the next exit north, there would be motels. Wrong, wrong, wrong choice. When we got on the interstate, the lovely tail wind that had pushed us along all day now, became a ferocious crosswind and both of us were blown off the road into the emergency lane. The wind was so fierce that my helmet was mashed up against the left side of my face and I imagined I looked like a fish with my lips pushed together into fish lips. My sunglasses mashed against my nose and that felt unpleasant as well.

The interstate fortunately had wide lanes and a very wide emergency lane. We stuck to the white line of the right hand lane as best we could. The only comfort I got was the fact that there were no trucks on the road and only a few cars but that still did little for my fear factor.

I knew that when planning the route that we would have to be on the interstate for about twenty miles and I thought I could handle that. Well, there were no exits and no hotels in the direction we were headed. I knew that the only way off that damned interstate was straight ahead. It felt like we had gone for miles and miles when another sign told me we had only gone five miles. I thought I would scream.

My only thought was to survive the nasty wind long enough to get off at our exit. Finally, we made our exit and when we got in between some of the small grassy foothills, the wind was easier to deal with.

Once again, we were in the middle of the grasslands on a back road, no civilization in sight, and no place to stay either. There were two small towns twenty miles up ahead and I hoped there would be something there.

As we came over a hill, I saw an orange road sign that made me very nervous. It said, "Seismic Activity In The Area." Great, that would just finish me off for the day. Not only was I getting blown to smithereens by the wind but now an earthquake was going to open up the ground and swallow us whole. I somehow imagined, quite well, the ground shaking and rolling. But it was just my imagination. I found out, that when we came over the next hill, that it was a survey crew measuring seismic activity for the purposes of oil drilling. There were wells everywhere and I guess they were planning the next place to drill. Now I wasn't worried about being swallowed up by the earth but turned my concentration back on finding comfort for the night.

We reached the first little town with a population of about four hundred and there was only a gas station and café and some homes. No hotel. Off we went to the next town, which was a mile up the road. That town had a population of one hundred and nine people but they did have a hotel. Yeah!

I didn't care what the place looked like. I did not expect much due to the desolate mining area. For forty-five dollars, we got clean sheets, towels, a shower, and a roof that didn't leak. I was happy as a pig in mud.

We went back to a place on that lonely road, called the Rim Rock Café, for dinner. The woman at the hotel recommended it and not given many choices in the area, we rode back several miles. The owner of the café told us that the only thing on the menu was prime rib. Oh, too bad.

The meal was outstanding. Two large pieces of Delmonico steaks were placed in front of us with baked potatoes and salad. We licked the platters clean.

With bellies full and a bed with nice clean sheets, we settled in for the night and slept rather well.

Grizzle Bear was crying his little eyeballs out he had been so scared by the wind. Then he pouted about not getting to go to dinner with us. I bought him some corn nuts from the hotel store and that shut him up. I heard him munching and crunching over in the corner of the room in his little bed so he went to bed happy too.

So until later, much love to all always,
Judy/Mom/Mommy

August 21, 2005
Sunday
Custer, SD
Mile 18,698

Dear Folks,

As we left the tiny little town with only one hundred and nine people and one hotel, the road immediately started up hill. As we crested the hill, I gasped at the land before me. For as far as I could see there were rolling hills of yellow grass, looking to me just like a yellow ocean. Up and down over the hills and foothills of grass we went. I felt like I was like riding on the ocean floor of yellow sand.

The road for miles was lined with wild sunflowers. Their bright yellow heads and black centers were turned toward the eastern sun and during the course of the day would turn their heads to follow the sun's ride in the sky. I had been seeing these wild sunflowers for days now and they sure are pretty.

I now know why rabbits multiply in the numbers in which they do. If they didn't, they would be extinct out here in the wild plains of Wyoming. For miles yesterday and more miles and miles today, dead rabbits littered the road, the result of being run over and flattened. Bits of white fluff littered the black asphalt like confetti scattered in the winds. I have never seen so much rabbit fur or rabbit road kill in my life. The road was polka dotted with rabbit fur.

To add to the squished rabbits there was an occasional flattened skunk in black and white. I would try to hold my breath when we went by one but it didn't help much as their aroma floated a long way. I usually wound up taking a big breath when I though it was safe only to find out the perfume was still in the air around me. Yuck!

Before we left the hotel this morning, the housekeeper told us that a town we were going to pass through, had only the week before, been hit by a very rare tornado, destroying the town and killing two people. We reached the town of Wright, Wyoming and saw the devastation. As usual with tornadoes, they are drawn to trailer parks for some reason. The area we saw destroyed was a trailer park right next to the road. People were still going through the rubble and one woman was taking a picture of what once was her home. I had to look away, it was painful to watch. In a field of the school, was a military medical helicopter still handing out supplies to a line of people.

I don't understand how, with all the open space around this town for hundreds of miles, and how, when a tornado is very rare in Wyoming, could one just happen to find this town and strike a trailer park. Would that be called fate?

After we made our next junction just a few miles out of town, I saw the mother of all signs. It scared me so much that I couldn't even stop to take a picture. The road took us right through the middle of a coalmine called the Black Thunder Coal Mine. Deep cavernous pits were dug into the hills. A crane as large as ten-story building was scooping up rock.

Anyway, the sign read, "Caution Blasting Area Ahead. Orange Cloud May Be Present. Avoid Contact."

Boy, my eyes were scanning the area for an orange cloud like you wouldn't believe. Just what were we suppose to do if we saw the cloud? There was no place to hide so I chose to run. There was digging underway, on both sides of the road and trains lined the road. One long train waited with empty cars for the coal and one was already full, ready to take off.

I only saw black clouds of coal dust not the orange one, but I scurried over that road like a bat out of hell. I did notice however, that in the direction we were headed, that the mined area had been returned to a natural state of grassy hills. So at least the coalmine was repairing the damage to the landscape when the mined coal was exhausted. I had forgotten how much Wyoming had in fossil fuels and I have been reminded very well in the last two days.

After the orange cloud scare, the road continued over miles and miles of grasslands. Small herds of antelope grazed on each side of the road. It was as if the road was ours as we rode for many miles before we passed another car. It was so enjoyable having the road to ourselves.

Riding on the plateaus here in the west suddenly ends and a descent is necessary. One minute we were riding over hills of grass and the next, we were descending a great plateau.

Before us were the Black Hills of South Dakota. One minute we were in yellow and green grass and the next we were in dark, grey rocks and green fir trees.

As we got closer to Custer, South Dakota, our stopping point for the day, we stopped at Jewel Cave National Monument and took a quick tour of one of the big underground rooms. We decided we didn't want to climb up and down seven hundred and fifty steps on the longer tour deep inside the cave. So we got a mini peak. Apparently, there are over one hundred and thirty-five miles of tunnels and rooms that have been discovered and so much left to explore.

After our quick tour of the cool, dark bowels of Jewel Cave, we arrived in Custer, found a room, and crashed for the evening.

Today, we played tourist. We decided to stay in Custer again tonight so we could wander around the area. We went to Crazy Horse Monument and looked around the site and the museum. The museum is one of the best ones I have seen in regards to the North American Indians. There were many artifacts that I found interesting and Ralph enjoyed the facts about the carving of the monument. Crazy Horse Monument is still a work in progress. Though started fifty years ago, it will probably take another fifty to complete. I wish I could be around when it is finished but that is not likely to happen. I didn't appreciate how much had been done to the monument since I was here with the kids thirteen years ago until I saw a picture of what it looked like then and now. The face of Crazy Horse is now finished.

Then we rode over to Mount Rushmore and took the usual tourist pictures there. The area around the monument has been completely redone since I was here last too. New marble building and walkways have given the monument a facelift.

But the best part of the day for me, was the ride around the surrounding area and then ride through Custer State Park. We rode first, on the wildlife loop. Just as we turned onto the loop road, a deer came running at full speed across the road between Ralph and me. I never even saw the darned thing. As habit, about every three to five seconds, I look in my rear view mirror to check for Ralph. On my check, I didn't see him so I pulled off the side of the road to wait for him. When he finally pulled up beside me, he told me of the deer. How could I have missed that?

The road rolled up and down lovely hills of rich green grass dotted with evergreen trees here and there. We saw many antelope on both sides of the road, some grazing, some lying down in the grass, resting peacefully.

The buffalo are doing very well in Custer State Park. I had just about given up seeing some when around the corner there were cars stopped in the middle of the road. A whole herd was right there on both sides of the road. Buffalo are very big and the people stopped to take pictures are in a car, protected by a cage of metal. We're not! Trust me, those suckers look even bigger close up. They raised their heads from chewing grass, some roll their eyes and drip snot out their noses as we went by.

A little farther up the road was another herd. I slowed to a crawl to view this herd, as there was a deep gully between them and me. There were hundreds of buffalo in the park today. There were plenty of new calves with protective mamas, too. The buffalo are so use to cars and people that they wander at will across the road and buddy you had better stop. I got an up close and personal look at many buffalo today. Many were too close for comfort for me. I could only imagine that the buffalo might view a motorcycle as a threatening animal. Thoughts of getting attacked crossed my mind many times.

Another part of Custer State Park goes through the Needles. The Needles are outcroppings of rock sticking right out of the trees, pointing right up to the sky with their "needles." The road went through tunnels cut right through the rock. Some of the tunnels were only eight feet wide. I was glad I was on a bike. When we reached the summit of the Needles, we went through the eye. It was like literally like threading a needle. The road was so very narrow that if the driver and passengers of the car in front of us stuck their hands out of the windows they would touch the sided of the needle rock. It was very cool. I wish I could have taken a picture of Ralph coming through that on the bike but there were too many cars and not a place to park nor a place for him to turn around and go back through.

The ride back down the mountains was nice. The sun was going down and the air was cooling quickly. Long shadows created by the late afternoon sun raced through the woods. Stripes of light green and dark green lined the forest floor.

After leaving the state park, we headed back into Custer passing Crazy Horse one more time. So ends another very pleasant day. Tomorrow when we leave Custer, South Dakota, we plan to see Wind Cave National Park and ride by the Wounded Knee Battle Site. Then it's on east through the southern part of South Dakota.

Grizzle Bear really liked the buffalo. I could hear him singing "yippee" as we rode through the park. He's begging for a little bow and arrow set but he's out of luck. Too bad for him.

So until later, much love to all always,
Judy/Mom/Mommy

August 23, 2005

Tuesday
Spencer, Iowa
Mile 19,226

Dear Folks,

Yesterday, after finally pulling ourselves out of a nice, dark, cool room and warm bed with clean sheets, we headed down the road to Wind Cave National Park. The park is adjacent to Custer State Park and the area looks the same with all the rolling green hills of wild grass.

After looking through the visitor's center, we decided to pass on the cave tour and wait until we get to Mammoth Cave in Kentucky. Since I did set foot in the park and did go into the visitor's center, I did collect a patch for my backpack. I have lost count on how many patches I have picked up over the last three months.

I wanted to spend a little time at Wounded Knee so we moved on down the road. As we left the park, another herd of buffalo grazed peacefully on the hills. Every now and then, a big bull buffalo was spotted close to the road, lying down chewing his cud I suppose, or else just enjoying the warm morning sun.

We rode about one hundred miles until the turn off for Wounded Knee. As we turned left onto the road, there were fields of hundreds of acres of great, big sunflower fields. All bright and yellow, their heads were proudly lifted to the eastern sun. The bright yellow was vibrant and the petals, I'm sure, were the size of my fingers. It was one of those sites that I just had to stare at for a long time. The color soaked into my eyes and brain and left me hungering for more. I think I could have stood there all day watching the yellow and orange swaying in the breeze, like an ocean of bright yellow waves.

Much to my disappointment, as with the Sacagawea site, the Wounded Knee site was hardly even recognized. We missed the site and had to turn around and go in the opposite direction to find a lonely marker. This site was well marked on the map I carried, but there was only a very weathered wooden sign with a very small amount of information explaining the history. Again, this was a big part of American history that had been just about swept under the rug.

On the main road again, heading east, we passed more fields of sunflowers in various stages of growth. Some were in full bloom with their bright yellow heads pointed skyward. Some were not fully formed and their little green heads the size of softballs hung down on their green stalk necks looking at the ground, as if saying that they can't look at the sky until the sunflowers wore a crown of bright yellow and orange.

We spent most of the day riding over several Indian reservations. I have found in my travels over many Indian reservations that, with the exception of only one I have seen, most are in such a state of neglect and trashiness. The houses along the road, for the most part are run down with junk and trash littering the area. Broken down cars, junked long ago stand rusting in the yards as well as broken toys and broken fences.

When riding through the small towns, trash and dirt litter the area. We pulled into a gas station and it looked as if no one had ever bothered to sweep the area, just letting the wind blow it away. Inches of dirt, blown around were caught by the curb along with discarded soda bottles and trash. It was a very depressing site.

It was immediately evident when we left the reservations. Yards around the farmhouses were neat and clean. The grass had been cut and farm equipment and machinery tucked away into out buildings.

We spent the rest of the day's journey riding through farmland. Rolling grasslands turned into seas of corn as their yellow tasseled heads swayed in the wind. Harvest time was approaching. Hay had been cut leaving the sweet smell in the air as we passed the newly cut areas.

The day was ending, the air cooling and the sun was turning everything honey yellow in the east. The map I had on my tank bag, showed many towns along our route. However, just because it's on the map doesn't mean there is a gas station or hotel in the area. We went through many a town that had only a population of seventy or ninety.

On we rode in the late afternoon and I was hoping that the next town would have what we needed. Just in the nick of time, a large enough town with about four hundred people came over the horizon and we stopped for the night. The hotel was very nice and considering it was the only one in the town, I was delighted that it was nice and clean to boot.

After dinner in the local restaurant, we settled in for the night. Ralph went to take a shower and found that we had no hot water. It was eleven P.M. and I was already snuggled in bed reading a book. He went over to the office, hoping beyond hope, that it would be open and was given a key to another room. We wound up moving all our stuff into a new room that unfortunately was a smoking room and reeked to high heaven. But it did have the hot water that Ralph required. I think I would have rather gone dirty than to spend the night breathing smoke.

We both woke up feeling as if we had colds due to the smokiness of the room and the irritation to our sinuses. It took a long while moving down the road breathing in the fresh air to clean out all the smoke from our systems.

The road I chose for us to ride on the last two days was far more remote than I expected and far more desolate than the map indicated. There were many dots on the map indicating small towns along the route. I'm glad that we came down this road, as it was a true piece of Americana. This was a road that ran right down the middle of the farm belt. This road belonged to the farmers and the big cattle trucks and farm equipment. It felt like we were moving through a day in the life of the mid-west farmer.

Big farm equipment, like plows, as wide as the road, cut the black earth up and turned over the dirt waiting for next year's planting. Hay was being cut and bailed. Oceans of corn and beans and wheat lined the road and expanded out on both sides as far as I could see.

After riding for several hours, we searched for gas and food. I wasn't worried too much about the food as I was sure that we would find it sometime during the day, but the gas was another situation. Not all the dots on the map had gas. As a matter of fact, there were more without than with.

Finally, we came to a little town called Menno, South Dakota, that happened to have both gas and food. After finding out where to eat from the owner of the one gas station, we rode one block into the two-block town and pulled into a space right in front of the café. I figured that this little town was so far out in the middle of nowhere that the food was probably all home made and not some processed crap.

I was right! We had homemade bean soup that was divine. The cheeseburgers were hand made patties and the bacon had just been fried. The dead giveaway about the homemade meal was the bright, red, juicy tomato slice that was on top of the burger. That sucker was home grown right out of the cook's garden. Oh boy, was it good. The meal was inexpensive at eleven dollars for two bowls of soup and two bacon cheeseburgers with fries and two cokes. The meal was all home cooked, not processed stuff. My tummy was very happy and satisfied.

As we were sitting eating our soup, we over heard a conversation that had us both laughing. Grandma and Grandpa were at the next table with their four grandsons that appeared to be about a year apart in ages. The grandpa was talking to a neighbor who was eating there also. Grandpa was telling his friend that his grandsons were going to be his helpers today. One of the boys piped up and asked what they were going to be doing and grandpa answered saying that they were going to be picking up rocks. A moment of silence passed and the boy said to grandpa in a small voice, "How many rocks"? Grandpa told the boy, "Well, I don't know, I haven't counted them." Again, silence from the boy. I almost choked with laughter. I had another flashback to my childhood, when my job had been to pick up rocks in the yard of the new house we had recently moved into. I thoroughly hated with a passion, picking up rocks. Mama had used it as punishment on me. I cannot even remember what I was being punished for, but I sure remember picking up rocks. I felt rather sorry for the four boys sitting at the table next to us.

I could only imagine these boys picking up mounds of rocks from a field somewhere. I wondered how their day was going to go and just what the rock count would be at the end of the day. Grandpa was also telling his friend that recently he caught two of the boys racing the tractors. One was on the John Deere and the other on the Snapper. I couldn't hear who won but I guess both had a pile of rocks to pick up after that race.

When we were back outside in front of the café, we were just putting on our helmets when an extremely loud siren went off. It is the kind we have at home that goes off every Wednesday at noon and when severe weather threatens. They are very loud when you are under one. Trust me, I've been there. Anyway, I looked at my watch to see what time it was and it was one-fifteen, so I knew that the siren was something for something else. The siren stayed on for probably two minutes, which is very long when you are right under it.

As we were climbing on our bikes, we noticed that a truck was driving rather fast down the two-block town, heading right toward us. A police car followed him. I thought the officer was chasing the truck. We backed out of our parking places and headed toward the stop sign at the main road when ambulance sirens started blaring.

Coming up behind us was an ambulance at top speed. We pulled over and waited for him to pass. No sooner had that one passed then another ambulance came barreling through the intersection, followed by a dinky fire truck and fire chief. It was then that I realized what we were witnessing. This was how the volunteer ambulance and fire system worked in this town.

I was extremely impressed with the speed in which the volunteers reacted in getting to the station and hauling butt to the scene. For such a small town, they had invested in two very nice ambulances. They looked like two of mine. Now the fire truck needed some help but the ambulances were in tiptop shape. I was amazed how quickly the medics reacted to the siren, got to the station, and got those ambulances moving.

Response times in Atlanta are supposed to be eight minutes to an emergency. These guys took their job seriously and I have no doubt they made the scene within that time frame. I think some of the city boys could take a few lessons from the farm boys. These farm boys made me proud to be in the profession.

After the dust literally settled from the ambulances and fire trucks, we headed back out on the road of cornfields. I saw succotash growing today. Not really, I'm not that stupid but the second planting of beans over the cornfield produced a rich green field of beans with a corn stalk growing here and there.

The cornfields got a little boring and the stench of the cow yards was enough to make me gag but it was still much, much better than a busy highway with trucks and fast moving cars and crazy drivers. I'll take the corn any day. And maybe the stench too.

We finally made it out of South Dakota and into Iowa and have made the turn south for a while. We will travel south until we hit Missouri and then head east some again. From there we haven't decided which route to take yet.

Yesterday, after seeing more buffalo than he could count, Grizzle Bear added a pinto pony to his list with the bow and arrow. I think he had visions of hunting the great buffalo on his Indian pony. Today though his thoughts moved on to the cornfields. I heard him smacking his lips as he recited, "yum, popcorn, corn nuts, corn on the cob, creamed corn, and caramel corn." He had me going there for a while until I heard him gagging, kacking, and hacking as we passed the stockyards. I could have sworn I heard bear vomit hit the asphalt. I wiped his little face off along with his dirty jacket when we found a room for the night. All is quiet on the bear front particularly since I saved him some vanilla ice cream with strawberries on top from my dinner.

So until later, much love to all always,
Judy/Mom/Mommy

August 24, 2005
Wednesday
Cameron, MO
Mile 19,523

Dear Folks,

Today we made the decision that, instead of staying out an additional week, we will make the final move toward home. We still have some pretty country to cover in the mean time and hope to enjoy the last four days. Ralph has been in a pretty foul mood since we left the wedding. He really does not want to go home.

Today was just a day we had to grit our teeth and get through. We traveled south on Route71 through the rest of Iowa and into Missouri. It was a hard day. The wind was blowing in from the southeast at a pretty constant rate and looked as if it would rain all day as dark clouds threatened constantly.

Market time for hogs and cows must be near, as I think we met every cattle/hog truck in the state of Iowa. Every one of them made me gag but the worst were the ones we had to follow. Trucks carrying sand or grit threw rocks and sand in our face, which hurt pretty bad. In addition, other trucks carrying supplies north and south came rushing up on our tails and passed us on the two-lane at remarkable speeds, sending us scurrying to stay in our own lane due the wind currents blowing off the back of the trucks. Very pleasant, huh?

But to me, I'm so sick of smelling pig shit, I could literally puke. I have smelled it for two days now and I have had a snout full. Today was one long road through rows of cornfields that smelled like pig crap.

On occasion, we would have a beautiful view from a hill of lush farm fields of corn and beans with the farmhouse tucked up in the trees high up on the hill. Now that was pretty.

As we got closer to Missouri, we actually got a curve in the road and a hill or two. The landscape was starting to look more like home with all the great big hardwood trees and green grass and rolling hills. Oh yeah, I forgot the humidity. I haven't felt humidity in three months and I recognized it immediately, like crossing an invisible barrier. On one side of the barrier was nice dry cool air, on the other damp, muggy, southern, summer air.

Tonight we found a cheap hotel room for thirty-nine dollars. I think we are the only ones in the place and it is rather spooky. The place smells rather musty and moldy too, but the room actually isn't that bad. Trust me, I've slept in worst during the last three months.

Today was a workday of sorts, just trying to get through the unending cornfields, dealing with the wind and trucks. The little musty hotel is a welcome haven for the night. I called all three kids tonight and gave them the heads up that we will be home by Sunday. Milissa told me that she would get the house picked up and I mentioned that maybe cutting the grass would be a good idea too. I can only imagine what the yard must look like after three months. I know the backyard only was cut once and I'm not so sure about the front. I know a neighbor cut it once, so I know the yard must have been pretty bad, huh? I'm sure all my flowers that I lovingly planted in April are long gone and dried up like sticks. I guess I will have to start over next year.

Grizzle Bear gagged and hacked his way through Iowa and I finally gave him a Ziploc bag in case he got sick again. I heard him complaining, saying he would gladly give up his pony, bow, and arrows if he just didn't have to see another cornfield. He was griping about the pig stench all day and I finally told him that misery loved company and to hush up. He's still pouting over in the corner of the room and I've heard a few grumbles about the smelly room. Too bad for him.

So until next time, much love to all always,
Judy/Mom/Mommy

August 26, 2005
Friday
Paducah, KY
Mile 20,070

Dear Folks,

Boy, what a struggle it was to finally make it out of Missouri. Yesterday wasn't too bad as we followed the Missouri River for quite a while and it was quite nice. All the cornfields have turned into lush bean fields and I think sorghum fields. The stalks on the sorghum are bright orange, rust, and mustard colors. The fields look like a blanket of fall colors.

I don't really know how we managed to do this but we have ridden on most of the Lewis and Clark Trail from Oregon to Missouri. The sky was overcast all yesterday and drizzled a little here and there. All along the road that followed the Missouri River, the martins lined up on the power lines like little black clothespins and when we went by them, they would peel off one at a time like a synchronized dance. I loved to watch them flying and darting over the land hunting bugs. They usually fly in pairs and match turn for turn, dip for dip, and climb for climb. It is amazing how they fly as one.

The cicadas were out in full force yesterday as well. I thought something was wrong with my bike at first. There was a strange noise and very loud as well, so close to the road, I was sure the bike was having problems. I then realized that it was the bugs making all that racket. We were so close to the river and the great big oak trees that lined the river gave the bugs a place to hide and sing.

Along with the lush green plants, trees and bugs singing, the humidity was like a wet blanket over the land and as evening approached, it got thicker and heavier. The damp earth gave off the familiar smell of damp dirt and wet rotting leaves and river mud. There are some smells that are just unique to the south.

We stopped in Washington, Missouri, for the evening just about the time it started to rain again. We managed to get some dinner without too much effort and decided to go see a movie since we were in a large enough town to have a theater.

All in all, it was a rather enjoyable day. The scenery was nice and we were riding our bikes. What more could one ask, I guess.

But today we paid the price. Today was a very miserable day for riding or for being outside. The road I picked to travel today was supposed to be a scenic route. The map indicated as much. I don't know who designated it scenic but they need their heads examined. It was one butt ugly road, with rough pavement and cruddy houses along the way with all their junk in the yards. We rode through so many small towns with old, broken down buildings and abandoned main streets with buildings falling in on themselves.

To make matters even worse it was close to one hundred degrees and there must have been ninety-five percent humidity. The day and ride was absolutely miserable.

We rode past two, very bad accidents today, both of which, the cars looked like they had rolled and the tops were crushed into the passenger area. At both accidents, fire and rescue were just beginning to cut into the car to remove the passengers. Even though we are very, very careful anyway, I became more so after seeing those accidents.

We stopped for a break after riding two hundred miles, got a drink, and cooled off a little. While we were sitting in the gas station, I noticed dark, black clouds building to the north of us. They had been threatening all day, but now looked serious. We got on our bikes and figured we might be able to ride ahead of the building storm.

We hadn't been on the road but five minutes when out of the north, off to our left, came winds so vicious that they blew me off the road several times and into the emergency lane. The land all around us was nothing but bean and cornfields for miles, so there was nothing to stop the wind. Worse than the wind, was the storm itself. Since the land was so flat, I could see for miles to the north where the storm was coming from and it was heading straight for us. Lighting was flashing everywhere and large white bolts lit up the sky like fireworks.

I was looking for the funnel cloud, big time. I'm not kidding, I was sure we were in for a tornado. Debris, paper, and leaves blew horizontally across the road. A flock of blackbirds was blown completely off the ground, into the sky and southward. The blackbirds couldn't even fly. They were at the mercy of the wind, as were we.

I was looking for a ditch or gully to go hide in as I watched the black sky to my left. The nearest town was fifteen miles ahead and I had serious doubts that we would make it there. Mile by mile we inched toward the next town and when I saw a sign for a Days Inn I got off the road and pulled into their parking lot. We would be much safer near or in a building than out in the open like we were. I was very frightened.

Just as we pulled into the parking lot of the Days Inn, the sky literally opened up and the hail and rain poured and the lightning threw bolts to the ground all around us. We hurried into the lobby only taking enough time to pull the tank bags off the bikes. There we sat for the next hour while the storm passed.

After thanking the lady at the desk for sanctuary from the storm, we got back on the road and rode for another eighty miles to Paducah where we stopped for the night. Before we got into Paducah though, we crossed the Mississippi River. The bridge was long and tall over the river. As we crossed over the water, the bridge continued up over green fields of crops growing in the flat flood plain. As I looked down at the green crops, it appeared to look like a flat green river. It looked as if half the river was brown water and the other half was green. The flood plains of the mighty Mississippi and Ohio Rivers are huge and flat and I'm sure very rich in minerals and good growing dirt.

Just as we had finished crossing the bridge over the Mississippi, the road turned to the right and we crossed over another big bridge, this time over the Ohio River. We were at the mouth of the Ohio where it empties into the Mississippi. Now that was a sight! Big barges were anchored in the Ohio River waiting their turn to be unloaded somewhere up stream. On the Mississippi, to the west, the sun was setting casting a light pink glow over the water and crops growing along the banks.

Grizzle Bear has promised never to speak to me again. Yesterday he complained about being drizzled by the passing trucks and today he started in about it being too hot but the final straw for him was when I left him out in the storm to face the lightening and heavy rain

329 of OTHER WOMAN

all alone. Gee, I thought it might toughen up the little fella a bit. I must admit though his fur was soaked and his eyes wide with fright when we got back on the bikes after the storm. I did dry him off good when we got to the room and I do hear him humming now on the other side of the bed. I gave him an entire bag of M&M's and a large order of French fries. Think he might forgive me? We'll see. Maybe I should throw in a hug or two?

So until later, much love to all always,
Judy/Mom/Mommy

August 27, 2005
Saturday
Kingston, TN
Mile 20,386

Dear Folks,

Wow, it's hard to believe that our journey is almost over. This will be the last journal entry from the road. We should be home by late afternoon tomorrow and one hundred days on the road will be over.

This will be a short entry tonight but after some of the dust has settled at home, I will be adding a few items to the site such as a packing list, some do's and don'ts and a reflection on the entire trip. So, for those of y'all who have been following along, please stay tuned, and check back occasionally.

For the past three days, I have been trying very hard to think just how I can summarize the wonderful adventure I have been a part of and I must admit I'm having trouble putting the enormity of it all into words. But I know the spirit will move me and I'll get it right.

We started out this morning in a light rain that ended soon but stayed overcast all day. I'm really thankful it did rain for once, as the clouds kept the temperature at a pretty comfortable seventy-five degrees instead of the almost one hundred degrees we experienced yesterday.

Once again, we rode through junky areas, small towns and some larger ones with plenty of traffic. We did go down a seventy-mile stretch of beautiful road called The Trace, not to be confused with the Natchez Trace. The Trace stretches right down the middle of a place called The Land Between the Lakes. It stretches between Kentucky and Tennessee and I think is one big state park. I sure wish we could have ridden down that all day, as it was nice and lonely with only a car here and there.

We have gotten so use to practically having the roads to ourselves and having the area so stretched out that coming back into such tight civilization and everything bunched together is quite an adjustment. I must admit I'm having trouble adjusting to the crowded roads, unsightly surrounding, and high humidity. Welcome back to the south.

As we neared home, the landscape looked very familiar, just like we could be in Georgia in the mountains. Everything was lush, green, and heavily wooded. Gardens have an abundance of weeds growing in them, something that is hard to control in the humid south. Vegetable stands are set up all along the roadside and if I could carry any, I would have stopped. I am looking forward to getting some of the last of summer's fruit and veggies that I have missed this summer. Boy, I am looking forward to sinking my teeth into a juicy peach or some ice-cold watermelon.

I almost hit a cat today as he ran lickity split across the road in front of me. Matter of fact I think that cat lost a few of his nine lives. A car almost got him too. I braked rather hard as he darted into my path and was wondering just what it was going to feel like when I hit him and I was also wondering if he was large enough to cause an accident. As luck would have it, the cat made it and I fortunately did not get to experience running over a good-sized animal.

Today we rode past a red barn on the side of the road that looked like it was on fire. There was a fair amount of smoke billowing out the roof and sides. I was about to stop and call 911 but I realized that I didn't see any flames and the other cars passing the other way didn't seem concerned. I then realized that it was a smoke house and the smoke was there on purpose. I had visions of turkeys or hams being smoked but found out later during lunch that it was tobacco that was being smoked to turn the leaves black for cigars. So much for my vision of large plump turkeys and hams. The bean fields and cornfields have been replaced with tobacco fields and I have no interest in tobacco at all.

All the small towns blended into one, the junky houses I could have done without but we did see some grand old houses in one town we went through. The houses were huge antebellum homes that had been refurbished. I was ready to move right in.

The town we picked to stop in for the night had only one motel and when we pulled into the parking lot, I got a bad feeling about the place. While Ralph was waiting for someone to come to the front desk, I was checking out the place. I motioned for Ralph to forget it and let's move on. I didn't feel safe in that place and it meant we had to drive another fifty miles down the road before we found a decent place to stay. Instincts are there for a purpose, and I listened to mine.

So here we are in Kingston, Tennessee, on our last night. We went to a place for dinner, around the corner from the hotel and it was a perfect way to spend the last night on the road. It was a juke joint with about six tables and a bar and reeking of cigarette smoke and greasy fried food. These kinds of places along the trip have produced some fun times and interesting people but tonight the locals weren't interested in anyone but themselves. Maybe it was the Georgia Bulldog hat I had on in a Tennessee town?

Tomorrow it's homeward bound on the very last leg of the journey. After the first hundred or so miles, I won't even need a road map, as I know the way home. Two hundred and forty more miles give or take. That is all that is left.

Grizzle Bear forgave me last night, especially after the bag of candy and a few hugs. I even let him sleep on the corner of the bed next to my pillow. All was forgiven this morning. Today on his perch behind me, he couldn't make up his mind which song he wanted to sing. First, it was Gee I Want to Go Home, and then it was On the Road Again. One minute he was giggling up and down with excitement of home and the next he was sobbing because his adventure was just about over. I know just how he felt. I promised to consider taking him on the next journey wherever that might take us.

So until then, much love to all always.
Judy/Mom/Mommy

August 31, 2005
Marietta, GA
Final Mileage 20,598

Dear Folks,

JOURNEYS END
MISSION COMPLETE
TRAVELERS ARRIVE HOME SAFE AND SOUND

Love to all, always
Judy/Mom/Mommy

September 1, 2005
Marietta, Georgia
Home

Dear Folks,

Yesterday was day one hundred, and the final day of our adventure. After sleeping to a respectable hour, we sadly and slowly packed our bikes for the last morning. The feelings were bittersweet. Our journey was just about over. So many pages had been turned in the corners of my mind. So, many new chapters written, so many new stories to tell family, friends and hopefully, someday, grandchildren.

I felt like I was coming out from under anesthesia. Had not our journey just started? But, now it was over, with just incredible, fantastic memories left in its place. Part of me was so anxious to be home and hold my babies once again, but another part was still back in the woods zooming along a desolate highway smelling and seeing my earth.

I have shared with my best friend, an astounding time in our relationship, one that, no one or no thing can take from us. I am grateful for the time we could spend together and the memories we made. The memories will always and forever be with both of us.

I know where my home is, and where my heart belongs. My children are my home; they constantly pulled me to them. Those heartstrings will never be cut. But, there is a part of me that knows where the road is too. The unknown of where that road into the wilderness leads, pulls me also. Both call to me in different ways.

My spirit and soul found healing along the twenty thousand miles of my journey. I have returned to my children and home a happier person, a calmer person and a more contented person. There is beauty and wonder in each day we are alive. Though I have always enjoyed the earth and noticed her uniqueness, I see more now. I have watched rainbows fall into the earth, eagles soaring on currents of wild air, wild animals hunting for food. I have seen the shafts and columns of honey, yellow sunlight filtering through thick forest. I have touched the raindrops that clung to the vibrant colored wildflowers and smelled the earth's perfume. I have noticed the way the grasses and wildflowers of the fields and mountains dance in the wind, nature's waltz. I have seen the raw earth of a prehistoric time and felt the magic of Eden and let its vibrant colored cloak surround me at sunset. I have felt natures icy fingers hold me in her hand on a barren tundra road and felt the pat on my back from her upon completion of riding to the end of the earth. I have felt the tingling joy of jumping into an icy mountain stream, the goose bumps racing all over my body. I have smelled my earth. Her perfume has many fragrances: sweet wildflowers, fresh cut hay, freshly plowed earth, the ocean, the frozen tundra and her grasses, the animals, pure fresh air, ozone, the smell of thick fir trees and the way the earth smell when the sun shines down on it warming the dirt, trees and flowers. The more of my earth I saw and experienced on my journey, the more my soul wanted and the more alive my brain felt. I have been forever changed. My heart, soul, and spirit faced changes and challenges along the one hundred day journey. Could any other woman have done it? I do not know. I have the answer for only one woman.

This journey was a challenge for no other woman but me.

Love to all of you always,
Judy/Mom/Mommy

BOOK OF LISTS

This section will try to enlighten the reader about such items as camping gear, riding gear, clothing, tool kit, first aid kit, and some overall practical advice.

RIDING GEAR

Over the years, we have tried several different types of riding gear. We have found all but the following listed items to be unsatisfactory for one reason or another. Our main concern was to stay warm and dry, which is generally the case with any rider. If you ride enough and long enough you will eventually find what works best for you. We have been the leather route and the rain gear that you wear over your clothes and heavy sweatshirts, etc. These did not work for us. Leather will get saturated if enough water falls onto it, then it takes forever to dry. One and two-piece rain gear is a pain in the rear to put on and take off. Both Ralph and I agree whole-heartedly, that First Gear absolutely makes the best outer riding gear. We both have the riding pants and Kilimanjaro jackets. Both have removable liners. The liner in the jacket is fleece and can double as a lightweight jacket if you are sight seeing or just hanging around camp. Both the jacket and pants are positively waterproof and warm. Even in some of the torrential rains we rode in, my clothes stayed dry.

The only exception was completely an operator error. I failed to snap the flap over the zipper in the jacket after a gas stop and in an afternoon rainstorm, my tee shirt did get wet. That was my fault and not anything to do with the design of the jacket. Also, I found my jeans would wick rainwater from around my boots. That only happened once and it was quite chilly. Just tucking one edge of my jeans into the top on my boots solved that problem. Again, that is not a design flaw in the riding pants, just something that was solved along the way. I also like the two-piece idea. The pants can always be removed if you just need a jacket. I did find though that both the pants and jacket felt mighty good in those cold evenings around the campfire in the cold climates we were in.

I would definitely purchase these two items all over again if given the choice. They get an A++ in my book.

For me, having wet feet has always been a big problem, as well as being just plain cold from the outside temperature. I tried on several types of actual riding boots and was not pleased with the fit for various reasons. I went to the Army/Navy store where I always purchased my medic boots, to see if I could find something one hundred percent waterproof. I purchased a pair of HighTech Magnum one hundred percent waterproof boots and all my problems have been solved.

Here again these boots are really all that they are advertised to be. They are really waterproof and my feet were tremendously warmer. The only thing I would change would be to add an extra pair of socks when the temperature drops below forty degrees. I actually put on my down booties when riding on the tundra and my feet never suffered the slightest bit of coldness. These boots also get an A++.

Along with my feet being a problem, my hands have suffered as well. Solving this problem has been more challenging than the rest. If my hands are cold, the rest of me is going to be as well. I carry three kinds of gloves. I wear a lightweight leather glove in warm weather, switching to a medium weight leather glove with a fleece liner when the temperature drops. I also have a pair of silk inner gloves to fit into the medium glove or heavy gloves. For the really cold and wet weather, I have a pair of Widder heated gloves. These combined with the silk liners are the bomb! Problem solved. No more cold hands and they as well are waterproof.

When the air really got cold, we both wore a silk hood under the helmet. Not only was the face and head warm, but the neck as well. That small area between the helmet and jacket seems to attract every whiff of cold air in the universe. Wearing one of these types of hoods solves that problem. Silk is particularly nice as it is light, takes up very little space, and is extremely warm.

Ralph carried his Widder heated vest, as he doesn't like to wear fleece of any kind. These vests are wonderful and work well for heating up the torso. For me, I like the fleece. It creates dead air space, is warm against the skin, and makes an extremely warm sweater that is lightweight and washes and dries quickly.

Helmets are very much a personal choice. They come in so many shapes, colors, types its hard to know where to begin, so I won't. I have a long history of being a medic, that gives you an idea of why both of us ride with a full-face helmet at all times, even in those states that don't require helmets. Buy the absolute best helmet you can afford to protect that noggin!

TANK BAG

Tank bags come in all shapes, sizes, and colors. Picking which one to carry is a personal choice. I have an Oxford Sovereign tank bag and I have been extremely happy with it for seven years. It has large magnets in the base and fits quite well over my tank. It has a large pocket on top for my maps and a large expandable compartment, which almost doubles in size when expanded. My bag comes off easily when stopping for food or gas but stays put when zooming down the road.

A tank bag to me is like a kitchen drawer, purse, and backpack all rolled into one. It's amazing just how much can be crammed into such a small space. I have managed over the years however, to figure out what needs to be in my tank bag. Generally speaking, it should be those things that you use frequently and want to get to easily and quickly.

Always, always, always remember to keep things in the same place where you can find them fast, particularly in the dark. I keep the contents of my tank bag in the same place within the bag so I can tell by feel alone what's what. This comes in handy when fumbling around in the darkness of the tent on a moonless night. You can immediately put your hands on your headlamp.

I don't pretend to even know what all Ralph carried in his tank bag. That is one of those places that women should not venture or even peak into. But, I do know that along with all the mystery items he carried in his tank bag, when he did unzip it in my presence, I could see the Dell Inspiron laptop computer with WiFi and Cingular PC card, two batteries for the laptop, a Treo 650 — Cingular phone, an AT&T cell phone, and various chargers for the computer and cell phones. On the bike handlebar was the Garman eMap GPS.

In my tank bag I carry my wallet, reading glasses and case, sunglass case since the sunglasses were generally being worn, a small cosmetic case whose contents include a clear, aspirin bottle filled with Advil and Excedrin, a small bottle of Pepcid for inflammatory meals, fingernail clippers, hotel size hand lotion and a fingernail file. Also, in the tank bag are two cameras, one digital, and one film, with three rolls of film. Other contents include one bag of candy mints, one bag of bubble gum, to replenish my candy dish on the outside pocket of the tank bag, cables for the digital camera, a twelve pack of AA batteries, two ink pens, one green highlighter for maps, a bottle of Deet, a paperback book, a headlamp, cell phone, two paper maps for the upcoming days, one paper map in the outside pocket, car keys, eyeglass repair kit, a baseball hat, a silk hoodie, and a small purse size Jansport backpack rolled up. A small spiral bound notebook of paper and a pen slipped into a plastic pencil carrier comes in mighty handy and will keep notes and receipts dry and safe. That was on top of everything inside the bag.

Then there are the extras that get thrown into the tank bag along the way and that is what makes it like a kitchen drawer. When you can find no other place to put something, just throw it into the tank bag. Upon arriving home, I found some other interesting items lurking in the darkness of my tank bag. There were several rocks that I lifted from the Arctic Ocean as well as a couple from the Pacific Ocean. There were some dried remnants of cottonwood fluff and a twig of crumbled baby's breath from the wedding. I found some empty, but clean baggies, a roll of electrical tape that I have no earthly idea how it got in there, my rally flag from the Road Kill Safari, four clips like mountain climbers use, some national park newspapers, some dead bugs, a small amount of dirt, rolled up chewed bubble gum, partially melted M&M's and an unusual aroma.

With the exception of the dead bugs, dirt, chewed bubble gum and the unusual aroma I would still pack and carry the same contents of my tank bag. This works for me.

CLOTHES

I'm sure there will be many varied opinions in this category. I, for one, not only despise doing laundry, I hate having several hours of traveling and vacation time tied up washing my filthy clothes. I will put it off as long as possible, sometimes wearing dirty clothes again. Therefore, the next time I venture on a long journey I will probably pack a few more clothes. Ralph agrees with me on this one even though I was the one that generally wound up doing the nasty deed while he was "working".

Ralph's packing list for clothing was:
Four pairs of jeans
One sweatshirt
Five short sleeve t-shirts
One long sleeve t-shirt
Six pairs of underwear
Six pairs of socks
One set of long underwear
One baseball hat
One large travel towel
One small travel towel
My packing list for clothing was:
Three pairs of jeans
One lightweight fleece sweater
One long sleeve t-shirt
One long sleeve denim shirt
Six short sleeve t-shirts
Eight underwear
Three bras
Six pairs of socks

One pair down booties
One fleece beanie hat
One baseball hat
One set of silk long underwear
One large travel towel
One small travel towel

In reality, of all the stuff we carried on this trip, our clothes took up the least amount of space when compared with everything else. Most of what we carried was camping equipment so the clothing paled in comparison.

TOILET ARTICLE BAG

The contents of one's personal toilet articles will obviously vary. While Ralph's bag was much, much smaller than mine, I still managed to cram all my necessary items into a relatively small bag for a woman. Ralph's list only states, "assorted toiler articles." I guess you will have to use your imagination. But mine however, is listed in full detail.

The first and foremost item that was put into my bag was the bottle of Oil of Olay Total Effects Age Defying Face Cream. I can't live without it, no way, no how and it would still be the first thing into the bag. After all, anything that is age defying is right at the top of my list. Some other obvious items that I carried were deodorant, shampoo and cream rinse, body wash and scruffy, one extra large, extra absorbent travel towel, hair brush, hair dryer, flip flops, toothpaste, toothbrush, mascara, two colors of eye shadow, one pair of earrings, tweezers, three razors, one hundred count bottle of Excedrin PM, one hundred count bottle of Advil, one hundred count bottle of Excedrin Migraine, one small Ziploc bag crammed full of Q-Tips, one small bottle of hand lotion and one bottle of Bull Frog sunscreen.

Of the contents of my beauty bag, there are a few items that I will leave at home the next time. Those items are the mascara, the two colors of eye shadow and the pair on earrings. I thought there might be some occasion that I might want to look a little more presentable and those items would come in handy. Though I wanted to look more presentable on a daily basis, it just was not feasible on a daily basis to get up and put on make up only to stick a helmet over my head and sunglasses over my eyes. The makeup went to the bottom of the bag on the first day. Has anyone tried to wear earrings while riding with a full-face helmet on? It hurts like hell when you pull the helmet over your ears and it hurts like forty hells when you take the helmet off. I was sure the lobes of my ears were being ripped apart. The earrings accompanied the makeup down to the bottom of the beauty bag.

Some might think that the hair dryer was another item better left at home. After all, who is going to see your lovely hair anyway? If you're like me, if the helmet isn't on my head then a baseball hat is. Between the two of them, they cover unsightly helmet hair, hat hair and bed head. Therefore, it was questionable whether I would even use my hair dryer. However, I have naturally curly hair and if not tamed by the hair dryer, I was afraid that any person within a mile of me would drop dead of fright.

I very quickly found out however, that when traveling in warm temperatures a head of wet hair kept the head cool for a good length of time. I learned to bravely forego the drying of my hair in the morning after my shower and just stick the helmet on and go. Generally, by the first gas stop, my hair was completely dry and completely flat as a flitter without the slightest hint of a curl. But it was still scary. I don't think my hair saw the light of day or night for very many minutes during the one hundred days of my journey.

Now, I had to learn the hard way just why that hair dryer came in handy. I did actually begin to use it when the temperature dropped below sixty-five degrees. The effects of wet hair under my helmet when the temperature was below a certain degree, was dramatic. While the ambient temperature was hot and I was sweating, wet hair felt grand. When the temperature was cool, wet hair under my helmet made me feel like I stuck my head into a bucket of ice water. The goose bumps started at the scalp and quickly scurried down my spine and out to my fingertips and toes. As I traveled down the road, the goose bumps, traveled their own road, like waves down my body, taking on a life of their own. The obvious remedy here was if the air temperature was going to be below seventy degrees, dry the hair before dawning the helmet and riding on down the highway. Otherwise, it will be one miserable ride.

Hairdryers are also useful when encountering cold bathrooms in the campgrounds, provided there is electricity in the bathroom and there is an outlet. There was more than one bathroom in several campgrounds along our journey that I warmed up quite nicely with my trusty hairdryer. They put off tremendous heat. I would hang onto the hair dryer if I were you.

Though it didn't really take up so much room, I'd leave the one hundred count of Excedrin PM at home too. I thought there might be some night when sleep would elude me and I would be in need of this crutch. I never even once opened this bottle. I was so exhausted at the end of the day that, with the exception of a period of time when it was daylight for twenty-four hours a day, sleep found me quite easily.

CAMPING GEAR

Traveling as a couple, each on our own bike, has many advantages. Not only do you get to share your experience with your best friend but also you get to share space on your bikes as well, which means you can carry more stuff. We would each carry our own gear on our own bike, but Ralph decided to be in charge of carrying the shelter and put me in charge of carrying the kitchen. Hum, what is wrong with this picture? What follows below is what worked for us and I'm sure that there are as many varied opinions as there are stars in the sky. We also discovered the hard way some things that didn't work. Those are discussed also.

Camping gear, as with most everything, comes in all shapes and sizes and all prices too. Depending on what your budget is, you can get just about anything you need for a reasonable price. You can also spend a fortune, if you so desire. Given our limited budget, we chose those items that we could afford, spending more on some of the important items and fudging on some of the ones not so important. The tent for example was not very expensive, at one hundred dollars, but it served us well. We invested in a good Therm-a-rest for its durability and reputation. We also invested in a good sleeping bag, as that might be the one item that saved our life if stranded in the middle of nowhere.

After looking at many web sites, in many stores and basically overwhelming ourselves with information, we chose a four man, three season, Eureka Tetragon 9x9 tent. It has a six-foot head clearance, which was important to us. If there was a chance we might have to spend some time in the tent due to inclement weather or just lazing around on some warm summer afternoon, we wanted the ability to stand up in the tent. It sure makes it easier getting dressed, undressed, or packing up gear. Since we were going to be sharing a tent, we needed something larger to accommodate our bodies and all our gear. In my opinion, it is best to pick a tent, one person larger than is actually going to be inside. For example: if there are going to be two people using the tent, then buy a three-person tent. The extra size is for all the stuff you will be carrying. Being the hogs we were, we chose double the amount of space. I stick by our choice as the extra space allowed some extra, elbowroom.

This tent was a perfect size for us and set up very quickly, even in the rain. The only thing I did not like about this tent was the flooring. I have been use to a Coleman tent, which has a waterproof boot for flooring that extends about six inches up the side of the tent. Even in the worst rainstorm, that Coleman tent did not leak a bit and everything on the floor of the tent stayed dry.

I was nervous about the Eureka, as it did not have this type of flooring. It later proved to be a problem, but I think that was mostly operator error with placement of the ground tarp and our tent being on an uneven area. Overall, the Eureka Tetragon preformed wonderfully and we were very satisfied with our choice.

We each used a large size Therm-a-rest that, at the time we bought these several years ago, was the widest they made. There are now wider ones on the market but just remember that the bigger things you pick, the bigger it is on your bike.

I experience residual nerve damage from a ruptured disc that was surgically repaired several years ago. After about three weeks of constant use on the hard ground, the Therm-a-rest was just not adequate protection for my back problem. I was in a good deal of pain and that pain was just about to interfere with the trip. I had the good fortune to actually sleep on a cot in one of our many varied accommodations. The cot combined with the Therm-a-rest was the ticket to my comfort. Ralph and I went to several places in Fairbanks before locating a cot that I could carry on the back of my bike. It made all the difference in the world and my back started to recuperate. Ralph chose not to buy one even though I ooohed and ahhhed every night when I stretched out on my bed. He was going to tough it out on the ground.

The cot, which we had originally purchased before leaving Atlanta, was shipped back to the store before we left town. It was shipped back due to the fact that we knew we already had too much stuff to carry. I found out the hard way that I should have kept the cot because I wound up with the exact cot three weeks later. I would not trade it for anything. The cot made a tremendous difference in my enjoyment of our camping experience. I think there are plenty of cots on the market to choose from if you are leaning that route. There are actually backpacking size cots available. Just keep in mind the higher off the ground they are the bigger they are and the more space they will take up on your bike. The one I found was eighteen inches off the ground and weighed ten pounds. The nice thing about one eighteen inches height is that underneath becomes an instant storage space for all the gear, leaving your tent nice and roomy. Also, in the event of a rainstorm, if your tent happens to leak, you are off the ground high and dry. Trust me on this one! Wherever I choose to travel next time, my cot will be with me. I will sacrifice the space on my bike for it.

We both had to purchase new sleeping bags for this trip. My nice down sleeping bag, that I had bought a million years ago, had been peed on one too many times by young children and animals. No amount of washing was going to salvage the down sleeping bag, so it went into the trash with a fond farewell. Ralph's old bag, I didn't think was up to the trip either. Besides, it smelled funny and I wasn't sure I wanted it in the tent next to me.

Since we were heading into a territory that was known to be cold at any time, at any moment, I didn't want to take any chances and be cold or worse, freezing. I did all the research about sizes, mummy bags verses rectangle, the filling, the pros and cons of down verses fiber filled. I ordered a beautiful mummy bag since I had never experienced the comforts of mummying and thinking since it would be smaller and lighter, it would stuff nicely into my waterproof bag. That mummy bag wasn't in my house more that ten minutes when I realized that I probably would have had it in shreds and its stuffing flying everywhere in the tent. It was like being in a straight jacket. I shipped the bag back the next day for a full refund. Ralph agreed that a mummy bag just wasn't right for either of us.

This is one item that I felt needed to be top notch. I wasn't going to take any chances since I had no clue where our journey would take us and into what kind of weather conditions. I chose a Summit, rectangle bag from Cabela's. I bought the long length since I'm on the tall side and the wider model since the smaller mummy size was too tight around my shoulders. My bag measured thirty-six inches by ninety inches. This was a good choice. My experience in the past in cold weather has not been pleasant, even with a down bag, so I chose the zero degree bag filled with Quallofil and lined with fleece.

I chose the Quallofil filling because it heats up quickly and if it gets wet, it will dry quickly, and still keep you warm. The fleece lining was another plus, as slipping into it when it was thirty degrees outside was like slipping into an electric blanket. True to its word, this bag lives up to everything it promised.

This was an excellent choice in my opinion but it is definitely a cold weather bag. There were many nights when it was cold, that I had to pull it off my shoulders or stick a leg out to cool off for a moment. If traveling in a cold climate I would highly recommend this sleeping bag. If traveling only in hot climates, don't bother, any old cheap bag will do. However, when we were traveling in hot climates we just used a cheap, two-dollar sheet I bought at Kmart before we left town, to cover up with at night. The sleeping bag made a nice padding on top of the Therm-a-rest during those warm nights. Even the desert can get cool at night though. Your shelter and bedding are items that you probably want to make a wise investment in.

In addition to a sleeping bag, don't forget your pillow. Ralph has a small square pillow that stuffs in with the sleeping bag, that he has used for years and he is satisfied with it. I on the other hand, haven't totally solved the pillow issue. I bought a small airplane size pillow from Kmart and it was just too small. I was really out of room on the bike for my standard pillow so I decided to use the reversible carrying case that my sleeping bag originally came in. It was suppose to double as a pillow when stuffed with items such as clothes. I would stuff the bag at night with my riding jacket and fleece liner. It worked ok, but I woke up more than once with a stiff neck as the contents were not exactly soft. This was not a perfect solution but it did work sufficiently enough. I will probably try something different next time.

We each carried a small folding chair for sitting around all those lovely, roaring campfires. If you are planning to spend any time in a campground, a folding chair is probably a good idea to take along. It's nice around the fire or just relaxing with a good book and tasty beverage. If your camping experience is only going to be limited to strictly throwing up a tent late at night and bedding down for a quick night's sleep, then maybe you should just leave the chair at home. Ralph is still debating this item. Though he used his chair every time we camped, he still is unsure whether he's taking his on the next trip. Like my cot, my chair will be safely secured to the bike.

Other camping items that Ralph carried were a nine by nine foot tarp for under the tent, twenty-five feet of rope, a battery operated lantern, a headlamp and one of those multipurpose, gadgets that has everything from a pair of pliers to a knife blade.

Since I was responsible for the kitchen, I dedicated one of my saddlebags for that purpose. If packed properly, it is amazing what can fit into a small space. I actually managed to pack it right the first time and only had to move one item from the bottom of the saddlebag to the top of the pile. That was the hatchet. The head of the hatchet was used to hammer tent stakes into the ground and the tent was always the first thing set up in camp. Below is a list of the contents of my kitchen:

Coleman duel fuel one burner stove
One small hatchet
Medium size bottled water for emergency use only
Two hard plastic nesting cups that can handle hot and cold liquids
Four plastic plates (one of which doubled as a great fan for the fire)
Two knives, two forks, two spoons
One set of tongs
One spatula
One can opener
Two wooden spoons
One expandable hotdog/marshmallow fork
One, ten inch frying pan
One set of nesting pots/pans
One 12"x 6" grill grate
One roll aluminum foil
One box sugar cubes
Six tea bags
Four bags Success rice
Salt, pepper, garlic salt, Montreal steak seasoning (be sure to store these inside a Ziploc bag.
One hunting knife

Five large baggies
Five small baggies
Three medium size garbage bags
Three large size garbage bags
Two square nesting food containers (Ziploc or Glad)
One roll paper towels
One roll toilet paper
One tablecloth
Gas siphon and funnel
Fire starter
Fire poker (found a discarded tent pole that works great for stoking fire)
Lighter
Three bags microwave popcorn
Small dustpan/broom for tent
Sponge
Dish soap
Corkscrew
One-gallon collapsible water container
One six pack size cooler with extra expandable pockets (Wal-Mart has one for $6)

Our original plan was to camp out for four nights and stay in a hotel on the fifth night. Given that plan, it was thought that when we stopped for lunch we would also at that time find a grocery store and purchase that night's dinner to be cooked at camp. The best-laid plans don't generally work out, at least ours didn't. Most of the towns we scurried through during lunch only had the roadhouse we were actually eating in at the time. There were no grocery stores most of the time. When we were able to find a store, the packed kitchen came in real handy and our meals around the campfire were positively gourmet and delightful.

While I am not a dainty creature and I usually can go with the flow in most circumstances, and I really don't mind getting dirty every now and then, there are some occasions where I just draw the line at setting up camp. I really have trouble with high temperatures and when the temperature is going to stay in the nineties or above, my bike, is naturally going to head directly for the cheapest hotel it can find. Also, a powerful electrical storm complete with hail, high winds and torrential rains tend to make me move in the direction of four walls and dry sheets. And then there is just a certain amount of times I want to feed the coin machine inside the shower and get a quick spray of water. I'm sorry but it takes longer than six minutes for me to lather up and rinse off. It takes that long just to get the road dirt off my face. I think that the price of the campground should include the water for the shower, don't you? There are also sometimes when nightly wanderings to the bathroom in the pitch black, with who knows how many creatures of the dark watching, gets really old. Its not much fun getting out of a nice warm sleeping bag when its forty degrees outside.

Having said all that, sometimes things didn't work out for us to camp every four nights and then find a hotel on the fifth night. We also found out that the further north we went and the more desolate the back roads became there were not grocery stores available. The towns that were marked on the map were not towns like you and I think of. The town actually consisted of a combination roadhouse and gas station. That was it.

As it turned out, we wound up eating two meals a day, either breakfast and dinner or lunch and dinner. The roadhouses along the route turned out to be very good and enjoyable. The food was generally tasty and since the road we were on heading to Alaska was basically the only one, we got to meet fellow bike riders. Both Ralph and I thoroughly enjoyed meeting fellow travelers whether they were bikers or others, traveling in campers or by car. Most everyone we talked to were so very interested in our journey, where we came from, where we were headed. It was fun to share stories.

The next time I make a trip such as this I am going to think real hard about carrying a kitchen or at least greatly scale it down. We also found out that when we did go into a grocery store for one meal it wound up costing us as much or sometimes more than if we ate out. There was no place for leftovers and we didn't want to attract any wild creatures either. For those occasions when a steak cooked over an open fire is just too good to pass up, I think I will carry just enough to get this done.

We were only caught a few times without resources for food which considering how many miles we traveled and the remoteness of the areas we were in, was quite remarkable. This was generally due to having to travel farther in a day than planned because of road conditions, storms, etc. On that very rare occasion however, my secret stash of goodies came in handy. I would hoard goodies along the way with tasty items I picked up at gas stops or the occasional grocery store. Ralph gave me a hard time more than once for the apples, oranges, trail mix, or bag of pepper jack cheese Doritos I bought and stuffed into the cooler or saddlebag. Guess who was the first one into my stash of goodies when food was not otherwise available? You just can't imagine how wonderful Pepper Jack Cheese Doritos taste when your stomach is empty and begging to be fed.

FIRST AID KIT

Given the fact that I am a retired medic, my first aid kit is probably more extensive than most people would normally carry. So, when packing your own first aid kit please keep that in mind if you use mine as a guideline. There are many, very suitable, preassembled first aid kits available just about in any store. My background dictates that I carry more items "just to be on the safe side." The following is what is in my kit. The contents may give you some ideas of some of the extras you might want in your personal kit or just might scare you enough to make you decide to go with one already preassembled.

After taking great care in assembling a personalized kit, making it as small as possible and hauling it all over creation and back, I, thankfully did not open it one time during the entire trip not even for something as little as a band-aid. But I was prepared!

My fanny pack kit measured nine inches by six inches by six inches and has two divided sections and one outside pocket. The contents are as follows:

Four pairs of rubber gloves

One emergency whistle

One Epipen

One tube Vaseline Petroleum Jelly

Twenty Alcohol Prep Pads

One .5oz bottle sterile eye drops

One emergency seat belt cutter (looks like letter opener with razorblade attached)

One first aid instructions for the untrained

One package of twenty count anti-bacterial moist wipes

Two, twenty-four gauge IV catheter needles (great for removing splinters)

Two petrolatum gauze non-adhering dressing
Two 3x3 sterile pads
Two 2x3 sterile pads
Four XL plastic adhesive bandages
One moleskin for blisters
Two emergency rescue blankets
One Protective Dressing Swab
One Benadryl itch relief stick
One Benadryl itch stopping cream 1oz
One Purell Hand Sanitizer
One fingernail clippers
Four Hydrogen Peroxide first aid wipes
Four packs three in one first aid ointment
One 2.7gm lubricating jelly
One 4oz bottle Burn Jel
One package Dramamine
Seven doses of 25mg Benadryl
Two CPR mouth barriers, pocket size
One wire splint
One high-risk emergency protection pack
Two ace elastic bandages
One 1" cotton tape
One 1" plastic tape
Two sterile Kling bandaging 3in x 75in
One package non-sterile 4x4's
One triangular bandage
One tweezers
One pair medic sheers
One forceps
One sharp point scissors
Two 5x9" sterile dressing
Six 4x4" sterile dressing
Two sterile eye pads
Four 3x3 sterile dressings
Two 4x4 sterile burn dressings
Ten regular Band-aids
Five small Band-aids
Five junior Band-aids

Ten Butterfly Band-aids
Six knuckle Band-aids
Ten fingertip Band-aids
Eight large Band-aids
Two sleeves Steri-strips

Thankfully, I did not use any of the contents of my first aid kit. However, going back through the kit and looking to see if there was anything I would leave behind the next time, I can say without a second thought, that I will keep it as is. The one item I might leave will be just the one I need in an emergency. As besides, you should have seen the things that I didn't take in the first place! I figured it would really be over kill to take my entire jump kit.

TOOL KIT

The tool kit for Ralph is probably a little more extensive than most due to the fact that Ralph is a certified motorcycle repairman. Like me with my first aid kit, Ralph carries more tools than are probably necessary. But just leave one of those items at home and that will be the one you need on some lonely back road in the middle of the desert. Unlike the first aid kit though, the tools were used on more than one occasion. Ralph put it in the saddlebag on his bike and stated that, that was the saddlebag we didn't want to open, because if we did, it would mean we had mechanical problems. Unfortunately, the bag was opened on several occasions.

The contents of Ralph's toolbox are as follows:

One BMW standard motorcycle took kit
One Honda standard motorcycle tool kit
CyclePump air compressor
Tire repair kit
Tire pressure gauge
Duck tape
Electrical tape
Five fuses — assorted amps
Test light
Five feet of electric wire
BMW oil filter wrench
Honda oil filter wrench
Two BMW oil filters
Two Honda oil filters
Four tie-down straps
Siphon for gas
Zip ties

Four pair of pliers —assorted types
Two pairs of locking pliers
Four screwdrivers — assorted types and sizes
Rachet handle
Set of metric sockets to 19mm
Set of Allen sockets
Set of metric wrenches 10mm to 19mm
Socket extension
Adjustable wrench
Torx set T-10 to T-40
Clymer BMW R100 repair manual
Clymer Honda Shadow repair manual

EXTRAS

Yes, there are always the extras that you just can't live without. In some cases you really must carry some of the following items, just find a space somewhere on the bike and then forget them. I actually tied two Jansport backpacks together and placed them on top of my hard bags and they worked great for catching all the extra necessary junk. They also came in handy for storing the extra layers of clothing that might have to come off during the day. Since these backpacks were not waterproof, I lined them with a trusty Hefty garbage bag. They both work great. Everything stayed nice and dry even during the worst rain.

After doing so much research over the internet about where we would be traveling and purchasing several books on Alaska, I settled on only two to take with me. One of them was the Milepost, which is a must, when traveling in Alaska and in northern Canada. I also took Moons Handbook about Alaska. I have used the Moons Handbook for other states and have been very pleased with the information they provide. I also carried a state map for each state I anticipated traveling through, as well as a nice Canadian map.

I will avoid traveling down an interstate at all cost and both Ralph and I really enjoy the back roads. I would take the map of the area we would be traveling in and highlight with my green highlighter, the route that we would ride that day. We traveled down some roads that were hardly pen scratches on the map but they turned out to be some of the best. We saw more beautiful country than either of us expected to find. Ralph likes to use his GPS but I am a believer in paper maps. On a paper map, I can read what landmarks are in the area. Also, on a paper map I can see where the campgrounds are in relation to the route we are taking. I like having that information. Ralph's GPS doesn't give that overall big picture. But, on more than one occasion, when the map was not clear, the GPS did come in handy. This was generally the case when we had to traverse a larger town. Using both, really worked well for us.

If you are going to be out on the road for long periods like we were, it is probably a good idea to have some vital information put in a safe place. I made copies of all our important information and put it into a nice bound report folder so everything would be in one place. The mistake I made was not taking it one step further and putting the folder inside a plastic bag. I put the folder inside my hard bag, which is watertight and has never leaked. It was in a safe place, so I thought. What I did not anticipate was, the bottle of water I had put in that saddlebag to drink later, springing a leak and soaking everything in that saddlebag. Just a little tip of advice here. There are different grades of plastic that water comes in. I bought the cheapest bottled water the gas station had and the plastic was flimsy, but it never occurred to me that it would puncture in my saddlebag. Well, it did and it only took a very small hole to cause big problems. My advice is first, if storing water, buy bottled water with sturdier plastic, and second don't put it with anything that it will harm, if it ruptures. I know, its only common sense, but you will be amazed at yourself, at the things that you don't think will happen in a million years.

My important papers were not ruined but extremely waterlogged and by the time everything did eventually dry out, they had grown mold spots and smelled like mildew. I did have to replace some preaddressed envelops but all ended well.

I made copies of our driver's licenses, passports, insurance cards, all credit cards, and gas cards. I carried business cards of our bankers, copies of eyeglass prescriptions, copies of medication prescriptions and pharmacy phone numbers. I also had a list of contacts at home including addresses, phone numbers, and e-mail address of friends, family, and attorneys. Since we would be gone for so long, I signed up to pay our bills electronically. A list of all companies with the login and passwords was included in our important papers.

This may seem like overkill but in order to handle personal administrative items while traveling these items came in handy. Just be sure to keep all these important information in one place tightly sealed within plastic.

ANIMAL LIST

The main purpose of our trip was not to view wildlife but a riding tour through the wilderness. If along the way, we happened to see any wildlife, then that would be an extra treat. We actually saw more wildlife than we thought we would, particularly since we did not go out of our way to seek it. We were delighted to be able to recall all that we actually had the pleasure to view.

Over a period of one hundred days we were fortunate to witness in their natural habitat a banana slug, seagulls, crows, ravens, starlings, hummingbirds, golden eagles, bald eagles, hawks, ospreys, martins, doves, ptarmigans, grouse, turkeys, vultures, bluebirds, wrens, Stellar jays, humpback whales, Dall porpoises, walruses, seals, puffins, otters, salmon, trout, Canada geese, loons, ducks (many varieties), wolf, foxes, skunks (all dead), a mountain lion (dead), several variety of deer, elk, caribou, moose, two black bears, one grizzly bear, horses, cows, llamas, buffalo, antelope, red squirrels, grey squirrels, chipmunks, prairie dogs, beaver, swans, desert lizard, blue tail skink, mouse, mosquitoes, Dall sheep, mountain goats, coyote, arctic snow geese, arctic fox, white and blue herons, and donkeys.

CAMPGROUND AND HOTEL REQUIREMENTS

Having stayed in so many hotels, I have lost count, Ralph and I came up with some criteria that helps us decide whether or not to pull into a specific facility. While I do enjoy the luxury of the fancy hotels, traveling on a tight budget does not allow for such accommodations. But even on a budget, there are just some items that are necessary. They may seem like small issues but these issues became big problems for us when we had to repeat them over and over.

For instance, if you are staying in a hotel that is over one or two stories, make sure there is an elevator. Carrying all your gear up three flights of stairs, making several trips, gets very old, very quickly. I just could not believe the amount of hotels that did not have elevators in them. If you are lucky to find a hotel over two stories with an elevator, make sure there is a cart to roll your gear to your room. Ralph and I got very good at seeking one level motels where we could park right outside the door.

Some of our other requirements are: positively, absolutely a non-smoking room, either a king size or two beds, air conditioning, hot running water, three prong electrical outlets, clean, clean sheets, a tub with a functioning stopper and under fifty dollars.

Yes, these motels do exist, we stayed in many. These types of motels are general run by mom and pop and are quite nice. I think most bikers like to stay in motels like these anyway. However, I have had the thrill of pulling up in front of five star places on my filthy, nasty bike, fully decked out in mud-coated gear. After telling the attendant in the valet parking that we had reservations, the look of one of disgust turns to one of service, and our bags are quickly and efficiently carried to our waiting room.

As far as campgrounds go, you have to be a little less picky. After all, you are sleeping outside in the dirt and elements. We like our campgrounds to be in the woods, hopefully next to a stream or river, surrounded by trees and very few human neighbors. Our ideal campsite would also have a fire pit, picnic table, a water spicket, electricity, internet and cell phone connection, showers(preferably ones that did not required being fed quarters), washer and dryer, camp store, all surrounded by unbelievable scenery. Now, I know that is asking for an awful lot, but we actually came very close on many occasions. Ralph and I were really amazed at the internet availability in Alaska. Most campgrounds used the internet. Communication in the remote areas of Alaska is king. We actually had more problems in the lower forty-eight than anywhere in Alaska.

FAVORITE ROADS

There are as many favorite roads as there are drops of water in the ocean. Some, we found to be incredible, for other people these might not be. In regards to this particular trip, however, we have a few favorites. If we have the good fortune to go back to that far away world of Alaska, Northwest Canada and the southwest in the United States, the below are just a few of our personal favorites we would like to travel down again:

The Alaskan Highway — from Dawson Creek, British Columbia to Delta Junction, Alaska

Alaska:

The Dalton Highway — also known as the Haul Road. Though the road was extremely brutal, the scenery was awesome.

The Glenn Highway — from Palmer to Glennallen

Highway 1 on the Kenai Peninsula

Highway 9 to Seward

The Richardson Highway to Valdez

California:

Highway 101 in northern California, through the redwood forest.

Idaho:

Highway 12 — running west to east from Lewiston, Idaho to Missoula, Montana

Missouri:

Route 19 running north and south

Nevada:

Highway 50 — running west to east from Reno to Salt Lake

Utah:

Highway 128 off I-70 north of Moab, into Moab near Arches National Park

Highway 191 to Blanding then Highway 95 to Natural Bridges National Monument, then Highway 261 south into the Valley of the Gods and Mexican Hat.

Printed in the United States
96368LV00005B/124-132/A